Spirits Of the Chesapeake

Jocelyn Miller

ISBN:10 0988621444
ISBN-13: 978-0988621442

DEDICATION

The colonization of America was a double-edged sword. Not only did the early European settlers establish the beginnings of what was to become the most powerful country on earth, but in turn, their arrival disinherited the native populations from their centuries old homelands and cultures.

Therefore, I dedicate this book with sincerity, not only to the first Americans who so cruelty lost their heritage, but also to the early settlers of the colonies to whom the inevitable march into the future would bring them face to face with adversities and challenges they could never have imagined.

ACKNOWLEDGMENTS

My sincere posthumous appreciation and thanks to Captain John Smith for his bravery, fortitude and foresight in his vision of a new world, and for the boundless intelligence he displayed in leaving behind a written and picturesque history of the early American colonies. His compassion for the native people of the Chesapeake Bay, and his wisdom in learning their culture and language, reflect on a man who not only forged forward, but did so with intelligence and honest concern.

Kudos to William Strachey, (Historie of Travaile into Virginia Britannia, 1612), whose translation of the Algonquin-Powhatan dialect has been so essential in writing *Spirits of the Chesapeake*.

Many thanks to June Robbins, a.k.a. *Morning star*, and Sterling V. Street, a.k.a. *Earth Keeper*, curator of the Nanticoke Indian Museum in Millsboro, Delaware, for generously taking the time to share cultural history and artifacts of the native people of the early Eastern Shore of Maryland.

Thanks to Daniel 'Firehawk' Abbott and the Restore Handsell Plantation Project in Vienna, Maryland, for access to the living history Chicone Indian Village, and for introduction into the culture of the tidewater people of the Chesapeake.

Thanks, as always, to my editors, Sally Bright and Carolyn Carson..

Thanks to Charles Ross for a beautiful cover.

A special thanks to my husband, Bernard, who is always able and ready to read my manuscripts, input his suggestions, and pull me out of technical slumps with his creative ideas.

Cover Graphic: Charles Ross

Remember me when I am gone away,

Gone far away into the silent land...

Christina Georgina Rosetti

Chapter 1

'Twas me," the old woman stood at the foot of the bed. "'Twasn't the others." To prove the point, she jabbed a crooked finger to her bony chest. "'Twas me," she repeated. Her hair, white as fresh snow, sat atop her head in a sloppy bun. Tendrils of frizz sprouted about the bun in such a haphazard way that it would have been laughable to see such a sight.

But it wasn't funny. Not to Cassandra Pratt, who pulled the covers over her face. "Go away!" she cried, but her voice came muffled through the layers of fabric. "You're not real. Go away!" *Surely this is a dream!*

All was still. Cassandra mustered her courage, flipped the covers off and prayed that the vision was gone; but the old woman's wrinkled face was now just inches from her own! Rancid breath filled her nostrils, prompting her to pull the covers up to her eyeballs.

"Don't ye forget!" the hag poked a menacing bony finger onto Cassandra's chest, and then… evaporated into air.

Cassandra was shaken, to say the least. She scanned the room, which had now brightened a bit with the morning sun. No hag visible, but she was confused as to whether the old woman had been a vision, a dream, or… or was she real? She ran to the bathroom mirror and pulled down her pajama top to see if the woman left a finger mark. Nothing, but she was sure she had felt the poke.

"Of course, it was a dream!" She was determined to let it pass as such. *It wasn't real—it wasn't*; but the vision haunted her as she applied her makeup and dressed into her finest white capris. These, she topped with a navy blue nautical-patterned top that hit her mid hip. To complement her pearl and diamond stud earrings, she prepared to slip on her Cartier wristwatch, but paused, wondering if it was a bit too much midday; but, *oh heck*, she loved glitz and wore her expensive clothing and accessories with pride, right down to her Gucci sandals, which were only outshone by her shiny red toenails. She was meeting her gossipy friends at the club for lunch.

After dressing, she called Bill. "I'm looking forward to the dinner dance tonight." It was a monthly event for her, Bill, and their other country club friends. Food, fun, laughs, dancing; ah, life was good!

"Me too, beautiful," came the reply. "I hope you're wearing one of your over-the-top sizzling sexy dresses tonight. Afterward, we'll…."

"Why, Bill Jensen, you're making me blush!"

"Oh, come now. Cassandra Pratt doesn't know what it means to blush!"

"Kiss, kiss, Billy Boy. See you later."

"Attic attack morning!" Cassandra opened the door to the 16 steps leading to the immense attic, which extended to nearly the entire expanse of the mansion, if one wanted to follow its twists, turns, and crawl spaces. She paused at the top to flip on an additional light to peruse the nearest contents, which was all she was interested in doing. The realter told her that she should take what she wanted before the crew came in to remove the discarded items—which she had put off until the last moment, and this was it.

"Oh, crap." She was tempted to leave it go. Did she really want any of this stuff? Dress dummies, sleds, childhood toys, window screens and other paraphernalia were tucked away in dim corners, and viewed through a maze of spider webs. These were the nearest items, and she was hesitant to investigate the furthest, darkest corners.

Then, she spotted an old trunk and decided to take a quick look to appease the realtor and justify that she had investigated the attic. After brushing away the spider webs, she turned the latch and lifted the creaking lid. A wisp of old dust wafted up her nostrils, causing her to cough.

Having no desire to sit on the floor in her white capris, she spotted a brocade padded stool next to a wicker rocker. Naturally, it was covered in years of collected dust and, as she brushed it off, it triggered a dreadful sneezing fit. Earlier, while dressing, she did not take into consideration that investigating the attic contents would require any physical contact with anything. The main thought was to give a quick look over the attic and then tell the realtor to have the men come in and remove it all. What could she possibly want in this dusty old place?

For a moment, she reflected on the oddity of having both parent's dead. First, she thought of her father, the smart and prestigious man whose family had entrusted a large and very healthy realty empire to him. With his business smarts he had expanded his inheritance into an even larger empire, worldwide; and it would support her in style for the rest of her days. It was the way she had grown up, with nannies, private schools, and trips to Europe. She had it all and loved her life.

Now that her mother was gone—a woman obsessed with having the best of everything— Cassandra was free to do as she pleased and live where she pleased. Her mother did her best to shape Cassandra into the perfect society woman, and succeeded; Cassandra relished her position. She wanted the best of everything, and had the best of everything. But the mansion was too large for one person, and expensive to run. She would sell the estate and purchase a penthouse apartment in Baltimore. First, though, she needed to get down to the task at hand, but only briefly; she wanted to get to the club in time to meet her friends for a gossipy lunch, and didn't want to arrive with dirt on her expensive white capris.

She set the stool next to the trunk and sat. "Okay, what do we have here," she said, lifting a manila envelope which was thick with papers—and dust. "Ah…ah…ach…!" A sneeze teased, but gratefully subsided; she didn't want to arrive at the club with red swollen eyes *and* dirty capris, either.

All she needed to do was take a peek inside the envelope, and the rest of the attic could go to the trash. She didn't care what happened to the junk, as long as she made this tiny effort. Job done.

"What am I looking at?" As she pulled the papers from the envelope, something metal hit the floor. "Now what?" On the floor lay a key—an old key. "You're a big one." She lifted it between thumb and forefinger. It certainly was larger than the keys she was familiar with, being about three inches long, and rusted. "What could this be for?"

First, she tried it on the trunk lock, but it didn't fit. Then she ruffled through the pile of items in the trunk— items that were of no interested to her—and, at the bottom beneath the debris, she spotted a wooden chest about a foot wide and eight inches high. Balancing the box on the front side of the trunk with her left hand, she inserted the key. "It fits!" Now she was hooked, and wondered why the box was locked in the first place. She gave it a turn and….

Chapter 2

Cassandra picked herself up off the floor. "What the heck?" she muttered, while dusting off her white capris with her red manicured nails. She turned to fetch the stool, but it was gone—vanished! In fact, *everything* was gone; the stool, the chest and key, the trunk...the attic...*what on earth?*

She turned a circle and then another, not at all registering her surroundings. "Where am I? What's happened?" *This is not the attic...am I dead? Did I have a heart attack?* "Help!"

She spun another circle trying to make sense of it all. Wherever she was, it was dark and gloomy, stale and dank. It smelled like a sewer; it creaked and rolled, causing her to fight for balance. The only light came from a continuous pattern of holes cut into the side. Then, with alarm, she realized that the holes were for several cannons that stood at the ready. *A ship? I'm on a ship?*

The hairs on the back of her neck shot to attention when a scream came from the darkness beyond the cannons. "Who's there?" she cried "Is someone there? Please, I need help!" There was no reply but for another hearty scream. She squinted into the darkness beyond. "Hello?"

This incredible scenario was startling enough, but then a woman appeared from the shadows and stood in the dust filtered beams of light from the cannon holes. Her hair, reddish in color, unkempt and wild, flew about her shoulders in disarray. A dark corset, tied in crisscross fashion down the front of the bodice, forced her breasts to plump like oranges at the neckline. Sleeves of ample fabric blossomed from the shoulder seam to tie at the wrist. Below the corset, a dirty apron cinched tightly at her waist. The woman's skirt hit mid-calf, exposing dark stockings and leather slippers. Cassandra was very attuned to the fashions of women and perused the stranger's attire in a microsecond, but the image before her sent her mind into a tizzy of confusion.

"Well, blimey," the woman placed her fists on her hips. "From where did ye come? Guess the blokes picked up a new wench, and just in time. Get over 'ere then, and give a 'and."

"Who are you? How did you get in here?" Casandra fought the quiver in her voice.

"I could be ask'n the same, miss, but 'tis no time. Come now, and 'elp a poor girl out." The woman jerked her head toward the darkness that loomed behind.

When a scream of agony again pierced the musty, dank, creaking hold of the rolling ship, the red-haired woman turned toward the sound and back again to glare at Cassandra. "Well, are ye feet nailed to the floor?" she yelled. "Move your arse over 'ere and 'elp!"

"Where am I? What is this place?"

"Are ya only good for questions? Lucy needs 'elp, and *now!*" The woman pushed her sleeves up to her elbows and stepped back into the shadows. "They could'na get a wench with sense now, could they?" she mumbled as she vanished into the darkness beyond. Then came the strange woman's voice. "Push, Lucy. Give 'er a push!"

Another scream. "Atta girl! I see it now….atta girl, another push…."

Cassandra took a few steps toward the commotion. "I can't see you. Where did you go? What's happening?" Fear gripped like a vise; she was definitely *not* in the attic.

"Atta girl, Lucy, nearly done!" Another scream echoed through the hold of the ship and then a baby's cry. "Lord be praised, ye done it! A beautiful little babe for ya. A lass, too!"

Cassandra followed the baby's cry, hoping that she wasn't putting herself in danger as she passed the light from the cannon ports into the dark, beyond. When her eyes adjusted to the change of light, she saw a prone figure on the floor, a woman, knees bared and raised, and the strange woman in the corset kneeling beside the figure. She appeared to be cutting the umbellic cord while the baby lay whimpering on the side. "Gimme da babe, Miz Izzie," the woman said, weakly. Once the baby was in her arms, she noticed Cassandra. "Who dat woman?"

"We's a new wench," said the woman named Izzie, as she massaged the prone woman's belly. "How she come about in the middle o' the bay, I can'no say." She stopped massaging momentarily and appeared to fold up a large soiled rag. "There now, 'tis done." She gripped the rag in her fist and stood. "Ach, me achin' backside!" she said, arching her back in a stretch and straightened. "Rest ye, Lucy, and I'll bring some vittles in a bit."

Izzie approached Cassandra, who was totally dismayed and on the verge of tears. She backed away through the streaming light of the cannon ports as the shadowed form neared. "Where…where am I?" Cassandra asked. Such confusion, a rude red-haired woman, childbirth, a baby and a ship; nothing made sense!

"Some fine 'elp from the likes of ya. Are ye deaf? Can'no 'elp a poor woman out?"

"Listen, I'm a little confused." She held her hands up as if to stop the woman's advance. "A few moments ago, I was in my attic clearing out an old trunk, and then, all of a sudden, I'm here." She straightened her shoulders. "Where *is* this place?" she asked, hands on hips in a spirited attempt at control of the situation.

"No 'elp, and ye talk nonsense. Git out o' me way." The woman pushed her aside with an armful of blood-stained rags. She then tucked a wad of her skirt and dirty apron into her waistband and climbed a ladder, rags in hand.

Cassandra followed suit, moving to the ladder and climbing upward. Once at the top, she spotted the woman at yet another ladder, pounding at a closed hatch. "Open up, ya lazy bunch o' pirates!" Izzie yelled, and shortly, the place in which Cassandra stood, brightened enough to see a rat scurry across the floor at the intrusion of light—and then another. A third rat managed to run across her foot, which forced a horrific screech from her lungs and a mad dash for the ladder. Quick as the rats, she scurried and climbed upward until she literally crawled on all fours out onto the top deck.

Legs. Hairy legs. Some light, some dark, some stockinged and oddly shoed, or barefoot; all stood about watching her emergence. The sun, well past high noon, and now a burning ball of red and orange, headed for the horizon, blinded her. Squinting, she held her hand as a visor against its brightness and rose from the hard-rolling deck of the ship— just as a swell caught her off guard, causing her to lose her balance.

"Steady as she goes!" a man said, catching her as she tumbled backward. His thick and hairy arms caught her in the armpits while his hands cupped her breasts in a most lewd fashion. "Let go of me!" she cried, but leaned helpless as a block of wood in his grasp.

"Let's 'ave a sample o'that!" someone yelled. "Can't let Donagal 'ave all the fun!"

Cassandra clawed at the man's hands until he dropped her — unceremoniously— onto the deck. "No gratitude in that one, but at least I got me handful!"

She stood and brushed the dirt from her white capris as the figures top deck came into view, black shadows against the blistering sun.

"A wench in drawers!" said a sailor, and the men laughed. "Whatcha been hiding down there, Izzie girl? Got more of 'em tucked away? One for each?"

Izzie stood a distance away on the rolling deck, and being that she was the only other person whom Cassandra knew (though vaguely) in this crazy nightmare, she moved to Izzie's side, somehow feeling safer. At this angle, with the sun behind her, the faces of the men belonging to the legs came into view. Once she was able to focus on the group of raunchy masculinity, her eyes grew large and she stepped backward until she felt the sidewall of the ship against her back. Bald or hairy, stout or thin as rails, the group represented the most distasteful and frightening display of mankind she had ever set eyes on. The woman, Izzie, had called them pirates, and Cassandra didn't have to conjure up an image of pirates in her head, as this was a motley crew if ever there was one.

Alarm rippled across her flesh, and she wished she would wake from this nightmare; she wished she was at the club laughing with friends and drinking mimosas. *How did I get here?* Who were these disheveled, scraggy and terrifying-looking men?

"Lucy 'ad the babe—a garl—if any of y'blokes cares to know about the poor thing. Lord knows one o' ya is the father, and Lord knows when this ship moors I'm taking me negro and her babe with me. None o' ye low-down scalawags is touchin' 'er again. Got me another slave outta ya's dirty deeds, anyways."

Cassandra listened to this brutal explanation of the woman and baby in the hold with sheer horror. *Slave? God almighty, where am I? Maybe I've been kidnapped into slavery!*

Izzie rolled her eyes up and down Casandra. "Tell me now— and don't be pullin' me leg. This 'alf dressed useless piece o'woman 'ood was fished outta the sea, aye?" This question was followed by silence as the men looked to one another and shrugged. "Well...I won't be forgettin' this little folly o' yours. Tis me 'ands what stirs the galley pots, aye? Tis me 'ands what can give ya the quick step!"

"We don't know where the wench come from," said another sailor.

"Well...ye can stick ya cocks in this one for aught I care. Stood like a statue, she did, when Lucy needed 'er."

"Wha...? How dare you!" Fury overtook Cassandra's fear at this offering of her body to the pack of barbarians that now practically salivated at the offer— or so it appeared in her mind's eye. She backed away to the rail again and subconsciously crossed one white-clad leg over the other. "Don't you dare touch me!" she yelled, erecting her head to the highest, most authoritative level. Her blond streaked shoulder length stick-straight hair flew in wild abandon about her head, the bay winds spidering strands across her mouth and eyes. There she stood, her authoritative moment crippled by a mass of unruly hair. The men laughed raucously, melting her ill-presented dignity. She trembled, and how she wished she were invisible to their eyes!

Izzie laughed with the men. "That'll teach 'er!" she said, and then, apparently satisfied that she had rid herself of the new cargo, she tossed her bundle of soiled rags overboard, and approached the men, hands on hips, staunch and forthright, red hair flying about her head. "Ye won't be layin' a 'and on me. Ye know I'll tear yer willies off 'an feed 'em to the sharks."

Cassandra was surprised to see the men take a step backward at Izzie's offense. The strange woman had power!

Where's our supper then, girl?" a hefty-bearded, round-faced man asked.

"John Petit, can ye not see tis been a bit busy below?" She raised two blood-stained hands.

Cassandra shadowed the woman to a large barrel nestled aside the forecastle, where she retrieved a wooden dipper that was tied by twine to the barrel. With dipper in hand, she filled a bucket and lugged it—sloshing over its rim with every step—to the sidewall, where she rinsed the blood off her hands and arms, then cupped her hands into the pink water and splashed it onto her face and neck.

"There, now," she said, wiping the water away with the dirty, blood-streaked apron. She lifted the heavy bucket, swinging it to toss the water over the side, nearly missing Cassandra's jaw. Cassandra quickly stepped backward, avoiding a possibly devastating injury.

"For Lord's sake, will ye stand away from me?" Izzie set the bucket down and stuck her face into Cassandra's. "Go! I got me 'ands full enough without a useless woman at me heels!"

"I...I don't know where to go, and you can't leave me with that pack of wolves, lady."

"Oh, can I not, now? And just who is givin' me orders?"

"Cassandra Pratt, that's who. I have no clue where I am or why I'm here, and I refuse to be left with those...those animals!" Cassandra pointed in the direction of the unkempt crew, only to find that they had dispersed and gone back to work about the ship. "Well, you know what I mean. I insist....'

"Pratt, eh?" Izzie interrupted and took a step back giving Cassandra the once over. "'Tis odd."

"Odd?" What's odd about it? Why should I want to be abused by that grotesque pack of beasts?"

"It an't that," Izzie replied. "Me name is Pratt, as well."

"A very odd coincidence." Cassandra was momentarily taken aback by that remark. "Surely we are not related in any way. It's entirely impossible that you and I...."

"Oh, 'tis now? Well I an't in no hurry to be akin to a useless, naked woman, neither!"

"Naked? I'll have you know that this outfit cost plenty at Neimen Marcus!" Cassandra was highly insulted, as she considered herself an authority on classy attire and spent hours perusing clothing in order to outclass her friends at the club. "Look at you! You look like...like a scrub woman!"

"Well an't you the fancy piper's wench with yer ear bobbles and bracelets."

Ear bobbles? "This is nonsense," she said. "Just answer my question...*please*. Where... am... I?" She asked this loudly, announcing every word as if Izzie were hard of hearing.

"We sail up the Chesapeake."

The reply came not from Izzie, but from above. She raised her eyes to see the figure of a man on the forecastle who peered down at the pair. As the sun was in her favor, he presented quite a handsome figure. His hair, brown and sun-touched, was pulled back into a ponytail at the nape of his neck, and flapped about in random fashion with the wind. The billowy, blowing sleeves of his ecru-colored shirt, crossed his chest over a dark leather vest that sat just below a belted pair of dark breeches. The breeches were met at the knees by sturdy, brown booted-legs planted firmly on the rolling floor of the forecastle.

At first, struck speechless by his handsome form, it took a moment before Cassandra was able to focus on his face, which the setting sun highlighted as having missed the razor. Instead, a neatly trimmed beard grew from the strong chin of his chiseled face. Cassandra did not miss the fact that he presented the most impressive figure she had ever seen, as he stood in the golden light of sunset.

"The...the Chesapeake?" She stumbled over her words at first, being so caught off guard and awed by his impressive appearance. "Good. The Chesapeake!" she said, gaining control. "You may take me to Baltimore—immediately. I can't make sense of any of this, but I would like to go home...*sir*." Surely, he was a figure of authority and she wanted to make a good impression, even if this was some stupid tourist ride that she found herself on. Perhaps the sleeping pill she took last night caused this insane blackout? She had heard of people sleepwalking under the influence of the drug and wondered if she had gone on some crazy escapade? Yes, that would explain the crazy hag in her bedroom, and this strange episode, as well.

"Come here," the man ordered.

"Gladly!" Cassandra sneered at Izzie as she passed.

"Lucy 'ad the babe, Cap'n, a garl." Izzie called from below. "I'm cleanin' 'er up and takin' the poor woman some sup. She has to feed that babe, not that any of these blokes could give a two-pence. Keep them animals o' yours away from 'er; she an't in any condition for tomfoolery."

"I shall give them a talking to, but you know how 'tis"

Exasperated, Izzie set her hands to her hips. "Better ye threaten 'em with the lash, cap'n."

Cassandra had climbed the forecastle and approached. Up close, she could see that the captain was a head taller than she and quite muscular. His hair was touched not only with gold from the sun, but his temples showed the early signs of gray, as did his beard.

"What's your name, woman?," he asked, eyeing her suspiciously.

"Cassandra Pratt."

"Hmph, 'tis odd."

"I know 'tis odd", she mimicked, "but that crazy woman and I are not—I repeat, *not*—related."

"How did you manage to stowaway aboard my ship?"

"Don't be ridiculous. Of course I'm not a stowaway—and you had better not be a human trafficker. I'm more a kidnapped victim, for your information. I'll pay for the ticket; just get me home. I'll pay *double* for the ticket. This is an insane tour anyway. I can't see how you could make any money doing it in the first place. Who, in their right mind would fake a horrid baby's birth in the stinking hold of a tour boat and have that crazy woman, Izzie, walking around with bloody hands? I don't know what company you're operating out of, but I will definitely review them online."

The captain stared as she gesticulated wildly while rambling on, and continued to stare after she had finished. In silence they stood, looking at one another until Cassandra could stand it no longer. "Well? Let's go to Baltimore!"

"Might I remind you, woman, that *I* am the captain of this ship, and that we are not seeking Lord Baltimore."

"*Lord* Baltimore? You are carrying this too far. Take me to any port along here and I will take a taxi home. No problem."

"Step below, *now*. Off with you. We shall speak later."

"Okay, I get it. I will pay you *triple* for the ticket if you return me to Baltimore, but your tour company will be hearing from me."

"Where are your clothes, woman? You cannot be flaunting thyself in such a way."

"Are you listening to me, Captain?"

"Your prattle makes no sense. Below with you, or I shall have you escorted."

"What? What's wrong with you people? I will not leave this spot until you promise to take me to Baltimore!"

"Cupid!" the captain shouted over her head.

"Cupid?" Cassandra looked about wondering if the captain had gone mad, but very shortly an extremely large and muscular black man appeared, shoeless, bare chested and wearing nothing else but knee length breaches. A map of tattoos crossed his chest and arms, as well as several odd lines inked into his face. To complete the picture, a large gold loop earring pierced his right earlobe.

"Take Mistress Pratt below," the captain ordered.

"Pratt?" Cupid replied. "'Tis..."

"I know! I know, 'tis odd!" Cassandra yelled, then grabbed the ship's wheel. "That man is not taking me anywhere," she growled. I will not leave this spot until you promise to take me home!"

"You are pushing my patience, woman!" The captain unpeeled her fingers from the wheel and physically lifted her to Cupid. "Take her!" he ordered, and Cupid flung her over a shoulder with very little effort, but not without giving her rear end a pat and squeeze.

"Put me down, you ape!" she cried. "Don't touch me! Help!"

Apparently, some of the crew watched from their various points on the ship, for spots of laughter rang out.

"Do not fondle the woman, Cupid," the captain said, less forceful than Cassandra would have liked to hear. "You are to leave all the women alone. Do you understand? Do all of you understand?" he yelled. Cassandra prayed his order was heard bow to stern; but most likely, it blew away with the gusty winds that now flapped the sails. "There will be a flogging if I hear otherwise! Understand?"

A few weak 'aye 'aye's' reached her ears, but certainly only those sailors within hearing distance. What about the others? She strained to hear more of a response, but none were coming.

"Get that woman's ass out of my face and down to the galley!" the captain ordered, his patience obviously having run the gamut. Cupid took the few steps down from the forecastle, with Cassandra bouncing along on his shoulder.

"And tell Izzie to get the woman some proper clothing!" the captain said in afterthought.

Casandra, totally at a loss of all sensibility of the situation, rode the muscular black back across a span of decking to an open hatch where Cupid set her down. "Go now," he said, indicating the ladder into the darkened bowels of the ship.

Being at least two hundred pounds lighter than Cupid, she realized that escape was ridiculous, as there was no place to escape to; they were surrounded by water.

First, she peered into the rectangular opening and then looked at Cupid, who stood impatiently with his arms crossed over his barrel chest. "Go," he ordered.

With no recourse, she descended into what hell, she did not know. Cupid followed close behind, and once on floor level she realized she was not in the same section of the ship as she had been previously. Glass-enclosed lanterns hung on walls, shedding an amber glow that revealed much improved conditions than she had previously experienced. Where the hold appeared to be of roughhewn wood, this section of the ship was civilly paneled and appeared to be more suited for living quarters, and not cargo.

The galley was a small space separated from the dining area by an overhead rack which held, by iron hooks, several utensils, such as ladles and serving spoons. The long dining table was of a thick hardwood that sat on stumpy legs secured to the flooring and surrounded by a dozen chairs. A rudimentary stove, built of brick and iron, sat against the ship's sidewall, its smoke pipe funneled out through the wall. Cassandra had never seen such a piece of work! Two large iron pots sat across an iron slab heated by the glowing embers in the hearth—the aroma none too enticing, as far as Cassandra was concerned.

Izzie stood bent at the waist tossing wood into the hearth of the apparatus. Her wild hair, now tied back with a string of cloth, created a large and fuzzy ponytail that sat like a strange animal upon her back. The heat of the hearth shone bright on her sweat dampened forehead.

She straightened and turned, once realizing she had visitors. "And why did ye bring this worthless woman to me?" she asked, wiping the sweat from her brow with the dirty, bloody apron.

"Cap'n say she is to help in da galley."

"She weren't a lick o' help birthin' that baby. I don't want'er. Take 'er out."

"No, Izzie. Cap'n says...."

"Cap'n says, cap'n says," Izzie mimicked, as Cupid's shiny black back departed the galley, leaving Cassandra to face her foe.

Izzie picked up a burlap bag from a dark wooden counter and flung it at Casandra, who caught it— just barely—as it was heavier than the red-headed woman had made it appear.

"Peel 'em."

She peeked into the dark opening of the bag. "Potatoes? You expect me to peel potatoes?"

17

"Do ye want to eat…" Izzie's eyes grew large, fists settled on hips "…or do ye want to starve? If ye do not lift a finger, then ye starve. I would not give a shillin' either way."

"Alright, alright," Cassandra said, defeated. She couldn't wait to get to shore and get home. She'd be on the phone pronto to report this rotten group to the tourism board. However, as nothing else had worked to speed her on the way home, she relented. "I need a potato peeler." She said as she set the bag down on the rough wooden counter.

"Oh, she wants a tater peeler, does she? 'ere!" Izzie said, stabbing the counter with a paring knife so close to Cassandra's fingers that she shrieked and jumped backward.

Izzie smiled for the first time, showing a few missing teeth in her brown-stained grin. "Thar ye go now, a tater peeler," she said, snidely.

Cassandra, determined to at least survive until the ship docked, composed herself and pulled the knife from the counter. "No problem," she said and reached into the burlap bag.

To her horror, instead of pulling out a potato, a brown furry object scurried up her arm to her shoulder, its long tail trailing like a snake! This sent her into a frantic high-stepping dance accompanied by shrill screams of terror. "Get it off! Get if off!" she cried, while her hands—one still holding the knife—waved erratically in the air— until the knife-yielding hand stabbed at the rat still perched and shaking in the crook of her neck. But, instead of stabbing the creature, who jumped to the floor and disappeared into a dark corner, Cassandra plunged the knife into her shoulder! Shocked at what she had done, she stumbled backward into the dining table and plunked herself into a heavy wooden chair as blood seeped through the fabric of her nautical top.

"Well, ye done it now!"

She vaguely heard Izzie say those words before the stars in her eyes vanished into darkness.

Chapter 3

Cassandra focused on the round, sweaty face of a man who peered into her own.

"So tell me, how the blazes did you manage that one?" he asked, seeing that her eyes had opened to slits.

"Wha...? Who are you? Where am I? Am I still on this damn ship?" Realizing she was lying prone on the dining table, she attempted to raise up onto her elbows, but a sharp pain in her left shoulder abruptly stopped her ascent. "Ouch! Oh, my God, the knife!" She reached to feel the handle of the blade protruding from her shoulder, but it was gone. Then, with horror, she realized she was wearing nothing from the waist up!

"How dare you!" she screamed. "Who are you? Where are my clothes?" Battling the sharp pain of her wound, she rose to a sitting position, throwing her arms crisscross across her chest. Nausea roiled in her gut, and she felt oddly light headed and dizzy.

"Don't git your dander up, deary; I seen plenty o' teats in me time...oh, yes indeedy, I have...." he added, dreamily. "And plenty bigger than those biscuits 'o yours." He nodded to her hidden breasts, causing Cassandra to press her arms even tighter to her chest. "But, back to the business of that nasty bit o' self-affliction. I put the needle to it, stitched it up, and you'll be good as new in a few weeks."

Cassandra's fingers felt for the knife wound. Three bumps indicated that she had three stitches. "Are you a doctor?" she asked, feeling as if she were about to pass out. "A *licensed* doctor?"

"Here and there. Most o' the time I cut the crew's hair, and shave the cap'n."

"What?" She felt herself weave on the table. "Did you at least give me a tetanus shot? That kitchen is disgustingly dirty, and there are rats! That knife probably hadn't been washed in weeks—or maybe *never.*"

The man looked confused. "Shot? You were not shot, dearie, you stabbed yourself!"

Cassandra thought the man was either totally in character, or she was losing it. "Tetanus shot," she said slowly. "A…tetanus…shot…. You know, sickness; lockjaw; death."

"Oh, lockjaw, you say. Well, an't nothin' we can do 'bout that but pray there is not infection." The man's voice began to fade away into the distance.

"Please…get me some clothes. I think I…I think…."

"I think you had best take a rest. The laudanum's gettin' to you. Get me a shirt, Izzie!" the man called. "Sorry, miss, but I had to cut your…uh…your undergarment off. I must say, taint never seen the likes of the harness contraption you was wearin'."

Izzie appeared from somewhere as a fuzzy blur, literally throwing a whitish cut of fabric at her. The man intercepted and helped to slide the large shirt over her head, and then guided her good arm through one sleeve.

"This may hurt a bit," he warned as he guided her other arm through the remaining sleeve, thus sending sharp pains through her injured shoulder.

"Stop! Stop!" she screamed, but to no avail since the other arm needed to go through or she'd be half naked without her bra.

"There now," he said. "Have yourself a little rest. We'll move you soon, due to it being supper time."

"Move 'er now!" Izzie yelled. "I got hungry men waitin' for their sup!"

"You people are taking this too far," Cassandra said dreamily, now that the sharp pains had subsided. "I want... to go... home." With that said, her mind cleared a moment. "I demand that this ship take me to port—somewhere—I don't care where. I need a tetanus shot, antibiotics, and you...you are not a doctor."

"Izzie, get Cupid," the man ordered.

"Cupid...I remember him...." The room began to spin.

"He'll take you to a hammock."

In her stupor, a hammock sounded wonderful; a hammock, Caribbean waters, Piña Colada...*oh yes, please....* Maybe they were coming to their senses after all, and were going to dock, were going to set her free?

Much to Cassandra's annoyance, she was awakened by snoring. Wherever she was, it was dark except for the golden light of lanterns, a few of which she caught sight of from her hammock as it swung gently from side to side with the rolling waters of the bay.

I'm still on the damn ship! With this realization, she attempted to remove herself from the hammock, but her wound thwarted her efforts as she struggled to rise to a sitting position. At last, with her upper body lying sidewise in the hammock, she was able to shoot a leg out and down to the floor. Now, holding the hammock steady with one foot on the floor, she rolled out of her canvas trap, landing on her knees.

Her squeaky scream of surprise and pain as she landed with a *thud*, startled the snorer and sent him into a different cacophony of sounds—none of which were pleasant to the ear.

"Damn," she whispered, fearful of waking the sailor. Upon standing, she noticed that there were several hammocks in this particular area, some with sleeping sailors, and some empty. In fact, there was more than one sailor snoring; and the entire situation was as baffling as it was annoying. Her patience was running very thin; her shoulder hurt like the devil and she wanted to get to shore, get home, and get medical help. Who knew what kind of doctor the joker was? Everyone on the ship was nuts. She would sue the lunatics!

The ship creaked as it rocked gently in the waters. The floor creaked too, as she slipped past the sleeping sailors, the hammocks, and left the area completely. She was surprised to come across an area she recognized—the galley! Apparently, the meal time was over, as there was not a soul in sight. In the lantern's glow, she saw that the chairs rested against the long table, the utensils hung in slots over the worn, dark counter, the ladles hung from their hooks, and only a slight warmth radiated from the brick oven. Remembering the rat, she quickly left the kitchen area to the ladder, and stood wondering if she could even climb. It wasn't a bit easy, climbing step by step, one armed. It wasn't fast, either, as she had to hug the ladder siderail with her good arm, take a step, then slide her arm up to hug the siderail at the next rung.

Once up, she was rewarded with a carpet of stars twinkling against the dark heavens. A mild breeze ruffled her hair, and she inhaled, thinking it was sweet and pure, forgetting for a moment that she was lost in the grip of a very unusual circumstance.

"Ah, you are awake, woman."

Cassandra focused on the captain who stood starboard, one arm resting on the sidewall railing. He was faintly outlined by lantern light, and she found it odd that only lanterns were used to light the ship, but perhaps this was a very authentic tour, down to the very nails.

"Oh, hello, captain. Why don't you stop referring to me as 'woman'. I have a name, as you well know."

"Of course, Mistress Pratt."

"Don't you think that due to the fact I have been injured on this tour, that you should get me to shore and to a real doctor?"

The captain laughed, which annoyed her greatly, as she did not find anything amusing about a knife wound in the shoulder— and especially *her* shoulder.

"The barber knows his craft. He has stitched up many of my men, and more than once, I might add."

"For what reason do you have need for his medical expertise, or lack, thereof?"

"Why, in my trade it is sometimes necessary for uh, unpleasant altercations."

She was exasperated. It was impossible to get a reasonable answer from anyone on board, they all spoke nonsense! The sleeves of the shirt she now wore were long and flowing, gathered at the wrist, but with such excess fabric that they folded over the wrist ties and covered her hands. The hem of the shirt ended at the bottom of her knees, leaving only a few short inches of capris peeking at the bottom. "Whose shirt is this?" she asked, holding up her hands and letting the excess fabric fall to gravity.

"It appears to be my shirt, one I gave Izzie to wash."

"Thank you, sir, for the loan of your shirt. I now insist you take me to shore so that I may get home and get real medical attention—and my own *clean* clothes."

"I'm afraid I cannot do that. You must remain with us until we are able to access land."

"Listen, Mr. Captain, I'm through playing this game. I need to get home to make sure that quack of yours, Dr. Nothing Barber, hasn't given me gangrene, or some horrid thing. There are hundreds of ports out there," she said, waving her arm across the expanse of darkness beyond the captain.

"Even if fires burned from shore, I could not leave you in the wilderness alone."

Lights. That's what was odd; there were no lights ashore! "I don't understand this," Cassandra said, as she moved to stand beside the captain, perusing what should be land in the distance. You said we're on the Chesapeake, but there are always lights along the Chesapeake."

"We are most certainly on the Chesapeake. We shall pull into a river for the night, so as not to be seen."

"Not seen? Why is this? I want to be seen! What the heck kind of a ship is this?" she questioned, looking up at the captain. Despite his somewhat overboard masculine appearance, his speech was peculiar to her, but refined compared to the crew; two plus two did not equal four in this circumstance. "What kind of ship is this, captain? Is it a tour boat, or are you some kind of whacked out modern day pirate? Am I a prisoner? Have I been drugged and kidnapped? Is it ransom you want? Well, my father is dead and you will have to deal directly through me."

The captain again laughed. "I think I am as confused as thee. Yes, you have been drugged, but for the purpose of relieving the pain of your self-inflicted stab wound. No, you are not a prisoner, and no, you have not been kidnapped."

"Where are you from? How did you hear about me? The newspapers? The society page? I demand to know!"

"'Tis my home, here."

"And what kind of a dumb tour is this? It's very un-American, you know, the way I'm being treated, and especially on a tour boat."

The captain laughed. "You are definitely a bit confused, woman. I can assure you this is not a 'tour boat', as you say."

Cassandra was getting quite huffy at this point. The more questions she asked, the more she thought to ask, and the captain's replies were not at all satisfactory. He seemed to find everything she said amusing. Indeed, she must have looked a sight: the long shirt, no shoes (which she just noticed), her hair blowing about her face, and then the ridiculous act of stabbing herself in the shoulder. *He must think me quite the nutcase.* She then reprimanded herself for even being concerned as to what the captain thought of her!

"Questions, questions. Izzie is right. You are a strange one and full of questions. To answer them, let us just say I am here working at my trade. I haven't a clue as to why you are here, and I honestly know not how you arrived on my ship."

"And just what is your trade if not tour boat operator?"

The captain straightened himself and stood with arms across his chest, stern and serious. "I can assure you of these facts; I am a ship's captain and have sailed these waters and the waters of distant lands for quite a spell. My crew did not have the good fortune as I, to be born into a family of gentility with access to a good education. Nonetheless, they may be a 'ruffians' as you say, and they may not speak proper English, but they are a hardworking and efficient crew."

Cassandra cradled her head in her hands. "I don't understand what's happening." She wanted to cry, but didn't dare show weakness in this circumstance. She straightened her body, shoulders back, chin high, and tried a new approach. "Please captain…uh…what is your name?"

"Captain Jonathan Percival Strongbow."

"Well, Captain Jonathan Percival Strongbow, in the morning I would very much appreciate this ship docking at any port along these waters. Eastern Shore, Western Shore, I really don't care. You will be rid of me, and I…well, I will be able to get to my doctor for a tetanus shot, and an examination of what Mr. Barber has done to me. There."

"And, Mistress Pratt, if you should care to disembark at St. Mary's, it shall be done; 'tis the only port I should sail to at this time."

"What? Why can't you take me to Baltimore?"

"You befuddle me, woman."

"Baltimore. Annapolis. Cambridge. St. Michaels…surely you can take me to a closer port than St. Mary's?"

"I know of no such ports."

"What? You have lost it, Captain; you are much too much into your character."

"I beg your pardon?"

"There have been ports here for centuries—I'm sure!"

The Captain stared out into the darkness, then turned to Cassandra. "Woman, I believe you are befuddled yourself. As captain of this ship, in the year of our lord, 1644, I can assure you that the ports you mention do not exist."

"1644? What kind of idiot do you take me for? You befuddle *me*, captain—if you really *are* a captain." Cassandra voice had now reached a high pitch, and her head ached. It was impossible to get any sane information from anyone aboard this ship! Izzie Pratt was a lunatic; the doctor/barber didn't know what a tetanus shot was; a poor woman gave birth in the filthy hold of the ship. Now the captain was telling her the year is 1644! "This is exasperating!"

Cassandra yelled. "This is the year 2018 and I just want to go home!"

"Calm yourself, woman! When it is at all possible, I shall deposit you—somewhere— but for now, you must stay onboard."

"Okay, okay." She took a deep breath. "I would like to go to bed, captain, and not with that gang of hoodlums in the hammocks. I require a private room and bath."

"I'm afraid that is impossible. Izzie has prepared a bed for you below."

"Below? You mean that dark, stinking, rat-plagued hell hole? Certainly not! What kind of crazy tour is this?"

"Now that you are up and about, it is important that the women are separated from the crew."

"Well, I'll go along with that," she said, remembering the salivating, disheveled, dirty men.

"Where's the door," she asked, tired of conversing in circles with the captain. Nobody understood her plight, and, worst of all, nobody cared.

The captain took a lantern from its hook, and she followed behind until he stopped to lift a heavy hatch door. "Mind your step," he said. "Two ladders down."

"Yes, I remember."

Traversing the ladder with her one good arm again was not a simple task, but at least the captain held the lantern overhead so she could see where she was going. Very carefully, did she tread the second ladder, and once down with the canons she took a lantern off its hook on the wall and scanned the floor near and far for rats. There were some things she couldn't abide, and rats were top on the list. After all, she had grown up in the lap of luxury, and that did not include rats!

"Izzie!" she called, scanning midship with her lantern. "Where are you?" Because of the dark night, the cannon ports gave little in the way of light.

"She sleep," Lucy answered. Smacking sounds from the baby indicated that the woman was nursing the infant.

Cassandra swung the lantern in the direction of Lucy's voice. "Where?" she asked, ignoring any form of courtesy. "Where's Izzie? She supposedly made a bed for me."

Lucy did not reply, but looked confused in the yellow glow of the lantern.

"You do speak English, don't you?"

"Yes," came the reply.

"Okay, great. Let's try this again." This time Cassandra paused between words in case the woman was slow witted. "Where...is...Izzie?"

The young woman nodded to her left, and Cassandra turned the lantern accordingly. A few feet away from Lucy and the baby was a lump covered by a blanket.

"Izzie, wake up. Where is my bed?" she asked, as she approached the lump. This woman here doesn't understand me."

No reply.

Cassandra nudged her with a foot. "Wake up!"

Izzie threw off her cover and shot to a sitting position. *"Trasna ort féin!*[1]*"* she yelled, and laid down, pulling the cover over her head. "On the other side," she said, muffled as it was.

"Well, thanks for imparting the information, imbecile. My bed is on what other side?"

"Dat way." Lucy, witness to the episode, gestured toward the bow of the ship.

Cassandra swung the light in the direction indicated and then back at Lucy. "I'm not sleeping all the way over there! Why, I can't even see where my bed is, and there are rats down here, you know."

"Rats, yes," Lucy replied, nodding.

"Whatever." Cassandra held the lantern outward as she slowly made her way toward the bow to retrieve her bedding; to her, it was better to sleep as a group—no matter how distasteful—than to sleep in the far end of a rat-infested ship, alone.

---

[1] *Téigh trasna ort féin'*: Go 'F' yourself in Gaelic

It was a creepy jaunt, to say the least. With only the lantern to guide her way, minimal directions, and ever watchful for rats, she gingerly made her way across the creaking, rolling floor, sidestepping the ballast rocks—which seemed to take up the entire width at this point— until she spotted a mess of rumpled fabric ahead. Once she reached the pile, she realized her bed was nothing more than a thin excuse of a pillow, and an even thinner blanket. As she lifted them from the flooring, a rat, apparently nestled in the limp blanket for the night, jumped to the floor and scurried away. Disgusted, she secured the bedding under her disabled arm and made her way back to the fold where she spread her blanket out a few feet from Izzie, set her sorry pillow at the head and painfully lowered her body. "What a nightmare," she moaned, as she shifted for a fraction of comfort—a nearly impossible goal on the hard wood floor. "I just want to go home," she whispered and began to cry.

"May God speed ye outta 'ere so I may enjoy a bit o' sleep!" Izzie replied from beneath her cover.

Chapter 4

Cassandra woke to annoying jabs at her ribcage.

"Get up."

She opened her eyes and looked to the cannon ports for the telltale filtered rays of morning sun; dawn was not yet beaming through. "What on earth for?" she asked, through a heavy sleep fog. "It's not even daylight yet; and stop kicking me! Leave me alone!"

"Git yer arse up. 'Tis time to cook for the crew." Izzie delivered a swifter kick to her behind. "Cap'n says ye's ta help in the galley, so git yer arse up."

"Oh, my God." She grimaced with pain when she tossed the thin blanket aside. "How am I going to work with this shoulder?"

"One 'anded."

"I need aspirin for the pain, and I have to pee—badly."

"In the piss bucket."

"And where might the piss bucket be?" she asked, haughtily.

"Git your arse up. If ye care to take charge of the emptyin', then ye can put it where ya like."

Begrudgingly, with the throbbing pain in her shoulder and every joint in her body aching, Cassandra raised herself off the floor. Her mouth tasted like low tide. She realized she hadn't had a drink of water or any food since…since when, she didn't know. This nightmare had turned her world topsy-turvy.

"If it's poopin' ye need to do, go to the poop deck."

"You are so crass, Izzie Pratt."

After relieving herself in the half-full, stinking piss bucket, with no toilet paper available, Cassandra staggered behind Izzie to the ladder, which she climbed one handed—and with great difficulty—to the next level. She couldn't help but wonder what would happen at the poop deck if there was no paper. What if the sailors were there? She dreaded asking Izzie the answer to that question!

Once on the middle landing, she realized she was near the galley, and a bit further beyond that would be the hammock section. It was good to get her bearings, even in this nightmare.

Izzie peered into the stove hearth and blew gently. "Hurry," she said, "bring the woodchips there in the bucket, and be quick!" She nodded to the shelf where the knives hung neatly in their slots. Next to the knives, was a large metal bucket, which Cassandra retrieved with some difficulty considering her handicap. Izzie reached into the bucket and grabbed a few chips, throwing them into the smoldering embers. Again, she blew gently, and suddenly, the chips burst into flame casting a warm glow into the galley.

Cooking breakfast for the crew was a grueling affair, literally. The large iron pots that sat stovetop were filled with water from a barrel and mixed with an unrecognizable grain. To her horror, Cassandra realized that the grain wriggled! A yelp of surprise slipped through her lips bringing Izzie to her side.

"What 'tis it now?"

"The grain—it's moving!"

"'Tis weevils; pay it no mind."

"We're going to feed the crew weevils?"

"The crew, the captain, Lucy, and we."

"I can't eat weevils. I would rather starve!"

"Pick 'em out then, if ye can, or don't eat a'tal, for all I care. Do the work and be done with it!"

This intercourse was interrupted by heavy footsteps on the ladder. Six men filed in, talking, laughing, pulling their chairs noisily from beneath the table. *Thump, thump, thump, thump.* The sound of their behinds making contact with the seats of the chairs brought to reality the advent of mealtime in the galley. Big and burley, small and wiry, smelly and unshaven, the men sat, pewter spoons gripped in strong and calloused hands ready for their morning meal.

"Gimme rum, woman!" a dark bearded man hollered, holding up one of the pewter mugs that sat by each place setting.

"Got me 'ands full, and two useless ones, 'ere," Izzie replied, nodding toward Cassandra, who felt quite intimidated contained in these quarters with a crazy woman and the present display of fearsome—to say the least—testosterone.

"Stop your idleness and get busy!" Izzie yelled, wiping her damp forehead with a corner of her apron. "Fill the mugs an' be quick now."

"I would be happy to," Cassandra replied haughtily. She was sick of Izzie's commands and superior attitude. "And what, pray tell, your highness, am I filling the cups with?"

"The grog in the barrel." Izzie pointed her frizzy head to a large barrel in the corner of the galley. "Stupid, useless woman," she mumbled.

With only one semi-working arm, it took time to fill the pewter mugs, one by one from the dark barrel, and serve as well, while suffering slaps and pinches to her behind by one sailor or another. The gruel was then ladled into bowls, which Cassandra also served to the men. By the time she reached the sixth man, the others were finished drinking their grog, and demanding more.

"Be off with ya!" Izzie yelled. "Ye knows the cap'n's rules. Cannot 'ave a bunch o' drunken sailors skulkin' about."

Eventually, the table emptied, thus allowing another group of six to tramp into the galley, settle their behinds on the chairs, and demand their meals. Cassandra's behind felt the repeated slaps and pinches through the narrow linen of the captain's shirt, and her white capris, which were quickly becoming splotched with spilt rum, gruel, and just plain dirt.

"This is disgusting!" she said, once all the men had disappeared. The galley was a mess, and Izzie was quite drenched in sweat.

"Disgustin', is it? This is the life, your greatness, until we leave this stinkin' ship. Not that I shall miss it for a bag o' gold coins. I shall make me own fortune in the new world."

"New world?" *This is crazy,*" Cassandra thought. "For your information, your *new* world is now the *old* world. You can read about it in school books—but, oh, you don't have any school books, and you probably can't read anyway."

"Lord in heaven, ye are a snide one, and I object to that remark. If weariness did'na 'ave a grip on me, ye'd be sportin' a fat lip!" She ladled herself a cup of the diluted rum and plunked herself down at the table. "Oh, me weary feet," she moaned, crossing a leg over one knee, and removing her slipper to massage her stockinged foot. "'Ave ya'self a cup o' grog and rest a bit. We've much work to do cleanin' up after those good-for-nothin' pirates."

"No thank you," Cassandra replied, though she felt quite thirsty. "I don't drink rum in the morning. Is there coffee?"

"Ha! Mi'lady wants coffee, does she? Coffee is for the cap'n and gents, not for ladies, and not for the likes o'you."

"Of course coffee is for ladies, too. I drink coffee by the gallons," Cassandra replied, exasperated. "I don't understand any of this; what in the world is happening?"

"'appenin'? Ye's daft, ya know. 'Tis us who cares to know what's 'appenin'. Ye come from the water, half naked, and talkin' strange. 'Tis a siren[2] ye may be for all we know, bringin' bad luck to the ship. Tell me the truth of it. Sit there." Izzie nodded to the chair across the table.

Cassandra relented, ladled a half mug of the rum mixture and sat down. She winced after taking a sip of the rum, but it was fluid, and she needed it. She gulped the rest down, her stomach rumbling as the rum hit her belly. She was starving, and thought of the lunch she missed at the club. Tears could have run like a faucet with the weariness she felt in this chaotic nightmare. "I don't know what's

---

[2] Siren: Greek mythology. Sea-nymphs who lured sailors to their deaths

happening. I don't know how I got here. I don't recognize anything…the ship, the food…the clothing."

Izzie's eyebrow scrunched together as she listened. "The 'ead is addled, is it? Well this is where ya be, aboard the schooner, Thunder, under Cap'n Strongbow."

"Do you always work on this ship?"

"Ha! An't 'ere for the pleasurin' o'these ruffians or cookin' their meals to me old age!" she replied, offended. "I work me fingers to the bone night and day for these pirates and the cap'n, and count the days 'til I can leave this bloody rat house—and I'm takin' me slave girl and her babe with me when I do. I won 'er fair and square. I'll not leave her to the 'ands of that murderin' bunch o' buccaneers. She can be me slave gal in the new world, and with the babe, I got me two in the bargain."

"Slave? There's no slavery. What are you talking about?"

"Cap'n tells me everyone 'as a slave in the new world— now I got me two."

Cassandra shook her head in exasperation. "How did you get here?" she asked, changing the subject and hoping by some miracle Izzie was as confused as she of her own appearance onboard.

"By King's decree!" Izzie laughed. "'Twas me punishment for pickpocketin' a gent who 'ad a jolly good time under me petticoat!"

"What?"

"You know…sticken' the old pego in me cock lane."

"What in the world are you talking about? See, this is what I mean; I don't understand any of this!"

"Do ye know nothin', woman? Stickin' the ol' horn up the…." Izzie spread her legs and gestured lewdly.

"Oh. Okay, okay. I got it, you can stop now." She felt a blush spread across her face. Izzie's character on board was obviously not just a wacko cook, but a prostitute!

"I stole from the wrong gent, is all." Izzie continued, justifying her situation. "How'd I know he was such big wig? He come to me with a pocket full o' Spanish silver and bullets in them twiddle-diddles. A garls got to make a livin', ya know. After a fortnight o' rottin' in Newgate prison, I, Izzie Pratt, is set a'sail with a bunch o' picaroons headed for the colonies, I am, and dumped off at Hispanola." Izzie sighed. "'Tis where Cap'n Strongbow made me acquaintance, and where me and Lucy hooked up. Perhaps 'tis a good thing."

Cassandra eyed her companion across the table. "Very convincing, Izzie."

"Aye?"

"You do a fine job of it, but I'm tired of all this playacting. All this crazy lingo, old clothes, creepy kitchen and pretending this is the year 1644, For Pete's sake. I've had enough; I just want to go home!"

"Play actin'? You really are daft; Me name's Izzie Pratt, born in Ireland, kicked on me bum to England, and this is the year 1644."

"This proves it!" Cassandra said, pounding a first on the table. "You are all nuts! This is 2018, for God's sake. What's wrong with you people? You are really taking this reenactment business too far."

Izzie looked very perplexed and stared at Cassandra questioningly for a moment or two before her brows crinkled together and her dark eyes narrowed into slits. "Now I gets it," she said. "Ye was in the madhouse, wasn't ya? Where'd they keep ya?"

"No, I was *not* in a madhouse. If anything, this ship is a madhouse!" The rum had now sent a nice buzz through her veins. No longer did tears well her eyes, but anger instead.

"Oh, Cap'n Strongbow!" Izzie said, shooting to her feet.

Cassandra twisted in her chair to see that the captain had now entered the galley. "Good morning," she said, following Izzie's lead and rising from her chair. "We're having a discussion going here, and I'm very concerned that I have been kidnapped to who-knows-where, by you and this vulgar crew of yours. Miss Pratt tells me, just as you have, that this is the year 1644. Now, I am sick of this. I have been forced to sleep in a rat infested—whatever that place is—and forced to work in this filthy kitchen with this crazy woman. I demand that you take me ashore...immediately!" The rum had fueled her anger, and she was tempted to ladle more into her mug.

"We won't be debating this again, will we, Mistress Pratt?" The captain pulled out a chair and sat. "Izzie, my food, please. I'll have it here, since you have neglected to bring it to my cabin."

"Oh, I do apologize, cap'n, but this daft woman 'ere is tellin' me that we are livin' in the year 2018!" Izzie laughed heartily as she removed herself to the stove to fix his bowl of gruel and cup of grog.

The captain raised his brows. "Still fixed on 2018, are you?" He leaned against the smoothly worn back of the chair, appearing to be deep in thought, but Cassandra was impatient.

"Yes, 2018. The game is over!" To prove the point, she plopped the fist of her good arm down on the table in front of the captain. "I will not take this any longer. If you do not take me to shore, I will swim!"

The captain's chair flew backward as he stood. "You are an insubordinate young woman! I remind you again that I am the captain of this ship. It is my duty to keep my crew and passengers— unruly as they be—safe. This is not a 'tour', as you continuously insist upon, but a working ship. If you cannot be...."

"Captain!"

Even Cassandra recognized peril in the voice of the sailor, who rapidly clumped down the ladder and ran to the galley. "'Tis the Windward, cap'n, in the middle o' the bay, straight off the bow!"

"Pull anchor. Make sail!" The captain ordered, and left without another word to the women.

"What does this mean?" Cassandra asked, turning to Izzie, who stood wide-eyed, and still holding the captain's bowl of gruel.

"We must get Lucy and the babe!" she said, setting the bowl on the counter. "Quick!"

"What's going on? You're scaring me!"

"Be quick, now!" Izzie raced passed Cassandra leaving her to stand alone and confused.

It was a madhouse of sailors that clambered down the ladder headed to the cannon deck. Izzie managed to squeeze into the melee and soon was on the gun deck herself. By the time Cassandra reached the bottom of the ladder—one armed at that— Izzie had the baby clenched to her chest. and was telling Lucy to climb. Izzie stepped in behind Lucy, leaving Cassandra to be last in line. She looked at the rows of cannons and the men scrambling with cannon balls, powder and shot.

"Make ready!" came an order from one of the sailors. "Three-pounders, all sides!"

Cassandra viewed the ladder as if it were the Empire State Building, but she certainly didn't want to be on the gun deck when all hell broke loose. The sore shoulder was making the nightmare even more of a nightmare; yet, she managed to climb the ladder again, prodded upward by the fear of something very dangerous about to occur. "Izzie!" she cried, once on the galley deck. "Where'd you go?"

"In 'ere!" Izzie's muffled voice called, and Cassandra followed the direction until she reached the stern of the ship, stopping at a heavy door. She knocked. "Izzie?"

The door creaked open. "Unless ye want your head blown to pieces, get in 'ere!"

Cassandra stepped inside to a paneled room with bowed windows at the stern. Nothing could be seen at this point, aside from morning light through thick and dirty glass. A large desk sat in front of the paned windows, with many books and papers sprawled about. Lanterns hung in several places against the walls, and an oil lamp sat on the desk. The cabin was large enough for a long rustic dining table with chairs to seat ten people, and in a corner, a bed covered in a faded quilt over a large, lumpy mattress. It looked much more comfortable than the pathetic blanket and pillow she was forced to use. "I gather these are the captain's quarters?" she asked, but Izzie was in the process of settling Lucy and the babe onto the bed.

"We gon die, Izzie!" Lucy cried.

"An't goin' to die, stupid wench. They an't got us yet, 'ave they?

"What the devil are you talking about?" A tremendous boom shook the ship, causing the women to fight for balance. "What's happening?" Cassandra screamed, her heart beating a mile a minute.

"Dem cannons!!" Lucy cried, setting the infant off into piercing wails.

The ship was moving—and quickly. Cassandra heard the captain shouting orders above. She ran to the bowed window to get a view of the oncoming danger, but the angle was wrong, and the small windowpanes were filthy from sea salt and foam. "Is this a reenactment?" she asked, sweat beginning to dampen the armpits of the captain's shirt.

"Most likely a big one," Izzie said, opening various cabinets in search of something. One after another, she opened and slammed shut cabinet doors until she found what she wanted—a bottle. There was no telling what was in the bottle as the glass was dark, nearly black, but she popped the cork and took a swig. "'ere," she said, holding it out to Cassandra. "be needin' this."

Cassandra didn't hesitate, she took the bottle and drank. She was terrified, with the captain shouting orders, Izzie's race to move Lucy and her babe, and the quick stampede of the sailors to man the cannons; this spelled trouble. It was all so real!

"How can we have a battle? This is a tour boat for God's sake." She took another swig from the bottle which brought on a horrendous coughing spell. "What the hell is in there?" she asked, once she could speak again.

Izzie took the bottle and poured a stream of the burning liquid down her throat, then wiped her lips with her apron. "I don't give a rat's ass what 'tis. I need it, and ye'll be needin' it too."

Boom! Boom! Boom! The cannons blasted, shaking the very ship and sent Cassandra shrieking, frantically running in a circle. "Oh, my God!" she screamed. "We're going to die!"

Lucy echoed her fears, while her baby shrieked with the commotion.

"Calm ya'selves," Izzie screamed, trying to override the cannon blasts and shrieks of the women.

A deep *thump* jarred the ship, sending Cassandra and Izzie to their bottoms. Izzie rose and ran to the door to slide a heavy wooden bar into place, therefore making it impossible for anyone on the outside to enter. Apparently, she had done this before. "Be still!" she ordered. "Screamin' like banshee's an't goin' to 'elp none."

"What's this all about?" Cassandra demanded, her face red from screaming. She had never been so scared in her entire life. "Damnit, you tell me, Izzie. What's going on up there?"

"Lord in heaven, can't ye 'ear? The cap'n's gone aside the Windward and now they fight and pillage."

"Of course, I can hear it, who couldn't?" Indeed, the shouting above, accompanied by gunshot, was horrific; but she wasn't sold yet. "Come on…this isn't real. I'm going to see for myself. You're all trying to make a fool of me!"

The sound alone, a cacophony of clashing metal, gunshot, and ear-piercing screams of pain, should have been warning enough, but Cassandra was determined to put an end to this farce and headed for the door.

"No!" Izzie cried, and ran at Cassandra, who was now attempting to slide the bar to unlock the door. Izzie pushed her away and shoved the bar back into place.

"Get out of my way!" Cassandra yelled. "I have every right to see what's happening up there. You lunatics are trying to confuse me!" She shoved Izzie in return, but the woman stuck to her spot as if her feet were nailed to the floor, and clawed at Cassandra's hand as she tried to slide the bar, again. "Dammit, Izzie, stop it!" She slammed her fist down on the woman's hands.

Izzie slid the bar open. "Go on, then!" she yelled. "Don't be 'spectin' to come back in. Soon's ya leave, the bar's goin' across. Off with ye!" Between the look on Izzie's fire-red face and the veins of her neck bulging in anger, Cassandra couldn't leave the captain's quarters soon enough. The door shut behind her, as promised, and even over the ruckus above, she heard the bar slam back into its cradle.

"I hope they slit yer throat!" was the muffled yell from the other side of the door.

She had to admit she was more than a bit nervous with the finality of the locked door behind her as she crossed the floor to the ladder. She had no doubt that Izzie would not let her return.

The ladder was a struggle with the one arm, but she climbed until her eyes had a visual of the upper deck. Surprisingly, even with all the frenzied racket of battle, nothing could be seen. She climbed another step higher, turning her head like a periscope until she thought perhaps all the fighting was on the other ship—until two grunting bodies tangled in battle fell before her eyes!

They fought viciously, and were so close that Cassandra could smell them; the putrid stink of men damp with exertion, fear and sweat. She took a step downward on the ladder, not wanting to be seen; it was important she not let the captain or crew think that she had been frightened by their shenanigans. The men continued to viciously swipe at each other with cutlass and curses. Metal scraped metal, grunts and curses prevailed, and then, in the blink of an eye, one sailor groaned, grabbed his belly and fell to his knees. Cassandra witnessed the blood oozing from between his fingers as he held his hands over the wound. *Is this for real?* He spotted her; a head sticking out of the hold. Whether he knew what he was looking at, or not, she did not know; but as he stared wide eyed into hers, his eyes slowly faded into blank orbs in his sweating face, and he collapsed to the floor, dead—or was he? Either he was a very good actor, or this entire scenario was real and she truly was stuck in the year 1644!

By her third trip of literally dragging buckets of water in which to clean the sickening accumulation of blood, flesh and guts from the upper deck, (a task in which she had been forcibly made to do, even with her bad arm) she was now one hundred percent sure that she had somehow, mysteriously— and horrifyingly— slipped into a bizarre time travel event from which she hadn't a clue of how to escape. Tears fell thick as the sloshes of water in the bucket. From the sailor who pulled the water up from the sea, to the sailor who tossed the water at the foul mess on the deck., she traveled weary and aching. The buckets, heavy to begin with, should have been carried with two hands, which was an impossible feat due to her injured shoulder. Therefore, she poked along, wondering how much help she could possibly be in this disgusting task. Izzie fared much better, having two arms to work with, and sneered at Cassandra at each pass.

Through all this, Cassandra searched for explanations of her predicament, but none made sense, and, how could they? How could anyone make sense of shifting from the 21st century to the 17th in the blink of an eye? The one thing she was sure of was that she had to escape this drudgery; Izzie was cruel, the men aboard were animals looking to rape and pillage at every turn, and the captain, though not a bad sort, had shut her out, presumably disgusted with her accusations of the date and consistency in pushing the tour boat topic. Perhaps he thought her insane, like Izzie did. Well, now that she had accepted the situation, she was not in a hurry to be set on land alone in the wilderness, which is how it appeared to be in daylight. No wonder there weren't any lights at night.

"She's still afloat," Izzie said, in regard to the ship, Windward, which had taken quite a beating in the skirmish, as told by the torn mainsail and the sight of the darkened, ragged holes left by the cannon balls. The women leaned on the starboard railing as they watched the pathetic shell of the Windward fade into the distance. The sun was a red ball on the horizon as the Thunder sailed up the Chesapeake and into a river that sliced a path in the marshy land. Thick vegetation and tall deciduous trees were still to be seen, until slowly they became one with the darkness of night; and the voyagers, themselves, an appetizing feast for the multitudes of mosquitoes that swarmed in buzzing menace.

Chapter 5

A kick in the ribs was no longer necessary to wake her in the mornings, as Cassandra had accepted the fact of her fate—at least temporarily. Surely there was a way to return to her real life, for she could not bear the thought of such an existence as the one that spread ahead of her like muddy waters. *I will find a way....* If anything could be said about Cassandra Pratt, it was that she *always* got her way.

"When do you think we'll get off this boat?" she asked Izzie, as the following few days after the battle had stretched into long boring ordeals with the Thunder hidden away in various small rivers, offshoots of the bay. "Why are we hiding all the time?"

"For the surprise attack, as if ye do not know." Izzie chopped away at the carcass of one of the skinned muskrats that the sailors had brought back from an onshore excursion. Three of the horrid looking red and raw critters rested on the wooden counter, which made Cassandra wonder just how sanitary this dinner would be. Black eyes stared from the carnage, which forced her to position herself out of their viewing range—not that the muskrats could see anymore. She had heard of muskrat as a meal, but that was country food, certainly not for a high society Baltimorean!

"Muskrat stew!" Izzie had exclaimed upon receiving the poor creatures, which at that time still wore their furs. She was obviously happy to cook something considerably more appetizing than the dwindling stock of rancid-smelling salted fish and pork, hardtack, and the never-ending wriggling barrel of gruel grain.

"Git your high and mighty arse over 'ere and 'elp chop these up," Izzie ordered, obviously annoyed at Cassandra's avoidance of the chore.

"I...I don't know about that, Izzie." At the time, Cassandra busied herself with peeling the few pathetic potatoes that remained in the burlap bag. Her shoulder, though sore from the knife wound, had improved immensely. Izzie needed help cooking for the crew; but the very thought of touching the red bloody creatures was nauseating!

"Ye must'a had a pile o' servants wherever you come from."

"Sort of...." Cassandra consistently tried to shut her prior life away; it only made her sad and nervous to think of what she was missing at home: real food, real drink, people who actually liked her (or said they did). She missed toilet paper that didn't scratch the hell out of her behind like the leaves that the sailors had brought back from their outing in order to refill the poop deck supply. Oh, the drudgery and inconvenience! The worst was yet to come, her period! Tampons and sanitary pads were non-existent!

"Whatever ye can get yer 'ands on," was Izzie's reply when asked about *that* upcoming event.

"You're not very helpful, Izzie."

"I got me own worries! An't got a magic box. I do what I can do! Use the captain's shirt. He won't be wantin' it back by the looks of it, all full o' dirt and food. Capn's got to look nice, ya know."

"Fat chance of us having the opportunity to look nice." Cassandra ran her fingers through her sticky, filthy hair and shuddered.

"In the new world..." Izzie began.

"New world, new world. I wish I *were* in the new world at this moment, in *my* time! We have tampons. We have real toothbrushes. We have toothpaste, coffee; and best of all, we have toilet paper in the real world!"

"Ah! Me aching 'ead to listen to yer blarney. Two thousand and eighteen," she said, shaking her head, disgusted. "Show me the…pons—whatever 'tis—the coffee for the women, and all the nonsense ye speak of! You'll see that it an't so."

"Maybe—by some miracle—you'll see that it *is* so. Ha! Then where will you be? Back in the past, that's where; long dead to the world."

Whack! The head of a muskrat lay severed and staring on the dark counter. Izzie, turned to Cassandra, the blood-smeared weapon gripped menacingly in hand. "Shut y'self up. I shall not be dead. I shall be prancin' around in me fancy clothes in one of them new settlements. I got plans, you see; I won't always be the Izzie you see befor' ye. Mark me words, lass. I'll 'ave me own home, me own land, silver in me pockets—and me own slaves to do me work!"

This was certainly a picture Cassandra couldn't fathom; the frizzy haired, vulgar woman standing before her, teeth missing, foul mouthed and unkempt. She could never—*ever*— in a million years accomplish that crazy dream!

Before Cassandra could come up with a snide response to Izzie's pipe dream, the first mate, Charles Updike—who looked not a bit of the sophistication his name implied— barreled his way into the galley.

"Ah, muskrat tonight!" He patted his paunch and licked his lips in a most disgusting manner.

"And what, might I ask, is the important reason for yer trespassin' into me galley?" Izzie asked, cleaver still in hand.

"Captain says to pack up and lock up tight tonight. In the morrow, we shall careen."

"In good cover, I take?"

"Aye."

"And yer mornin' meal?"

"He says to lock up tight this night."

"Aye," Izzie continued to chop the muskrats, as Charles Updike had delivered his message and departed.

"What does this mean, careen?"

"The cap'n 'ill beach the ship. The crew will turn it to its side for the scrapin' o' the barnacles and weeds."

"On its side? How is that possible?"

"Ye shall see," she said, tossing the severed pieces of muskrat into a huge black pot.

The heat fell like a blanket as the women set foot on land. Cassandra watched as Cupid helped Lucy off the dory. She clung to the babe—her precious cargo—and Cassandra wondered if Cupid could be the father, considering he was dark as night, and the baby appeared to be without a tinge of white blood. Judging by the sweet look Lucy shot him as her bare feet stepped safely upon the sandy shore, was it possible that a union with consent passed between the two?

But there was more to think about than Lucy and Cupid, and one thing was keeping one's balance! "I'm weaving!" Cassandra said, reaching out to Izzie to steady herself, her sea legs having not yet adjusted to land legs. Izzie shook the hand off her arm and proceeded up the sandy beach through the tall grasses and into the forest of red cedar and sweet gum trees, leaving Cassandra to follow like a drunken sailor as her legs adjusted to the steady earth.

The path—and it did appear to be a path, though narrow and edged with brambles—wound its way through the trees, over fallen leaves that that lay like a carpet before them. When at last Cassandra caught up with the woman in a small break of the thicket, she stopped and stood silent, an outsider, as one who instinctively knew the barrier between herself and the subject, which in this case was Izzie.

"Ah, 'tis good to smell the trees and feel the earth beneath thy feet, aye?" Izzie raised her head skyward, spread her arms and spun a circle. "'Tis heaven!" Beams of sun reflected off the red of her frizzy head; and for one brief moment, as Cassandra trespassed into Izzie's moment of bliss, the crass woman appeared as a magical and beautiful spirit of the forest, spinning her circle of red and gold, weaving a memory that embedded deeply into Cassandra's mind. Though she didn't know it at the time, it was a birth of realization that there was more to a person than expensive clothing, perfect hair, and even perfect teeth. She wanted to spin a circle of her own, but felt—*knew*— her spirit fell short of such perfection.

"Where's Lucy and the babe?" Izzie asked, the magic spinning circle having played itself out.

Cassandra shook loose from her moment of self-pity.

"Uh...I don't know. I assumed she was behind me."

"Well, she an't, as ye can see."

"Perhaps she's staying on the beach. I think she and Cupid may have a thing going."

"Oh, those beastly men. And what good would it do her if they did? They are pirates, and what awaits pirates? The cutlass, the pistol or the gallows; 'tis the grave for the lot o'them. Come, let us look for berries, roots, or some such thing. Nuts, maybe...anything aside from rotten meat and hardtack."

The further they walked into the forest, the more the hairs stood out on the back of Cassandra's neck, but she refused to show any signs of weakness to Izzie, who trudged ahead, her feet crunching last winter's debris. Broken branches and twigs caused much twisting of ankles, along with the occasional curse, but onward they went. Squirrels scattered up trees and seemed to fly from branch to branch as the women tread through their domain. Occasionally a swarm of mosquitoes attacked which sent them into a frenzy of self-affliction; arms swung, hands slapped, and feet jumped in furious animation.

"How will we get back?" Cassandra asked, arms spotted with lumps from the thirsty insects. She felt that perhaps they had gone too far and turned to look behind, but the trees and brambles had become so thick, they blocked what few rays of sunshine had managed to penetrate through the lofty tree branches. While it was a relief to escape the full weight of the heat, it was also a fear of the unknown upon which they tread.

"Do you think there are bears or wolves here?" Cassandra asked.

"Are ye daft? How's a lass from Ireland to know?"

"Forget it."

"I see not a berry, a nut, or nothin'! I had it in me mind that a forest was full of food."

"Stop," Cassandra whispered, taking hold of the back of Izzie's blouse as she was about to step over a fallen log. "Look."

Izzie followed the direction of Cassandra's pointed finger to witness a doe in the distance. The doe stood nearly camouflaged between the trunks of sweet gum with two spotted fawns by her side. Their ears pricked to attention at the sound of the approaching intruders, but within a micro-second the doe's tail flicked and away she leapt into the depth of the dark forest, the fawns following without hesitation.

"We would be livin' high off the hog, aye? Muskrat stew last night and venison stew tonight! Ah, but we cannot send the men after a doe with babes now, can we?"

"No, I suppose not. They'll never find her anyway. We don't know where we are, or how we'll even get back."

"Oh, but ye are a worrisome creature. We return the same way as we came. Can ye not see 'tis a path?"

Cassandra stopped in her tracks and looked back at the thick brush. "Apparently not the way you see it."

"Look ahead," Izzie said. "It looks to be a clearin'! Lord in heaven, let it be a field o' berries!"

As they approached the clearing, the indisputable sound of children playing reached their ears. They stopped, as their feet crunching through the leaves and twigs were a distraction. "What are they saying?" Cassandra whispered.

"An't the King's English...." was Izzie's reply, and they crept softly forward until they were near enough to hide behind the brush of prickly brambles that caught on their clothing and scratched their arms.

"Oh, my God!" Cassandra whispered. "It's Indians! What do we do?"

A village of sturdy huts, built of tightly bound vertical reed topped by dome shaped roofs of the same, dotted the clearing. Children chased one another in play, and a few women meandered about, apparently at their day's tasks. In the distance were circular gardens that looked to be thriving with vine laden squash. The vines crept up and along the woven branch fences; healthy, ripe squash of green and yellow hung as decorations, while stalks of corn stood tall above the fence line.

"We get to the garden, I say."

"You're insane," Cassandra whispered. "Go if you want, and end up in a pot with the squash, but I'm headed back to the ship. Aren't you afraid of *anything?*"

She locked eyes with Cassandra. "An't nothin' as fearful as an English dungeon," she replied, deadpan. "If they come at me screamin' as banshees, then I might find the fear o'God in me, but...."

A rustling in the thicket caused the women to turn.

Cassandra grabbed Izzie's hand out of sheer terror. A moment passed as her mind shuffled through a hodgepodge of escape plans, but, of course, there were none; they were trapped between sticker brambles and a half dozen Indian men holding wooden spears sharpened to fine points. It was a terrifying sight. The men were short and muscular, and wore nothing but a loin cloth to cover their genitals.

It was not their muscular bodies, nor their dark piercing eyes that gave the women a fright, but their strange appearance: half shaved heads topped with a black fringed mohawk dividing the bald right side of the skull, from the knot of hair on the left side, which was decorated in odds and ends of natural sources: an animal bone, feathers, shells, and, to the horror of the women, one native had what appeared to be the skeleton of a human hand placed so in the knot that the bones of the fingers stretched across the ear to the hairline, framing the man's face in macabre fashion.

Their pierced ears were just as grotesquely decorated with the bones of animals and other items of nature.

It was a dual stare down that ensued—the strangely dressed and decorated native men holding their ground, and the women waiting for the next move.

"Top o'the mornin' to ya!" Izzie finally blurted, to which there was no response aside from a few of the men casting confused glances at one another.

"We was just admirin' that nice garden you got there and wonder if you would not mind sharin' a squash or two?"

"I don't think they understand you," Cassandra said, a tremor of fear causing the quiver in her voice.

"What can we do for ye gents today?"

"Really, Izzie!"

"I don't hear ye makin' friendly conversation with the heathens," she whispered through the corner of her mouth.

"Cheskchamay![3]*"* the man closest to the women—the one with the horrifying human skeletal hand ornament—suddenly grunted while simultaneously extending the spear toward them.

This unexpected action caused both women to forget the backdrop of brambles and jump backward, only to find themselves falling into the brush! Cassandra shrieked as the thorny branches sliced and pricked her body through the thin layers of clothing. Izzie had a bit more protection with her petticoat and long skirt, but her face and arms took quite a few pricks before she settled completely into the thorny brush.

"Trasna ort féin!"[4] Izzie screamed, her arms waving, as the thorns caught and ripped at her blouse. "Get us out of o'ere, ya blasted savages!"

---

[3] *"Cheskchamay"*: *All friends.* Algonquin language collected by William Strachey

[4] *"Trasna ort féin!"* Gaelic for "go 'F' yourself."

As Izzie screamed curses, Cassandra lay tucked away in the brush like a bird in a nest, afraid to say a word for fear the natives would spear them on the spot. The brambles pricked as needles with every tiny breath or movement, but this she preferred to a death by spear.

Their horrid circumstance appeared to be of great amusement to the natives, who broke into wide grins and belly laughs. It was when the spears were lowered and helping hands reached for the two entrapped women, that the fear level lowered.

"Could it be the savages are of friendly nature?" Izzie whispered as the men signaled them forward into the village of huts. As they entered the compound, the appearance of the strangers—and women at that—created quite a frenzy. Native women gathered, stared and snickered. Some reached out to touch the captain's tattered, filthy shirt, Cassandra's only clothing aside from panties and capris. Of great interest, was Izzie's frizzy red hair, which inspired much chatter. "Ouch!" she yelled, brushing away the grabbing hands of the women. "Be off with ye, now, before ye pull me hair outta me 'ead!" she exclaimed

"Be nice," Cassandra whispered

"'ave 'em pullin' yer own hair then, and you be the nice one."

Children ran in front of the parade, chattering and jumping in the excitement of the moment. The very young were stark naked, whereas pubescent boys' and girls' genitals were covered in deerskin flaps, or skirts which tied at the waist. The girls' hairstyle was closely shaven to the scalp with a lock of hair at the back, grown long.

The captive parade stopped at a hut typical of the others, except for the plethora of embellishment that decorated the frame of the doorway: feathers, beads, shells and a few animal bones.

The lead man, "Claw Face," as Cassandra would think of him—due to the human hand décor—spoke a few loud words in his native tongue.

Seconds later, the hide flap door spread to one side and a native man stepped out and straightened. He was as sturdy in appearance as the others, and dressed much like the others, only more so; not only did he decorate himself with shell jewelry and animal bones, but a live snake had been threaded through one of the larger holes in his left ear!

"Holy St. Patrick!" Izzie said, placing a hand over her heart. "The man's wearin' a snake!"

"My God!" Cassandra exclaimed, stepping backward and onto the bare foot of a native man standing behind her. This unexpected feel of something beneath her foot, caused a squeak of surprise to slip between her lips. Claw Face, who stood between they and the apparent chief, turned to stare her in the face and said a few words of his own—none understood by Cassandra, of course, but she considered it to be "shut up," in their language.

"He must be an important fella, considerin' his…his…." Izzie began.

"…snake earring." Cassandra finished.

The man now spoke, while the snake, approximately one foot in length, slimy and green in color, wriggled and dangled, its head turning upward to brush against the prickles of the shaved side of the chief's head, and its tail investigating the man's neck. It was quite difficult to concentrate on the man and his words—though totally foreign—while the snake's animated activities caught the eye.

Claw Face stepped aside, fully exposing the captured women to the chief, who bent forward and sniffed Izzie's hair like a dog on the track of an animal.

"Do you think he's wondering if we'll taste good?" Cassandra whispered, chills running up her spine as the chief now stepped to sniff around her own head and neck. He made a face and spoke to someone in the tent. A woman stepped forward through the open flap.

If the men were highly decorated, there was no question in Cassandra's mind that this woman was a queen. Exotic tattoos of plants and flowers crept like vines up her arms and legs. Her face was intricately tattooed, as well as her naked breasts. Between her face and breasts lay a string of shells in various shapes, the largest toward the center, and the smaller to circle and tie at the back of the neck. The hide flap that fell from her plump middle to mid-thigh was fringed at the hem, and from it hung many shells that tinkled as she stepped forward.

The chief spoke to the woman, and she walked off leaving Cassandra the urge to watch her leave, for surely her backside was as decorated as the front; but Snake Ear was speaking and fear of reprimand from Claw Face kept her attention drawn to the chief.

Soon, the queen returned with several women, and the captives were shuffled off by the group. As they walked in a line through a narrow trail, similar to the one upon which she and Izzie had arrived, the native women chattered and giggled, which irked Cassandra to no end.

"They're talking about us, and I hope they aren't discussing torture tactics," she said to Izzie. They were separated by a short native woman, of whom Cassandra was able to study from behind as they marched along. She was young, as told by the smoothness of her skin and a rump that still bore the muscle of youth, as it did not sag and jiggle. Two strings of sinew were tied together at the small of the woman's back to hold the flap of animal hide that the women of the tribe wore to cover their frontal private parts. It was a wonder to Cassandra how the women could spend a day, a night—a lifetime—with such delicate parts of their bodies exposed to the elements.

"They won't be layin' a 'and on me," Izzie replied, matter-of-factly. "I got a knife in me garter."

Soon, they came to a pond that lay as still and smooth as glass, nestled in the tall trees. At the waterside, the native women began pulling at their captive's clothing, an indication to strip.

"I'll not be takin' me clothes off 'ere in the middle o' heathen country!" Izzie exclaimed while slapping away the brown hands that pulled at her skirt and blouse. She crossed her arms over her chest in defiance.

Meanwhile, Cassandra, shaking with fear of what was to come, pulled the dirty shirt over her head, threw it to the ground and folded her arms across her chest as well. The native women, obviously curious over Cassandra's white breasts, came close, moving her arms away to view these new objects of interest. Cassandra stood still, totally embarrassed, standing tall amongst the black-haired females as they murmured in wonderment and poked at the white of her flesh.

With the native women preoccupied, Izzie stepped backward and away from the group. Three of the women did not miss her hasty exit when she bolted for the trees. She did not get far, as the native women pursued as fast as startled deer and tackled her to the ground. When the tumbling and screaming were done, Izzie stood naked, her amply endowed white body, glaringly bright against the deep green of the forest.

Aside from Izzie's red hair and huge breasts, the native women were fascinated by her filthy clothing, one holding the skirt to her waist, another investigating the shift and petticoat, and another the corset that Izzie wore on the outside over her billowy sleeved shift. The knife and stockings lay in the dirt until another woman plucked them up and exclaimed loudly over the weapon. The natives hovered around the knife, whispering amongst themselves and glancing at their captives, until one young woman took all the items and ran off down the path with the filthy bundle.

"Bring me knife back, ya filthy thieves!" Izzie yelled, but to no avail as the remaining women now took her arms and led her to the lake. She fought like a tiger. "The savages shall drown me!" she screamed, but the native women, strong as oxen, ignored her screams and half dragged her into the water.

"I think they want us to bathe, Izzie," Cassandra yelled. "Do as they want, *please*. We're in enough trouble, as is!"

"And just what will we be wearin' after?" she yelled over her shoulder. "I an't marchin' back into that crowd 'o heathens naked as a babe. I an't fornicatin' with nothin' o' the kind, neither; I'll slit me own throat." Then, as an afterthought, "What can they pay with anyway, shells?" This she was able to say only seconds before she was dunked beneath the surface.

Cassandra held her breath waiting to see Izzie's head pop above the surface, and it did, with Izzie coughing and cursing. The thought of rape had not occurred to Cassandra and she wished Izzie had never brought the subject up. What if it were so? New fears ravaged the raw fragments of her nerves.

Izzie's screams brought her attention to the river again, where the women now scrubbed her head with what appeared to be fistfuls of grass, or vegetation of some sort. They dunked her time and time again into the lake, much to her loud objection; there was great commotion every time her head resurfaced.

"I'll kill every one of ye!" she yelled. Or, *"Go hifrean leat!"*[5] Only when they felt she was sufficiently clean, was she allowed to leave the lake, where she stood shivering and coughing, her arms crossed over her chest in an attempt to warm herself.

The women now motioned Cassandra to remove the rest of her clothing, which she did, peeling off the tattered, spotted capris, which, at one time had been white as snow. Next, her undies, which, had gained much attention and snickers from the women. Then, entering the water of her own free will, she found it cool; but considering the warm humid air, it was bearable and refreshing. However, when the group of smiling, giggly women came at her with plants in hand, she stepped backward. There was something ominous about the approach of an unfamiliar breed of human, but considering there was no escape, she stopped and bore the next step, the mysterious plant shampoo.

Afterward, admittedly feeling clean and refreshed, she ran her fingers through her hair, fluffed it about to dry, and stood with her arms outstretched, enjoying the heat while her skin dried. Her eyes roamed the perimeter in search of native peeping Toms. It crossed her mind that the native men may be curious about naked white

---

[5] *"Go hifrean leat!"* Gaelic for 'go to hell', or, to 'hell with you'.

women, just as the women were, but she encountered nothing suspicious.

"*Matchcores. Matchcores⁶,*" said the young woman who had previously absconded with all the filthy clothing. She had returned with garments made of animal skins, which she now held out to the women.

"Oh, mercy. Heathen' clothin'; and just what is it?" Izzie asked, holding up a flap and turning it about. "An't no bigger than a kerchief. I an't wearin' such a thing!" she held the flap against her belly and crotch. What about me blouse?" She pointed to her ample breasts hoping the woman would catch on, but she just nodded and giggled and handed Cassandra the same animal skin apron.

Once the skirt flaps were in place, tied at the back with sinew, they were marched back into the village covering their breasts with their hands, a move that seemed to bring only more giggles to their captors.

"What are we going to do, Izzie?" Cassandra was close to tears, as she had never been in such an embarrassing predicament! The cheeks of her behind jiggled with every step through the path and she dreaded entering the village in such an exposed manner. "This is inhumane!" she cried, but the native women, having no understanding of the English language, continued to chatter amongst themselves in a high pitched, excitable fashion, while Izzie marched ahead, grumbling in English and Gaelic.

The dreaded moment arrived as they approached the village center. The children, bouncy, joyful things, ran gaily aside the group of women, while men gathered and watched, conversing with one another.

"This is so demeaning!" Cassandra cried, tears streaming down her cheeks, while the cheeks of her behind jiggled to the beat of each step. She wanted desperately to place her hands over her backside, but that move would have exposed her breasts

---

⁶ "Matchcores:" Garments, as translated by Captain John Smith

54

The group paused at the chief's house, where one of the native women called through the closed flap door.

"Maybe they were cleaning us up for the slaughter," Cassandra said as they stood waiting for Snake Ear (as she thought of him) to appear.

"They won't be slaughterin' us and we won't be fornicatin' neither."

"You sound sure of that."

"Long as I got breath in me body...."

The chief appeared, his signature snake still wriggling, still trying to find an escape to its entrapment. Snake Ear indicated the two captives to enter, which they did, lowering their heads so as not to bump them on the door frame.

For Cassandra, it had been a nightmare, paraded through the village half naked—literally—but the memory of that jaunt gave way to total shock and mortification as her eyes adjusted to the dimmer light inside the long house, to see none other than Captain Strongbow and first mate, Charles Updike! They sat on fur-lined benches across from one another, a small fire from a shallow dirt dugout between them. The low fire sent a thin trail of smoke upward through a smoke hole in the top of the abode.

Cassandra gasped and pulled her naked breasts tighter against her chest in embarrassment, a movement which only caused them to balloon out at any route accessible behind her crossed arms.

"Heaven be praised, Cap'n Strongbow!" Izzie yelled.

The chief was obviously annoyed by the loud outburst and quickly reprimanded the women by a few loud foreign words of his own. He sat himself at the head of the fire—which was surprisingly warm for such a small fire, and hardly necessary considering the temperature outdoors— and lit a pipe by holding a slender stick of wood into the flame. He then indicated for the women to take seats on either side of the fire, which they did, Cassandra sat next to the captain, as she had been on his side when they entered and was far too embarrassed to turn her back to him to cross over to Updike, thus exposing her naked behind. With her breasts still hugged tightly to her body, she timidly sat, ignoring

Jocelyn Miller

the lewd peer from Charles Updike, who did get an eyeful of her rear end.

"May I present," Captain Strongbow began, "*Weroance Arathkone*. The weroance[7] is willing to return you to us bathed and no longer obnoxious to the nose—his indication, not ours—but for a price. We are now bartering for your release."

"An't you the calm one!" Izzie exclaimed. "And us pawns, helpless and naked!"

"If you control yourselves from meaningless outbursts, I may be able to return you to the ship." He said this calmly, but the undertones and control of his voice were accusing, and angry.

Izzie pouted, looking much like a part of the native décor against the furs, her red hair a mass of frizz and curl that could have been upon the back of some wild creature of the forest. "I just want to be gettin' out o'this heathen camp and back on that rat-infested ship o'yours. Please get the return o'me clothin' and me knife, cap'n, while at the barterin'."

"If you hold your tongue, I may be able to accomplish just that." The look in his eyes put the clamp on her voice, and she sat still, clutching her breasts which, a few sizes larger than Cassandra's, were quite difficult to obscure from view.

The heat in the longhouse was intense, as told by the sweat beginning to roll down the faces of the captain and first mate; or perhaps it was the stress of the situation. At least they both seemed to have a knowledge of the king's language, as all conversation was made in sounds and movement of the hands, similar to a game of charades.

Cassandra sat as if awaiting a firing squad: nervous, sweating, praying, and trying to control the ragged nerves that caused her to tremble with fear. As the bartering went on, voices became louder between the captain and the *weroance*, as well as hand gestures

---

[7] *Weorance:* Algonquin word meaning 'Leader', or 'Chief'

which became more erratic. The louder the voice, the more twists and turns of Cassandra's stomach.

"Alright," the captain said, standing. "Agreed."

"What's agreed?" Cassandra blurted. "Are we free?"

"Yes, but for a hefty price."

She didn't care a hoot what the price was, just the fact that they were free was enough! She stood, only to be reprimanded by *Weroance Arathkone*, who motioned for her to sit. "What is it, captain? I thought we were free to go?"

"You shall be free, tomorrow. In the morning, we shall return with the trade items."

"No!" Izzie shouted, leaping off the bench, her arms gesticulating wildly, having totally forgotten the fact that she was naked from the waist up. "You won't be findin' me sleepin' with the likes of these animals! I an't fornicatin' with none o'them, neither. You tell 'em cap'n! That an't part o' the price, is it? You get us out o' here, *today*!"

Cassandra's eyes popped with embarrassment at the sight of Izzie's heavy breasts released from their hold and swinging with every gesticulation. She didn't miss the look on Updike's face, either, or even the weroance himself!

"Cover yourself, woman! Don't expose the goods and you won't be bothered!" Strongbow ordered—quite strongly.

Izzie, realizing what she had done, quickly slapped her arms across her chest while the captain had a brief conversation with the *weroance* (who could not keep his eyes elsewhere than at the redheaded female). Once Strongbow achieved the *weroance's* full attention, the *weroance* called to his wife, who apparently stood outside the door during the bartering. After a few words, he sent her away and, when she returned, she carried with her two shifts made of deer hide, and handed one to each woman.

"You have now raised your ransom. These women work hard making their dresses and now you have taken their unfinished work in your foolishness."

Cassandra and Izzie ignored the reprimand and hurriedly pulled the hide dresses over their heads.

"Thank you, captain," Cassandra said, so relieved to no longer feel exposed, that she began to cry in gratitude.

"No need to weep, woman; you shall be back onboard tomorrow. "Night falls soon, and we go now to gather the trade goods."

"Gather? What are they, then?" Cassandra asked.

"Shells, game, metal and anything else we can combine to compensate for their loss of two foolish women."

They had to put their faith in the captain, and felt safe until sunset when they were herded to the center of the village, where a large fire— near bonfire size— was lit with piles of wood gathered by the women, including the captives; work they were forced to do.

"Earnin' our keep," Izzie said at the time.

"Or gathering wood to cook us...."

They had no clue as to whether the preparations that had occupied the villagers for most of the day were for the captives' benefit, or if it was a nightly occurrence, or just a simple coincidence that fell on the night of their capture. Worst of all, Cassandra couldn't help but worry if the chief had lied about release and planned to burn them alive! Her fears were calmed when, with most welcomed relief, they were instructed to join the other villagers by seating themselves in a circle around the burning flames.

"I wish I had me knife," Izzie whispered. "If 'harmin' us is what they plan, I would stab the first to try!"

Before Cassandra could answer, a high-pitched warbled yell filled the night, preceded by the men of the village creating an inner circle about the fire. As if a button were pushed, they all began to high step simultaneously twisting, shouting, hooting and hollering as they danced around the fire.

"An't they actin' the maggot!"[8] Izzie said.

"I can't believe I'm seeing this." Cassandra watched as the men passed, their dark skin brushed amber by the glow of the fire. All eyes turned to her and Izzie when the occasional young man stopped in front of the women to perform solo. At this juncture, the entire circle of dancers danced in place allowing the solo dancer to complete his routine before continuing.

"I don't like the way they look at us," Izzie shouted over the hullabaloo. "Like we's the prize at the end o'this melee."

As the spectacle of the dancers circled the fire, the captives were served a clay bowl of stew that appeared to contain squash, corn and some sort of meat. Cassandra scrutinized her serving in the firelight, contemplating the edibility of the mess. After all, she was in a strange time, a strange land and with strangers of whose friendship she was not sure, and now, strange food! She and Izzie were apparently the property of the natives, a commodity to be bartered, so would their captors have reason to poison them?

"Me 'ead is hurtin' from all the hollerin'," Izzie said, taking a chunk of (unknown) meat from the clay bowl and popping it into her mouth.

Cassandra watched Izzie for any signs of poison, such as clutching the throat and gasping for air—like she had seen in the movies— but Izzie continued to pop chunks of vegetable and meat into her mouth with no effect.

"Will ye stop the starin' and eat!" Izzie blurted. "Leave me eat me supper without yer eyes upon me! Ye are such a daft creature."

Next, the women were served a clay cup filled with an unknown liquid. Cassandra sniffed, dipped a finger into the cup and licked the liquid off with her tongue.

---

[8] *'Acting the maggot.'* Irish slang for acting in a particularly foolish manner. *Most common Irish Slang* www.slang.ie

"What is it?" Izzie asked.

"I think it's a grog of sorts."

"Ah, just what me spirit needs!" Izzie said, taking a swig. With Izzie still breathing after consuming the food and grog, Cassandra did the same. She, who had eaten in all the finest restaurants in Baltimore—and other places around the world—assumed the food would be disgusting; but to her surprise, it was quite palatable—or else she was starving and even shoe leather would have tasted like prime rib.

"'Twas a powerful grog last night, aye?"

Cassandra lifted her head from—she wasn't quite sure from what she lifted her head—but it was something hard covered by something soft. "Where the hell are we?" she moaned. "What time is it?" A bit of memory found its way to her mind's eye, and she vaguely remembered something about a fire and lots of dancing. "Was I dancing?" Then, "Oh, my God, I was dancing with them!"

"Drunken sots, we were." Izzie replied. "Oh, for the love of Jesus take care when you sit up. Your head may roll away, and good riddance."

Whatever their actions the night before, it apparently endeared them to their captors, for no sooner had the pair risen to sit upon the hard fur covered benches in one of the longhouses, when a trio of women arrived bearing items of food and clay cups filled with another unknown liquid.

Cassandra took one look at a questionable bowl of a mushy substance and ran for the doorway. Once out, she searched for the edge of the woods and ran like the wind to vomit into the brush. When she returned to the longhouse, one of the native women held the clay cup out to her and nodded.

"Drink it," Izzie said. "An't grog."

Cassandra drank it just to get the taste of bile out of her mouth, and found it to be refreshing water.

"The gruel an't bad, neither," Izzie replied, scooping it out of the bowl with her fingers.

"No thanks," Cassandra said, nodding "no" to the smiling woman who still offered the bowl of food. She patted her stomach in pantomime, an attempt to make the woman understand that she couldn't eat. The woman nodded in return and spoke to the other women. They laughed, and one left the longhouse returning later with two narrow twigs[9] and held them out to each captive. The woman pantomimed chewing on the branch, then touched her head. She repeated this motion several times before Cassandra caught on.

"I think she's telling us that this will help our hangovers."

They took the twigs and, timidly at first, began to chew on the ragged ends. Later, as they stood outside Snake Ear's house waiting to be invited in while the captain finalized their release, the twigs still protruded from their mouths.

"I don't know what this is, but I feel so much better. Don't you?" Cassandra asked

"Aye, for sure...but...."

"But what?"

"I'm thinkin' that I may 'ave let me guard down in me drunken state last night, and let one of them savages stick the ol' horn up me cock lane. Now I'll be worryin' me 'ead 'till me next monthly!"

---

[9] Willow branches

61

Chapter 6

Why am I here? I just want to go home! Cassandra thought these words as she stood sweltering in the morning sun. The day was humid and mosquitoes buzzed madly about her head. They feasted on her face, neck, arms and legs; and she had plenty of exposed flesh for their feast. What she would give for a can of bug spray!

The careenage camp was set up upon the sandy beach of an island edged with marsh grasses and water fowl. The women were instructed to help unload the dory when it came ashore, as it continuously returned to reload from the ship, which sat afloat offshore waiting for the correct time and tide to bring it in. So much had been taken from the ship, that the beach resembled a dockyard laden with goods to be shipped out, and yet the items that continuously arrived seemed endless.

"And just how much junk are we taking off this floating rat trap?" Cassandra asked, as she set a small trunk onto the sand.

"Till the ship is light enough t'be pulled on its side for the cleanin'", Izzie replied.

Cassandra looked at the Thunder, which seemed as big as an ocean liner at the thought of turning it on its side. "How the devil is it possible?"

"In time ye'll see. Well, don't stand like a lump, keep movin'! It an't for Lucy and me to do all the work," Izzie marched back to the waiting dory with Lucy on her heels.

The baby let out a cry, which caused Cassandra to walk to where she lay on a flour sack beneath the shade of a red cedar tree. The baby had filled out some and now resembled less a scrawny, wrinkled newborn, than a burgeoning human. "I suppose Izzie would be making you work, too, if you could walk."

"Git your arse over 'ere!" Izzie yelled, obviously impatient.

"Gotta go. God calls," Cassandra said to infant, who's little face scrunched in anger. Her chubby legs and arms flailed maddeningly as her cry reached a sharp and piercing wail. "Lucy!" Cassandra called. "What's wrong with the baby? Maybe the mosquitos are getting to her?"

"She hungry!" Lucy yelled in return. "I'se comin'."

"Hell of a thing," Cassandra mumbled. "Babies, pirates, Indians, no tampons, no toilet paper...." This tirade spewed for the length of her walk to the waiting dory.

"'Bout time." The sailor in the dory handed her a wooden crate that turned out to be quite heavy—so much so that it took her down with it onto the sand, where she landed hard on her knees.

"Ouch!" she yelled, feeling the pull in her back and bits of sharp shell digging into her flesh. Frustration set in, as usual. "Why am I here?" she cried, a hint of tears gathering. She wasn't born to do this heavy work!

"The devil cares not why ye's 'ere, and neither do the blokes or meself. Git yer arse up and 'elp, what little good ye do." Izzie, true to form, showed little compassion

Finally, in the late afternoon, it appeared that enough cargo had been taken off the ship. The tide was in, and the Thunder sailed forward with it. When it could approach no further, heavy ropes were thrown to the sailors on the beach. While Captain Strongbow yelled orders, the sailors on shore pulled and heaved the ropes until the ship began to list to its side. Thick trees had been cut into logs which were vertically positioned in deep holes dug into the sand by three of the sailors, to prop the ship as it listed, so that it did not roll completely to its side.

"God Almighty!" Cassandra said, later. She was totally exhausted and still there was work to be done! Cupid had built a pit, loaded it with wood and started a fire with his flint. The women were now responsible to make the evening meal, as the crew would certainly be looking forward to one when their work was finished for the day.

As soon as Cupid felt the flames were satisfactory, he left to help the rest of the crew, who were still scraping barnacles off the ship's bottom guided by bonfires set onto the beach.

Izzie placed a large iron grate over the pit and topped it with two of the black pots from the galley. She popped the cork on a small barrel and poured its contents into the pots, and then opened one of the smaller crates to remove bundles tied in cloth—dingy cloth—Cassandra noted.

A whiff of stinking meat wafted up Cassandras nostrils and she stood back. "What are you cooking? That stuff is rotten!"

"Twill boil a while," was the answer, as Izzie tossed the contents into the pot. She then untied another bundle. "Cut these up."

The heat of the fire was intense as Cassandra leaned over the pots, cutting up the few potatoes that had been therein. At one point, she pulled out a thick object that appeared in the firelight to be a root vegetable.

"What is it?" she asked.

"I do not know...found it at the Indian town. There's squash in there, too. Make speed now; the men will be wantin' their supper."

Two hours later, the men were lined up at the black pots where Cassandra ladled stew into their pewter plates, along with a biscuit of hard tack which had been concealed in one of the other bundles.

When the women finally sat for their own supper, Cassandra hesitated. As always, when something supposedly edible had a nasty odor, she waited for Izzie and Lucy to take their first few bites. If the women didn't run to the bushes to vomit—or clutch their throats—then whatever the mess, it was apparently not poisoned, at least not immediately.

Cassandra closed her eyes and bit into a piece of meat and immediately spit it out. "It's rancid, for sure!"

"Eat the squash then, fancy lady!" Izzie replied from across the fire. "I care not if ye eat! I'll not be taking insults from ya," she growled. "I work me fingers to the bone while ye do naught but complain of the toil. Do ye not see where we set? Do ye not see the beach and the forest? Do ye not see that food is what we can find?"

Cassandra shrank back at this retort. She looked at Lucy, whose head was pitched downward over her plate, but her eyes were dark spots in globes of white as they rolled from Izzie to her, and back again. It was no use raising Izzie's temper; after all, the woman had saved her time and time again. "I'm sorry," she mumbled, and spooned a piece of squash—she hoped it was squash—into her mouth. It was palatable, at best.

Chapter 7

After the rescue of the women and the careening of the ship, which, in Cassandra's mind, took a tedious and annoyingly long nine days, the Thunder set sail, heading up the Chesapeake.

Did it really happen? Cassandra stood at the stern of the Thunder as it sailed away from the group of natives who had tread the path to the banks of the Chesapeake to watch them depart. Never in her wildest dreams could she have envisioned the events of careening a ship and capture by Indians; not she, not Cassandra Pratt of Baltimore! What a story it would make on her return to the real world, *but, will I return?* And who would believe the story anyway?

The crew members, who had hunted to bring fresh meat to the galley, were forced to relinquish much of the game they shot for their own use, as it was used in payment to free the captive women. This, of course, was high payment for the foolishness of the women to wander off in the first place, and it did not sit well with the crew or the captain. To make matters worse, the captain, aside from the game, was forced to give up much of the booty taken from the Windward in the last battle.

Three days passed before the alarm was raised again for the pirating of another ship on the bay. "Man the sails!" the captain ordered, and the men set to work like the scurrying rats in the hold. The winds, which were quite high at the time, set the ship in motion at an alarming speed, one that portended an event most imminent.

"Not again!" Cassandra cried, after slipping away from the galley to view the object of alarm. The enemy ship looked quite large in the distance, as it was in full sail and appeared to be of a greater size than the Thunder.

She could quickly scurry up and down the ladders now with ease, thanks to the repair of her shoulder wound, and the short deer hide shift from *Weroance Arathkone;* it made physical movement so much easier than the captain's long and loose shirt, though one had to be cautious to not climb the ladders within view of the crew, as all undergarments were long gone with the natives. Now, as she viewed the ship approaching, chills ran up her spine.

Lucy, having rejoined the work force in the galley, added one more body to the already cramped galley conditions, making it feel even smaller. Her baby, whom she named 'Free'—in the hopes that one day the child would be free—was tightly wrapped and asleep in a length of cloth that Lucy had miraculously knotted against her back, leaving her arms and hands free for work.

"Back into the cupboards with the lot of it!" Izzie ordered, waving her hands over the mess of food that sprawled across the warped wooden counter.

"And the food will be full of roaches when we return—*if* we return," Cassandra was fully disgusted, not only with the thought of being blown to pieces in another century by cannonballs, but also with the filthy countertop and dank, dark, roached filled cabinets as well. She slammed a cupboard door shut and turned the short wooden lock that would keep the doors closed during the interchange of warfare. "How the hell I get out of this place, I don't know...." She mumbled.

"When ye do, twill be me on your shirttail."

With that said, the women headed to the captain's cabin for safety, where Izzie again tracked down a bottle of grog. After three hearty swigs, she handed it to Cassandra. "I got a bad feelin' o' this one."

Lucy, always on the jittery side of things, let out an ear-piercing squeal at those words.

"Lord, wench, ye's breakin' me ears!"

"We's dead!" Lucy cried. "Po' Free!" The baby scrunched her face and let go a high pitched wail, obviously feeling the panic in her mother's frantic outburst.

Cassandra ran to the bowed windows behind the captain's desk and strained to see if anything of the impending battle was visible; but again, the windows were splattered with salt and foam. Obviously cleaning the windows was not required at the careening of the ship.

Following Izzie's lead, she took three swigs from the bottle and wiped her mouth, replacing the cork just in time; for at that moment a tremendous boom rocked the Thunder. The enemy ship had apparently fired the first cannon, as there was significant jarring, sending the women battling for balance. The splintering of wood from the cannon blasts was so loud that it caused the women to duck, though they were protected in the cabin. Men hollered overhead and on the cannon deck as well, which now returned fired with maddening force. *Boom, boom, boom!* One after another, the balls flew to their targets, and the Thunder received hits in return. Each hit was a terror to be reckoned with, but the biggest terror came when, after a tremendous hit, the ship listed severely to one side.

"We go'n drown!" Lucy cried as she, holding the baby to her chest, slid to the listing side. Cassandra and Izzy slid downward as well, until all were huddled together in the crook of the floor where it met the side wall. The captain's desk, bed, chest and dining table were, thankfully, secured to the floor, but like a band of wooden soldiers, the chairs and other debris regrouped into a clunking, mangled mass of legs and spindles and sundry that formed an ominous wall of debris. The floor planks groaned as the grotesque wall became a monstrous weapon that scraped, slid and tumbled its way toward the trapped victims. Free wailed as Lucy tried to regain her footing, but the baby's squeals were overshadowed by the screams of all the women as the horrific wall of debris came crashing toward them.

"Fire!" The worst of the worst had occurred! One of the lanterns came loose from its hook and crashed into the captain's desk. Oil spewed a fiery stream of flame as the lantern broke and then rolled and bounced toward the pinned group, trailing its dragon flame of death behind it.

"We have to get out!" Cassandra screamed, her heart beating out of her chest.

Izzie grabbed the lantern, tossing it aside, but the fire had taken a hungry bite out of the debris thus adding fuel to its flames. Lucy managed to remove herself and Free from impending death by crawling away from the fire. The papoose arrangement on her back had all but unraveled, and the baby now dangled precariously to her side as she laboriously scaled the entrapments.

As smoke from the fire thickened, Izzie clambered and clawed her way over the pile of trappings. She, too, on all fours, climbed like a spider up the tilted floor, grunting, cursing, sliding downward and then pushing herself upward with a foothold on the fallen debris. When she slid downward a third time, she screamed in anger. "We must reach the door!"

Cassandra climbed over the mounds of furniture trappings to reach her. "Use me!" she yelled, bracing herself upon the pile of rubble she had just managed to conquer. Izzie found her footing on Cassandra's shoulders and pushed her body up the incline trying to reach the door. Just what she could accomplish there, Cassandra couldn't imagine, as the severe tilt of the ship and laws of gravity, would prevent the ability to stand and slide the heavy bar that locked the invaders out, but now, trapped them inside a burning hell. But it was a natural instinct to fight for any outlet that held a hope of survival. If they did not try, they would perish.

Izzie finally reached the bottom of the doorway and slid her hands into the thick crack between it and the floor, hanging on for dear life, the fingers of both hands gripped tightly to the bottom of the door.

"Climb...up...me," were the strained words that reached Cassandra's ears.

"I can't!" The smoke had followed its natural course and rose upward, thick and choking; it was imperative they free themselves—and quickly!

"Climb...up...me...." Izzie repeated, coughing through the smoky haze.

"Watah comin'!" Lucy yelled. "It comin'!"

Sure enough, the force of the bay had pushed its weight against the bowed window with such a horrifying force that the paned glass imploded. The water rushed through the broken panes as though a dam had broken. It was a dire situation to say the least: Lucy with the tiny babe, Izzie hanging tightly to the bottom of the doorway, while Cassandra bore the brunt of Izzie's slippered feet digging into her shoulders.

The ship shifted again, and there was no doubt that they were sinking. The water had killed the fire, but Lucy and Free were sure to drown first if they failed in unbolting the door.

The cannons had stopped firing, but all was not quiet as the sounds of disaster rang all about the women locked in the captain's cabin. Men shouted in the distance from adrenalin, pain or fear. If they were still aboard or in the waters, Cassandra could not tell. *I will not die here!* she promised herself. Escape consumed her, and as if by a force of magic she set to motion, struggling upward on Izzie's body, mindful of the pain the woman must be suffering with knees and elbows digging into her flesh; but Izzie held tight.

"Hurry...hurry..." Izzie whispered, barely audible. She was surely strained beyond endurance from the weight of her own body, as she no longer had Cassandra's shoulders for support.

When Cassandra reached Izzie's head, she used the wild red hair as a hand-hold and painfully worked against gravity to pull herself high enough to reach the wooden cross bar.

With such weight pulling on her hair, Izzie's head snapped backward, but Cassandra did not have time to worry about breaking the woman's neck in this effort; the water was rising, Lucy was screaming that she couldn't swim, while Free wailed in her mother's arms.

Miraculously, Izzie bore the weight with what surely was, by now, excruciating pain. Cassandra could feel the spasms of Izzie's muscles through the handfuls of hair gripped tightly in her fists. "I'm sorry...I'm sorry...I'm sorry," she muttered repeatedly, while slowly she inched her way upward reaching for any grip or handhold on the wooden door. Being that the door was worn and scarred from its life at sea and battle, there were enough cuts and grooves from which she could grip.

There was not room nor time for error. Every nook and cranny of the battered door brought her closer to the wooden bar. *Don't fail...I can't fail!* It was life or death, and she, Cassandra Isabel Pratt of Baltimore, had the lives of four people in her hands, including the most important—her precious own. *Please, God, please,* she prayed, when at last she had her feet at Izzie's shoulders and two hands on the wooden bar. She was exhausted, and surely Izzie was at the point of collapse.

Because of the odd angle of the ship, Cassandra was half suspended, hanging for dear life, one hand on the bar and now one on the metal door latch, her feet anchored on Izzie's shoulder. Any further shifting of the ship would make the task impossible to accomplish; if that occurred, she would then hang from the bar like a trapeze artist and all would be lost.

Time was the key to survival, and she set to work. The bar was heavy, but supporting herself with the iron door latch, she strained to slide the bar to the left; a daunting task! It was heavy and difficult enough to maneuver when using two hands, but one? Guttural sounds escaped her throat in unfamiliar grunts as she expended every effort to slide the bar sideways. The veins of her neck bulged thick through the white of her skin. She was right handed, and her left was weak from the knife wound; yet she endured with every muscle in her body.

"Get... ready. The door... will swing... open." go... now! Later, she would wonder how she managed to do it; but with super-human force Cassandra put her entire body into sliding the bar from its slot. She took a split second to gather her strength, for shifting it to the left, heavy as it was, would take every inch of strength she could muster. She pushed, then pushed again, residual pain from the knife injury cutting again through her shoulder as her arm strained to move the bar to the side. At last, it unlocked. The door, now free of restraint, fell open with the powerful force of gravity. It hit Cassandra with such weight that she fell backward, sliding down the tilted floor until her head rested between chair legs. Izzie followed suit, sliding downward until she, too, came to rest at the army of twisted chairs and rubble. Cassandra looked at her partner in this endeavor, but Izzie laid in the debris as a snow angel, her red hair splayed as a fan over the seat bottoms, arms and legs of chairs. Her eyes were closed, but she was breathing.

Cassandra quickly rolled over and pushed herself away from the mangled mess. She looked at the open door above and wondered how they could manage to reach it now that their only path to freedom was visible. They would have to push Lucy through first, but what awaited them once free of the sinking ship? Were there life boats? Would they have to swim? Could the others swim? What happened to the men? The unknown was as frightening as their present situation, but it was the only alternative.

"Watah comin'! Be quick!!" Lucy cried.

"Me achin' bones." Izzie spoke, much to Cassandra's relief. She had been afraid to look again in case the woman had expired in the past few seconds. Luckily, some of chairs had managed to tangle themselves in such a way that several of the seat bottoms faced upward thus avoiding impaling themselves. With great difficulty, they raised their bodies to stand very precariously upon the pile of debris. Cassandra prayed the ship would hold its position long enough for their escape, but as to how they would escape was uncertain.

Lucy was up to the waist in water now, holding Free above her head; but even though the ship was holding steady, it could not be trusted to remain so. Lucy handed Cassandra the baby, and Izzie pulled her up and out of the water and onto the pile. It was a desperate balancing act, as the chairs shifted with the weight of the three women. They clung tightly to one another, but should one go, she would take the rest with her, along with helpless Free.

"What now?" Cassandra asked. It was a desperate situation, as they could barely stand on the mess of chairs as it was, and the door was above them at a 45-degree angle.

In that moment of great desperation, as all three women looked yearningly at the distant door, the angel of mercy looked down upon them; his face was wide, brown and tattooed, and his name was Cupid.

"Help!" Cassandra yelled. "Get us out of here! Hurry!"

"Lucy?" Cupid asked.

"Cupid, me n' Free is alive!"

"Move yer arse, Cupid. Get ye a rope, get a ladder; help us up before we sink like the rats!" Izzie yelled, and Cupid quickly disappeared.

They counted the moments he was gone. Lucy kept her eyes glued to the water, which slurped and sloshed around the rubbish with every ripple of current and wave, bringing with it a few water weary rats. But rats were the least of their worries.

"Can you swim, Lucy?" Cassandra asked?

Lucy's eyes grew ten times wider. "No swim," she said, as if it were the most ridiculous question to ask.

"You, Izzie?"

"Now what would a garl from Ireland be doin' in the water?"

Free, who had finally quieted, again began her incessant squealing.

Lucy tapped a breast. "Hungry," then looked anxiously from the baby to the door above. "He comin'? Yes?" she asked.

I hope, I hope, I hope. "Cupid!" Cassandra called.

The chairs shifted, sending Izzie to her knees. She grabbed a thick chair leg and held for dear life, while Cassandra fought to keep her own balance. Lucy wavered, and with only one hand free, as the other held the screaming baby, she managed to keep herself from tumbling by squatting quickly onto the unsteady pile, which was all that kept them from drowning.

"Cupid!" Izzie screamed. "Git yer fat arse over 'ere before we drown!"

Thud...thud...thud. The sounds came from above.

"He come!" Lucy exclaimed.

Rungs of a ladder began to show themselves through the gaping doorway. It slid down the tilted floor until it could reach no further, stopping a foot or so from the waiting women. Cupid held tight to the top rung.

"Go!" Izzie ordered. "Give me the babe. I'll bring 'er up."

Once Lucy was able to get a foot on the first rung by leveraging from a tumbled chair, she climbed quickly and then, climbing over Cupid, disappeared from view.

Next, Izzie instructed Cassandra to go. "Wait at the top to take the babe."

Cassandra climbed until she, too, climbed over Cupid. Izzie stood below with Free tucked under an arm. "Hold tight, Cupid," Cassandra said, for indeed, strong as he was, his clenched teeth and sweating brow displayed the stress of holding a ladder full of women. Once Izzie was within reach, after what surely was the most difficult climb of all with a babe in arms, Cassandra took Free and handed her to Lucy's waiting arms.

With all women safe from entrapment, the group sat precariously on the outside of the severely listing, creaking ship.

"Oh my God, it's horrible." Cassandra shield her eyes from the grotesque scene before her. A raft of debris and bodies floated atop the water; bodies, barrels, planks of wood rose and fell with the flow of the bay. Sea birds flew and dove from above, some landing on pieces of the remains of the Thunder, and some on bodies to pull a strip of flesh from the victims.

Did none but us survive?" Izzie asked.

Cupid shrugged his shoulders, expanding his arms to encompass the bay. "Mos' dead or drowned."

"Where's the bloody cap'n, then? Drowned with the rest of 'em?"

"Dey took 'im away. Cupid replied.

"Who took him? Took him where?" Cassandra asked. "Who were they?"

"'Twas a ship wid a foreign flag, took 'im."

"They won't be showin' 'im the mercy, then. 'Tis over, I suppose. 'Tis done. He'll be danglin' at the end o' rope." Izzie said, matter-of-factly.

"Oh, no!" Cassandra could hardly believe her ears! The captain, young, strong and—she had to admit—handsome, could come to such an end?

"I told ye," Izzie said. "'Tis the end of all who pillage the seas: the cutlass, the pistol or the rope. We won't be worryin' our 'eads about the fate of Strongbow. Better we worry 'ow to get us off this sinkin' ship."

It was obvious, by the creaking and shifting of the Thunder, that she could go under at any moment. Cupid scaled the side of the ship as a mountain goat. He ripped planks of wood from blackened holes shattered by cannonballs, and piled them near the women.

"We keep a'float t'shore. Da big one fo' Lucy and da babe. Come."

The water was cool and dark as each person set about on their charred kickboards. Cupid propelled his to be near Lucy and the baby, who was swaddled in the ragged piece of cloth and lay atop her float, while Lucy hung on for dear life. After a while, the gentle roll of the bay appeared to have rocked the infant to sleep; but Lucy was terrified and cried softly as she kicked her board along, trying her best to keep the bay water from washing over Free's board.

Terror wasn't confined to just Lucy. Cassandra tried to control her fear of dark waters and concentrate on reaching the nearest land, which seemed a hundred miles away. She tried not to think of what swam beneath their floating hub; but when mysterious tips of fins began to surface, first sparingly, and then with more and more frequency, she could not control the sheer terror that brought the hairs of her neck to attention.

"What is it?" She cried. "Sharks? Oh, my God, sharks!"

"No, 'tis rays." Cupid assured her. "'Tis only da rays."

"Rays...you mean stingrays?"

"Dey gots barbs. Hurt."

"That's a relief," she said, sarcastically, but when it appeared the rays were headed directly for their water caravan, fear took over. "No!" she screamed. "Oh my God, get us away from here, Cupid!" She kicked her board frantically trying to move away from the oncoming mass of fins, but there were too many—perhaps hundreds, thousands—and they seemed destined to mingle regardless of her efforts.

"Be still, woman!" Cupid yelled. "All of ya, be still!!" He had by now maneuvered his board to Cassandra's and grabbed hold. "Stop!" he yelled. "Still ya'self!"

"Okay...okay. Sorry." Her body trembled against what was, already, a lifetime phobia of aquatic life. Never did she ever swim in the dark bay waters, and here she was, a refugee from a sinking ship in the 17th century, paddling a broken piece of timber across the Chesapeake Bay through a fever[10] of stingrays! "I want to go home," she cried softly. "I just want to go home...."

---

[10] 'Fever' of stingrays, refers to a group of stingrays.

Chapter 8

It wasn't home, but it was land! No words could express Cassandra's sheer joy at surviving a fever of stingrays without so much as one stick of a barb. It had been a terrifying experience, hanging onto a makeshift paddleboard in the middle of the bay and staying stone still while the fever of rays swam through their shipwrecked group, silky, slimy wings brushing her arms and legs. Lucy especially had a difficult time of it, and by the time they reached land, she was sobbing uncontrollably.

Land! Cassandra wanted to kiss the very ground upon which she stood, drenched through and through, and chilled to the bone as she was; but ever so grateful, all the same. "Not much of a beach," she said, taking in their surroundings. Instead of sand, the beach was composed of clay, dark earth, and a'clutter with washed up sea grass, driftwood, and other debris. Behind them stood the forest.

"Gather ye wood," Cupid ordered. "We make fire."

The words were barely out of his mouth before the women were scattered into the thick of trees, all shivering from their duration in the waters of the bay. Even tiny Free was soaked, triggering them to hurry at the task of gathering the firewood.

Cassandra focused entirely on her own situation, bemoaning the fact that she was stuck in such a predicament: wet and freezing in the wrong century, starving, thirsty…the list went on and on, as well as the shivers, which did not abate. This propelled her to quickly gather an armful of dry twigs and branches, while Izzie, who had returned to the beach with her own armload, dug a pit in the sand.

Cupid walked along the lapping waters of the bay, climbing obstacle after obstacle of beached debris and driftwood. When he returned, he did so with his hands full of oysters, the size of which Cassandra had never before seen.

"Plenty mo' where dis come from. Crab, too. Get us a fire going."

Without a match, or lighter, Cassandra had no clue as to how this would occur, but occur it must. Her deerskin shift was as heavy as it was wet, and even though the air was not chilly, their time in the cold water had taken its toll. Soon it would be nightfall, and without fire…well…she didn't want to think about that event; it simply couldn't happen!

With teeth chattering, she watched Cupid gather items that any other time would have been ignored: a wide branch into which he dug an indentation with an empty oyster shell plucked from the beach. Then, an armful of sturdy looking sticks, bits and pieces for kinder, and a handful of debris from the forest floor, which very much resembled a fluffy bird's nest. He handed Izzie the fluff, as she had hunched down next to him by the fire pit.

"Hurry up, we're freezing!" Cassandra said, rubbing her hands together.

This comment ran the wrong way with Izzie, who stood, looking the mirror image of Cassandra in her wet, stringy hair and soaked shift. "And who's ye to be tellin' us to hurry up, ya a lazy, shiftless horses arse?"

Cassandra cringed. She was simultaneously embarrassed and ashamed, but then pointed to her offering. "Well…here's my wood, right there at your feet."

"So, gather ye more," Izzie said, "but don't be tellin' us to hurry up so we can warm yer precious skin. The fire is first to warm the skin of that little babe there, not yer own."

78

Izzie hunched down again while Cupid placed the tip of one sturdy stick into the dent in the branch. "Keep yo' hands here, and here," he said, pointing to both ends of the horizontal branch as it lay in the sand. "Keep it still, now." He then rubbed the stick rapidly back and forth between his palms until Cassandra thought the friction alone would burn his hands right off his arms; but on and on he went, tirelessly, until smoke appeared at the intersection of the stick and indent.

"Quick!" he said to Izzie, and she brought forth the ball of fluff in her hands and gently placed it near the smoking embers of fire. Once the spot of embers was gently tapped onto the fluff— and with some gentle blows from Cupid— a burst of flame brought cheers from the small group huddled around the bulky sailor.

The burning fluff, highly guarded and cupped in Cupid's hands, was now carried to the waiting pile of wood and kinder. Again, the group huddled together and prayed silently, waiting for the beginnings of a fire to warm their bodies and dry their soaked clothing.

Later, as darkness fell, after the fire had sparked to flame and burned comfortably, and with Free unwrapped from her soaked swaddling and asleep near the warm fire, the women continued to gather twigs and sticks at the edge of the forest while Cupid gathered the heavier branches.

"There are probably Indians here, too." Cassandra said, later, eating the last of her share of the giant oysters, which were roasted so nicely at the edge of the blazing fire. "I hope they're as friendly as the last group."

"Sometime," Cupid said. "Sometime dey an't."

"What do you mean?"

"Sometime dey fire arrows. See?" he said, pointing to a scar on his chest that flickered silver in the light of the fire.

With her newly acquired comfort zone shattered by the reality of Cupid's words, Cassandra looked about the camp and into the dark forest. "You'd know if they're out there, right Cupid?"

"Maybe. Maybe not."

"You're not very encouraging."

"We gots notin' to trade and dey an't gonna like dat."

Cassandra looked to Izzie, who sat next to her on the sandy beach; but Izzie stared into the fire as if hypnotized, showing no reaction to his words. Lucy sat across the fire by Cupid, hugging little Free close to her breast.

"Definitely not the Marriott." Cassandra mumbled in the wee hours of the morning as she lay on her bed of branches, which Cupid was kind enough to retrieve for the women. He had set them about the fire pit with the intention of keeping the fire going throughout the night, not only for warmth, but to keep the insatiable mosquitoes at bay.

Cassandra raised to her elbows when she noticed Lucy sitting by the fire. "You're up," she whispered. "And you fixed the fire."

Lucy nodded, the baby suckling at her breast.

"Do you miss your home, Lucy? I miss mine. I wish we were at the Marriott, it's a nice place to stay when travelling. I guess you've never been to a hotel." *Of course not, idiot.*

Lucy continued to suckle the babe.

"I wish you could talk."

"I talk," Lucy replied, the baby now asleep in her arms. "Not talk English good."

"That's the most you've said since we met. How did you hook up with Izzie?"

"Her win me."

Cassandra had to think on this one. "Playing cards?" She could imagine the woman playing cards, ace's up her sleeves...cheating.

"No. Me massah wan fuck her. She say 'you gimme dat blackie woman, I fuck you.' She done it and we go on da ship."

"Oh! Well... that was blunt and to the point."

"She good, Miz Izzie."

"Is Cupid the baby's father?" After Lucy's tale, she didn't think the question was rude.

"Mebe. Baby not from Massah. He Dutchman. Mean."

"Do you think Cupid is Free's father?" she repeated.

"Tink so, mebe. She black, like me, like Cupid. Izzie say she be free one day."

"Somewhere in that mean, scrawny woman, beats a heart."

"Whad?"

"Nothing. Goodnight, Lucy. Get some sleep."

"Git on up, negar[11]."

It was an order, but from whom? Cassandra opened an eye and then the other. In the predawn light she focused on what was either an apparition—which would not be a surprise in her present predicament—or, there really was a scruffy looking character standing over Cupid pointing a long pistol at the fellow. She found herself surprisingly offended by the term *negar*. After all, the big lug of a brute had saved them all.

"His name is Cupid, and who the hell are you?" She stood and crossed her arms over her chest, as it was a bit chilly in the predawn—not to mention that another dangerous situation had presented itself and she needed to look tough.

Cupid had awakened by now and shot to his feet, towering over the unkempt stranger. He quickly whacked the pistol out of the man's hands, letting it fall to the ground. Within seconds, Izzie leaped on the pistol and scampered away on all fours like an

---

[11] *Negar:* Negro. First used in Colonial times

animal, until she stopped several feet away. There, she stood, pistol held in two hands, the hammer cocked.

Cupid, by this time, had the man in a choke hold.

"Show ye 'ands or I'll be blowin' the top o' ya 'ead off." Izzie said, sounding quite authoritative.

"Now, don't git thy dander up" the man said, his voice stressed with the weight of Cupid's arm pressing on his windpipe. "Don't see strangers here much, 'tis all; just the savages. Could ye kindly tell (cough) this black beast of a man to leave go? You have the pistol now, and I am not a fighting man."

"Stand aside, Cupid," Izzie ordered. "This bloke an't goin' to hurt no one."

"Thank you, mi'lady," the man said, bowing as he was released. "I appreciate your kindness," he said hoarsely, rubbing his throat.

"What business 'ave ye in this place?" Izzie asked.

"Me name is Phineas Barnett, at thy service and pleased to welcome thee to our bonny shores."

Free began to cry, and Lucy, who had been frozen to her spot next to the fire, now stood with the baby in her arms and stepped further away from the group as if ready to flee—if necessary.

"And just what is your business, Mr. Barnett?" Cassandra asked.

"Why, I have no civilized business in this wilderness—not as yet. 'Twas the pirate crew that left me—the meanest cutthroat mangiest group of animals you ever did see. They sank the ship I sailed on, but spared me. After trading with the savages, they gave me my pistol—with no powder—and left me here to die by the hands of the savages."

Izzie lowered the heavy pistol to rest at her side.

"As ye can see, I am not dead, and do not plan to be, mi'lady. All I desire is a means of transport away from the native peoples."

Everyone jumped at a sudden alarming scream. It was so shrill that the hair on Cassandra's arms shot to attention. Baby Free howled, and Izzie turned the pistol to the direction of the frightening sound.

Next to Lucy stood a native woman, naked at the breast and heavily tattooed, as could be seen clearly now in the rising light of day. Her dark hair disappeared behind her shoulders, and around her middle was tied the traditional flap of deerskin.

Lucy's eyes were wide with fright, even though the woman did nothing to harm her, except stand as an inanimate object—a statue—staring at the hubbub that transpired at the fire pit.

"Me wife," Phineas said. "Her Indian name I cannot pronounce, so I call her Pillar. Do ye not agree that she is like a pillar, staunch and upright? She follows me hither and yon, her mouth shut tight like a clam. I sometimes wonder if there is anything in there."

"'Tis odd," Izzie agreed, as the group stared at the woman. "And how be it ye have a savage wife?"

"I trade me skills for the comfort of a longhouse. The chief has thanked me with my...uh...beloved Pillar." He motioned the woman to come to him, and she obeyed.

Lucy followed next, to stand in the safety of Cupid's shadow.

"What is your skill?" Cassandra asked, and then stepped back as Phineas—without a verbal response to the question—suddenly moved his hands in mysterious motions, leaving her to wonder if he was going to pull a knife or other weapon from somewhere on his body and slay them all. But when his hands stilled, he presented to the group, palms sides up, two coins.

"Ye's a trickster!" Izzie exclaimed.

"Magician...trickster, whichever ye prefer to call it, it has saved me skin from the savages. They think 'tis mystical powers I possess, and 'tis me hope that they continue to think so."

This gets stranger and stranger by the minute, Cassandra thought, eyeing Phineas in his nicker-length trousers, tattered stockings and shirt that appeared to have once had a laced collar and cuffs, while his wife, Pillar, stood nearly naked by his side. *A visual oxymoron, if ever I saw one.* "So, you do tricks for the natives?" she asked.

"'Tis their great pleasure to present me as evening entertainment; that is, after their great ballyhoo event of dancing and hollering." With that, he walked past the small group, Pillar following close behind. "Come. We go to the village."

Natives, both young and old, male and female, gathered as quickly as if conjured by Phineas' magic, as the group made their entrance into the village. As occurred previously, the arrival of their strange entourage raised great excitement with the native women. Of interest was Izzie's red hair, and Lucy's, whose black, tight kinks brought many hands to touch and pull. Much commotion was expressed over baby Free, as well, and so much so, that Lucy was forced to stop in her tracks so the women could get a good look at the dark infant.

Nothing about the group garnered the men's attentions more than Cupid. He was the last to enter at the heels of Lucy. The native women made many loud exclamations as the black, tattooed giant of a man strode forward. His tattooed torso seemed to fit in with the natives, as they, too, bore the tattoos of their tribe. A few of the native men ingeniously cut him off from the party as if he were a stray beast.

"They just want to look you over, my good fellow; you shall be fine," Phineas said.

"Fine, my arse!" Izzie appeared ready to battle the small army of natives with the empty firearm. "The savages may be plannin 'ow to slaughter the man."

"No!" Lucy shrieked at Izzie's words, and the smattering of women who walked beside her, shot off in a flash at the alarming sound of her voice.

"Do not show aggression, woman!" It was the first sign of anger that Phineas had shown throughout the entire encounter with the shipwrecked party. He then said something to the men in their language, and they dispersed.

Cupid rejoined the troops. "Don' you worry, Lucy," he said. "I'se stronger den the strongest of 'em."

"Not bad," Cassandra said, noticing the neat rows of native longhouses. In the distance were the vegetable gardens that appeared as neatly placed as were the houses.

"This is no village, it must be an Indian city," she said to Phineas, with whom she tried to stay abreast, perhaps feeling safer with him next to her. Pillar followed solemnly behind.

"It is quite large, and the native's friendly. There is plenty of food, and yet, I miss the comfort of my own kind, and the ways of my people. 'Tis an odd life with little means of communication, but I have learned a few of their words, and they a few of ours. That you and the Irish lass are here, brings joy to my heart.... and the slaves as well, of course."

"And what blarney goes up 'ere?" Izzie asked, stepping forward from the endless petting hands of the native women, to fall in step with Cassandra and Phineas. "Are we to be amongst the savages now?"

"Do you have another suggestion?" Cassandra asked.

"Nay, I do not." Izzie admitted. "There is food here, and water, but I'll not be livin' amongst the savages for long. 'Tis here I come to make me fortune, and 'twill be so. And not as ye's thinkin', neither," she added, when Cassandra scoffed at her remark.

"We must speak to the *weroance*." Phineas led the group to native man who stood aside a longhouse waiting for their approach. The *weroance* would have suffered extreme deafness to not hear the excitement and commotion as Phineas led them into the village, and now to his abode.

"I present to you, *Weroance Meqwanoc[12].Netab[13],*" Phineas said, thumping his heart with a fist. *"Netab."*

---

[12] *Meqwanoc:* Long Feather, as translated by William Strachey.

[13] *Netab:* Friend, as translated by William Strachey.

The *weroance* stepped forward to examine his new guests. He appeared much interested in Izzie's frizzy red hair, reaching his hand out to gather a fistful, scrunching it tightly to watch it spring back into its normal state. Izzie stood as still as a rock, much to Cassandra's relief. Lucy's black, tight curls were also a fascination, as well as the baby, who seemed to return the *weroance's* interest by delivering a toothless smile. Judging by the look of surprise on the *weroance's* face, and the smile he returned to the little one, Cassandra noted a complete metamorphosis in the man's face; one moment, stern, the next, soft as cotton candy.

She forced herself to stay still as he approached, and even when he put his face to hers, lingering much longer than he did with the others, she held her breath.

"I think he's impressed with your blue eyes," Phineas said. "Let him look."

Cassandra stared back, and finally the chief resumed his place by the door of the longhouse. "*Netab,*" he said, thumping his own heart.

"Now what?" Cassandra asked.

"One must have patience when dealing with the savages."

The group stood impatiently waiting for the next move, while the *weroance,* having called two women from his house, rattled off words in his language before they walked away. Their costume was typical of the ones seen at the previous village: tattooed bare breasts and deerskin flaps secured in the back with sinew

As they waited for the next move, Cassandra was able to appreciate the fine figure of the *weroance.* He was taller than any of the other Indians she had seen. His face was strong and handsome—*in a foreign way, of course*—she added. Many feathers of eagle and turkey were fastened to a long ponytail that hung from his left shoulder, as the right side of his skull was shaved short. This seemed to be a strange, yet universal, hairdo for the men of the area. Around his neck he wore many necklaces of animal claws and shells that lay upon his muscular chest. In all, he was a fine-looking man, obviously well-toned from his life in the forest. He pointed to Cassandra, and opened the flap to his tent.

"*Crenepo, caumorowath*[14]" he said, indicating for her to enter.

"Now wait a minute; what's he saying?" Cassandra asked, nearly afraid of the answer.

"Hmmm." Phineas thought a moment, while the chief began to look a bit irritated.

"Hmmm, what, Phineas? What's going on?"

"I know the language," Izzie pipped in, a wide grin on her face. "He wants to bed you!" She said, breaking into raucous laughter.

Cassandra felt her face go white. "What? I will not! Phineas, tell him I will not!" She gripped his arm in sheer terror.

"Izzie may have come up with the answer, my dear. The chief has apparently taken a fancy to you and your blue eyes."

"He can take his fancy and stuff it. I'm not going into that tent!"

"*Crenepo!*" the chief repeated, loudly.

Laughter rang out behind the group at the tent door and they turned to see what appeared to be the entire village watching this scene with interest and amusement.

She swore it was the chief's wives who had ganged up on her. After being pushed—and none too politely—into the longhouse, she had turned in an attempt to escape and saw the two women who had previously left the tent, glaring threateningly, blocking her escape.

"Help! Phineas… Cupid!" she yelled.

"Do not make a move, Cupid." Phineas shot out an arm to block his advance. "She won't be harmed, but ye may find an arrow in the heart if ye proceed."

"A little bang o' the balls an't goin' to kill the lass." Izzie said with great amusement.

---

[14] *Crenepo, caumorowatch:* woman, enter.

"Just you wait, Izzie Pratt!" Cassandra yelled. "I'll wipe that sneer off your face!"

Inside, she walked backward, away from the door, making room for the chief. He said something she didn't understand, and when he walked toward her, she stepped backward, only to trip on something that flung her into another something hard. She fell to the dirt floor and cried out in pain as she landed on her rump.

"Is ye alright?" she heard Cupid yell.

'Of course not!" she screamed, at which she heard Phineas raise his voice to Cupid, and much muttering from the native group outside the longhouse.

The *weroance* came at her, the palms of his hands extended and speaking in a low voice, as if to calm her. He extended a hand to help her off the ground, which she did not accept.

Afraid to turn her back to him, she struggled to raise herself up, while the *weroance* crossed his arms over his toned chest and waited. When finally she stood, he placed his hands on her shoulders and pushed her backward until she plunked on a blanket of deer hide. He then did the unexpected; as the inside of the longhouse was composed of two long pelt-covered benches along the sides, and one at the far end where she sat, he took a seat on the long bench to her right, allowing her to sit alone.

"Don't touch me," she said, knowing full well that he wouldn't understand. She had to admit, even in this nerve-charged circumstance, that the chief was an impressive and regal figure. from the eagle feathers in his black, shiny hair, to his hide moccasins, he was as handsome as any man she had ever seen in her modern world, though *in a primitive and ethnic sort of way*, she reminded herself.

He stared into her eyes and then touched his own.

"Blue…eyes." She wondered if that was what he wanted to know.

"Bewf." He puckered his lips and tried to repeat her words, but they came out more as a 'pfff' sound.

"Blue," she repeated.

"Lew."

"That's a bit better, but it's "blue" with a 'b' sound." She stressed the 'b' hoping he would catch on. Perhaps he only wanted an English lesson and not sex—she hoped.

"*Arrokoth.*" He pointed to her eyes and pointed to the ceiling of the longhouse.

She looked upward, but not understanding his words, she didn't know what he wanted her to see.

This time, he reached out toward her eyes— his index and middle fingers in a 'v', resembling snake fangs—and then pointed upward again. "*Arrokoth*".

"*Arrokoth?*" she repeated, confused.

When he suddenly rose and took her by the arm, her heart raced. But instead of assaulting her, he led her to the outside of the longhouse where he pointed to her eyes and then upward to the sky. "*Arrokoth!*" he said. "*Arrokoth!*"

"The sky," Phineas said, still standing outside the tent with Izzie, Lucy and Cupid. "He's saying thine eyes are the color of the sky. That may work in our favor; he may think ye a goddess!"

"Sky blue." She pointed to the sky and then to her eyes. "Sky blue."

From there on, she was known as Sky Blue to the native peoples.

"And how fares ye Holy Highness on this day?" Izzie asked, two days later.

"It's just a shame your eyes are brown, Izzie. Otherwise you may have been the privileged one to sleep in the chief's house."

"We were quite comfortable with Phineas, thank you. At least we did not taint ourselves by sleeping with the savages. And which one of the savage women was poked in the night—or was it ye?"

"Now, now ladies," Phineas said. "Put thy grievances aside, we have business to do. We must make a plan."

Phineas did not consider the black members of the shipwreck party as equals, forcing Cupid to stand off to the side.

"Really, Phineas. We owe our lives to Cupid. You wouldn't get away with this in my century," Cassandra said, ignoring Izzie's remark.

"Whatever do you mean?"

"She's daft, that's what. She thinks she comes from the year 2018," Izzy said, beating Cassandra to the punch.

Phineas eyed Cassandra as if she had sprouted horns. "Perhaps she is a goddess after all," he said, shrugging his shoulders. "But daft or goddess, we must find a way to reach civilization. Surely there are our own kind in this land."

"Cap'n Strongbow told of such a place, but where? Where are we now?" Izzie asked.

"I could not say, and the heathens have other words for places that our kind hath given Christian names." With knitted brows, Phineas stared at Cassandra. 'Hmmm…I wonder…."

"You wonder what?"

"I think perhaps with thy status as the goddess Sky Blue, you may be able to convince the chief that we would like a boat."

"Listen, Phineas. I don't do a darn thing until you put Cupid right here where he belongs. Just who the devil do you think will pilot a boat anyway? You? A broken-down magician? Or perhaps, Cupid, who has, God only knows, how many years' experience at sea? I put my money on Cupid."

"Aye, that goes for me, as well," Izzie said.

Chapter 9

Why am I here? The days in the village passed as an odd foggy dream. *Am I here forever? Am I dead?* There were so many questions, and no one to answer them. Cassandra fought the depression of being alone in a strange world, in a time that was not her own; she found little comfort in Izzie.

As Sky Blue, she obtained many privileges, one of which was sleeping in the longhouse with *Weroance Meqwanoc* and wives, instead of in Phineas's overcrowded longhouse—which was packed to the front door flap with Cupid, Lucy and Free, Izzie, Pillar and Phineas himself.

Her attempts to learn *Weroance Meqwanoc's* name were fruitless, even after practicing it over and over again. It continuously came out as *Makanock, Quemanock*, or some such nonsense. Because she could not get it straight, she therefore had Phineas translate it into English. It was only fair; if she was Sky Blue, then the chief could be Long Feather. In fact, he seemed pleased with his English name and answered to it proudly, though it did take some getting used to.

Knowing not what else to do with her time, she absorbed herself into village life. The woods were a thick and unknown territory, making escape questionable; and where would they escape to? Long Feather's wives tolerated her existence—but barely. She knew they spoke of her, and poked fun in their strange language. After all, she had usurped them from Long Feather's attentions. Though he didn't touch her, she quickly became the object of interest in his attempts to teach her the ways of the native woman, a job that, in most cases, would have been left to his wives. He was proud to add this new addition to his small harem: her sleek body (due to many diets and personal trainer), her hair, oddly streaked with sunlight (from the hair salon), and the eyes…he sometimes stood and stared into her eyes as if seeking the answers to the world's most perplexing questions. She, in turn, chastised herself in these moments, for perhaps seeking the answer to her own personal questions in his eyes. *Stop, stop, stop!* Her brain screamed, when the pull of his odd charisma brought her near to the point of imagining herself with him beneath his deerskin blanket.

"He an't bedded ye yet?" Izzie asked on one of their many firewood gathering journeys into the surrounding forest. Cassandra avoided her as often as she could; but there were so many tasks all the women were required to do, that they ended up together on most days.

"Why do you insist on being so…so vulgar? What business is it of yours, anyway?"

"Won't be long, near as I can see. 'Tis not a bad looking fellow with them muscles and fine 'ead—not for a savage, as i'tis. The marriage bed is on his mind. Even Phineas says so. Surely you could make a trade? Perhaps thy favors for one of them little boats? 'Tis not difficult; I have done it many the time, meself."

"Don't be ridiculous. And, no, he hasn't touched me." *But he sure touches the other one….* It seemed Long Feather couldn't get enough of nightly encounters as judged by the moans and groans she was forced listen to in the dark. One wife, Ussac, meaning 'Crane', according to Phineas, was obviously pregnant, her brown belly protruding outward above her hide flap. The other wife, Cuttack, ('Otter'), was kept rather occupied beneath the deer hide blanket nearly on a nightly basis. After two weeks of living in his tent, it was getting rather annoying; she hated to admit the fact that, at times, she wouldn't mind it being herself, and wondered if her growing annoyance weren't for that fact.

"Phineas and meself been conversin' or' the predicament, and the point of the matter is that because ye are so close to the *weroance*, that surely ye could give him a go at it and make a bargain."

"You and Phineas are very loose with my virtue! Why don't you 'give him a go at it', since you don't seem to care who you 'go at it' with."

Izzie threw her stack of firewood to the ground, and came at Cassandra at the speed of light. Cassandra stood back, fully expecting to be tackled, but the red-haired woman stopped a breath away, fists plopped hard on hipbones. "Don't be pointin' a finger at me discussin' virtue. I been on me own since fourteen and there an't much a poor lass can do to make a quid. It weren't me first choice, but ye see me standin' 'ere, aye? I an't no fancy lady, but I got me some courage and I got me plans."

Cassandra sighed. "I'm sorry, Izzie. It's just that in my time, I don't...don't fornicate with every man that comes along—and certainly not to make a bargain. You and Phineas are asking me to prostitute myself to get us a boat. Sheesh."

"Boat." Cassandra said.

She had taken a break from the endless task of weed-pulling in the squash garden, to venture to the bay where Long Feather and some of the other men were fishing. Some were in a dugout canoe several yards off, spearing fish, but Long Feather and his group had come ashore. The men stepped out of the beached canoe with several large fish and headed for the village.

"Boat," Cassandra repeated, pointing to the rugged dugout.

"Acomtan?"

"Yes, *Acomtan* is boat." The 'b' words were sometimes difficult for Long Feather to pronounce, even though he had given her the name of Sky Blue. Once in a while, he would call to her as Sky Lew, and then quickly correct himself by pursing his lips and forcing the 'b' sound.

"Tangoa acomtan. Give me boat." It had seemed as good a time as any to ask Long Feather, as he was standing by the water next to the very item she desired.

Long Feather look confused, so she repeated: *"Tangoa acomtan."*

Long Feather smiled a broad smile that exposed remarkably fine teeth. He was obviously amused by her request.

Good Lord, what did I say that should make him smile? She struggled to remember the words Phineas made her practice and wondered if she had said them correctly.

"Me, Sky Blue," she pointed to herself. Then, "Cupid, Lucy, baby" (here she folded her arms, as if holding an infant) "Izzie and Phineas. *Cawcawmear."* Here, she pantomimed rowing an imaginary boat. *"Cawcawmear.* We go."

Long Feather's charming smile turned to a frown, his brow furrowed, his eyes darkened in his handsome face, and his strong hands grabbed her shoulders. *"Matah[15]! Sky Blue, noungasse![16]"* He thumped his chest.

This does not look good.

He thumped her chest, and then his. *"Noungasse,"* he repeated.

---

[15] *Matah:* No!

[16] *Noungasse:* wife

Whatever he said did not sound promising. He indicated she was to stay standing, while he secured the canoe. She watched, momentarily entertained by the ripples of his muscular back and buttocks, while he finished the task. Rear ends were always in view in camp, due to the frontal flaps that both men and women wore, and which left their behinds bare.

Izzie found great fun in shamelessly critiquing the behinds of the natives, and especially choosing her favorites of the men. "Now that's a good, strong bum, aye? Bet it rides well. If time allows, I may have to try one, savage or not." Izzie spoke so often of this, that Cassandra found herself now lost in Izzie's fantasy before shaking herself loose of that possibility.

When Long Feather had finished securing the dugout, he gripped her upper arm and led her down the path and back into the village. She felt herself flush in embarrassment as the villagers stopped to stare as they passed; the *weroance* pulling Sky Blue along like she was a naughty child! Obviously, he was very, very angry.

When they arrived at his longhouse, he literally tossed her through the door flap and yelled a few words she couldn't possibly understand, aside from the fact that she was pretty sure she wasn't to leave.

When he returned, Phineas was with him.

"Oh my, I believe we have an issue here, and one I have been concerned about, Cassandra, dear."

"What's happening? He's furious!" she said, glancing at Long Feather and then back to Phineas. She didn't like the way Long Feather was staring, like she was about to be burned at the stake. "Did I say something wrong? I tried to speak the words you taught me...."

"He understood."

"He doesn't want us to leave? Is that it?"

"He does not wish *thee* to leave, and this puts the others, and meself, in a bit of a pinch. The rest of us can go, but ye must stay—as his wife."

Cassandra was speechless—but not for long. "Of course you told him you won't do that, right?"

Silence.

"You will not leave me here, Phineas. Don't even think it for a minute."

"Surely ye will think of the others?"

"And surely you are thinking of your own hide, Phineas Barnett. I will not stay here, and you are not leaving without me. Fix it with Long Feather, or I swear... I swear I will use my goddess power to have you cooked with tonight's supper!"

"Do not be...."

"Do not be, *nothing*, Phineas. I don't even belong in this God forsaken century and you will fix it with him." She pointed to Long Feather who watched the fired up interaction between the two with quiet concern, his arms folded over his chest.

"Fix it!" she yelled. "Use your ridiculous magic, for God's sake!" She rose, wanting to run out the doorway back into her own century; but when she attempted to leave the longhouse, Long Feather barred her entrance with one outstretched, muscular arm.

"Sky Blue, noungasse," he said, thumping her chest.

"Cawcawmear." she said, pointing to herself. We go. Sky Blue *Cawcawmear."*

Long Feather indicated (rather strongly) for Phineas to leave the longhouse. As he passed, Cassandra felt a shudder of raw fear ripple through her body. The thought of being alone with Long Feather in his state of mind did not fare well with her at the moment, even though Phineas was showing his traitorous colors and no help at all; she wanted to ring his neck for even thinking of leaving her behind.

"I swear, Phineas, if you leave me here I'll hunt you down and kill you...even if you are already dead!"

He shook off the hand that had gripped his forearm. "I don't know whatever you mean by that remark. Do what the *weroance* sayeth, and save us."

Long Feather pointed to the bench at the narrower end of the house. *"Nawpin,[17]"* he said, a bit more gently.

---

[17] *Nawpin:* Sit

What now?

He gave her a little push toward the bench. *"Nawpin,"* he repeated.

She took the hint, walking slowly across the matted floor and sat on the bench and wait; but for what, she wasn't sure.

He stuck his head out the door and yelled a few words to whomever was within hearing distance, and closed the flap. She translated his words in her head as 'do not disturb', which certainly disturbed her to the highest degree!

Wide eyed, with brows raised, she watched as he approached, her heart pounding in her ears. "What are you doing?" she asked in an unsteady voice. "What do you want? *Netab, netab.* We are friends."

"Noungasse," he replied.

"Matah! Matah noungasee!" she said. I am not your wife!"

Long Feather lifted her to a standing position, reached the bottom of her deerskin shift and tried to lift it over her head, but she shot her arms to her sides and held tight with all her might.

To counteract her move, he grabbed a wad of hair at the back of her head and pulled tightly.

"Ouch!" she cried and reached up to grab his hand, but in doing so, she had given him access to pull the shift completely over her head, which he did; and there she stood, naked, embarrassed, angry and afraid. *This can't be happening. I'm going to be raped by an Indian weroance in 1644!*

But Long Feather did not immediately throw her to the bench and leap on her—despite the newly extended position of the frontal flap, which she could not help but notice, and which he could not miss her noticing. Instead, he ran his hands up and down the front of her naked self, caressing her breast, then her private parts. He watched her eyes as he did this, and she, his. "Sky Blue," he whispered. *"Noungasse."* He turned her around so that she faced a side wall, and ran his fingers down her back, and over her hips. He pulled her to him, her back resting against his solid chest, wrapping one strong arm under her breasts while he caressed her privates with the other hand. He massaged in a most tantalizing way until she felt a heat spread through her body as her resistance dissolved into the faintest of memories. *No!* her conscience screamed. *Run away*! But she did not want to run away, and there was nowhere to run to, even if it had been her desire.

As he bent her every so subtly forward until her hands rested on the soft, pelt covered bench to her front, she realized that perhaps his nightly exploits with Otter had been a way to sway her to this moment. Had it been inevitable? She knew now, with his magically caressing hands— with his resolve to have his hands on her body, and his resolve to make her his wife—that she had wanted this moment! She had found him attractive since the moment she set eyes on his noble stance, his strong, handsome face, his eyes, even his odd hairdo with the tall feathers that gave him his name; she had considered this event, and now it was a reality.

She blushed. She blushed often with the memory of what transpired in the longhouse. In fact, she had not even left the longhouse since she and Long Feather had begun their marathon of mutual adoration hours before. She wondered what Izzie, Phineas and Lucy were thinking. Were they thinking she was dead, perhaps? Perhaps she *was* dead and had been all along? The thought had occurred to her time and time again, but she certainly didn't remember death happening. If so, she was gloriously dead.

The moment Long Feather had entered her as she bent over the fur covered bench, began an odyssey of positions and pleasures that she had never experienced before. *Where did he learn this stuff?* she wondered afterward, as she lay naked, stretched out on the pelts of animal hides as soft as she felt inside.

Long Feather had left the tent earlier, and when he returned, he carried a drinking bowl filled with fresh water.

"Thank you," she said, rising to sit on the fur. She took the bowl from his hands, and scanned the floor for her shift, suddenly feeling very exposed and bashful. As he stood before her, she reached beneath his flap to feel the instrument that had brought her such pleasure. He smiled, but pushed her hand away with a harsh word.

They all know. She felt their eyes upon her as she walked through the village from the *weroance's* longhouse to Phineas's. *They all know what we did....* It was embarrassing, to say the least, and it took her a good long while to muster the courage to open the flap and step outside into the village. She expected the snickers and whispers of the natives as she passed, but carried herself straight and tall as she walked through the gauntlet of curious onlookers. A union between the chief and Sky Blue was big news.

Izzie stood outside Phineas's longhouse, her hair a crazy mass of frizz—surely a result of the suffocating humidity— and eyes that watched with humor as Cassandra approached. "You got them whirligigs[18] now!" This set her off into howling laughter. "An't no secrets in this savage town!" More laughter.

"Shut up." Cassandra replied. There was nothing she could deny. "Where's Phineas?"

"He and the chief's 'avin' a little talk, they are. Me thinks it's a bargainin'—a tradin' talk; her highness, Sky Blue, for one of them rickety boats. Me and the others are leavin' this pit o' charm, yer Holy Highness, but ye whilst be stayin' 'ere birthin' savages for the rest of thy days." Izzie smiled, satisfactorily.

"Why do you hate me?"

Izzy thought a moment. "Ye's weak, and on a high horse. Prancing around like ye's too good for the rest o' us. *'I'm not from*

---

[18] *Whirligigs:* testicles

this century'!" she mimicked. "*'I come from the year two thousand...'* what was it now?" she asked, stopping her charade.

"Two thousand eighteen, and you, you foul mouthed slut, are dead! Long dead!"

A small crowd of women stopped their chores to gather at the scene. It was an amusing distraction, the red headed white woman and Sky Blue, arguing.

"'Tis not true!" Izzie approached Cassandra, hands on hips, face as red as her hair. "Ye art a liar! Am I not standin' 'ere a'for them holy blue eyes?"

"You are nothing but an apparition, and for what reason I have been thrown in with the likes of you, I don't know."

"Listen 'ere, ye Saintship, go back then. Go back to where ye come from, as ye's not needed nor wanted. Rot with the savages; me and Phineas 'ave plans, but they do not include the likes of you."

"He'll betray you just as he's betrayed me."

"I ain't no puddin' 'ead. No need tellin' me 'bout the deeds o' men; I know 'em all." Then, turning to the crowd of onlookers, "Go away ye heathen whores!" She yelled these words, stomping her foot into the dirt. The group scattered like rabbits, leaving Cassandra to wonder if Izzie's wild red hair and disposition had planted a seed of fear in some of the villagers. If she, Cassandra, was a goddess with her blue eyes, Izzie, with her crazy red hair and temperament, could have been the devil.

Chapter 10

Cupid pushed the dugout off the beach. At knee deep he climbed aboard, his weight forcing the dugout deeper into the water, but not enough to sink their means of escape.

Cassandra stood sadly by Long Feather, holding back tears that begged to fall as Cupid and Phineas paddled the canoe further into the bay. She would have waved, but for the sly smirk Izzie directed toward her as they faded into the beyond of freedom. Phineas, Cupid, Lucy and the babe, and Izzie, her longest known acquaintance, off to where, she couldn't tell, while she remained in the Indian village as Long Feather's wife.

I may as well be mute, she thought, turning away from the sad sight. *I've been traded for a boat, and here I am in a primitive village with people I can't even communicate with.* That reality, above all, seemed the saddest; and so much so that tears began to trail down her cheeks. She wiped them away and continued toward the village.

Back to work; endless frigging mundane work. "Damn it!" she said aloud, and then realized that Long Feather walked by her side. She felt his eyes on her as they proceeded along the path. He reached out to catch a tear and rubbed it between his thumb and middle finger. "Sky Blue *neighseum*[19]"

She didn't know what he said, but kept walking until they entered the longhouse.

"*Paseme uppooke*," Long Feather sat at his usual place on the hide-covered bench at the far end the longhouse.

She fetched his pipe and tobacco, as these words she knew well. He was always ordering one wife or another to fetch things for him. Otter and Crane were away at one of their endless tasks, leaving Cassandra with the *weroance*. Her new life as Long Feather's bride did not hold promise for a wonderful future. Of course, she had no intentions of staying put; this was not her life, not her future. Her infatuation with Long Feather was running thin.

"I'm going to leave you," she said, knowing full well he couldn't understand her words. *Izzie Pratt hasn't seen the end of me.* Long Feather stuffed his pipe with tobacco grown from the village garden and now struck the flint and tinder until the dried, crushed leaves sparked and lit. He inhaled deeply to distribute the embers, thus sending a spiral of acrid smoke upward toward the smoke hole.

"At the first opportunity, I'm leaving." She smiled, and he returned the same. "I don't belong here," she continued. "You have Otter and Crane to care for you, and I can't be one of three. I'm not like you." *I'm certainly not like them, either.* She was sure the wives hated her, and was *positive* that they had stolen her Cartier watch. She had searched everywhere: the gardens, the entire longhouse, and even while out wood gathering, in case it had fallen off, but to no avail; it was gone, and so was her concept of time.

"I don't come from this century," she continued. "I'm not an Indian, I'm a modern American woman. I don't live like this." She spread her arms to indicate the inside of the longhouse. "I miss my people...my home...." Just the word 'home' caused the tears to well in her eyes once more.

---

[19] *Neighseum*: to cry

Long Feather cocked his head, his carved pipe gripped between his teeth. *"Nawpin,[20]"* he said, patting the bench beside him.

She sat, and the two stared into each other's eyes. "What kind of relationship is this?" she asked, eyebrows raised. "With Phineas gone, we can't communicate." *Except under your blanket, but what kind of relationship is that?* "You're a fine man, Long Feather, but this will never work; I can't live like this." *Maybe I'm not alive... maybe I'm dead and don't know it? Oh God, please don't let me be dead! Is this some crazy kind of hell?* Her head screamed for answers to her dilemma.

Long Feather's confusion at her words was evident by the expression on his face. Then, realizing that her thoughts—her sadness and stress—had written themselves across her own face, she smiled, hurriedly patted his thigh and stood. *"Mecher,"* she said. "Eat." She pantomimed putting food into her mouth, and left to join Otter and Crane; surely it was time to prepare the evening meal. To shirk work responsibility in any form was frowned upon, and she needed to keep in good graces while she planned her escape.

Plan? Ha! There is no planning. Woods, marsh and swamp, that's all; and I need to get through it to where the people are—*my* people. What if there are only Indians? Oh, good Lord, why don't I know more of history? I should have spent less time at the club and more at the library!

Thoughts tossed like stormy seas through her mind. Anxiety grew to gargantuan proportions as she lay on her pelt-covered bedding in the dark of the longhouse. Nearby, Long feather snored intermittently, while Otter and Crane slept silently, aside from the occasional wisp of exhaled breath from either.

---

[20] *Nawpin:* Sit

Finally, on a night when the moon glowed full, its silver light blanketing the earth, she stole the pouch in which Otter kept her important items, such as flint and steel, herbs, bones, and most important, a razor-sharp clam shell that served as a knife. *Forgive me Otter, but I need this more than you.*

Cassandra crept from the longhouse and set about her chosen path along the bay northward, the direction Phineas and the others had chosen. At least travelling close to the bay, she could gather the large oysters that flourished so prolifically in the waters; perhaps even catch a crab or two. *Thank you, my fellow wives, for teaching me to gather and open oysters!* She owed Otter and Crane that, even though they thought her lazy and ignorant, laughing behind her back. She knew nothing of survival in the wilderness...*and, why should I? I wasn't born into this insanity.*

Perhaps departing on the night of a full moon was a mistake, but the thought of entering unknown territory in total darkness was not appealing; she would chance the moonlight. Three weeks had passed since the others had left the village. How far could they get in a day, she wondered? It was impossible to answer the question, since she had no experience whatsoever in paddling a dugout, or in figuring the distance one could travel in a selected period of time. Traveling by foot was another matter altogether.

The night was chilly as she crept through the forest of red cedar, sweet gum, pine, and the horrid brambles that poked and tore at her flesh. The path was no doubt created by the natives, weaving alongside the bay, perhaps hidden from view of encroaching ships, but close enough to the bay to gather food. This, she followed, knowing full well that come the morning light she would need to venture away from this safety zone and deeper into the forest, or else a search party—or Long Feather himself— may track her down. Then what would happen? *Would he kill me for running off? Could I be killed for running from a village that doesn't even exist?* "They're all dead, for Pete's sake!"

Every crunch of twig or leaf, fallen branch, and worst of all, animal sounds, caused her to crouch low to the ground for fear that Long Feather had discovered her tracks. Or, perhaps worse; wild animals had picked up her scent. But neither bear, nor wolf, nor any creature of darkness crossed her path through that long night, aside from raccoon and deer.

Her worst enemies were the mosquitoes that buzzed in droves about her head and body. The constant hum of tiny wings nearly drove her mad as she swatted and cursed. Itchy welts raised from foot to ear; blood seeped and scabbed from constant scratching. Next, were the ticks, and then the invisible chiggers that burrowed into her flesh. Before the final light of day, she checked her body, cursing for lack of fingernails—which had long since broken to the quick—to pull the buggers out. In Otter's pouch, she dug out the sharp clam shell. With this in hand, she scrapped against the menacing insects until the ticks either backed away or their bodies shredded, leaving the heads imbedded in her skin; it was the best she could do, for between the chiggers and ticks, her legs were covered in red itchy bumps. There was no cure but to wait for the incessant itching to pass.

When the first light of day pasted the thick forest against the purple-blue sky, she made her way to the water, making sure that the imprint of her moccasins dug deep into the mucky shore. Covering her retreating tracks was not as simple; the natives were cunning, and she had no doubt Long Feather would be on her trail. If he thought she had swam away or drowned, she could relieve herself of the burden of capture.

Exhausted, she gathered an assortment of pebbles, and luckily found a fallen branch with a few smaller, leafy branches still attached. With this, she attempted to brush away and cover her retreating prints. She sprinkled pebbles and debris over her work and hoped the incoming tide would make her walk into the water more realistic. Looking into the forest, she mustered her courage; and still holding the sweeper branch, she began her trek. *At least I know which way is north.*

Though the sun would not be visible for a while, its dawning rays edged fluffy clouds with pink and gold in the eastern sky. As she walked further into the mass of trees, she brushed away her footprints until she dropped the branch and continued into the thick of forest and the unknown future.

"Three friggin' days!" Scratched, bloody arms and legs, her deerskin shift filthy and torn, her hair matted and full of twigs and leaves, her mouth a foul and gritty place, and her stomach rumbling from hunger, she gathered leaves and branches to make a bed. "I'm going to die of encephalitis, Lyme disease, thirst or hunger—or *all*—before I see another human." The memory of the cozy longhouse, food aplenty, the bitter wives and Long Feather, all hung close in memory. Compared to what she endured at this time, it was a pleasant memory.

Darkness fell, and once again she curled into a ball upon the leaves and branches. It was little protection against a fear that spread like wildfire throughout her body. She had given up night travel after she was satisfied that Long Feather did not have a search party in action.

"Could he not have missed me?" More often as not, she rambled aloud to keep herself company, and to keep her head in check should the fear of the darkness of night run rampant. The sounds of unseen animals—creatures possibly watching her through the thicket—ran chills up and down her spine.

These thoughts consumed her as she lay in her curled position on her bed of leaves and branches. The nights were cool, and she had no blanket but the shift, which certainly did not do the job. She did not like exposing herself to the elements—or the animals.

The first two days and nights were terrifying. Thirst consumed her until she came across a pond on the third day. Hoping it was safe for drinking, she drank slowly at first, and then   quickly, until she could hold no more. *So far, so good.* At times, she felt uplifted and proud of her stamina and will to reach civilization; but at other times, desperation and fear of the night overwhelmed her, as it did on this night.

"It's hopeless! I'm lost...lost...lost.... Soon I'll be dead," she cried, and was answered by the hoot of an owl. But instead of death, dawn broke, and with it, her spirit, as she woke to another day in the nightmare. "Oh," she groaned, rising from her lumpy bed. Leaves and twigs stuck to her shift and hair. She relieved herself behind a log— privacy still a matter of importance, though there wasn't a soul nearby. *Just in case, but... I wouldn't even care if anyone caught me peeing, as long as I were saved!*

"Get it together. Another day. No pain, no gain. Put one damn foot in front of the other. I must find more water today. Wait...what is that?" She had spotted dark dots on a nearby bush. As she approached the bush—daring not to get her hopes up—she realized there were more and more dark spots popping against the green. "Oh, my God, please be blueberries!" In her exalted state, she dropped to her knees and picked the berries, one, two—three at a time— stuffing them into her mouth as quickly as her hands could work. Nausea struck briefly as the tart juices ran a purple trail down her chin, but her stomach adjusted; she was rejuvenated, and rejuvenated she headed north, Otter's pouch bursting with berries.

Later, as night approached again, Cassandra, exhausted to the bone from another day of dodging thorns and forest debris, her arms and legs a crusty, red-stained stinging mess of pain from biting and embedded insects, stopped her painful trek to prepare her camp for the evening. "And now I lay me down to sleep," she said, stooping to kneel onto the blanket of leaves, when a familiar odor wafted up her nostrils. She straightened, inhaling deeply, desperate to find the direction of the source. "Campfire!" she said aloud, then covered her mouth in case there were Indians nearby.

The odor of burning wood came from the east. She crept silently—or as silently as the brush would allow—until the smoke from the fire spread thickly toward her, and she was close enough to hear the crackling of wood from the flames. That was not all she heard; she stood still as a deer...*humming?* This new sound required further investigation, as it was a woman's voice. An Indian camp? She lowered herself to her hands and knees hoping for camouflage within the brambles. It was a challenge to not scream out when the thorns scraped against the already raw flesh of her arms and legs as she crawled toward the sound. Once, to the edge of the brambles, she lowered herself to lie on her stomach and spread the brambles with her bleeding hands, hoping the crackling of the flames would muffle her sounds.

"Oh! Oh, thank you, God!" she said, backing away from the brush, this time mindless of the painful tears of her shredded flesh. Once able to stand, she maneuvered her body around the brush and trees to a clearing where a comforting, crackling, orange-red fire danced upon the dry logs. It was the most welcome vision!

"Izzie, it's you!" she said, running at the woman full speed before crumbling to the ground.

Chapter 11

hen Cassandra next opened her eyes, orange-red flames leaped in daggered splendor before her. It was heaven, the crackling fire, the comfort. The sounds and smell of the burning wood brought tears of relief to her eyes.

"Izzie...." She raised herself onto an elbow and perused her surroundings; dirt, trees, and more dirt. "Where are we? Where are the others?"

"Ah, ye's awake now. I nearly lost me flesh with the sight of ye springin' from the bush like a witch or the devil hi'self! As to where we be, I could not say. As to the others, I could not say, neither, except that they are again in the hands of the savages."

"Long Feather?"

"No, I had no knowledge of them, and them being not as friendly as the others."

"How did you escape?" Cassandra raised herself to a sitting position, all ears.

"I did not. They come in like a team of banshees, screamin' n' wailin'. Rounded us up like sheep. I took it upon meself to protest the interruption with some hollerin' of me own, and they cut me out o' the fold. They took the others, then pointed their sharp spears at me and backed away like I was full o' the plague."

Cassandra eyed the woman across the fire, the woman with hair as wild and red as the flames, and eyes that pierced like a panther. "It doesn't surprise me," she said. "You look a little, uh, scary."

"And ye don't? I told ya, I nearly jumped out o' me flesh at the sight of ye running at me like a wild beast o' the forest!"

"You left me there," Cassandra said after a long pause of silence, enough time to recall her pain on the banks of the Chesapeake watching the group depart in the dugout—without her. Izzie's departing glance at that time had been nothing short of a smirk. "If I weren't so damn tired, I'd pull your hair out for leaving me behind."

"Am I correct to assume 'twas not wedded bliss with the *weroance*?" Izzy cracked a sly smile, not unnoticed by Cassandra.

"I want to be with my own kind—and that does not include you *or* an Indian tribe. I want to be back in my world with my own people and not a bunch of uneducated, ignorant ruffians, such as yourself—not to mention dead ruffians, at that."

Izzie jumped to her feet, fists clenched at her side. "Am I not standin' a'fore ye?" she shrieked. Then, to Cassandra's total surprise, she placed her hands over her belly. "I got a life growin' in me, you see, so I an't dead."

"What? You're pregnant?"

"Aye, an't bled in a while."

"How the…? oh, I remember, you and the Indian."

"Aye. 'tis not that I'm proud." Izzy sat again and stared at the fire. It was the first time Cassandra had witnessed any remorse whatsoever in the strange woman.

"I would rid meself of it, but there an't a midwife or witch-woman near abouts…unless ye…. unless ye could help a garl out?"

"What? Impossible! I could do no such thing; and, besides, I wouldn't have any idea how to go about it in the first place."

"Useless woman," Izzy mumbled, taking a long stick from her kindling pile and poking the fire.

"Serves you right," Cassandra mumbled in return, all the time wondering if it could happen to her? There were simply too many issues to worry about without the thought of pregnancy; but now she added that possibility to her list of growing horrors. Could she become pregnant in a different time with a long dead Indian *weroance*? How could she explain it to her friends, *if I ever see them again?* So many mysteries!

"What have you been eating?" Cassandra asked after a long stretch of silence. "I'm starving."

"Not a morsel for two days. Whatever ye thinks o'me, tis not me world neither. I would give me tattered shift to be back on the Thunder cookin' up a supper for those bandy-legged pirates."

"Oh, don't mention food..." Cassandra groaned, her stomach growling at the memory of Izzie's stew simmering on the stove. "We need a plan, Izzie; and whatever you may think of me, we will have to put aside our differences. We need to find civilization—if one exists here."

"Aye, I'll not be disputin' that, but don't take it in yer 'ead that I'm beholdin' to yer company."

Dawn broke, shooting splintered rays of sun through the forest's lofty branches. Birds trilled and chattered as the women woke, damp from morning dew, dirty from days lost in the wilderness, their bellies crying for food that could not be found in any simple manner, and tongues parched from want of water.

"North," Cassandra said, her voice dry and brittle, in desperate need of fluid. "We have to find fresh water." She stood and brushed away the woodland debris from her filthy shift.

Izzie coughed and smacked a dry tongue against her palate. "Me tongue is parched," she said, flitting the muscle in and out of the dark and semi toothless hole of her mouth. With her tongue still smacking and darting like a snake, she rose from the forest floor and attempted a stretch. "'Tis a piss I need," she said, and headed for the nearest tall pine where she stood, spread her legs, and peed a long stream of urine.

Gross woman, Cassandra thought, as she headed to her own outdoor commode, a patch of bramble and brush amidst the rough bark of the lower trunk of a tall cedar. Here she squatted, her thighs feeling the pull of weakened muscle; the lack of food and water had taken its toll on her bedraggled body.

Relief done, her thighs refused to project her body upward. She wavered, her hands reaching backward to brace against the harsh forest floor. "Oh, God!" she moaned, the full reality of their desperate predicament hitting full force. Tears filled her eyes and raced down her filthy cheeks until she tasted the salt in her own parched mouth. Then, as if the last ounce of fluid had been spent with the outflow, her tear ducts ceased to produce, leaving her eyes as dry as the Sahara.

"Quit your ballin', woman. Take me 'and; we cannot be lettin' this inconvenience be the death of us."

The thin, white hand that pulled her back into the surreal reality was surprisingly strong. Ashamed to have broken so pathetically, she mustered her courage, looked northward, and followed Izzie's lead with eyes blinking; a futile attempt to replace the precious fluid so ridiculously spent.

"Damn!" The words exploded from Cassandra's mouth as she tried in vain to expel the relentless mosquitoes that swarmed about her head and welted body. Even though they had rubbed moist soil on their bodies to conceal their body odor, the unwelcomed guests to their small, weary caravan of two, engulfed them in a cloud of buzzing, biting torture as they trudged through the seemingly endless wilderness.

Storm clouds had gathered overhead, the humidity rose and the atmosphere became heavy, as if air had gained substance and weight to push against their earthly forms. Flies, that appeared to Cassandra to be house flies, now joined the menacing cloud in an ever-increasing cacophony of noise, and stung even more painfully than the mosquitoes. "If I live through this...." she started to say—flinging her arms like a wayward marionette—but was stopped by a tremendous explosion of thunder overhead.

The sky broke. Rain poured in gallons upon the pair, washing away the torturous insects. It streaked days of dirt down their uplifted faces, into their thirsty mouths, opened to catch the downfall of life giving fresh water onto their parched tongues.

"Thank ye, God in heaven!" Izzie yelled to the treetops. She ruffled her crazy mane of red frizz, then pulled the filthy deerskin shift over her head, leaving her white body naked amongst a background of bark and green. "Clean thy shift!" she yelled, over a crack of lightening. Cassandra reluctantly did the same, pulling the tattered, dirty shift over her head.

They laid their shifts over a log, letting the pounding pellets of rain beat the dirt and grind away. Then they washed. Armpits, necks, behind ears and privates, scrubbing with soapless hands the cracks and crevices of their thinning bodies. Cassandra looked to Izzie's white, flat belly, seeing not the signs of the growing babe Izzie had referred to; but it was much too early to tell.

When the thunder diminished and the storm moved on, they wrung the excess water from their shifts and dressed, the shifts now clinging cold and clammy to their refreshed bodies. The wind had increased, the humidity blown away, and the temperature had dropped dramatically.

"Feast or famine," Cassandra said, shivering, and trailing behind Izzie as they proceeded their onward trek. "Now, if we could just find food...."

As the sun lowered behind the thick forest, Izzie stopped and turned to Cassandra, wide eyed, putting a finger to her lips. "Shhh. Listen."

Sure enough, a low buzz of human voices reached Cassandra's ears, yet impossible to tell which language was spoken.

Following Izzie, they crept ahead, crouched low, tiptoeing gently over the leaves and woodland debris, ignoring the thorns of bramble that scratched and pierced their tender, wounded flesh.

Then, "Heave, ya lazy negar!" were the first words to reach their ears.

"English!" Cassandra said, overjoyed to hear a language she understood— despite its context.

The women now stood at the edge of the forest. Ahead, land was in the process of being cleared of brush and trees. A man wearing a wide brimmed straw hat held taut a rope of which was tied to a fallen pine. His long muslin shirt cut into a deep V at the chest, with sleeves billowy in the style of the day. These fell over breeches which were met at the knee by tall boots of leather.

Between the man and the fallen log stood a powerfully built black man, naked to the waist, his muscular chest glistening with the sweat of labor. His face appeared marked by tattoos, and in his right earlobe, the setting sun reflected on a gold earring.

"Cupid!" Cassandra and Izzie both yelled at once. They burst from the edge of the forest like frightened deer, racing to the one man who had saved them from a watery death.

A smile broke across Cupid's face, displaying his rows of fine teeth. "Izzie! Miz Pratt!" He dropped the rope and ran to meet the pair of women, circling them in his thick arms. "How…what….?"

"Who's that man," Cassandra asked, nodding to the stranger in the straw hat, who now stood with arms crossed over his chest, the once taut rope laying at his feet.

"Dat man buy me from da savages. Tis not a good one; savages better."

"Where are Lucy and the babe?"

"Dey's here, too," he said, wiping sweat from his brow.

"And Phineas?" Izzie asked.

"No, da savages keep him."

"Git ye back to work, lazy negar!" the straw hatted man yelled as he approached the group.

"Hold yer wicked tongue," Izzie hissed at the stranger. "The man's name is Cupid, not 'negar'."

"And hold thy tongue, woman," the man replied, spittle spewing through his crooked yellow teeth, "or I shall hold it for ye." This he demonstrated by placing a fist before her face.

Cupid maneuvered both women behind his shirtless frame. "Dem's me friends," he said, crossing his powerful arms over his chest in a stance that surely was understood across all language barriers.

Cassandra peeked around Cupid to witness the response, and was satisfied that the stranger had received the full impact of the message, as he had taken a few steps backward.

"If it's food ye be wanting, women, then gather the rope and heave. I shall not feed those who do not work. Come, *Cupid*," he growled the man's name, glaring over his shoulder at Izzie, who looked very pleased with herself at standing up to the stranger.

Food! Just the word threw Cassandra's stomach into a painful, gnawing state. How could it be so utterly difficult to get food? It had to be fished, scavenged, grown, or shot, if one wanted to eat; and now it had come down to doing a man's work!

Cassandra rolled her eyes. "Do you honestly expect we women to move that log?" She, too, had now crossed her arms over her chest, and shook her head haughtily, tossing her straight-and-now-stringy head of hair from her eyes in hopes of showing her superiority and breeding. "We're weak, we haven't eaten in days, and...that woman is with child," she added. "We have no strength!"

The man turned and glared through beady eyes of blue, sweat running rivulets down his cheeks. A scraggly beard and mustache framed a mouth that displayed his crooked yellow teeth. "Then set ye both down, but ye shall not take one morsel from the mouths of those who spill our sweat into this wretched land; thy shall sleep with pain in thy bellies!"

Izzie, looking thin and peaked, stepped forward. "'Tis work ye need? 'Tis me can work like the ox," she said, then whispered to Cassandra. "Do not be takin' it upon thyself to spread the word of me savage bastard."

Cassandra sighed, defeated, and wearily followed Cupid and Izzie to the limp rope at the fallen log. Chivalry was certainly dead in this time zone, too.

With four people tugging at the stubborn log, it moved, much to Cassandra's amazement. The heat and humidity had temporarily lessened, but then returned with a vengeance, even with sunset approaching. She wiped sweat from her brow with a clammy hand, now blistered from rope burn. "Don't you have a beast of some sort to help with this kind of work?" she asked the planter, then heaved the rope again with the group.

"The savages took it upon themselves to confiscate the beast and what foul I hadst, then offered me this beast and the woman and child in return," he said, indicating Cupid. "There was naught a choice but to comply with the heathens."

Lucy cried with joy to see Izzie and Cassandra, as told by the tears that flowed from her large brown eyes. Baby Free had grown in the few weeks since Cassandra had seen her last, and now had eyes that focused and stared with curiosity at the new faces. Her chubby legs kicked beneath the loosely woven blanket of flax, while her arms waved erratically with excitement from her basket cradle set to the left of the fireplace hearth. Izzie lifted her from the basket to bounce her on a hip.

The fireplace was aflame, even in the heat of the outdoors. This made the cabin barely tolerable, but the aroma of baking bread set above the fire in a raised black skillet, mingled with something bubbling in the pot, rendered it tolerable enough.

The planter's cabin was a shambled construction of slats of pine. Its high peaked roof was thatched with dried grasses, and its floor nothing but dirt. Along the wall were pegs which held an assortment of items: a finer hat than the planter wore at present, breeches and a filthy looking waistcoat; apparently, he had retained one good set of clothing to wear on special occasions, none of which occasion Cassandra could conjure in this time and place.

The rest of the hooks held an assortment of tools; hatchet, hammer, saw, rope. A wide slab of roughly hewn wood balanced on two barrels, created a table of sorts. Only one oddly constructed rustic chair sat at the table, and an additional overturned barrel set against a wall. The fireplace was large enough to roast a skewered pig—should they have one—along with the black iron pot of bubbling stew hanging from an iron arm that extended either into, or out of, the fire.

Beside the low framed door hung a flintlock pistol. Two narrow windows cut into the walls on either side of the door, allowed a view into the yard from the front of the cabin. Narrow windows of the same fashion were placed strategically on the sides and back walls, thus bringing in daylight while allowing views for approaching savages.

On a sidewall shelf sat two trenchers, two wooden noggins and what appeared to be eating utensils. "Does the planter have a wife, Lucy?" Cassandra asked.

"No," she said quietly, her eyes suddenly cast downward.

"What's wrong?" Cassandra asked wondering why the simple question should cause such a reaction.

"Has the beast put himself upon ye?" Izzie was quick to read the silent language of the woman.

"Please, don' tell Cupid. When he work in' field, da planter come take pleasure."

"Oh…well, Christ." Cassandra threw her arms into the air and tried to obliterate the disgusting picture in her mind; the middle-aged planter dropping his breeches and forcing himself upon poor Lucy, who already had her share of worldly troubles. "How long have you been here? How many times has this happened?"

"Been here six, seven day. Don know fo' sure. He come to me two time."

"Well, there won't be a third time, and Cupid should know this," Cassandra said, remembering how the two had looked lovingly at one another back at the careening of the ship. "Cupid would not allow this to happen! What if you become pregnant; what then?"

"Please, say notin!" Lucy begged. "

"Let the bastard try again," Izzie growled. "Ye belong to me, not to the likes of him. Ye art mine, fairly won at the cost of me virtue!"

To this, Cassandra scoffed silently, but Izzie, satisfied that she had resolved the issue, now stood in front of the fireplace, baby Free still in her arms. "What shall we eat, Lucy? We have walked so many days without a morsel."

"Bread bakin' and meat in da pot. Mus' wait fo' planter."

Cassandra's mortification at the thought of Lucy and the planter faded to the back of her mind as the surety of real food came front and center. "We'll help," Cassandra said, just moments before a spell of dizziness caused her to plunk herself onto the one chair at the table. "My head is spinning," she mumbled. "Water...."

Lucy was quick to pour water from a dented pewter pitcher into one of the noggins. Cassandra drank until her cup was empty. "Thanks," she whispered. The water was surprisingly tasty. "It's very good. Where did it come from?"

"Da crick. Good watah."

Izzie handed the baby back to her mother. "How much land has the planter?"

Lucy shook her head. "Don' know."

"Hmm. Land with fresh water. A man with no wife...."

Cassandra stared incredulously at her companion. "Hmm, what? What are you thinking?"

"I shall have me land, one day. Land and fresh water. I shall have it all, but not in this place with the likes of that buck-fitching[21] buffoon. I'll get me a man with silver in 'is pockets!"

---

[21] *Buck-fitching*: Old, lecherous and nasty fellows. The First English Dictionary of Slang, 1699

"Which you'll pilfer right out of there, no doubt." Cassandra replied.

Izzie stared straight-faced at Cassandra. "Aye. Me life's been one suffer after another, and 'twill be no more."

Chapter 12

ore rum, woman!" The planter banged his noggin on the table as he worked a piece of meat in his mouth, the stew gravy trailing a brown line into his beard.

Lucy scampered to her feet from her place on a small braided rug at the side of the hearth next to baby Free. Only the planter sat at the table, while the others sat wherever a spot was available in the dimly lit cabin. Cupid sat upon an over-turned barrel, while Cassandra and Izzy roosted on the edge of the planter's cot, each awaiting their turn for the extra trencher to be passed from person to person. When the food was finally in their grasp they ate like the starving animals they were, their fingers greasy from the gravy.

"Even the Indian village was more civilized than this," Cassandra said between mouthfuls.

"There 'tis the door!" The planter nodded in its direction, scowling at her remark as he broke a chunk of bread from a round load. "I did not invite ye," he said, his words now garbled by the wad of bread.

"Nay, and ye won't be seein' the backs of us, old goat—not unless Lucy, Free and Cupid are in our company." She finished her turn at the trencher and rose to pass it along to Cupid.

"Stop baiting him," Cassandra whispered. "You're making it worse."

The planter leaned back in his chair "'Tis no hardship for me to gain more hands these past three days for clearing the field." The planter glared at Izzie on her short trek across the room.

"No more!" Izzy spat. "Clear thy own field! We shall take our leave on the morrow. The woman and babe are *my* property, not for ye to do with as ya like."

Without warning, the planter's arm swung outward, forcefully smacking into the small of her back as she passed. This action sent her flying forward until she—and the trencher of stew—splattered against Cupid, who shot upright, knocking Izzy to the dirt floor.

"Téigh trasna ort Féin!" she yelled, while Cupid attempted to wipe the remnants of stew from his bare chest.

Lucy grabbed the baby, who had begun to scream angrily, having been woken abruptly from her sleep, and pressed herself against the wall next to the fireplace. Cassandra jumped to her feet and stared wide-eyed at Izzie, who was now on all fours, red hair covering her face like a wild animal. And, animal like, she crawled the few paces to the hated man eating his meal. He rose swiftly, sending the one chair flying sidewise onto the dirt floor, then grabbed a fist full of the red mane and yanked her to standing. "None leave, ye foul-mouthed whore, except for thee!" Bits of food flew from his mouth to her face as he spewed his angry words. In return, Izzie pursed her lips and spit a wad, hitting him on the chin.

"Curséd be ye!" the planter yelled, and gave her cheek a mighty wallop.

Cassandra was horrified at the mad scene and attempted to pull the planter away from Izzie, but Cupid intervened with a thick arm around the planter's neck. "Leave go," he growled into the man's ear, wrenching his arm an inch tighter. The planter struggled for breath and quickly released Izzie, who stumbled a few feet's distance before racing to the table to retrieve the bread knife.

"I say we cut 'is throat." she poked the tip of the knife a fraction into the planter's juggler. "'Tis a comeuppance for being the wicked soul he is, fornicating with poor Lucy at his whim—and her with a babe."

Lucy gasped, her eyes wide in fear at the mention of her name. She held the baby tighter, pressing harder against the wall.

"Izzie, stop!" Cassandra yelled. "Stop!!" She was dizzied with horrification at witnessing a possible murder.

"'Tis true, Lucy? Dis man been at ye?" Cupid tightened his grip.

"Don' do murder, Cupid! Please don' do no murder!" Lucy cried.

"Ye been at my woman?" Cupid yelled, and with gritted teeth he again tightened his hold on the man's neck. The planter tried in vain to pull away from the death grip, but the more he struggled, the more he choked. With eyes bulging, face shiny with sweat, and losing oxygen by the second, he now fought weakly against his attacker,

Cassandra felt faint. The sight of Cupid's strength and anger, Lucy's fear, and Izzie's determination to kill the planter, all played out as a macabre scene enhanced by the glow from the fireplace. *This cannot be happening. It's a dream— a nightmare!*

Cupid's face morphed into a knotted ball of anger as the muscles of his arm bulged on the ever-tightening chokehold. The planter's legs weakened; he was nearly unconscious, his tongue protruded grossly between his lips.

"Stop! Stop, Cupid! This is murder!" Cassandra ran to the macabre trio, Izzy and Cupid, locked in one evil goal, the planter, his face the color of death. In vain, she attempted to pull Cupid's arm from the planter's neck, but he was strong as an ox. "Stop!" she screamed, and battered her fists against his broad back.

"Get away," Izzie threatened. "I want to see 'im die—a just punishment!"

Lucy set Free into her basket and joined Cassandra. "Please, Cupid, no! 'Tis murder—you hang!"

By some miracle—perhaps the sound of Lucy's beseeching voice—Cupid released his prisoner, who fell to a clump at their feet.

"Damn ye to hell, woman," Izzie yelled, pointing the knife at Cassandra's face. "He should be meetin' the devil hi'self!"

"Is he dead?" Cassandra whispered ignoring Izzie's threat and brushing the knife-wielding hand away. With the frenzy ended, they stared at the planter's body at their feet. "Is he breathing?"

"Please, no dead," Lucy moaned. "You hang, Cupid!"

Cassandra stood frozen, her head bent to the floor, her mind miles away. *Why am I here? Am I here? Am I dead? Is this hell?* Then, "Good God, Cupid, look what you've done! Somebody somewhere is going to wonder what happened to this man, and if they're not stupid, they'll be looking for you—maybe for us. We have to bury him. Get a shovel, do something! Don't stand there like dummies!"

At her words, they dispersed. Cupid left the cabin to search for a shovel. Lucy, trembling in fear, again retrieved the crying baby from the basket.

Izzie walked to the fire, staring at the embers. She then turned and dug the knife into the tabletop with one hard stab. "Her righteous ladyship," she said with venom. "Ye weren't aboard the Thunder when poor Lucy was passed from scum to scum. Ye did not 'ave the occasion to listen to the bawlin', nor see the pain the wench suffered. Y've not been at the 'ands of devil men who don't give a farthin' for thy soul, but lust the body. Y've not been spit upon, nor starved, nor beaten, nor scorned for the rags upon your back. Y've not suffered." She spat a wad of spit into the dirt at Cassandra's feet. "Righteous ladyship who appears in the bowels of a ship in naught but her skivvies, and looks upon us like roaches."

"I'm suffering now, crazy lunatic!" Cassandra leaned over the table, fists planted on its top, the vertical knife between them. "I don't know where the hell I am!" she yelled. "I don't know who you are, or these people, or why I'm here at all. So far, I've survived a shipwreck, been captured by Indians—and, for Christ's sake—even married an Indian! I've wandered lost in forests, and yes, I've starved. I'm tired, I'm filthy, I'm lost and...and I just want to go home!" Tears filled her eyes with the verbal reality of her state of being. *Please don't cry...don't let her see you cry.*

"I gots a shovel." Cupid said, bursting through the door, tool in hand, and just in time as Cassandra wiped away a tear.

"Let's get to work," she said, hoarsely.

Izzy scowled and crossed her hands over her chest. "I don't take me orders from the likes of ya, she said haughtily.

"Oh, cripes," Cassandra mumbled. She pulled the thin cover from the planter's bed. "I'm going to pretend this is not really happening. I'm really not here, but lost in a nightmare with a bunch of crazy people." She laid the cover over the body. *This isn't real. I will not feel remorse...* "Oh!" she jumped backward. "Listen..." she leaned an ear toward the man at her feet. "I heard something." If the floor had not been dirt but wood, the ping of a dropped pin would have reached the ears of all those who now stared at the planter's prone body. When Cupid tapped his body with his foot, the planter groaned.

"He's alive! Thank God, he's alive!" Cassandra sighed a sigh of relief, while Izzie wasted no time; she ran to the table and yanked the knife free.

"And he'll be gettin' 'is just reward."

Cupid swiftly removed the knife from her hand as she barreled for the planter.

"Cupid, put him on the bed and then let's all get out of here. Get your stuff, Lucy." Cassandra glanced at Izzie who stood with arms crossed, dark beady eyes expressing nothing short of hate at the lost opportunity of giving the planter his comeuppance.

"Got nothin' but Free." Lucy said, then removed the cover from the planter. Gripping one end between her teeth, she attempted to tear into the cloth, but to no avail. Cupid handed her the knife, which she took and proceeded to jab and cut at the fabric with desperate force.

"What on earth are you doing?" Cassandra asked.

"For da babe, gots to swaddle her bum."

"Oh, I never thought of that." *What do I know about babies?*

While Lucy ripped swaddling from the planter's coverlet, Cupid lifted his heavy body and placed him onto the bed. Wheezing, guttural sounds from the man's throat signaled that he was having some difficulty breathing, but, hopefully, he would recover in a day or two—when they were far, far away from repercussion.

Lucy threw the remaining bit of bedcover over the man. "Done," she said, and they ran from the farmhouse with nothing but the clothes on their backs — except for the flintlock that Cupid had removed from the mantle over the fireplace. With Lucy's knapsack full of swaddling, they ran from the ramshackle cabin into a moonless night, which gave a grateful cover should the planter recover quickly and give chase.

Chapter 13

"Are ye sick, Izzie?" Cupid asked, watching as she squatted on the shore of a wide river banked with acres of tall grass. Far back, on either side of said river, the forest grew tall and stately. At this moment, waning rays of setting sun poked through the timbers.

Izzie cupped the river water in her hands and splashed it onto her face, wiping the bile from her mouth, then wiped the back of her neck with a cool palm and stood, shaking her hands to dry in the still and humid air. "Aye. Sick o' this endless journey through forests and rivers that 'ave that no end."

"Sick, my foot," Cassandra mumbled, knowing full well the cause of Izzie's recent nausea. For two days and nights they had walked in Cupid's shadow in hopes of coming across a settlement. For two days and nights Izzie had slipped into the forest to gag as her stomach expelled...*nothing,* for they had not eaten since the final supper in the planter's farmhouse, of which most had spilt to the floor. The sound of her retching— the emptiness, the nothing—of her belly, sent shivers up the spines of the weary, starving travelers.

"An't none 'ere but savages? No villages? Her ladyship..." Izzie threw a snide smile in Cassandra's direction, "...sayeth she is from the future, yet she wanders hopeless as a lost lamb. Would she not know this place? Lies roll from 'er tongue like rain."

Cupid raised an eyebrow. "'Tis true, woman? If ye know this place, we go to village."

Cassandra sat on flattened marsh grass along the riverbank, knees to her chest, arms wrapped about them as if to shelter herself from the strange world into which she was rudely deposited. "Don't you think that if I knew this place I would not be sitting here in the dirt with a bunch of people who have been dead for centuries? Would I be wearing this filthy animal hide? In my own time, there are cities, roads, cars, gas stations, hotels, restaurants...bottled water, nice clothing, and supermarkets, so we don't have to wander like animals through the woods looking for food." She rested her head onto her knees. "God, why am I here?"

"Listen to 'er words!" Izzie plopped her fists onto her hips. "She speaks not our tongue. 'Tis a madhouse she needs!"

All sat in quiet contemplation until Lucy alerted them to possible danger. "Look, a boat!" She pointed upstream, and all eyes focused on a dugout paddled by a single form.

Cassandra jumped to her feet. "Indians! Get back!" They retreated quickly from the water's edge into the brush, but when the dugout paddled closer, Cupid literally leapt from the brush and bolted like a flagtail deer over the tall grasses to the riverbank.

"What are you doing?" Cassandra shrieked. The thought of recapture by Indians did not appeal in the tiniest bit—not to one who yearned for the 21st century.

"Cap'n! We's here!" Cupid yelled, waving his thick arms wildly about his head. "Here!"

Without a second thought, Izzie leapt from hiding and joined Cupid in his frantic attempt of rescue.

"It da Cap'n," Lucy said, as if it were an obvious fact. She gave Free a loud kiss on her tiny cheek. "It da Cap'n. We go now."

"I hope you're right," Cassandra muttered as she joined the others. She stood squinting, trying to bring the figure in the boat into focus, and at the same time wondering what it was about the figure that made the others think he was the captain of the

Thunder, as she could decipher nothing familiar of the form. The man's hair hung unruly below his shoulders. He appeared to have an immense beard, and not the tidy one Cassandra remembered.

Upon hearing the yells from shore, the man at first appeared to duck into the bottom of the dugout, but then recognized the large black man waving frantically at the riverside. He waved an acknowledgement and turned the dugout in their direction.

"He comin'," Lucy whispered in relief, and added a little two-step to indicate her joy at the prospect of salvation. Baby Free, feeling the excitement of the moment, interjected a yelp of sorts, as if realizing rescue was on its way.

"Oh, my God, it *is* him!" Cassandra said, as Captain Strongbow paddled closer to their station. As he approached, his features sharpened into memory. Though the vision before her was not the chiseled face, hair neatly tied at the neck, blousy shirt and tidy beard that she had known, there was still a familiarity: the set of the shoulders, square and muscular; the strong arms and large hands paddling the dugout. The blousy shirt was no longer white, and the sleeves that once blew in the breeze of the bay, were now rolled to the elbows.

The captain was nearly upon them now. It was not Cassandra's fervent dream come true—to return to the 21st century— but it was a welcomed relief to know that they would be saved from the endless forest and marshlands; for surely the captain had knowledge of the land, and could bring them to civilization.

The river was deep enough at this point to handle the dugout's shallow draft, and he was able to row up to the bank where the relieved group stood watching with great anticipation.

"Ye's alive, cap'n!" Cupid held the bow of the dugout steady as Captain Strongbow set one booted foot, and then another, onto land.

"I am indeed alive, Cupid. 'Twas a challenge to escape the blackguard, but a compromise was met." He looked at the wide-eyed trio of women. "'Tis wonderful to see that ye are all alive as well. I feared you had drowned in the sinking of the Thunder, and it has weighed heavily upon me. 'Tis good to see that you have not been killed by the Indians, as well. The Susquehanna are in uprising on the western shore and most likely will visit the eastern shore when the carnage is complete." He then bent to get a look at Free. "The babe is healthy, Lucy, tis good."

"What is this, chitchat hour?" Cassandra was astounded by the civility of this greeting under such dire circumstance. "Thank God you're here, Captain. Take us out of here— immediately! We been lost for days. We're starving, we're thirsty; we're dirty, and we're dead tired." She pointed to the dugout. "Will we all fit in that thing?"

The captain ignored Cassandra, and instead motioned for Cupid to follow. "Give us a hand." The men lifted the dugout from the river and hid it in the tall grass, out of sight.

Meanwhile, Cassandra fumed at being ignored. "Good Lord, Captain, I don't see why we have to stay here. We've been stuck in these woods forever."

At last, he turned to face here. "I see you are as contrary as before, Mistress Pratt, but it will be far too dark to travel on the river. We shall camp here for the night."

"Here? Must we spend one more night in this mosquito-infested land?"

"Is there another?" With that, he raised his brow, widened his eyes and stared a moment into hers, which was long enough for Cassandra to realize that she was receiving an order.

Izzie snickered.

"Gather firewood, women," the captain ordered. "Cupid and I shall search for food and fresh water, but if none is found, we shall have a fire to keep the mosquitoes and animals at bay."

Lucy was quick to respond. Perhaps the thought of wild animals approaching in the dark did not settle so well. Her fear of the night rose sharply at sunset, as witnessed by the others on the trek from the farmhouse. She quickly followed as Izzie led the way into the darkening forest, while Cassandra stood fixed to her spot.

"Be hasty, woman!" Captain Strongbow barked. "The sun hath set!"

"Captain, sir," Cassandra said, taking her stance of crossed arms in a pose of superiority. "Much has happened since we last met, and I have managed to care for myself alone in these God-forsaken woods—and survived—I might add.   I certainly don't require a pirate sea captain flinging orders at me. Perhaps you can boss the others, but...."

The captain was upon her now. "Mistress Pratt, you test my patience. I may not be in possession of my ship, but I am still responsible for the well-being of my passengers; and in the morrow, you shall be my passenger. Might I suggest that you follow Izzie and Lucy into the forest and gather firewood? Otherwise, you leave no choice but to section you away from our companionship—and our fire."

"You can't do that."

"Cupid! There lay a hemp rope in the bottom of the dugout. Bring it to me." He grabbed her wrists, holding them together with one powerful hand.

"Wait a min...."

Within seconds, Cupid arrived with the rope, which felt thick and scratchy as the captain wound it about her wrists.

"Wait! You can't be serious!" Cassandra cried, and kicked the captain in the shins. His reply was to jerk her hands as the knot tightened.

"You are not the only one to undergo dire circumstance. I, too, have had my share. I am tired and hungry as well, and I shall not allow a foolish woman to prevent me from setting up a fine and safe camp. If you cannot not help, you do not eat."

Through his angry words, she fought hopelessly against the rope, yet he continued pulling her toward the forest. Even then, as she tripped and fell to her knees, he continued to drag her a few short feet to a thickly trunked tree where he wrapped the long end of the rope around the trunk and secured it with a knot, leaving enough slack for her to stand or sit.

"I am indeed serious," he said, nodding politely before turning away. "Let us go, Cupid."

"Come back here!" Cassandra screamed through the twilight, but to deaf ears as the men were now out of sight.

It was not long before the insects discovered their feast. Mosquitoes came in massive clouds to swarm about her head, in her ears, inside her nostrils, but with her hands tied she could not successfully swat them away.

"Damn you, captain!" she yelled. "Help!"

In frantic frustration, she brought her hands to her mouth and tried to bite the knot loose; it wouldn't budge. "Damn it..." she whimpered, shaking her head madly as the hungry insects continued to bite at her exposed flesh. She cried loudly and unabashed, but silenced when the breaking of twigs caught her attention. "Izzie? Lucy? Oh, thank God. Cut me loose and I'll help gather wood... *please,* untie me!" She shook the strands of filthy, oily hair from her tear-stained cheeks and focused on a pair of legs that first appeared in her field of vision. In the gathering darkness, she could see that it was not Izzie, nor Lucy, nor the captain, or Cupid who stood before her, but an Indian! "No!" she screamed, terrified of recapture, and hoping that her screams would quickly bring the rest of her party. "Get away, savage!" she yelled at the intruder, and kicked her legs toward him, though she was seated by the tree and her kicks were nothing more than pathetic frantic jerks that did nothing but scuffle dirt.

The man was dressed in the familiar clothing of animal hide loincloth, his chest bare, and hair adorned with shells and bones.

Another Indian appeared in similar dress, and the two stood a few feet away conversing in their tongue, but made no move to untie or kill her. Though she was familiar with some of the language of the Indians she had lived with, the men spoke rapidly, and she did not understand their words.

Much to Cassandra's relief, the captain and Cupid returned rather quickly. *"Wingapo netab[22],"* the captain said, and the Indians approached him. They conversed briefly in the native language.

"Don't let them take me!" Cassandra pleaded, thinking perhaps the captain was trying to make a deal to get her off his hands.

---

[22] Wingapo netab: *Greetings, friend*

"Have no fear, 'tis not you they want; they think you are crazed. Twas the shrieking that brought them forth, and came to help if there was a person in danger; but they have found naught but a woman tied to a tree. They are curious as to the reason."

"I *am* in danger! I'm tied to a tree while the mosquitoes eat me alive. I demand to be released!"

The captain apparently repeated this message, as the Indians then broke into laughter. It was now, with the captain and natives side by side, that Cassandra realized how small the natives were as compared to the tribe she had lived with. The men were slight of build, though muscular, with their height coming no higher than the captain's shoulders, thus making the captain look as if he were a foreign god.

"Who are these men, captain?"

"They are the *Choptank* passing through, and they are harmless, a peaceable tribe.

"Well, thank God," she said and held her hands up to be released. "Please," she said. "I will help the women gather wood."

Total darkness set in. With the black of night surrounding them, they sat in a circle around the fire consuming the oysters that the men had gathered. The native men had joined them for a while, and then dispersed back into the forest.

"They tell me there is a small farm to the north by which we can reach by boat." Strongbow said. "But they also warn of the Susquehannock tribes of whom they have spotted coming from the western shore in their dugouts. We must be on alert."

Cassandra shivered. "Just how bad are they, that we have to be on alert?" she asked.

"Bad," Strongbow said. "And brutal."

"I can't say I've seen a plethora of white folks around these parts. All we've seen are Indians, more Indians, the fake magician, Phineas, one creepy planter, and us. That's all. Who the heck are these Susquehannocks going to fight?"

"They come to raid the other tribes, and as long as they are about, they shall try to kill us. My apologies for being blunt, ladies, but 'tis the truth and ye should know." Strongbow poked the burning wood with a long stick. The flames crackled and brightened at this move, and they sat silently watching the fire.

Cassandra searched the faces of the other women. She, herself, was terrified. Lucy's eyes were big as saucers, as she sat holding Free tightly to her breast. Izzie stared blankly into the fire while throwing broken pieces of a dried stick into the blaze.

"What a comeuppance!" Izzie exclaimed, breaking the silence. She then began to laugh.

"What could possibly be so funny, Izzie Pratt?" Cassandra asked, annoyed that Izzie could laugh with the threat of murder at any moment.

But Izzie laughed so hard that tears, flickering silver in the firelight, rolled down her cheeks. Then, totally out of character, she began to cry.

"A comeuppance! I am hastily put upon a ship out of London, banished for me discrepancies; win meself a slave girl in Barbados then put upon another ship...." She stopped her rant to hiccup a sob. "I come to the Americas to make me fortune and live like a lady. Ha!" She stood and brushed the dirt from her deerskin shift. "And where am I now? Lost in a land of savages with a heathen babe in me belly, waiting to be hacked to death! 'Tis not fair!"

Chapter 14

The following morning, ever aware of the threat of the Susquehannock raiding parties, the group settled into the dugout to search for the plantation of which the Choptanks had spoken. Cassandra, Izzie, Lucy and Free, sat between the two men who lifted the carved wooden paddles and rowed in a westerly direction until they reach the bay.

The river was smooth, but upon reaching the bay, whitecaps spiked upon the water and set the little dugout on a rolling course. It rocked from side to side as they glided over the small swells, making their way north along the jagged coastline. Cassandra was most anxious for any sign of civilization. *'Plantation'*, the Indians had said. White pillared mansions filled her head. Salvation! After all, those were the only plantations she could envision; but then, there was the cabin of the planter they left behind, which was not at all grand. *Think positive!* Perhaps there were real and civilized people at the new plantation—*even if they are long dead.* But, in the back of her mind, the realization that danger lurked on land and sea from the Susquhannocks, made short work of elation.

After what seemed hours of rowing, the first sign of civilization was spotted. "Look!" Cassandra yelled, most excitedly. "There's a shack—see? There, in the distance. There must be a plantation house in there somewhere!"

Through the thick brush and trees, a section of wooden structure appeared—barely—but enough to signal a structure of European origin.

Captain Strongbow and Cupid rowed toward the bank, and upon reaching it, beached the dugout. Cassandra was so eager to find her salvation that she began to run through the brush, only to be stopped abruptly by Captain Strongbow, who grabbed a fistful of her shift. "Do not hasten thy step!" he ordered. "We know not what lies ahead." His grip was tight and held fast until she relaxed her body.

"Do not do that again, Captain," she said, tuning to face him—and Izzie, and Lucy, and Cupid, who stood watching from the shore. "We have reached civilization, so why can't we hurry?"

"Do you not see the smoke ahead? 'Tis not a good sign."

Cassandra turned to view the structure, which could only be seen in fragments visible through the brush and trees—*and smoke*; she had not noticed it before in her excited state. "Smoke," she said under her breath. "What do you think it means?"

"The women shall remain by the dugout while Cupid and I investigate," The captain looked again toward the smoke. "If 'tis necessary to escape, take the dugout and do not attempt to find us."

Suddenly, Cassandra wasn't too sure of herself. What did the smoke mean, she wondered? She looked to Izzie, but she and Lucy had already made their way back to the dugout. She, too, returned to find Lucy sitting in the craft with the baby, and Izzie with one foot in the boat looking as if she were ready to shove off.

"What do you think it is, Izzie?"

"I place me bet on the damned savages."

Cassandra shuddered. '*Brutal*', the captain had said of the Susquehannock. "This is hell, isn't it?" she said, looking up to the heavens. "What did I do to deserve this?" She gripped her head between two clawed hands, closed her eyes and shook her head violently, as if to shake herself free of this nightmare; but when she opened her eyes again, she was still standing by the Chesapeake Bay with a crazy redheaded prostitute, a black servant girl and a baby named 'Free'.

Strongbow and Cupid returned to the dugout so quickly, it caused the hairs on the back of Cassandra's neck to stand on end.

"What is it?" she whispered. "Are they coming? Tell me they're not coming!"

Strongbow edged her backward quickly until she had no recourse but to step into the dugout. Cupid pushed the boat back into the water, and Strongbow shoved them off. The feel of danger was so thick that not a sound was heard, aside from the heavy breaths of exertion from Strongbow and Cupid. Their faces glistened with sweat as they rowed quickly northward, until they came to an inlet banked with the tall grasses so common to the marshlands.

"It was the Indians, wasn't it..." Cassandra said, breaking the terrifying silence that fell over them in their escape.

"Yes," Strongbow said, "'Twas the Indians. The cabin is charred from fire, and there are three bodies upon the ground; a white man and two negars."

"We goan die!" Lucy moaned.

"Not if I can 'elp it," Izzie said. "Are they gone, cap'n?"

"They were departing," Strongbow replied. "When we feel they are gone for good, we shall return to bury the dead."

"What? Why would we return?" Cassandra asked, and none too politely. "You're going to get us all murdered!"

Strongbow's head snapped to her direction, his brows furrowed, his eyes penetrating. "Mistress Pratt, it is out of respect for the souls of the dead that we return. We cannot, in good conscience, leave them to rot where they lie to feed the creatures of the forest."

Don't look at me like that! She turned her eyes away. She was terrified, that was all. *I don't want to be disrespectful to the dead,* she told herself, but the thought of recapture—or brutal death—

took precedence over the souls of strangers. "They're dead, captain. They won't know if they're buried or not."

Strongbow's brows now raised in arches over his blue, dark-lashed eyes. "*We* shall know, Mistress Pratt. *We* shall know that we left them to rot."

She pouted. All eyes were on her now, awaiting her reply. "Well," she said, straightening her body—as if it were possible with her bottom smack on the floor of the dugout— "Far be it from me to cause a guilty conscience amongst those who have been dead for centuries."

"See, cap'n? Izzie blurted. "She sayeth we are dead, and yet she speaks with us as the living. She is daft, sir."

"Daft or not, she is in my care." Again, he turned his penetrating eyes to hers. "Mistress Pratt," he said, "We shall return to the plantation to bury the dead. You may remain in the dugout, if you so desire."

They bid the afternoon together in the craft, nestled amongst the marsh grasses. Aside from the call of birds and the shrieks of eagles and osprey, the buzz of the mosquitoes ebbed and flowed in harmony with the slaps and curses of their hosts.

At last, when the sun sank a bit lower into the western sky, Strongbow and Cupid rowed the craft back to the landing of the plantation. The women stepped into the shallow waters to lighten the load as the men pulled the craft onto the shore. All were silent, lest the Susquehannocks were nearby, but only as a precaution. Strongbow was certain they had left the area, having accomplished their task at hand. He pantomimed for the women to stay, and the two men returned to the scene of the massacre.

Soon thereafter, Cupid appeared. "'Tis good. Dey gone. Come."

Cassandra, Izzie, and Lucy, (holding dearly to Free), followed Cupid through a narrow path in the brush. Cassandra's heart raced! Plantation! Civilization! She briefly chastised herself for forgetting the three people who lost their lives, but her joy at reaching at least something that resembled civilization, overshadowed all.

At first view, was a small charred cabin, the one she had spotted from offshore. Most of the cabin was standing, aside from a partial wall that managed to survive the failed burnout. At second view, there was...*nothing*...nothing but a dilapidated shed and a planted field. Cassandra searched all corners of the planted field for the plantation house, but saw none.

"Where is the big house? Did they burn that as well?"

"It stands before ye," Izzie said, pointing to the cabin.

"Where's the plantation house? Surely there will be food and beds to sleep in. That little shack is nothing but servants' quarters."

"That 'little shack' is the plantation house, Mistress Pratt." Captain Strongbow said. He and Cupid had returned from the forest, one holding a shovel. Sweat glistened their brows. "The dead are buried; may they find eternal peace."

With those words, Cassandra's hope for relief from hunger and thirst, shattered. Her shoulders slumped along with all hope of salvation from the treachery of the endless wandering. There was no plantation house to bring them comfort.

"Cap'n," Izzie said, looking over the field of healthy green leaves, "what 'tis that grows in the field?"

"Tobacco," the captain replied. "A valuable crop. 'Tis a pity the farmer is dead because the field looks fine and healthy."

"So 'tis." Izzie stood a long time staring at the field before walking toward it, and then into the furrows between the crops. The plants were tall and full, with leaves long and wide at the base, narrowing to a point at tip's end.

"Oh, God," Cassandra mumbled, watching her nemesis stroll between the planted rows. "What is she thinking?" she whispered, and turned to Strongbow. "Where do we go now, captain? Perhaps there's a real civilization further north?" She was anxious to leave this place—this disappointment.

"First, we shall see if there is anything to recover in the cabin. We need the planter's name so that we may report him dead."

"Report to whom? The Indians?"

"St. Mary's, across the Bay. They shall know who farms this land."

"If there *is* a civilization, then why don't we head that way? I'm tired of this roaming. Look at me, captain. I've never looked this...this...horrible in my entire life! My hair is filthy, my clothes—if one could call these clothes—are filthy and...and...unbecoming to say the least. I need food! I need clothes—*real clothes*—and I need comfort!" With this tirade came tears. She fought them, but the dam broke; she sank to the ground and sobbed.

"Don' you cry, Mistress," Lucy said. "We gon find someplace to res'. We gon find food and watah. We gon be fine."

Cassandra looked up at the woman standing above her with babe in arms, and suddenly felt very ashamed. Lucy, the quiet companion; Lucy, who had been passed around shipboard from sailor to sailor. Lucy, who had given birth to her baby in the filthy bowels of a ship. Lucy, who had no future but one of servitude...Lucy, won at a game of sex by a crazy prostitute...Yes, Cassandra felt very ashamed.

She wiped the tears from her eyes, stood and brushed the back of the deerskin shift, then straightened to her superiority pose. "My apologies, Captain. My apologies, Lucy. I have been very selfish, and I'm ashamed. There, I've said it."

"What if the Indians return? Did you think of that, captain?" Apologies aside, Cassandra now stood outside the burnt plantation cabin while Izzy searched the charred remains inside for any items of importance.

"They shall not return," he replied. "They have done their work, there is nothing left of interest for them."

Still, Cassandra could not help but constantly peruse the boundaries of the planted field for any sign of the savages. This, she accomplished, by standing outside the charred structure, fearful of moving physically in any which direction without Cupid or the captain as guard. Cupid had taken their only weapon to hunt game, and that alone made her fearful should the savages return, and they with no protection whatsoever.

"Here!" Izzy held a charred document as she stepped out of the cabin. "Look, cap'n!"

Strongbow took the papers from her hand and appeared to read intently as Izzy stood by, anxiously waiting.

"Well? 'Tis a grant?"

"Indeed, Izzy. 'Tis dated 1636, and states that this land is granted by William Claiborne of Fort Kent, to John Highgrove of…. The rest is missing."

"Does it show a wife? A child?"

"If it did, they have gone to the ashes, but I must tell yo…."

"'Tis providence!" Izzy exclaimed, quickly taking the singed paper from the captain. She walked to the edge of the tobacco field. "I claim this land!" She directed her proclamation to the field and then turned to the others. "'Tis now mine!"

Cassandra and the captain stood dumbstruck. "Can she do that?" Cassandra asked.

"Not to my knowledge," Strongbow replied. "Lord Baltimore now holds the grants, and Fort Kent is no more.' 'Tis solely the jurisdiction of Lord Baltimore."

"Well, you'd better tell Izzie that if she claims the land, she is doing so illegally."

+

"'Tis not of importance to me." Izzie carefully folded the charred remains of the grant and placed it between her breasts. "It matters not that Master Highgrove is dead, because I will now and forever be known as Mistress Highgrove."

The camp fire crackled and snapped. Spikes of flame danced in chaos as each piece of broken branch or dried twig was added; the forest had been kind with its bounty of food and fuel. Now, the travelers sat in stunned wonder at Izzie's proclamation.

"What?" Cassandra stared at Izzie across the rabbit that roasted skewered on a makeshift spit created by Cupid. "What?" she repeated. "You can't do that…can she, captain?"

"The answer to that question lies across the bay in St. Mary's, Izzie. There is no record of your marriage to John Highgrove."

"'Twas burnt in the fire," she replied. "What proof is there that I am not the wife of Master Highgrove? I am with child, am I not? I am with the child of Master John Highgrove."

Cassandra thought of the babe that could be born with the skin of the natives, and hair to match. "Seriously, Izzie, what if the baby…"

"Stop! I shall not hear of it!" Izzie replied most adamantly. "'Tis the child of Master John Highgrove!"

Cassandra looked to Captain Strongbow, who appeared to be mesmerized by the flames. With a long stick, he directed the kindle and branches into a neat, even pile beneath the roasting rabbit. She found herself suddenly intrigued by the handsome man. His hair, brown and gold, graying at the temples, was now pulled into the signature ponytail at the nape of his neck and tied with a string of hide. In profile, his features were strong and masculine and so much more detailed by the light of the flames. The billowy shirt, once clean, but now splotched with dirt, tattered and torn, was a sure map of their treacherous journey; and yet, as quiet and as proper as he was, Cassandra couldn't help but feel that there was another person beneath the façade. Perhaps he held so much inside that it painted a picture of who he thought he should be, how he should portray himself. What was the real man like, she wondered?

He must have felt her eyes upon him, for his head pivoted in her direction. The feel of his eyes, moist and reflective by the light of the flames, caused an electric flash of excitement to race through her veins. Not a word was spoken for a second that passed as an hour; Their eyes locked in a strange and indisputable recognition; and it was in that precise and fleeting moment that the bare truth lay before her; they were connected, not just in this journey, but in the journals of time.

As it came, it went. Cassandra shook herself loose from the hypnotic state, but all had changed; the way she viewed the captain, had changed. She could not see him as a stranger, as an obstruction in this, her search for escape from the 17th century. No, there was something more…something more to come. It was the past, the present, *and* the future.

Chapter 15

This is ridiculous!" Cassandra stood in the doorway of the cabin while Izzie scavenged its interior. Three and one-half walls stood, as the fire had burned a large and misshapen window into the fourth. The light from the hole in the wall made obvious the fact that the Indians had done a fine job trashing its interior. Izzie tread slowly, making her way back and forth from one wall to the other, tossing burnt and damaged debris through the jagged hole to the outside. and non-damaged items in a pile by the fireplace. Cupid did the same, beginning at the opposite end.

"You simply cannot stay here. There are dangers...Indians...and not to mention that you're pregnant!" Izzie ignored her remark and continued scavenging the wreckage.

Lucy, with Free lumped into the makeshift papoose style carrier slung around her back, had foraged the nearby edges of the forest gathering kindling and broken branches. She now carried an armload to place on the ever-growing pile of firewood. "I stay, too," she said. "We's Izzie's."

Cassandra looked to Cupid, bent over as he pillaged, his back shiny with sweat. "And you, too, I suppose?" she asked.

"I stay," he answered.

It wasn't that she was so fond of Izzie, for the woman riled her no end; but despite the mutual dislike between them, she somehow felt that they should stick together in this strange land. After all, Izzie was the fire, and she, but a burning ember, a tag-along. She looked long into the woods pondering her dilemma. The thought of returning alone to the wilderness with the threat of death or recapture by Indians, was enough to give her second thoughts.

With no other response from the dissenters, she threw her arms into the air in exasperation, and set off to search for the captain. Surely, he could talk some sense into her! "You are a disaster, Izzie Pratt!" were her parting words.

"Me name is Highgrove," Izzie shouted. "Mistress Elizabeth Highgrove, to one and all!"

"The problem is, Captain, that I am stuck in this time zone, and I don't want to be here. I want to return to *my* time. I can't stay here with the others, waiting for some magical moment to deliver me to my own life. I must keep moving — I must keep searching; if only I knew what brought me here in the first place!"

The two stood in the thick forest where the captain was felling thinner trees for logs with an axe that was found in the small toolshed that still stood, despite the carnage left behind. It was obvious the Indians had pillaged the shed, as many tools were missing by the count of empty wooden pegs on the walls. Yet the axe, which would have been highly prized by the marauding Indians, had, by a stroke of good fortune, fallen behind a wooden box and out of sight.

Captain Strongbow wiped his sweaty brow with a corner of his muslin shirt. "You are a paradox of mystery, Mistress Pratt. You speak in riddles to which I have no reply."

"Are you staying?"

"Long enough to patch the wall for Izzie and the others, but then I must be on my way. I am a man of the sea —of the bay— and yet I no longer have a ship."

Her heart sank at the thought of him leaving. "Well…where will you go?"

"To the island settlement north of this place. There, I shall secure supplies for Izzie, with promise of payment from Highgrove's tobacco crop. I shall also find a man with knowledge of tobacco to return with me when I bring the supplies. But, then, I must depart. I shall return to the island settlement and procure passage to Barbados."

"Why Barbados?"

"I shall find a ship and crew."

"If there's a settlement north of here, then I'll go with you. Maybe I can find a way to return to my life." While the thoughts of an actual settlement were exciting, her heart sank at the thought of the captain—or her— leaving and never seeing him again. But what did it matter? The man was not of her time; he was dead, four centuries past!

"This, you cannot do," Strongbow said. I am familiar with the bay and the natives, and the journey will be treacherous. For speed's sake, I must go alone."

"Then take me with you to Barbados. Please, take me, I can't stay here forever!" *What if he's killed by the Indians and never returns? Perish the thought!* She had to believe that he *would* return, and with supplies as promised. She still had time to convince him to take her along. Perhaps in Barbados she could find the answer to her time travel mystery, and return home—*home!*

Log by log the burnt wall was patched, the cracks filled with a combination of mud and ash, and even grasses and weeds. The fireplace was still in usable condition, but the roof was a difficult and time-consuming matter altogether, for burnt holes glared above as skylights. The men ventured to a wide, fresh water river that snaked through the marshlands to collect the bulrush that grew tall and profusely in its water world. The rush was tied together in tightly bonded bundles and secured to the existing roof.

"He'll huff, and he'll puff, and he'll blow your house down!" [23]Cassandra said as the group stood appraising the final structure.

"Who say?" Cupid asked.

"Over me dead body," Izzie crossed her arms defiantly.

Lucy's eyes grew large as she perused the perimeter of the tobacco field for the enemy who could blow their house down.

"Relax!" Cassandra said. "It's the story of 'The Three Pigs' and I guess it hasn't been written yet. It's not real. Relax."

The structure was rudimentary and primitive at best, according to Cassandra; but to Izzie, it was a palace. "Me first home!" she exclaimed, dancing a jig.

There was no guarantee that the structure could withstand a significant windstorm, or even a rainy day, but it was what it was, a shelter.

During the reconstruction, Izzie, and Lucy spent their days scavenging for food in the marshlands. They had access to a seemingly endless supply of fish and other water life, including turtles, crabs, oysters and clams. Upon experimentation, they managed to catch a few eels with crudely made baskets made of

---

[23] "He'll Huff, and he'll puff, and he'll blow your house down!" From the fairytale 'Three Little Pigs'. Author unknown.

reeds and grass. Cupid fashioned spears as he had witnessed the making of during their time at the Indian camp. Izzie and Lucy enjoyed the challenge of spearing. It was a sight very amusing for Cassandra, who watched from a distance as the women waded knee deep in the marsh.

Cassandra claimed the job of caring for Free, while the other women fished. It was the unwritten law: if a person did not participate in catching food, or building the cabin, or, in this case, childcare, then they could not eat.

"I will watch the baby," she told the others. "I simply cannot touch those slimy eels!" And so it was that she participated by sitting with the baby in trade for food—food that was, for the most part, bland, disgusting or unpalatable. The thought of eating eel and muskrat turned her stomach, and at times she found herself remembering fondly not the food of her true place in time, but more the recent memory of the food at the Indian camp. There, she was privy to a diet of corn, squash, beans, and even venison. Their present state fared poorly in comparison. She wished she had requested from the captain salt, or pepper—or anything of flavor—that would spice up their bland diet.

"Can ye not catch us a muskrat, Cupid?" Izzie asked one night after three consecutive nights of roasted eel.

"And a Caesar salad?" Cassandra asked in jest. "And while you're at it, how about some oranges and bananas? Chocolate layer cake? Starvation is not my preferred method of dieting."

Izzie rolled her eyes in response, while Cupid looked totally perplexed.

"We need some citrus and vegetables, or we'll all end up with scurvy. We can't eat the damn tobacco." On top of being in the wrong century, living with the threat of massacre by Indians, not to mention starvation, Cassandra was seriously worried about vitamin deficiency. She checked her teeth daily, hoping they wouldn't come loose. There was not a chance of gaining weight with a constant diet of eels, crabs, fish and muskrat. Already, her worn and stained shift sagged from bony shoulders. "None of my friends would recognize me!" she moaned, combing her fingers through hair that was in a perpetual state of stringy disarray.

Ammunition was nearly depleted for the pistol Cupid took during the escape from the planter, and the captain promised to return with flint and gunpowder. Until his return, they would be at the mercy of their own resources. Cupid stood guard day after day, night after night, should the Indians return. He also trapped small game, such as raccoon and muskrat; he was saving the ammunition for big game, such as deer—and Indian.

"He'd better be coming back," Cassandra mumbled. She wanted to cry her eyes out. It was raining—no—it was *pouring*. The reed roof was leaking in several places onto the dirt floor below, and onto *her*. The fireplace sizzled now and again from stray raindrops that found their way down the chimney. *This will be a muddy mess in the morning.*

She lay atop her makeshift bed in the darkness. All the leafy branch beds, one for each of them, were placed against the walls of the cabin. When the captain returned, there would be five.

"Quit your gripin' and go to sleep." Izzie replied from across the room. "

"Seriously, when he returns—*if* ever he returns— I will leave with him. You can have your little shanty and tobacco field; I'm going to find my way home."

"And a good riddance," Izzie replied, then yawned.

"He's been gone a month now. Maybe he won't return. Maybe he'll find a ship and sail away and leave us to this hardscrabble life. Maybe you call this living the good life, but not me. You can't even imagine, in that Neanderthal brain of yours, what life is like four centuries ahead."

"Wha'd ye call me?"

Cassandra nearly jumped out of her skin; she didn't hear Izzie cross the room and materialize beside her. The firelight barely framed an outline of her figure.

"I didn't call you anything. Go back to your pile of twigs."

"You did! you sayeth what of me brain?"

"Go away. You're going to wake everyone up."

"I'se awake," Lucy said.

"Aye," Cupid said.

"See? Go away Izzie, I was just rambling."

"No. Wha'd ye call me?"

"Good grief." Cassandra sat up and faced Izzie's knees. "I said that you couldn't imagine what life is like four centuries ahead—in the far away future. Don't worry about it, you're dead already."

Cassandra didn't see the foot that slammed into her ribs, but she surely felt it. "Stop it!" she screamed swinging her arms outward to block another kick, but Izzie had already returned to her bed.

"I an't dead!"

"You *are* dead. You're all dead and I'm living a nightmare!"

All was eerily silent. Then, "If we are dead, then ye are dead too." Izzie said smugly. "Ha! There's a comeuppance for ya!"

Silence returned, but Cassandra's thoughts ran helter-skelter through her head. *I've thought of that, you red haired witch. God, please, don't let it be true, don't let me be dead! I just want to go home!*

"He comin'! He comin!" Lucy ran barefoot from the marshlands, where she and Izzie had been fishing.

At that moment, Cassandra was silently cursing her role as babysitter, as Free was now at the crawling stage. How the baby arrived at that stage of development so quickly was a mystery. It seemed that the passage of time was at the whim of time itself, and she had no other option but to accept the fact.

Presently, Cassandra barely had a moment for her own needs, for she was forever chasing the crawling baby. Never in her prior life had she desired to have children; and, darling as baby Free was, with her black, tightly curled head of hair, big brown eyes, and impish grin, she most definitely required a sharp eye to keep her safe. Had her own mother done this? Had her own mother spent her days chasing a crawling babe? That was a picture Cassandra couldn't fathom; her mother, coiffured and polished, chasing baby Cassandra? *Impossible! I had nannies to chase me.*

Now, with Lucy running at her like she was on fire, Cassandra took her eyes from Free. "Is it the captain?" she yelled. "Tell me!"

"Yes, da capt'n, and he an't alone." Lucy stopped to catch her breath. "He...he an't by h'self...der's a man wid 'im...where my Free?"

Cassandra looked to where she had seen the baby last, and she was gone! "Oh, mercy! Free!" she yelled. "She was just here...I swear!"

The women scrambled in different directions calling the baby's name. Cassandra's heart beat a mile a minute; it was *her* responsibility to keep the baby safe, and look what happened!

"You must be looking for this," Captain Strongbow appeared from nowhere, it seemed. In his arms was the chubby baby, clutching the captain's beard in her fat little fists.

"Thank God!" Cassandra said, nearly collapsing as a powerful wave of relief washed over her. "She was here a minute ago."

Lucy ran to her baby and relieved the captain of his charge. "She good. Don' worry, Miz Cassie. She quick like da lighnin'." She said, and then meandered toward the cabin.

Cassandra expressed shock at the figure standing in the Captain's shadow. She had been so concerned about Free's whereabouts that she hadn't even seen the man—the Indian—appear.

"I hope that's a friend standing behind you." She nodded toward the Indian. He was taller than most, and perhaps around her own age of 30. *A sturdy fellow*, she thought, eyeing the man from head to toe. His attire was entirely familiar to her; the deerskin clout to cover his privates; his chest was bare and sported tattoos that she could not decipher. Through one ear was pierced a thin bone, most likely a finger bone from an enemy. His head was shaved on one side, and secured into a braid on the other. The braid was embellished with beads, bones, and an eagle feather. Of course his appearance brought back memories of time spent with Long Feather, and *that* brought the heat of a blush to her face.

"This is *Opotenaiok,* but he answers to 'Eagle'. He is to be your helper; he knows tobacco."

"You mean *Izzie's* helper, don't you? I go with you, remember?"

Captain Strongbow shot a quizzical look her way. "No, I do not recall making such a bargain."

"I can't stay here, Captain. I'm not a farmer, I'm not a pioneer. I'm a city girl. I need a city and friends, and...clothes!" She was suddenly embarrassed at her appearance; her shift was filthy, which was something the Indians frowned upon. Her hair was stringy and needed a good washing—another cardinal sin in both worlds, old and new.

"I go see tobacco," Eagle said.

This caught Cassandra off guard. "You speak English?"

"Little," he said. "I go tobacco."

"Finally, an Indian who speaks English," she said as she watched him head toward the tobacco field. "Where did you find him?"

"At the island. He serves as translator for the English, and he knows this country well—and tobacco, of course."

"Well, surprises never cease. I'm sure he'll be of great help to Izzie. Now, when do we leave?" she asked, shifting her eyes to the captain.

Captain Strongbow shot her such a penetrating stare, that she shifted her position, crossing her arms over her chest, chin up. "Well? When do we leave?"

Strongbow cleared his throat. "You are a perplexing woman, Mistress Pratt. I cannot take you to Barbados. It is not a proper place for a woman unless...unless she is married and mistress of a plantation. Perhaps you will not find your, uh, *'own time'*, as you say. How could you survive such a place?" His broad shoulders and powerful arms gave life to a new muslin shirt beneath the leather waistcoat as he, too, mirrored her stance with his arms across his chest.

Despite her determination to change her present circumstance, she couldn't help but take in the fine figure of the man standing before her. From his dark-lashed blue eyes to the tall, scuffed brown suede boots folded over at the knee, she found herself momentarily mesmerized; he nearly took her breath away. *I'm losing it,* she thought, and cleared her throat, regaining her composure and jumping back into the present situation. "And if I don't try, then how will I know?"

"My apologies, Mistress Pratt, but I will not be responsible for leaving a young—and confused—woman alone in such a place as Barbados. Your request is denied."

"I'm not confused!" she said in anger. "I'm lost! No one believes me. You all think I'm crazy, and I don't know how to prove to you that I'm from the 21st century, but I *am,* and I don't belong here!" Cassandra, suddenly drained, covered her face in her palms and fell to her knees. "I don't know how to return to my life; I don't know why I'm here, but maybe you're right, maybe it won't make a difference if I go to Barbados. Maybe it will still be 1644? Maybe I'll be stuck in this God-forsaken time warp forever...maybe this is purgatory...maybe I'm dead."

Captain Strongbow pulled her to her feet. "Tis best you stay here with those you know."

She turned away and headed toward the cabin, wanting to reach it before she broke into sobs, making even more of a fool of herself. How could they believe her anyway, and what difference would it make?

"Wait," he said. She stopped in her tracks, but did not turn to face him.

"I have tried time and time again to determine how you arrived on the Thunder, but the truth evades me," he said. "Let us leave the answer open, and perhaps the mystery shall resolve itself to both our satisfactions."

She smiled to herself and turned. "Thank you, Captain. If you can accept the possibility that I'm from another time, I will try not to mention it again." *I will try...I will try...* she promised herself. *"Are you coming back? Will we see you again?" Why do I care? What's wrong with me? The man is dead, for Pete's sake!*

They stood in silence a moment, their eyes locked in the strange, faint recognition that Cassandra had felt before; it was almost as if the moment was frozen in time, for neither moved until Cupid's voice broke the spell.

"Cap'n, ye's back!"

"Yes...yes, Cupid. Come help, I brought many supplies."

With that, Cassandra watched as the men disappeared down the path to the bay.

Chapter 16

"ookie' dis!" Lucy exclaimed, her delight plainly witnessed in the pearly white smile beaming from her dark face. "Mo' trenchers!"

Cassandra couldn't hide her own elation at the fact that they now had more of the wooden plates to go around, considering that the previous planters dinnerware was quite limited. But, as primitive as trenchers were to her world, she, too, sported a grin. "What else is in that sack? Maybe spoons and forks?"

Again, Lucy grinned as she pulled out four two-pronged forks. "Dey's mo'," she said, and pulled two metal spoons, then two more, and then three more forks. These were not the silver utensils of Cassandra's 21st century home, but they were at least recognizable.

On the floor sat a squat iron pot on three legs, a basket of eggs, a tarnished copper kettle, a metal ladle, an iron frying pan, an extra-long two-pronged fork, and a several sacks of unknown contents; the bounty that Captain Strongbow promised. On the wooden table (that Cupid had literally slaved over for days), sat five copper mugs, a large copper bowl, a burlap bag of salt, one of sugar, and one of Guinny Wheat[24].

Izzie peeked her head through the doorway. "Quick, come see!" The excitement in her voice was not wasted on the women, who ran outside to witness three hens and one rooster busily scratching and pecking at unseen morsels in the dirt.

"We gits eggs!" Lucy squealed with delight.

"And chicken! How did you accomplish this?" Cassandra asked the captain, who stood nearby watching the happy reactions of the women. "How did you fit everything into the dugout?"

"I shall show you. Come, there is more bounty in the boat."

On the landing at the water's edge sat a log canoe[25], much wider than the dugout in which the captain had set off on his venture to the island settlement. Cupid was busy emptying the boat and setting bags and small crates ashore.

"It's different," Cassandra said. "Bigger than the other."

"This was made from a larger tree than the other." He then proceeded to peek into several sacks until he retrieved a certain one and handed it to her. "Here," he said

It's kind of heavy. What's in here?"

"'Tis for you and the women. I believe you will find it satisfactory."

"So mysterious." She smiled her best smile, and carried the sack back to the cabin, where she dumped its contents onto the table. Izzie and Lucy stood wide eyed, as lumps of cloth tumbled from the bag. Before Cassandra could toss the empty sack aside, Izzie was rifling through the pile, much like the chickens outside scratching in the yard. "Garments!" she cried, clutching handfuls of fabric. "Bless ye, cap'n!"

---

[24] Guinny Wheat:, a term used by the colonists for corn meal.

[25] Log canoe: A boat created in the Chesapeake Bay, originally used for oyster tonging.

"Clothes?"

"Aye, clothin'! The cap'n 'as blessed us with clothin'!" The words were barely out of her mouth before she lifted the filthy hide shift from her body, tossed it onto the dirt floor and, stark naked, searched frantically through the pile for something appropriate to wear.

Cassandra gasped at the sight of her naked foe. "You're starting to show, Izzie." Even though the woman was slight of build and thin from weeks of minimal food, Cassandra saw immediately that Izzie's belly had swollen, obliterating her once narrow waistline; her breasts jutted outward and full, with nipples puffy, dark and wide.

"Aye," Izzie agreed, concentrating on her search through the pile of garments. "Now, where do ye suppose the cap'n come across ladies' clothin' for the askin'?"

"For God's sake, put something on before the men come inside." Cassandra began her own search through the rumpled pile of fabric until she realized that Lucy had removed herself from the table, along with the other supplies, and was working at putting the new utensils and cooking supplies in convenient places—not an easy task in such sparse quarters. "Get over here, Lucy, and choose something to wear."

"When ye's done. I gots tings to wear." She wore the same clothing she had worn on the Thunder: long gray skirt that had apparently been adjusted for her pregnancy. Now, the skirt was held together with a ragged sash tied about her waist..

"Come here, now," Izzie piped in, apparently having finished her search, and now clutching her chosen garments. "Ye need a change. Me wench shall not look as if her mistress cared not!

Cassandra felt as happy as if she had purchased a $2000.00 outfit at Prada. Having bathed in the bay, washed her hair with bay grass—as the Indian women had taught her—and fitted herself with a full-length linen shift, she felt as if she had stepped into a new cleaner and more civilized chapter in this nightmare. The shift's fabric was lightweight enough for the hot, humid bay air. Normally, it would be covered by a waistcoat or corset, and a long skirt, but those would be saved for the winter. Instead, Lucy ripped apart three long strips of fabric, and these they wore around their waists as sashes. Izzie had to tie hers just below her breasts, due to her expanding belly.

Lucy was overjoyed in the newly designated kitchen area, for she had put Cupid to work immediately making pegs for hanging her new (but obviously used) culinary items. He also added three rough shelves to one logged wall for the trenchers and utensils. All cooking was done outside, but now, with the three-legged pot, Lucy could make one-pot dinners in the fireplace that would feed the lot of them. On this first night of celebration it was a rabbit stew *with* vegetables, thanks to the captain and his bounty from the island settlement. He had returned with a small supply of potatoes, carrots and a few turnips.

Captain Strongbow and Cupid felled two dead trees for firewood. They also cut four five-foot logs from a thicker felled tree to place around the fire as seating. By supper time, all were exhausted from the day's labor, yet excited to share their very first civilized meal cooked in a real pot, served in real trenchers, and to be eaten with real utensils. *If only we had marshmallows!* To Cassandra, it was as if she were sitting around a chimenea with friends in her own time.

"You didn't tell us how you were able to gather all these supplies, Captain." Cassandra said this while seated next to Izzie on one of the log benches. The captain sat alone across the fire, while Lucy and Cupid shared the log to the left. Baby Free was sound asleep in the cabin on Lucy's branch and leaf bed.

"How did you manage to get these clothes—for which we humbly give our thanks, by the way. Who did they belong to?"

"'Tis to the kind women in the settlement, to whom ye owe thanks."

Cassandra couldn't resist. "Take me to the settlement then, and I'll thank them in person,"

"And a good riddance to the daft one!" Izzie pipped in, before taking a spoonful of rabbit stew.

Cassandra shot her the signature daggered look, only to witness the most sinister grin cross the woman's face.

"I jest." Izzie smiled her toothless smile.

"I do not believe you will find your '*true time*' in the settlement, Mistress Pratt; but if you do so wish, perhaps I should find a family that will take you in."

Cassandra sighed. Another family? Another bunch of dead people to become acquainted with?

Lucy sat wide-eyed and pensive. "Don' go," she said, shaking her head. Cupid also seemed to wait with bated breath.

"Well, on second thought, maybe the settlement doesn't hold the answer I'm hoping for." Agreeing to remain in her present state was a difficult choice, but was there another, better choice? Would another group of strangers be an improvement? Was there a portal hidden somewhere—one that would return her to her life? Would she know it if she saw it? Perhaps it was best to deal with Izzie and her foul temper, than with strangers; at least she was familiar with the red-haired witch.

"A wise choice." The captain turned to Izzie. "The clothing is your own, a gift; but for the pots and other supplies, there is now a credit at the trading post on the island. When the tobacco is ready, it must be taken there where you can clear your credit and receive more for new supplies."

"What is it we'll be receivin'?" Izzie asked, her fork in midair between trencher and mouth.

"Credit."

"By who? I want no credit, I want me sterling!"

"'Tis done in this way."

"I can't be makin' me fortune with credit as payment! Who is gettin' me sterling, then?"

"*You* are getting it in trade."

"Blarney!"

"Then maybe you're ready to give up this ridiculous tobacco idea and move to the settlement? We could all go." *It's worth a try,* Cassandra thought, since Izzie's dream of coins jingling in her pockets apparently was not panning out.

"Éist do bhéal!"[26] Izzie shouted at Cassandra as she stood, throwing her trencher to the ground, which sent Lucy scrambling to retrieve the precious object.

"'Tis me home now, and I shall make it pay—in sterling!" Izzie bunched the front of her shift into her fists, stepped over the log from which she sat—then stopped abruptly. Eagle had materialized and stood before her "Out o' me way, heathen!" she yelled.

Unfazed, he stepped aside, stone-faced, watching her disappear into the cabin. "She spirit like fire hair!"

Cassandra stood at the edge of the tobacco field watching Eagle instruct Izzie on the fine points of growing tobacco. *What would we do without him?* she wondered. *Nothing!* He was the only person amongst them who had good knowledge of tobacco farming. Occasionally, Izzie's voice reached her ears, but nothing that could be deciphered into English. *She's probably cursing him out* for *some stupid reason;* which certainly rang true, considering her temperament..

The captain was leaving for the island on this day, which was another reason Cassandra was standing at the edge of the tobacco field; she was sad. The captain had, for her, been the glue that kept

---

[26]"Éist do bhéal" Irish Gaelic for 'Shut Up!"

her here. After all, he had convinced her that Barbados was a foolish dream (her words, not his), and that her best choice was to stay on the plantation with people she knew.

"Perchance your place in time will find ye here," he had said on one of their talks, and talk they did, many times during his stay. She sought him out when he was chopping wood, or fishing in the creek, or gathering oysters at the bayside.

"I must bid you goodbye, Mistress Pratt." His voice brought her quite out of her self-pity mood and directly into one of regrets: Regrets he was leaving; regrets that she may never see him again—*ever*; regrets that he had never been enticed by her...by what, her beauty? Hard as she tried, she was still a misplaced woman with stringy hair, no makeup, no tooth whitening, and wearing an unattractive outfit of homespun.

"Oh, Captain," she sighed. "I don't know what to say except that I am—*we* are—so sad to see you go. You have been a great help to us." She looked away, biting her tongue, swallowing her desire to declare her feelings; but again, she had to tell herself that he was a ghost, a man long dead, and he had not pursued her, even in this crazy nightmare. "I'll walk with you to the canoe." She waited while he bid his goodbyes to Eagle and Izzie, and then followed him to the cabin where he bid goodbye to Lucy, and picked baby Free up to give her a kiss on the cheek.

"I have already bid farewell to Cupid," he said. "I shall miss him on my voyage back from Barbados, as he is a fine sailor and a boon to my crew. 'Tis best you have a man about for protection."

"Back?" Are you coming back?" Cassandra asked, trying to muffle her excitement.

"The bay is my home, and it needs protection."

"Protection from whom, the Indians?"

"Aye, that too, but protection from pirates, protection from foreign navies or any others who feel privy to our waters."

"But, *you* are a pirate!"

"I protect the bay, Mistress Pratt. 'Tis me work."

She walked behind him to the water's edge, every step bringing her closer to the log canoe that sat beached on the shore—and his departure. She loved the way he looked from behind; the broad shoulders adorned by the muslin shirt and leather vest; the breeches cut short at the knees by the suede boots; and the ponytail tied with a leather strip. Just the sight of him was electrifying; she had never before experienced such a feeling, not even with Bill, whom she professed to love.

"Wait!" The words were out of her mouth without prior thought of *why* he should wait.

The caption, who had stooped to push the canoe back into the water, turned. "Yes?"

"Uh, how long will it take you to return?"

"However long it takes to procure a ship and crew."

That's no help. What's time in this crazy place? What's time to these...these ghosts, anyway? A year? A decade? A century?

"Oh," she replied, thinking of nothing else to say that would keep him any longer. It nearly broke her heart to see him standing tall and strong, one booted foot in the dugout, one planted firmly on the ground. He was the only person she could truly communicate with in this curséd nightmare, and now he was leaving! A breeze ruffled the pony tail at the nape of his neck, as well as his shirtsleeves. She never liked bearded men, but there he stood, bearded, mustached, and *oh so handsome!*

"Well, then, I'll miss you Captain. May you have a safe journey." She couldn't even muster a smile, and turned to leave. Maybe three steps were taken before she felt his powerful hands on her shoulders, hands that turned her to face him, hands that brought her forward, hands that pressed her to him as he brought his lips to hers.

The world spun. If he was dead, she wanted to be dead, too; she wanted this moment to freeze—to never end! Inside, she was a world of fluttering butterflies as he pulled her tighter. Her breasts melded into his chest as if they had finally found their home, and she cursed the fabric of her shift; it was a wall between them. She wanted to rip it off, to lay in the woods and have him. She didn't care a wit of the dirt and leaves, or fallen branches that would cut into her flesh; it didn't matter, she wanted him—and desperately. But then, it was over, and she stood dazed as he pushed off into the bay, never turning to see her standing numb on the shore; never uttering a word of farewell.

Chapter 17

Cassandra flew to a sitting position; surely they were under attack by Indians! As dreams and reality mixed into a surreal state of being, she felt—and terrifyingly so—that an Indian was waking her for the slaughter, kicking her shoulder should she miss the event of her demise; but when she opened her eyes, daylight filtered in through the small glassless windows of the cabin, backlighting none other than Izzie.

"Her high and mighty is up now, is she?" 'ave ye forgotten 'tis harvest day?"

"Oh, it's just you," she moaned. *I'm still here.* "Harvest?" She rubbed her eyes and focused again on Izzie. "Good lord, your belly grew overnight!" Once her mind adjusted to the present moment, it dawned on her that perhaps time had jumped a month or two; she did not remember Izzie's belly having been so large the night before. Cassandra had no choice but to take each day as it came, for there were mysteries involved that she did not at all understand, and this was one, the passing of time. She could hardly believe that today was harvest day already.

On went the old deerskin shift—washed and stiff. She pulled it on over the homespun shift, hoping that the hide would soften up;

it felt like cardboard on her skin and she was grateful for the softer homespun shift beneath. She laughed to think how ridiculous she would look to her friends at home; they would be aghast to see her in such an outfit!

Outside, Cassandra was shocked at the size of the tobacco leaves; they, too, had grown threefold and practically obscured the furrows between the rows. She viewed the site with great distain. *I was not born to farm tobacco; this is more Lucy's work....* That thought brought extreme guilt after it came to mind. Lucy had her hands full between caring for Free, and her responsibilities of cooking and laundry. Lucy was no more born to harvesting tobacco than was she. *Shades of the old life,* she thought. After all, she had maids and nannies all her growing up years, and they did everything for her; whatever she asked, they complied.

Izzie and Eagle approached as Cassandra, sweating already from the humidity, stood staring at the field and the work yet to come. Though daylight was right around the corner, it would be a far stretch in months before toil in the heat during daylight hours became tolerable, and she dreaded the day's work ahead. "Good morning," she muttered, not feeling at all good about it. "I'm here. Let the party begin."

What a horrible party it was! Eagle managed to bring— in trade of promised tobacco, of course—several sharp tobacco-cutting knives. The plants were then cut at the base and laid upon the ground over the plant stub. Row after row, sweat after sweat, thirst after thirst, she, Izzie, and Cupid worked cutting the stalks. Having initially started each row at the same time, it became an undeclared contest to see who could reach the end of their row first.

"This is not a game I enjoy!" Cassandra said wiping the sweat from her brow at one third of the way through her second row. Izzie and Cupid were several feet ahead in their own respective rows. "My back is killing me, and I'm taking a break."

After her break, Cassandra commenced the tobacco harvesting, but stopped after completing just one row. "Oh, my aching back. I need another break."

Izzie, too, stretched, belly straight out. "Ye hear, Cupid? Twice she must stop and rest, poor creature, and me with a babe in me belly."

"Isn't it lunchtime yet?" Cassandra shaded her eyes for a look at the sun's position." *Please be lunchtime.*

"Aye, 'tis," Cupid stabbed his knife into the ground. "Lucy comin' now."

Seeing that the harvesters had noticed her approach, Lucy stopped to wave them forward for the afternoon meal, then backtracked to the cabin, Little Free following behind, for she was now able to stand and walk quite quickly, much to Cassandra's surprise.

It was then, on the walk to the cabin, that Cassandra noticed a new shed of sorts perched at one edge of the woods. "Where did that come from?" she asked.

"How could ye not recall the buildin' o' the tobacco shed?" Izzie shook her head in dismay and continued toward the cabin.

No, I do not remember. "Time is passing quickly for me, Izzie. I don't expect you to understand, and I don't understand it myself, but I have no recollection of that shed being built."

"Ye are befuddlin', Cassandra Pratt. I shall tell ye, then...."

Prior to the harvest, Cupid and Eagle had constructed a rudimentary open air shed for the curing[27] of the tobacco. In the necessity to keep the rain from the leaves, they had thatched the roof in similar fashion of the cabin, which was not promising, considering that the cabin roof leaked in the rain.

Eagle, feeling that the cutting of tobacco was below his station, accepted the job of gathering the cut stalks and hanging them over a thick, long, stripped branch for transport to the tobacco shed. There, they were hung to dry by their stems over the rough-cut poles that ran from side to side the entire length of the shed.

---

[27] Curing of Tobacco: The process is to hang the tobacco from its stalk until the leaves are brown and the center vein is brittle.

It was all so confusing to Cassandra. The appearance of the tobacco shed, the growth of the tobacco leaves, Izzie's large belly, and Free, able to toddle behind her mother; this was all so new. At times, she wanted to run screaming into the woods, for the jump ahead in time was perplexing, something she could not justify in her head. She was constantly having to jump forward into whatever was transpiring at that particular moment in time.

Weeks passed—or so she imagined— since the tobacco leaves lost their green and turned brown; they were cured, and now it was time for a journey to the island. Excitement was in full force as two boats were loaded with their bounty at first light. Cassandra didn't ask where the dugouts came from, for it was too bewildering to even think on. She told herself that Eagle brought them at some point during the mysterious void of time, and left it at that. She was just glad that they were there, and overjoyed at the prospect of visiting an actual settlement. But first, they must make the arduous journey, with Eagle leading the way in his dugout.

Eagle sat center, in one dugout, while Izzie took the back, and Cassandra the front. Between she, Eagle and Izzie, were stacked crates and sacks of the dried tobacco leaves. Prior to the journey, the leaves were stripped from their stalks and packed into the crates and sacks in which the captain had brought their supplies. The hope was that rains did not come to spoil the leaves throughout the journey, for they were covered poorly with what was at hand: strips of bark, skirts and whatever other fabrics could be mustered from the captain's original gift of clothing.

Lucy and Free sat in the back of Cupid's dugout, nearly invisible for the stacks of tobacco that hid them from view until the boats paddled side by side up the Chesapeake.

"What is wrong with the child?" Izzie yelled, across the watery expanse to Lucy a few hours later, for Free had been fussing and crying for the longest time.

"She don' wan' sit," Lucy yelled in return.

"Give her over then and we'll have a game or two. Row closer, Eagle!" The child was passed from one boat to the other, much to her delight, as Cassandra could hear the giggles over the crates, sacks, and Eagle's head. Izzie seemed to have a knack with the child, which surprised Cassandra no end since the woman had little tolerance for anything.

Cassandra, too, was bored, as the journey was very long. They were not in possession of a map or GPS, so she hadn't a clue of the time it would take to get to the anticipated destination. She couldn't pinpoint where, on the eastern shore, the cabin sat, so could not judge the distance, and wasn't sure as to where they were headed, except to 'the island', which she thought perhaps was Kent Island. There were no bridges, no water traffic, no houses by which to judge. Besides, how could she calculate such a rowing distance without a GPS to tell her their time of arrival?

"How much longer to you think, Eagle?" She chose this moment to ask because, for one, she had to pee desperately, and for two, she needed to stretch her cramping legs. She half stood, and only half because she didn't want to unsteady the dugout. Over the top of crates she turned to see Eagles eyes burning into hers. "Sorry, Eagle. I had to stand a moment." He replied by a nod of the head and a grunt. He stared at her quite often back at the cabin, and it was very disconcerting. *Does he know about me and Long Feather? Have I a reputation with the natives? Does he think I'll have sex with him?* All these thoughts crossed her mind as they traveled along.

That night they camped alongside the bay. Eagle appeared to know exactly where to beach the dugouts; and in his quiet, knowing way, had rowed to shore with Cupid following close behind. It was a relief to stand, stretch, and pee, but she'd had enough of wilderness camping for a lifetime, during her lost journey through the forest.

"I know the drill," she mumbled, as Izzie and Lucy proceeded into the forest to gather wood for the fire. Free ran ahead on chubby little legs, totally delighted to be ashore and *free*, just like her name.

After an uneventful night—no marauding natives, no wild animals—and a paltry dinner of Lucy's hardtack and dried-hard-as-nails-venison jerky, the party took off again in their dugouts, grateful that the waters were calm and the sky, clear.

The land was so changed from Cassandra's time that she could hardly believe she was really on the Chesapeake. There were no mansions or houses along the shore, just miles and miles of wilderness on both sides of the bay, as they traveled northward. Osprey called and flew overhead, as did the eagles and seabirds. When schools of fish rippled and churned the bay waters, flocks of seabirds dove and soared, circled and dove again to catch their bounty. When the schools of fish moved further into the distance, the short entertainment gave way to the return of boredom.

The sun sank lower and lower until Cassandra was afraid they would need to camp another night. But then, with dimming daylight upon them, she caught sight of firelight ahead. "Is that it, Eagle?" she asked, rising halfway to see him over their cargo. "Is that the island?"

"Hmph," he said, which she took as a 'yes'.

"You must be exhausted from rowing for such a long time."

"Hmph," he replied.

"We're here!", Cassandra yelled, unable to contain her excitement. Ahead were the first signs of civilization she had seen since the Indian village. In the fading light, there were houses, small, and not at all like the houses in her real twenty-first century life, but dwellings just the same. This meant *real* people, not crazy red-haired witches full of contrary moods and nasty temperament. This meant *other* people, *real* people. *Really dead people,* she reminded herself, but she didn't care a wit. "New blood," she said, under her breath.

'New blood' appeared to work both ways, as several men had gathered dockside to watch as the two dugouts approached. Perhaps it was unique for an Indian and black man to arrive at port with women as cargo. The onlookers stood on the beach looking as actors in a Thanksgiving production. These were the first finely dressed men the women had seen in quite a while. Felt hats shadowed their faces, which were further held in shadow by the twilight of the hour. All sported waistcoats of dyed linen, with knee breeches and stockings held in place with ribbon garters. Cassandra blinked twice, for the scene before her was surreal, leaving no doubt that she was, indeed, embedded in a century far from her own.

"What have ye there, Eagle?" one of the men ashore asked.

"Tobacco," Eagle replied, in his blunt manner, as he and Cupid both jumped out of their dugouts and into the shallow water, pushing the dugouts further onto the shore.

The women stepped out, barefoot, into the shallow waters of the bay; two white women and a Negro wench with child. Cassandra would have loved to read the minds of the men who stood gawking at the new arrivals, for surely, they presented an uncommon sight: shoeless, skirts much too large and tied in place with cords of fabric. The same for the waistcoats that overlaid the smudged shifts beneath. They sported no bonnet or cap, and their hair was as untamed as the wilderness from whence they came. Izzie's hair rose in a wild frizz and kink that haloed her small face. Even in the fading light, Cassandra could see the eyes of the men fall upon Izzie's bosom, as she refused to secure the shift at her throat, instead letting it lay open, thus exposing the cleavage of her breasts.

"Greetings, gents," Cassandra said, and the eyes of the men shifted to her person. "We have come to trade the tobacco. I am Cassandra Pratt and this is…." Cassandra raised her eyebrows, shot a glance toward Izzie, took a breath and let the words go: "Mistress Elizabeth Highgrove, widow of John Highgrove of Highgrove's Chance." This introduction had been rather forced upon Cassandra by none other than Izzie.

"Yes, we have heard of the Indian raid through Captain Strongbow. Our condolences, Madam Highgrove." The man removed his hat and gave a sweeping bow. "We have, thus far, managed to keep the savages at bay. May I present myself, Gideon Broome. May I also present Ezra Hemingford, and Josiah Staples." Ezra and Josiah removed their hats and staged their own sweeping bows. "Captain Strongbow did mention that the survivors of

Highgrove Chase would bring tobacco for trade.

"Aye, and, as you can see, we have come," Izzie said.

"John Highgrove never mentioned a wife," Ezra said, matter-of-factly. Cassandra thought she heard a hiss from Izzie's lips.

"'Tis no concern of mine, sir, if Master Highgrove had not the courtesy to mention meself. I have come to trade 'is tobacco, and that 'tis all," Izzie replied, with a touch of venom in her voice.

"Have ye come as well to sell the plantation, then?"

"No, good sir." Izzie's arms crossed defiantly across her chest. "Come to trade, 'tis all."

Cassandra cringed. She could see that this interchange may get a bit too personal for Izzie, so she interrupted the men to introduce Cupid, Lucy and her babe, "Lucy is maid servant to Mistress Highgrove," she added—another forced introduction which evaporated into thin air, for all the acknowledgement it received.

"Did Master Highgrove have a will?" Master Staples interrupted the introductions.

"I'll not be answerin' your questions, sir. I have come to trade me tobacco, and a fine quality i'tis. Eagle will agree." She turned for a nod of agreement from Eagle, but he was gone. He apparently felt he had done his job for the day and had quietly disappeared. Izzie turned again to the men. "Your questions on me marriage an't of concern. I am the goodwife of Master Highgrove, and carry his child in me body."

Stupid, stupid, stupid idea Izzie, posing as Mrs. Highgrove! "Could we trouble you for the name of a hotel? We're dead tired and starving," Cassandra interjected, even more anxious to avoid what appeared to be an interrogation. "We've come to trade tobacco, to find a hotel and to have dinner."

When none in the trio replied, she thought perhaps 'hotel' was the wrong word. "*Inn*, do you have an inn here?" *Catch more flies with sugar...*she reminded herself. The men were getting on her nerves with their questions, but she had to control her temper. Her bottom hurt from the long ride, and night had fallen. The only lights were faint shadows coming from the candles and oil lamps in the distant houses. She was also very hungry and assumed the others were as well. Her stomach rumbled for food, and her head for sleep.

"We are but a small settlement and have no need for an inn at present, but we shall find you comfort for the night," said Ezra Hemingford.

Izzie was taken to the home of Gideon Broome, Lucy, Free and

Cupid to Ezra Hemingford's barn, and Cassandra to board with Josiah Staples and his bouncy young bride, Arabella, who appeared to be more than a decade younger than her husband, and delighted to have Cassandra as company.

"What joy to have companionship from a new face in this dismal place!" Arabella exclaimed, her arms full of quilt and pillow, which she placed on the floor in front of the fireplace.

It was surely a feast fit for nobility, according to Cassandra. Upon her arrival at Josiah Staples' home, and the introduction to his fair bride, she was fed a divine supper of leftover ham and potatoes, and a glass of beer to chase away the heavy salt of the ham. She was to sleep by the fire beneath a real quilt, and lay her head upon a pillow of feathers. *Awesome* was the wooden floor, since they still walked upon a dirt floor at Highgrove Chase. Never had she been happier to see something as mundane and every day as a real floor and furniture!

Even though young Arabella talked incessantly, Cassandra was in heaven; she wondered if the others were having such a fine experience?

"...and Goodwife Hill is as contrary a person as you could hope to meet." Arabella said, disgusted, though Cassandra could not follow the young woman's train of thought, and hadn't a clue as to whom the Hill woman was, or the 'why' of her contrariness, for she was so enjoying the comfort of the Staples' home that she had blocked out Arabella's chatter.

In Cassandra's mind, Arabella appeared as a fashion plate; a skirt of finely woven, yellow colored linen matched her waistcoat. The peplum, or little skirt that flared at the waist from the waistcoat, was embroidered with daintily stitched orange and blue flowers that followed a vining trail of green, which encircled the entire circumference of the peplum. The shift beneath her attire was laced at the throat and at the cuffs of the billowed sleeves. An added touch of fashion, were the blue ribbons secured just above the elbow. This added a charming double 'puff' in appearance to each sleeve. Cassandra couldn't help but wonder where in the world the woman could find an outfit of such grandeur in a settlement such as this. Upon the walk from the dugout to the Staples' home, she did not notice even one structure that resembled a retail store, though what one would look like in this settlement and time was beyond her imagination.

She looked to her own mismatched skirt and waistcoat, all too large and unattractive, and suddenly wondered if here was an opportunity to beg clothes that fit? "Your attire is lovely," she said to Arabella, who had suddenly become quiet. "Do you think it possible for my friends and I to trade for clothing that fits? As you can see, this is not my own outfit. When the Indians raided Highgrove Chase, they either stole or burned everything." *Lie, lie, lie.* "We have nothing left but these." She held out her skirt for Arabella to inspect. "As you can see, this is much, much too big. "Of course, we're grateful to Captain Strongbow for bringing them to us on his last trip here, before he left for Barbados," she added, not wanting to offend her hostess in case she had donated an item.

"Oh, Captain Strongbow," Arabella said dreamily. "He is a fine picture of a man; do you not agree? And such a gentleman!" She held a slim, white hand to her throat. "Why, when he visits us here on the island...." Her sentence was cut short as her husband entered through the front door with an armful of firewood.

It was enough said for Cassandra to understand that her, yes, *her* captain was a dreamboat to this young bride! She felt a slight pang of jealousy, which she tried to overcome. *The man is dead. You have no claim on the him, and he is not your lover!* But looking at young, vibrant and pretty Arabella, with her beautiful name, and clothes to match, Cassandra felt old, doughty, filthy and ugly. While Arabella's hair was light brown with a tinge of gold, tied back into a mysterious array of bun and curls, her unlined face framed with wispy ringlets, she, herself, now had below-the-shoulder hair, previously highlighted to the highest level, and now darker roots having grown at least five inches in this mysterious passage of time. How could she think for a moment that the captain was serious about that kiss...that wonderful surprise of a kiss that left her breathless on the shore at his departure?

"It is so pleasant to have a new face in our presence, is it not, husband?"

"Indeed," he replied as he kicked aside the charming bed that Arabella had arranged at the foot of the fireplace. "Woman," he said, whereas both Casandra and Arabella came to attention. "What have you done here? I have yet to prepare the fire."

"I am indeed sorry, husband. My excitement at company has made me forget the correct order of things."

Good lord. Cassandra wanted to kick Mr. Hill's butt into the fire as he knelt before the fireplace, her comfy looking bed now a rumpled pile of quilt and pillow. She glanced at Arabella, who seemed very embarrassed and suddenly shy in the presence of her husband. Obviously, obedience was priority when he was around, as her demeanor had changed dramatically.

Now, without his hat, Cassandra was able get a good view of Mr. Hill. He was not entirely unattractive of face, and most likely in his early 40's, with brown hair tinged silver at the temples and thinning at the crown. When he stood, having prepared the fire to his satisfaction, she could see that the buttons of his waistcoat appeared strained over the protrusion of his belly. Certainly, he was old enough to be Arabella's father!

He then nodded to Cassandra. "Off to bed," he said, which she felt was an order. He left them and entered the small bedroom that Cassandra had peeked into upon her arrival.

As he closed the bedroom door, she and Arabella both knelt to redo the quilt and pillow. The fireplace crackled comfortably as the kindling took to flame. Suddenly, Cassandra was hot and moved her bedding a foot or two away from its prior position.

"I bid you a good night, Mistress Cassandra. I do hope you will remain with us for a while." She tiptoed to Cassandra and whispered in her ear. "I dare say I am starved for company closer to my own age. The women in the settlement are far older and have much distain for me, though I can't imagine why."

I know why, because you're young and pretty. "How long have you been married to Mr. Staples?"

"I arrived in the Bay in July, when it was blistering hot, and was married soon after," she said, her voice lowered to a near whisper. "My father was acquainted with Mr. Staples in England, and this marriage was pre-arranged when I was but a child."

"It was brave of you to come this distance alone." She, herself had been terrified, having been thrown into her own circumstance, but Arabella was barely out of childhood and married to an older man! "Did you want to come so far from home?"

"Certainly not," Arabella answered, her shoulders slumped and her expression dim. "I had an interest in a boy, much to my father's dislike, as he had promised me to Mr. Staples."

Arabella's story now had her full attention. "And?"

"And...I am now here, so far away from home and the boy I loved." Tears rolled down Arabella's pretty checks.

"I'm so sor...."

"Arabella!" Both women jumped at Mr. Staples' gruff interruption from the bedroom. "Come to bed!" he demanded.

"Good night, Mistress Cassandra," she said, wiping her tears away as she left.

Cassandra stood transfixed by the fireplace. *Poor kid,* she thought, grateful that time had changed the fates of young women such as Arabella. Of course, things had changed dramatically by the twenty-first century; but here she was, stuck in 1644, and things had changed in reverse for her!

Chapter 18

It was a good thing that she had moved her bed back a few feet from the hearth, because when she woke, Master Staples knelt between she and the fireplace, stoking the fire.

Quickly, she threw the quilt off and sat up. "Good morning, sir." She said. "Sorry if I'm in your way." She then looked to the window by the front door and realized it was still dark outside. She didn't want to ask the time, should he have a watch in the first place. In fact, she didn't want to ask anything from him for fear of his bark; but did he bite as well? *Stop being a sniveling chicken; he's a ghost!* "What time is it?"

"Time to rise," he said, without turning to look her in the face. She wondered if he ever said anything that didn't sound like an order. On the walk from the beach to the house the night before, he hadn't said a darn thing.

"Is Arabella up? I'd like to see her before I leave to meet the others."

"She hath been up an hour already feeding the chickens," he said, and left through the front door.

"Rise and shine," she said aloud. *I wonder if there's an outhouse?* She really had to pee. They didn't have an outhouse at their own cabin, but they had talked about it often enough. There, sanitation was controlled by each person responsible for their own area, but Cupid promised he would build one. Cassandra hated it, the fact of no running water, no toilets, and no toilet paper, but there was nothing she could do until someday (she hoped) she was whisked back to civilization.

Taking her own lead, she crept around to the back of the Staples' home, held her skirt out and away—the best she could, for it was way too much fabric to lift—spread her legs a bit and peed in the dirt. She then made her way toward what looked like, in the dim dawning light, a chicken house.

"Oh, Mistress Cassandra, I bid you good morn, and do hope my husband didn't awaken you." Arabella was her lively self, gathering eggs into an apron pocket.

"No problem, Arabella. I must be going to meet the others, anyway. Do you always get up in the dark?"

"Oh, yes. When husband rises, I rise. When he beds, I bed. Would you like porridge? We mustn't let you leave without nary a crumb."

"Well, yes, I guess I should. Food is hard to come by, especially in our neck of the woods."

"Oh, naught! We have much food; our bellies are full."

"That's the advantage of town living, I suppose."

"From where do you come, that you have not food to eat?"

"I wish I knew," she said, wishing she had a map of the area so she knew where the heck her cabin sat in this wilderness.

"You have no recollection?"

"I'm new," Cassandra replied. "I don't quite know my way around here," *in this century, I mean.* "We came by boat, as you know."

"You do have a distinct way of speaking. How many are in your party?"

"Five—uh, make that six. The baby makes six."

"A baby? Oh, I should love to see the baby!"

Now that day was dawning, Cassandra could see that the young bride was fully dressed and coiffured, only today she wore a long, brown, light woolen skirt and linen bodice over her lacy shift. Over her skirt was pinned a white, deep pocketed, slightly stained apron, and around her shoulders a cut of triangular muslin, pale yellow in color and large enough to tie at the breast with a bow.

"You're looking very put-together so early in the morning, Arabella."

"Thank you, Mistress Cassandra. We must find something nice for you to wear. Come with me, as I have many pieces of clothing brought from home."

Arabella finished feeding the chickens, and off they went to the Staples' bedroom. It was not a large room, but cozy: a real bed with a lumpy mattress covered nicely with a quilt, the pattern of which Cassandra didn't have a clue, being that she had never, *ever,* considered making a quilt, herself. She especially noticed the embroidered edges of the pillowcases, and sighed; it was all so civilized, warm and comfortable. The lacy window curtains fluttered in a slight breeze, as the shutters were opened unto the new day. The wood paneling lent a rustic touch that nicely framed the atmosphere of the room. It all worked together, the curtains, the paneling, the quilt, and even a beautiful dresser with an ornately framed mirror that sat against one wall…*mirror….*

"It was in my bedroom at home," Arabella said, seeing that Cassandra now stood at the dresser viewing herself in the oval mirror. She opened a large trunk beneath the bedroom window and began taking items of clothing out and laying them over the quilt. "Let me see…," she said, as Cassandra continued to stare into the mirror.

No! It can't be me…please, God, that isn't me I'm looking at… is it? She moved a hand to pull on a string of hair; the image moved with her. She felt faint. She was horrified at the stranger staring at her from the mirror, and stepped backward until she felt the lumpy mattress at the back of her knees. "It can't be!" she said aloud. "It's not me!" The gaunt, poorly dressed, stringy-haired woman in the mirror could never be her!

"Whatever is wrong?" Arabella asked, a skirt from the trunk drooping in her hands. "Are you ill? Please sit!"

She did. Cassandra sat, sinking into the feather-down mattress, covered her face with her hands, and cried.

"Oh, my! Whatever is wrong? Have I offended thee?"

"No...no...I'm sorry. I scared myself in the mirror." Cassandra attempted to wipe away the tears. "That can't be me. I used to be pretty. I used to have nice clothes, nice hair...who is that person? She's ugly!"

"Why, you are not a bit ugly. You need new clothing, and perhaps we can do something with your hair." She took a seat next to Cassandra on the bed, which caused their behinds to sink ever so deeply into the mattress. "This is a difficult country for one's appearance. It is harsh. There are no shops; there is nothing here but heat and mosquitoes. There are no parties or pretty dresses. This is why every morning I fix my hair. I find something clean and nice to wear. I, too, want to feel pretty, as well as *be* pretty. It is far too easy to let one's appearance go in this place. I hate it!" Her voice rose at those words, and she slammed her hands down onto her lap, the drooping skirt still clenched in her fists. "If I think too hard on it—that I am here, the wife of...of *him*—I sometimes would rather be dead." She whispered the last words, perhaps knowing that it was a sin to even think of doing oneself in.

Cassandra eyed the young bride, noticing that she, too, had tears running down her cheeks. Then, realizing she had created a pity party, suddenly shot to standing. "We must stop this!" she said, and reached for Arabella's hand. "Let's look at the clothes and get happy. Clothes make women happy, right?"

Arabella looked up at her guest, her blue eyes reddened and watery. "You are so very right."

"Well, an't ye the fine lady," Izzie sneered, upon seeing Cassandra in her new and stylish attire: a dark green skirt with matching bodice and peplum, which was beautifully embroidered by Arabella at some point in her prior and happier life in England.

Cassandra replied with her own smirk. "Aren't I, though?" She spun a circle, the long green skirt twirling with her. She lifted the skirt to show Izzie (and Lucy, and Cupid) the petticoat that Arabella had given her, along with a pair of worn slippers. "I have many," Arabella had said of the petticoat and slippers, when Cassandra tried to dissuade her from giving up such lovely things.

Cassandra tossed her head about to emphasize the clean shine of her hair, as Arabella had shampooed it with her own blend of vinegar, water and an aromatic oil.

"Will ye not introduce us to yer acquaintance— if ye be done with the prancin' and showin' off of the new clothin'?" Izzie asked.

Arabella had come to the meeting place along with Cassandra. She was anxious to meet the others and to see the baby. "This is my new friend, Goodwife Arabella Staples, wife of Master Josiah Staples. And these are my...well...my companions, Iz...I mean Goodwife Elizabeth Highgrove, widow of John Highgrove of Highgrove Chance.

"Very pleased to make your acquaintance, Madam." Arabella showed her good manners by performing a brief curtsey, to which Izzie replied with a grunt and a run of her eyes from the top of Arabella's coifed head, to the dainty slippers peeking from beneath her brown woolen skirt.

"And this is Cupid, Lucy, and baby Free."

Arabella did not quite know how to greet the dark ones but, after a slight hesitation, she performed her little curtsey. "So pleasured," she said. "May I hold the child?"

With Arabella delighted to play with Free, Izzie and Cassandra left the two women at the waterside, and instructed Cupid to begin unloading the tobacco.

"'Tis the tradin' place ahead," Izzie said, breathless, and nodding ahead to a building near the dock. Her pregnancy was obviously beginning to affect her activities, as her quick pace created a shortness of breath.

"Slow down, Izzie! I don't think the trading place is going anywhere. Let's not be worn out by the time we get there, please!" The boned bodice Arabella had given her was seriously affecting her own oxygen as well. She was not used to such restrictions and thought that she would remove the boned bodice before heading back to the cabin, saving it for special occasions—*like there will be a special occasion?*

"We are to meet a man there, and I don't fancy being late; and I will be doing the bargainin', so don't open that mouth o' yours."

"So why am I here with you then, if I must keep my mouth shut?" Cassandra asked. They had arrived at the door where Izzie paused, her hand on the latch.

" Ye can read and write, 'tis why."

"*Amrae n-amrae!*"[28] Izzie exclaimed.

"Holy smokes!" said Cassandra. "I don't believe it!"

"Strike me down with a feather!" Phineas Barnett stood from behind a desk framed by crate after crate of trade goods.

"How, by the love o' God, how did ye escape the savages?" Izzie stood frozen to her spot. "I can'no believe me eyes! For sure, I thought the savages made a sup of ya!"

"Ah, but you forget me special talent, Izzie dear." He then waved his hands mysteriously in pantomime and presented a feather plumed pen to the dumbstruck women. "Me magic has saved me time and time again in this savage land. But, here I am, a humble man with honest occupation. Here, I have food fit for the likes us," he said, spreading his arms to include them. "Food to the English palate, and ale, and a bed to sleep in. But come...come. Ye stand away as if I am the devil hisself!"

---

[28] "*Amrae n-amrae!*" Gaelic for 'wonder of wonders'!

Phineas gathered two empty crates and set them on the floor by his desk. He then pulled his chair around and they sat in a circle, sitting in awe of the consequence that brought them together again. "Tis me turn to question ye both, for surely I worried meself sick thinking of poor Izzie in the forest alone after the savages came. And what hath become of your marriage to the *weroance*, Cassandra?"

"I should bat you over the head with this crate, for leaving me to live with the Indians—and a marriage that *you* arranged! I snuck away, that's what. I snuck off in the dark and starved for three long days and dark, scary, cold nights, lost in the forest before I chanced upon Izzie. And the whole time, I planned on wringing your conniving neck, Phineas, if I ever saw you again."

"Yes, yes. 'tis old news and circumstance, dear Cassandra. Let us forget it, for you are here now—and Izzie as well, surviving the brutal forest to sit afore me."

"An't much can bring me down, Phineas. I 'ave me plans, and I shall see them through."

"Was the babe in your belly part o' the plan?" he asked, his eyes glued to the large swell of her stomach. "Is it...."

"Hush!" Izzie said, and so strongly so that Cassandra nearly leaped from the crate she sat upon.

"Is it what?" Cassandra questioned. "Is it wha...? Wait a minute..." she said, eyeing the two suspiciously. "Don't tell me that this baby could belong to Phineas? You two? Good Lord, do you stop at nothing, Izzie? You get drunk, screw an Indian you don't even remember, and then Phineas, too?"

"A savage?" By the look on his face, Phineas was truly shocked. "You fornicated with a savage?"

"Stop this!" Izzie jumped to her feet. Wha' 'tis done 'tis done. I'll hear no more of it! Her highness bedded a savage herself, so don't be casting no stones at me. We come for the tradin', not the tellin' o' stories and not to lay judgement upon Izzie Pratt Highgrove, the Mistress of Highgrove Chase. Yes, 'tis is I, Phineas, the *Mistress* of Highgrove Chase, and I am 'ere for the tradin' of me tobacco."

"Highgrove?" Phineas looked incredulous. "John Highgrove who was slaughtered by the savages?" Phineas laughed deep and long. "Well, well, well. So 'twas to *you*, Captain Strongbow took the supplies and sent the native, Eagle. I know naught what to say to this fabrication of yours, Izzie Pratt. I shall keep me lips sealed to the good wives and men of this settlement, but...." he stared at Izzie's swelling belly. "If that child you carry is tanned as a savage and has hair the color of midnight, I'd like to see you present it as heir to Highgrove Chase." He was silent a moment, leaving his comment to sink in. "But, being a good businessman meself—and an acquaintance to Master Highgrove *and* the Mistress Highgrove—and knowing of what fine character she doth possess— I believe we can make a fair bargain between the two of us—*just* the two of us—for our own peace of mind."

Izzie shot to her feet, her face as red as her hair. "Peace? I'd like to give ya a piece of me fist, Phineas Barnett! You'll not be takin' the food from our mouths, nor a shillin' to line yer pockets, ye cloying[29] land pirate."

"The pot is calling the kettle black," Phineas said, standing to meet her face to face. 'Tis thievery you do, presenting yourself as the widow Highgrove."

"'Tis thievery *you* do, takin' livelihood from Izzie Pratt!"

"Stop!" Cassandra said, tired of the bickering, and getting nowhere in the trade of goods. She wasn't about to take the long trip back to their cabin without all the supplies they needed. "Stop! This is getting nowhere. We need those goods, Phineas. Just what do you propose?"

"T'aint no....."

"Shut up, Izzie. Let's listen to him, lying cheat that he is. We need the supplies."

"Now there's a smart one," Phineas said, dragging his chair around to the back of the desk. He sat, producing a loud smacking sound as his behind met with the chair seat.

---

[29] *'Cloying'*, thieving;

"Smart, my arse!" Izzie yelled, glaring at Cassandra. "Her highness, herself, is thinkin' to give me tobacco away to the likes of Phineas Barnett? Over me grave!"

"Just what are your terms, Phineas?" Cassandra asked, ignoring Izzie's fury. With Phineas behind the desk, the crates sat far too low to the floor for eye contact, so both women stood before him, one waiting for an answer, and one glaring at the pudgy, smug man who held her fortune in his hands.

"John Highgrove had a fair good crop of tobacco growing in his field. 'Twas through Highgrove, hisself, that I am privy to this account, as we were of good acquaintance. Considering the gravity of Izzie's crime, I believe a fifty-fifty share would suit me nicely."

"You'll get half o' nothin' from me, Phineas Barnett!"

Cassandra ignored Izzie's outburst. "A fifty share of *what*, exactly. Our goods?" "This is a commodity deal, not money."

"An't no sterling nor coin to be had in these parts. 'Tis the Spanish silver[30] that rules," he replied.

Spanish silver? What are we talking about? "I don't understand, Phineas."

"He's lyin' through 'is teeth." Izzie growled. "An't no Spaniards here."

"We don't *have* Spanish silver," Cassandra said, still totally confused over the conversation.

"'Tis true, no Spaniards, but Spanish silver? Yes, indeed, you do have the coin."

"He's full of the blarney, he is." Izzie said, leaning over Phineas's desk. "And how shall I be sharin' half o' me Spanish silver with the likes of you, if I have no Spanish silver, eh?"

Phineas rose from the desk and, without a word, walked past the bewildered women and opened the door to the outside. Cassandra assumed he was looking about for eavesdropper. "Cupid? I've set me eyes on Cupid! He is in your company, as well?"

---

[30] *Spanish silver* held the highest value in the 17th century

"Aye, and Lucy. 'He's deliverin' the fine tobacco leaves for the tradin', which is why we come in the first place, and not this blarney talk of Spanish silver."

"Well, I am overcome with surprise this day. What a miracle i'tis that we have survived the harsh cruelties of this land and joined together again. We shall make fine partners!"

"What in hell are you talking about?" Cassandra asked, totally perplexed by now.

"May ye burn in a fiery hell, Phineas Barnett, that you should be a partner to me!"

"You'll be agreeing, for I know what character you truly are, Izzie Pratt; I know your hunger for riches."

"Lay it on the line, Phineas," Cassandra said. "What is this all about?"

"Master Highgrove came to this land with riches. This I know, for when he come to the settlement, his purse was a'jinglin' full of Spanish coin. When 'tis not tobacco season, he still come to purchase goods with his jinglin' coin."

Cassandra and Izzie looked to one another, the latter's eyes wide and bright a moment, before her eyebrows knitted together and the bright eyes turned to slits from which she peered menacingly at Phineas. "If 'tis blarney ye speak, ye'd best be preparin' to meet the devil, hisself."

"Me word 'tis good as the silver in Highgrove's pocket, may he rest in peace."

Cassandra sat herself down on the wooden crate watching the two characters exchange a battle of words over the mysterious riches of Master Highgrove. The arguing pair became muted— background noise—to her ears. *What does all this mean? I can't wake up from this nightmare. Am I truly dead, and why? How? I don't remember!* She felt herself an apparition in this time; one not there, and yet, she experienced it—she *lived* it. She communicated with these people, these ghosts, and yet, it was as if she were watching a movie she didn't understand, a movie in which she played a part in a bizarre and seemingly endless movie.

"...'tis there, I tell ye, for never was the purse empty but for the times he left with his goods, it having been spent for such.

When he come again, the purse is full." He stopped his recount of observations to wipe his brow with a kerchief. "There lies a treasure in that land, and I am deserving of my fair share for imparting the knowledge."

"Where does it lay?" Izzie asked.

"'Tis there, at Highgrove Chance."

Cassandra broke her spell of thoughts and stood. "But *where*, Phineas? How can we share a treasure that's invisible?"

"Aha!" he said, as if he were about to pull a treasure map from his sleeve. "I know not."

"That's a total let-down," Cassandra leaned over the desk. "That's it, then. We can't share what we don't have, so back to square one; we've come to trade tobacco." She turned and walked to open the front door for the weighing and inspection of the tobacco, but Phineas wasn't finished yet.

"Do not be hasty, woman. We have not resolved our problem as of yet."

"The problem being that Highgrove had some Spanish coin, and you are determined that there's a treasure box buried somewhere on the property? *That* problem? Do you know how large that property is, Phineas? Have you ever been there?"

"And are we to sweat and slave for yer 'alf?" Izzie said. "I say, not. If 'tis treasure yer wantin', come with shovel and spade to search; sweat and slave among us."

"I would not trust ye, Izzie, not for all of Highgrove's silver, for your heart is as greedy as mine. I shall take me leave when the tobacco trading is done in the bay, and come with shovel and spade in hand, as ye say."

"Well, good," Cassandra said. "The issue is now resolved between the two greedy ghosts. May we now proceed to the tobacco trading? I'm sure Cupid and Lucy are as anxious to get out of Dodge, as am I."

"What sayeth?" Phineas asked. "Dodge?"

"A slip of the tongue. I *sayeth* let's get down to business, *please!* This town full of pricks is not for me, and we need our goods—desperately. We need to start for home, and it would be nice to get going before nightfall."

Once the bundles of cured tobacco leaves were brought into the building, the bargaining began.

"As ye can see, Phineas, 'tis high quality tobacco."

Phineas weighed the leaves and marked the weight in the ledger that sat upon his desk. "'Tis good, as ye say. Captain Strongbow was wise to send such as Eagle; he has vast knowledge of the land and tobacco, but he is of the Susquehannock, a warrior tribe, so 'tis best you keep on good terms with the savage, but do not put full trust."

"What do you mean?" Cassandra asked. She had felt safe with Eagle on the property, but now, with Phineas's warning and the Susquehannock on the uprise, she wondered if she could even look at him without fear of torture or death, and especially remembering how the Indians had slaughtered Highgrove and his servants. She had never given it a thought before now.

"Ye never know what lies in the native head and heart."

"The list," Izzie commanded, getting down to business.

Cassandra was forced to put her fears away and pulled a ragged piece of woven fabric from her cleavage. At the cabin, there was no pen or pencil with which to write, and no paper to write upon, so she had ripped the fabric from one of the supply bags and now borrowed Phineas' plume and inkwell, preparing to write. It was awkward, having never experienced such writing with plume and ink; but at the same time, it was all that was available.

"Shovels, of course." Izzie said. "Needle and thread, A pair of scissors...fabric for which to make clothin'...." On and on she dictated until Cassandra was forced to write—and extremely small at that—on the back and edges of the fabric swatch. When finished, the swatch resembled the rantings of a crazed person, as the weave was loosely woven and the ink and plume difficult to maneuver on such a base as uneven fabric; each word blurred into the other. Nevertheless, the list was necessary so that nothing was forgotten.

Of course, Phineas was not in possession of all the requested items, but as the two dugouts were filled with crates containing such things as a large sack of sugar, of salt, of guinny wheat, of dried peas, cobs of corn, a barrel of beer and other sundry items for the inhabitants of Highgrove's Chance, even Cassandra could barely contain her excitement. Though many items were primitive compared to the 21st century, they were still an extravagance, or a necessity that she had been so long without. Even a homely bar of lye soap was wrapped carefully in the fabric list and gently packed into a crate.

Arabella, still enjoying her morning (which now headed toward the noon hour) with baby Free, was amazed at the excitement the traded items brought her new friends, but her joy was short-lived at the sight of Master Staples walking forthright atop the incline that sloped downward to the group on the beach. His approach did not seem at all amicable.

"Wife!" he said loudly. "I have come home for my sup but there is naught in the pot, nor bread on the table. While I toil, you play with negars!"

Arabella's face turned bright red. "So sorry, husband, I have lost track of the hour! I come now." She hurriedly handed Free back to her mother.

Just to emphasize his anger, Staples literally jerked Arabella away from the group by an elbow and dragged her up the incline at such a pace that she could barely keep up with her small slippered feet.

"Is that necessary?" Cassandra yelled after him. Her face also red, but from anger, not embarrassment.

Staples stopped short at the top of the incline.

"What sayeth thee, woman?"

"Is it necessary to show your manly control in such a cowardly way, by abusing a woman half your size?"

Phineas, who also stood with the group by the dugouts, gasped. "Mind your mouth, Mistress," he whispered. "Master Staples is well respected here."

"Shut up, Phineas. The man is a beast."

"Oh, let her," Izzie said. "'tis good amusement!"

Master Staples left Arabella at the top of the incline, and retraced his steps down to the group. Lucy quickly sat herself and Free in the dugout out of harm's way, while Cupid busied himself rearranging crates.

Cassandra took a step backward at his approach, but Staples came right up to her, his face in hers. "This," he said, a shower of spittle spraying her face, "'tis no affair of yours. I suggest you keep out of my business as it is between husband and wife."

"It's everyone's business when a helpless woman is being abused."

"Right!" Izzie offered, nodding her head in agreement.

"Nor your business," he said, turning to Izzie, who then, not one to be bullied, crossed her arms over her chest and raised her chin defiantly.

Arabella tottered down the incline. "'Tis alright, husband. I beg your forgiveness. Let us go, and I shall fix your sup." She slipped an arm through Staples arm, but he pushed her away.

"Leave me be, woman. Go to the house!"

"Please," she begged. "Mistress Cassandra has been a friend to me. I wish no harm come to her." Again she put her arm through her husband's, and this time he not only shoved her, but delivered a blow to her face with the back of his hand. "Go!" he yelled.

Arabella cried out in pain as she stumbled backward, falling onto her behind. Immediately Cassandra rushed to lift her struggling friend from the ground, as the abundance of her clothing had hampered the ability to rise on her own.

"Truly, Mistress Cassandra, I am fine," she whispered. "Please go before he becomes angrier!" She brushed the dirt from the back of her skirt, but still bore a red mark from the force of her husband's hand.

"You do not belong here, woman. Go and leave us to our ways," Staples ordered.

I definitely do not belong here. "How right you are, sir. But I can tell you that your bullish act would land you jail time in the 21st century, and were we there, I'd sic the cops on you."

A look of confusion flashed across Master Staples face. "You speak in puzzles, woman. Perhaps you dabble in witchery? Perhaps you have bewitched Arabella to your own design that she wouldst deny her husband his sup?"

Izzie, Phineas and Arabella all gasped—quietly, but audibly—at his words. "Come," Izzie said. We must go *now*." She then grabbed Cassandra by the sleeve of her new frock and pulled her toward the dugout.

"What's wrong?" Casandra whispered, turning her head to see Master Staples and Arabella walking up the incline, arm in arm.

"Do ye want to burn or hang? The man has witchery on his mind. Do ye not know?"

"Know what? I read all about the witch hunts back in the 1600's, and it has nothing to do with me."

"Aye, so you say; but we know you as a *daft* woman, not as a witch," Phineas offered. "If he speaketh the word, ye shall not set one foot off this soil, but be bound for trial."

"Trial? For witchery? Oh, come now, this is ridiculous."

"In't ridiculous when the fire is lit at your feet. In't ridiculous when ye dangle at the loop end of a rope." Izzie gripped her own throat, and smiled maliciously. "...and I an't burnin' with ye."

Cassandra stood a moment, pondering the ridiculous possibility of a charge of witchcraft. *I guess anything is possible in this crazy time.* "Okay, okay, let's get out of here. Where's Eagle? We won't get anywhere without him."

As if by Phineas' magic—or the confusing passage of time—Eagle appeared next to her as if on cue. "We go," he said.

Cassandra glanced behind at the village. She could barely see the tops of a few houses, smoke trailing from chimneys to blend into a gray afternoon. "This is a creepy place," she said to herself, then sat, facing Eagle as he pushed off from the beach. "You don't say much, Eagle." He looked her in the eye, his arm and shoulder muscles flexed and rippling like separate animals as he gripped each side of the canoe, pushing it further into the bay, saying nothing, just looking into her eyes; and she wondered what was on his mind. "Why are...." She wanted to ask why he stared at her, but he released his grip on the canoe and jumped in behind her, taking up the paddle.

'*Warrior tribe*....' Phineas' words shook her. She was already vulnerable in a land she didn't recognize. Although she had surprised herself with her ability to survive in the wilderness for the amount of time she had done so, she was not set on murder-by-

Indian. This she could not—would not— tolerate, and especially murder by Indians long dead!

She turned on her seat to face Eagle. "Why do you stare at me? I need to know."

He looked confused, so she rephrased the question, along with pantomime. "Why - do – you - look (she pointed to him then she forked her middle and index fingers to point at her eyes) at me," then poked her chest.

"Like," he said, and went back to the business of rowing.

Chapter 19

The snows came, and with it, a cold wind roaring across the bay from the western shore. Eagle had returned to his people—or to the island. They didn't know for sure, and he rarely shared. He said he would come again at planting time, and as he had proved himself—so far—to be trustworthy. They believed him.

It was on this cold, snowy, windblown day, with a fire crackling in the fireplace and a fine pot of stew cooking there, that Izzie's baby decided to be born.

"Ach! Me water!" Izzie cried, loud enough to raise the devil. Lucy's knitting needle flew through the air, the ball of yarn rolling off her lap and across the floor collecting bits of twig and dirt as it went. Baby Free stirred in her cozy crib (one that Cupid built), and Cassandra let out a sharp yelp, thinking for a moment that the Indians had come for murder.

Cupid dropped the log he was about to add to the crackling fire and stared wide-eyed at Izzie as she stood lifting her skirt to see the water first hand, but it had seeped into the dirt, leaving just a darkened spot as viewed from the firelight.

"Holy shit, Izzie, you scared us to death!" Cassandra said, rising from one of the chairs Cupid had fashioned with wood and vines from the forest. She was still scared to death, as she had been dreading this day. What did she know about birthing babies?

Nothing! She couldn't even google the question to see minute by minute instructions online. "Lucy, let's get a pot of water boiling," she said, remembering this from the movies, though she wasn't quite sure what came after the boiling water. *Rags...yes.*

The inhabitants of the cabin had been sitting comfortably and quietly as close to the fire as space allowed, when Izzie's water broke. Now, they were a frenzied beehive of activity with Cupid adding more kindling and logs to the fire, Lucy removing the pot of stew from the fire and replacing it with a pot of water, and Cassandra running circles in search of rags.

Since the trade of goods on the island, the settlers had busied themselves making the cabin as comfy and homey as the trade goods would allow. Lucy had surprised them with a talent for knitting, a craft she learned in Barbados; a most useful craft considering the onslaught of winter at the time. With the trade of the tobacco, they were able to acquire knitting needles and several balls of yarn imported from England, from which Lucy spent the fall knitting simple capes for the women, blankets for Free and Izzie's baby, who had not yet been born. For Cupid, she sewed a shirt of heavy linen.

With new tools, Cupid made pallets of wood to raise their beds a few inches above ground level. A few chairs had been crafted to sit around the rustic table that he had constructed in the beginning of their venture. They now had blankets to cover themselves through the cold winter nights, and fabrics from which they fashioned clothing. With Eagle's help, a bake oven was constructed outside of the cabin, and Lucy could now bake biscuits to accompany their stews. All in all, it was a far cry from the lonely, frightening nights Cassandra had endured during her escape from Long Feather's camp, and she was grateful for each improvement toward comfort and civilization, no matter how small.

"Damn the drink!" Izzie screamed through a contraction. "Damn the savages!"

Cassandra wiped the sweat from Izzie's brow—and from her own—as the night wore on. She and Lucy had piled the blankets on the table with Izzie atop; the pallets were simply too low and inconvenient for an important event such as childbirth. Izzie's contractions were now coming so close that neither Cassandra nor Lucy had time to think or fret, because the baby was coming and instinct took over; they were as ready and waiting as they would ever be.

"Da head!" Lucy cried, and sure enough when Cassandra peeked, there it was, a dark head of hair forcing its way into the world.

Izzie let out a bloodcurdling scream, a final push, and there he was, right into Cassandra's waiting hands with his full head of black hair and a scrunched-up howling face; baby boy Pratt, aka Highgrove.

She grimaced while Lucy cut the cord, feeling rather faint from the experience, now that the adrenaline rush of terror had passed. This had been a messy ordeal for Cassandra, and here she was, right smack in the middle of it, and not knowing a darn thing about childbirth! But, she was the first one to hold the baby, who continued to screech at the top of his lungs. "He takes after you in the complaint department," she directed at Izzie, who was, for once, too exhausted for a comeback.

Cleaned up and swaddled, Cassandra held the squealing infant up for Izzie, who had fallen back onto a thin pillow stuffed with leaves and grass. "Heaven be praised," she whispered, exhausted. "'tis done." A pause. "Is he white...or dark?"

"In-between. Look."

"He a fine boy." Lucy said, massaging Izzie's stomach to help discard the afterbirth.

"I'm glad you know what you're doing," Cassandra whispered into Lucy's ear.

"Gots ta feed dat boy, Miz Izzie."

Izzie sat against the log wall by her pallet, pale, disheveled and obviously exhausted. It had been a rough three days since the birth. Her milk had come in, and now that the baby—still unnamed—had his taste of food, he was fussy and insatiably hungry if he wasn't sleeping.

"Oh, give me the wee savage," she said, begrudgingly, holding out her arms. "He sucks the life out o' me," she complained, as he hooked onto a nipple.

"He fine and strong," Lucy said—at least for the 100th time—as Izzie was experiencing extreme difficulty accepting the role of motherhood.

"You play, you pay," Cassandra said, standing aside the cot watching Izzie's ordeal. "You're going to pass on your distemper through your milk, if you're not careful. Speaking of which, he needs a name. We can't call him 'boy' or 'baby' forever, you know."

"I care not what we call him, the little savage. There! 'Little Savage.' 'Tis a good name."

"I'll tell you what; Lucy and I brought him into this world, so we'll name him if you won't. Right, Lucy?"

Lucy cast a look to Izzie for approval. "But he Miz Izzie's babe…."

"'ere, take him. Ye can have 'im." Izzie said, holding him outward. He had released the nipple and appeared to doze off.

Cassandra wrapped him in her arms, holding him close to take in the sweet smell of new life. She sat on a chair by the fire, wishing it were a rocker. *Look at me, so domestic!* Though she had tired of watching Free during the early times—the times when this nightmare was new and her anger hot—she now felt quite happy and content holding the small bundle in her arms, and proud, proud that she had done the unexpected, bring a baby into the world. She looked down at his round, tanned face and jet black hair, black as coal....coal...Cole...Kole! *Beautiful!*

"Lucy, I think I have a name!. *Kole,* what do you think? His hair is black as coal, but we could change the spelling, spell it K-o-l-e." She spelled the name and waited for approval.

"Now the fancy one is spellin' out the word for us. Do ye think we can spell? I had no schoolin', and neither did Lucy. Call 'im what ye like. I care not."

"'Tis a good name, Miz Cassie."

"Kole. Good!" Cassandra was quite proud of the name she came up with. Now, after three days, the baby was a person, one of the fold.

Spring. It was a beautiful word and a beautiful, sunny, cool day when Captain Strongbow appeared at the edge of the yet unplanted tobacco field. Cassandra had convinced herself that she would never see him again, that he was gone from their lives— *her* life—gone for good no matter how deeply she had felt a connection with him.

"Da cap'n!" Lucy called. "Da cap'n come!"

Cassandra literally dropped the spoon with which she was going to stir the stew in the black kettle, and ran to the doorway.

"Der!" Lucy pointed across the field to where he stood, in person. Someone was with him, but Cassandra was so excited she didn't stop to look, but literally gathered her skirt and ran halfway across the field before she had to stop to catch her breath. *Idiot, what the hell are you doing? Don't look so eager— so easy.*

By now, Izzie was standing next to her. "An't ye the saucy one, runnin' after the cap'n is such a way? Surely, he will think ye a harlot behavin' in such a fashion."

"A harlot? You mean, like you?"

Izzie gave her the usual dirty look, then shaded her eyes against the sun. "Well, kiss me arse, I believe 'tis Phineas with the cap'n."

Cassandra followed suit, shading her eyes. "It is! I guess he's here for the treasure hunt. I wonder if he's told Strongbow?"

"Ha! And share the findin's? 'Twould not 'appen." Izzie turned to look her in the eye. "Do not be trustin' that dolt'ead.[31] He would just as soon sell his own mother as give up Spanish silver."

"You're probably right. Come, let's say our hellos to the captain and Phineas.

That night, Cassandra watched from her low pallet as the captain spooned rabbit stew into his mouth. With two extra mouths to feed, the stew was split five and one-quarter ways, the one-quarter being a portion to Free, who sat next to her mother on their pallet. Luckily, there were trenchers enough, but the chair making

---

[31] 'Dolthead'; a fool *The First Dictionary of Slang, 1699*

196

was still a work in progress and there were not enough for each, as yet.

Before Cassandra could count to three, Izzie, in her usual, pushy manner, had taken a chair at the table along with the men, so she sat upon her pallet from where she watched the captain in profile.

"'Twas unbeknownst to me that you had an acquaintance with Mister Barnett." Captain Strongbow addressed this to Izzie, who sat aside him.

"Aye, we had a time together at the Indian camp." She glanced in Cassandra's direction. "It was there *she* married the savage king and stayed, while the lot of us went forward to seek a settlement."

"Wait just a darn minute." Cassandra set her trencher on the pallet and stood. "I want to clarify this." She approached the captain. "That woman and that man, Phineas Barnett, bargained my life away for a canoe. They made a deal with Long Feather to leave me behind in trade for freedom, while I was forced in marriage to an Indian, for Pete's sake."

"And not one complaint slipped between thy lips...."

"And just where did Kole come from? You should watch who you're pointing fingers at!"

Izzie's face turned bright red in anger. She stood, letting the chair fall backward onto the dirt floor. From there, she sped toward Cassandra, but was stopped in her tracks when Captain Strongbow stood between them.

"Would it not be best to accept the circumstance of past events? 'Tis a rough country and balance with the natives is precarious at best." This he said to both women.

Izzie grumbled, lifted her chair from the dirt and sat again at the table, but not without casting a threatening look in Cassandra's direction.

"Thanks, Captain." Cassandra was embarrassed to the color of tomato. She didn't want him to know of her carnal relations with Long Feather; in fact, she could barely believe it herself, wondering at times if it had really happened. *Take the good and let the rest go.* After all, she certainly had learned a few things from the Indians. Just the fact that she was *there,* observing and working with Long Feather's wives, was an education in itself, regardless of their disdain for her in regard to the chief's infatuation and preference for *Sky Blue*. If she hadn't had the experience of the Indian village—and the use of Otter's pouch—she wondered how she would have survived her lone trek through the wilderness.

She took her seat on the pallet and continued to watch Captain Strongbow in profile. *A strange man,* she thought. They had not had a moment alone since his return, and he had not shown any indication of the feelings he had expressed in the surprise kiss at his departure for the island last summer. *What was that about?* she wondered. His only comment upon their greeting this day,Stron was that the women looked 'well, and in good health'. *Was that a compliment?*

"What is your plan, now, Captain? Will you stay a while?" *I hope....*

"Aye. There is unfinished business here."

She hoped that meant her...or did it mean the Spanish silver? Did Phineas tell?

"Oh? And what might that be?" Izzie piped in, her mind most likely running along the same lines regarding the Spanish silver.

The captain turned his gaze to Cassandra. "I shall stay a time to help with the field," he said, his eyes locked in place on hers.

Boom...boom...boom. Cassandra's heart pounded in her ears. *He stays for me!*

Izzie followed the Captain's focus to Cassandra. "As I can see, Cap'n."

Strongbow returned his attention to the group at the table. "'Tis late to start the tobacco properly, seeded in a separate bed. We shall prepare the field, plant directly and pray it takes a healthy hold."

"The year past was Highgrove's first go at tobacco," said Phineas. "It proved a fine crop; the man knew his task. We shall hope the mistress does as well...and in more than one path," he said, eyebrows raised.

"An't no failin' for Isabel Highgrove," she replied. "And you, Phineas? Perchance ye have come to plow the fields as well?"

"In a manner of speaking. There is not much trading at the island as yet. I felt the need for a different atmosphere, and thought I could perhaps be of help."

"Well," Cassandra stood. "Come, Lucy. We'll clean this mess up."

With the trenchers washed and set aside and the black kettle wiped clean for tomorrow's meal, Cassandra left Lucy with the children and walked to the field where the captain, Izzie, Cupid and Phineas stood gazing at the stretch of work before them. The last wink of sun had sunk behind the trees and the hidden horizon beyond, but still the twilight rendered its last faint glow before the onset of darkness. It outlined the stubs of countless tobacco plants that needed plucking before the seeds were planted.

Cassandra now lived by the sun and cycle of the moon. No longer did the Cartier watch sparkle from her wrist; no longer did it matter the hour that she rose, or the hour that she slumbered, for it was all determined by the sun and moon—and the season. For now, in the birth of a new spring, it was the season of love and sowing the earth. Cupid's arrow had pierced her heart, and she was determined to steal the captain's.

Chapter 20

The winds found them. Cassandra, Izzie, Lucy, Captain Strongbow, Cupid, and even Phineas who begrudging proclaiming himself a merchant, not a planter, stooped over the field, row by row, pulling last season's cropped tobacco plants. The winds blew the dirt that clung to the roots of the plants, up their nostrils, into their eyes, their hair, their clothes, and yet they pursued, as time was of the essence if Highgrove's tobacco was to be successful.

"Not again!" Izzie complained, as her baby squealed in hunger from a basket, which was set aside the field. "Is he never satisfied?"

"He's a growing boy," Cassandra answered, across the wind and two rows away.

Izzie tromped over the few rows to her child, sat with her back to the wind, and pulled a bare breast from her blouse to feed Kole. He was a robust and healthy baby, handsome and strong—and with an insatiable appetite that Izzie found quite annoying, but which Cassandra found quite amusing.

"Perhaps we shall have a chance for an evening stroll after the sup?" Captain Strongbow had gained on her from his row. He now stopped to stretch his back, hands on hips, elbows bent, and head facing the blue heavens above.

If we're not dead from exhaustion by then. She mimicked his stretch, heart again thumping to the beat of desire. "Of course!" she replied, nonchalantly. *It's about time you made a move.* After three hard days of work in the field, and with very few words between them, she was beginning to think she had misread his intentions.

"I shall look forward to it," he said, as if telling her nothing more than the time of day, and resumed pulling the tobacco stubs.

He was a mystery; he had kissed her passionately out of the blue, that time, but now…now, he seemed almost shy, silent as a schoolboy with his first crush. In fact, he seemed so distant and so out of character from her first conception of the man, that she had to wonder where the real captain of the Thunder had gone? His physical stature—so strong, handsome, and virile, was an opposite to his present mental state. Still, her heart thumped in anticipation. She wondered if she was just lonely for a man, and then looked at Phineas, hunched over, plodding along his row and grumbling. *No, I am not looking for just any man....*

"Shall we have that stroll, Mistress Pratt?" the captain asked later as she and Lucy cleared the trenchers and utensils from the table.

"Of course," she replied, giving her best smile.

Izzie sat at the table sipping her watered rum. "I'm supposin' it an't *this* Mistress Pratt you'll be askin'."

"My apologies, Izzie. I do sometimes forget that we have two Mistress Pratts."

"But you're Goodwife Highgrove, now. Remember?" Cassandra asked, her eyes a warning as she jerked Izzie's trencher from the table causing the three-pronged fork, to fly several feet toward the fireplace. "No need for you to come along."

"Soon the little savage will be sucking me life away as i'tis." she replied, standing. "He hath worn me to the bone. There shall be no more babes from this body!"

Cassandra ignored Izzie's outburst, as Izzie constantly complained about her status of motherhood. Then, removing the stained apron from her skirt, she tossed it over a chair back and took her knitted cape from a peg on the wall. "Captain and I are going for a stroll."

They departed the cabin, she, following his lead. A full moon peeked from above the tree line as they headed toward one side of the field. "We shall circle the field, with your permission," he said.

"Lead on," she replied. She didn't care where they walked, as long as they were together.

"'Tis a bit chilly, but the wind has died."

"Tobacco is so much work. Look at that field." She stared at contempt at the moonlit disrupted rows, literally bringing to light the task that still lay ahead. "Tomorrow we will slave again to ready the rows. Do you think we can finish it in a day?"

"I shall help with the rows until they are finished, and then…then I must depart."

"No!" she replied, without realizing the words had slipped from her mouth.

"British ships come with supplies, and I must protect them from the scourge of pirates that plague the waters."

"But *you're* a pirate!"

"Aye," he said, stopping to gaze into her eyes. "I am a pirate for the good of the colony; I protect the bay."

"Will you return?"

"If you wish it so."

"…if I…" *enough!* the man was exasperating! "Captain Strongbow, could we not play this game."

"I beg your pardon?"

"As much a gentleman as you are, I can't go on and on with these little looks and innuendoes that go nowhere. I live in a different century; you don't have to be so…so proper and dignified where I come from. Well—yes, nice and mannerly—but you take it beyond the beyond. What happened to the strong and forceful man from the Thunder? What happened to that guy?" She stopped her tirade, embarrassed; but at least she had expressed her feelings—in a 21st century sort of way. She felt kind of silly in the silence that followed. He looked flustered in the moonlight, and she was immediately horrified that she had ruined her chance.

"I...I was raised to be a gentleman in the presence of ladies."

"And I appreciate that fact. But...I can't tell what your feelings are for me, or if you have any for me at all."

He was silent a moment, and she wondered if she had been too forward for this century. *Have I ruined it?*

But then, she was taken aback when he gripped her shoulders and held her firmly between his strong hands "I *am* the very same man of the Thunder. Because I don't throw myself upon you does not mean I do not harbor feelings. I have lusted—yes, lusted—for you since you first appeared so mysteriously upon my ship. If 'tis me you want, you must speak the words. Pride in my conduct forbids me to act aggressively and selfishly toward you." Then, contrary to the very words he spoke, he kissed her. He kissed her hard, and with passion, and when he let her go, she stood back, consumed by said passion, and so much so that she could barely speak the words.

"I want you," she whispered. "I want you badly."

For the first time in her life, she was literally swept off her feet. No sooner had she whispered the words, than she was whisked into his arms and carried into the forest. He set her down next to a red cedar, and there he kissed her again, her back against the tree. She was faintly aware of the bark biting at her neck—but only faintly. His arms circled her waist, and they were on their knees, then she on her back, then her skirts lifted, then the weight of him upon her...in her...then....

The moon was higher now. She watched it, and its bright companion. Venus? she wondered. So appropriate, if so. Goddess of Love. Oh, how she was smitten! The captain lay beside her on the fallen leaves. The ground felt hard and sharp, broken branches stabbing her entire backside, part of which was exposed. She pulled her skirt down as he leaned toward her, resting on an elbow. "Am I man enough? Am I what you desire?"

She reached to run her fingers along his cheek, his beard, his shoulder. "That, and much, much more. Please don't think me a slut."

"No, do not think such a thing. I do not think of thee in such a way." He traced a finger around her face. "The moonlight becomes thee."

"And you as well, captain," she said, pulling him to her. "I love the way you say 'thee'.

The nightly 'strolls', as she and the captain referred to their passionate unions, came to an unwanted end when the tobacco rows were finally plucked of the old plants. The captain gathered his few belongings and bid goodbye. "When you are ready to sail again, Cupid, I shall be waiting."

"Soon, cap'n. Now I help wid da tabacco."

Cassandra followed him to the shore of the bay where a small flat-bottomed boat waited, beached and secured by a rope tied to a tree. "Where is your ship?" she asked, thinking that his ship should be moored off shore.

"It remains at the island with the crew."

"You've come far to help us. Having been at the island myself, I can't imagine what they've done for entertainment."

"Ha! At best their entertainment has been hunting for game, and bartering with the natives to supply the ship for our departure."

"Be safe, Captain. Please come back to me."

He gathered her to him; she never wanted to let him go.

"'Tis I who fear you shall disappear, just as magically as you came to me. I beg you, be here when I return." One final prolonged, passionate kiss, and he pushed the dugout off shore.

"What is the name of your ship?" she called out.

"I have christened it *Spirit of the Bay*," he yelled. "'Tis in honor of a beautiful woman, a spirit who appeared from another world!"

Her heart swelled at his words, and she walked toward the cabin, inflated, in one way, to think that he had named a ship in her honor, but deflated that he had gone.

It was early yet, and Lucy was outside stoking the oven for the morning meal of biscuits and gruel. "He gone now? He come back, you see."

Cassandra sighed. Lucy seemed to know what was in her heart, while Izzie did nothing but torment. She entered the cabin to prepare for the breakfast.

"And were ye spreadin' your legs for the cap'n at the sad goodbye?" Izzie sat at the table fingering a small sack.

"You're disgusting," Cassandra said, stirring the pot of gruel. "Why do you insist on being so vile?"

Izzie ignored the question and concentrated on the sack that sat before her. "The tobacco seeds, they are so small. 'Tis me fear they will blow away. We shall plant today, even without Eagle, the blasted savage. He should have returned by this time."

"Where's Phineas?"

"Soon's the cap'n was out of sight, 'e took 'is spade and set off to search for the silver, thief that he is. He shall not leave this place but over me corpse, should he find it while we toil in the field. I shall kill 'im first."

"No doubt," Cassandra replied, for surely the woman was capable of murder. "I hope you know how to plant the seeds," she said, changing the subject.

"Cap'n told me as much as he knows hisself, but 'twould help to have the savage here."

205

By the time they ate their breakfast and reached the field, Eagle was waiting for them. Cassandra thought that perhaps Eagle was the *Spirit of the Bay* and not she; his abrupt appearance ran shivers up her spine.

"Well, blimey, would ye look at that, the savage, hisself!"

"Always here when you need him."

Greetings aside, Eagle instructed the method of planting the seeds. With the captain gone, Phineas off to discover the silver, and Lucy watching Free and Kole, it was down to the four of them; Cassandra, Izzie, Cupid and Eagle.

As the day wore on, Cassandra felt that something was amiss. Throughout the morning, she noticed that Eagle seemed edgy, and continuously looked about into the forest, or appeared to be listening—for what? She didn't know, but was concerned. He was a mystery at best, but the way he stopped to look and listen put her on edge.

At noon, Lucy brought corncakes and watered rum. Little Free ran at her skirts, while Kole was slung on her back in a papoose type blanket arrangement. It was one of the many times Cassandra wished she had a camera. From where she sat on the side of the field, it was a sight worth—at the very least—a painting; Free running toward them on her chubby legs, a big smile, and full of delightful shrieks of joy reaching their ears. Lucy had wrapped her own kinky hair into a kerchief she had cut and sewn from a flour sack. It matched the dull white of the skirt and blouse she had fashioned with the quickly depleting supply of fabrics they had obtained from the tobacco trade. A red sash defined her waist, its tails hanging brightly as kite tails. Kole bounced along in his papoose, his black hair sharply contrasted against a blue sky. A wave of sheer contentment passed through Cassandra as the trio approached. She could not remember a feeling such as this, except, of course, in her liaison with Captain Strongbow.

While they ate, Cassandra kept an eye on Eagle, who skirted the edge of the forest before he would accept a corncake for himself. "Did you notice that Eagle seems on edge today? He's giving me the willies the way he keeps looking into the woods."

"Perhaps he looks for Phineas?"

"I don't think so. Why wouldn't he ask, then?"

"He look for somptin," Cupid said, rising. "I go talk," he said, and walked away toward the Indian.

"Perhaps he knows of the silver?" Izzie shot to her feet. "He'll not be havin' me share!"

"Relax, Izzie. Sit down. Phineas is probably on a wild goose chase looking for silver that doesn't exist."

"If it do, 'tis mine. 'Tis me land."

Cassandra rolled her eyes. She seriously doubted there was a hidden treasure on the property, and Izzie could not expect her to dig along with Phineas. As soon as the seeds were planted, she knew Izzie would head out in search of the treasure herself.

Eagle finally returned for his corncake, Cupid in tow, but his eyes continued to peruse the perimeter of the open land.

"What do you look for, Eagle?" Cassandra finally asked.

His reply was a 'grunt' as he consumed his corn cake in two bites.

"You're making me nervous, the way you poke your head into the woods. If there's something we need to worry about, you'd better let us know."

"Where Phinis?" he asked, without answering her question.

"Did I not tell you?" Izzie looked to Cassandra. "He is lookin' for Phineas, because he knows what a cloying bastard he is, and knows what he's lookin' for."

"Phineas is in the woods hunting." Cassandra answered.

"Umph." It was all Eagle said, and Cassandra knew that there was no sense in pushing him for more information, for his staunch and quiet stature alone spoke a very strong language.

Throughout the next day, Cassandra watched as Eagle continued to peruse the forest as they worked. "He's not searching for Phineas. I tell you, something is wrong, and I feel like we're in danger."

"'Tis me in danger of losing me fortune if Phineas finds it."

The following day, as they completed the planting, Eagle was preparing to leave, when Phineas stumbled from the woods, yelling incoherently.

"Look!" Izzie exclaimed. "The fool has found the silver! He'll not be takin' me share," she grumbled, and raced off toward Phineas, her shift gripped tightly in her fists. Suddenly, she stopped short, frozen in place. Phineas had fallen to the ground, face down.

Eagle shot into action. "Go!" he yelled, waving toward the cabin. "Go, now!"

"What is it?" Cassandra was covered in gooseflesh. "What's wrong? What's happened to Phineas?"

"Go!" Eagle commanded.

"I stay," Cupid said.

"You go. I come back. Go!"

Izzie flew past the trio, screaming as she went. "Do what the savage says! Phineas has arrows in his back!"

"Oh, my God…let's hurry!"

At that moment, what looked like an entire tribe of wild, half-naked, painted, screaming men sprang from the woods—some jumping over Phineas' still body as if he were nothing but a log in the way—and all raced toward their homestead.

Whooping and hollering they came, some shaking tomahawks while others shot endless streams of arrows that screamed past Cassandra's ears as she ran. All the while, she prayed her legs to move faster. *Don't fall! Don't fall!* She knew a horrid death awaited her if she did—*or am I already dead?* Her thoughts flew in microseconds across her mind while her body felt as if it moved in slow motion, the cabin appearing further and further away; and yet she ran toward it like lightening. It was all the women could do to reach the cabin door alive—and they did—but of what use was the flimsy door with a tribe of crazed savages running at them?

The women shrieked with terror when Cupid and Eagle crashed through the door, nearly knocking it off its hinges; but relief was short lived. They had little, if any, protection.

"Don' let 'em in!' screamed Lucy, clutching Free in her arms. "Da baby, Miz Izzie! Git da baby!" Both Free and Kole were hollering from the commotion, but there was no time to comfort them.

Cupid loaded the gun he had stolen from the planter so long ago, and braced it on the open window sill.

"One shot isn't going to do anything!" Cassandra yelled.

"No!" Lucy cried. Miz Izzie, he takin' da baby!" Eagle had plucked the screaming, red-faced Kole from his cradle and headed for the door.

"What are you doing?" Cassandra barred the door with her body.

"Give me the babe!" Izzie screamed, tugging on the child's arm.

"He takin' Kole!" Lucy yelled.

The cabin was a cacophony of maddening voices of panic and anger as Eagle pushed Cupid, Cassandra and Izzie from his way. The door flew open, and he stood outside holding the squealing Kole up over his head like an offering to God. The baby's brown arms and legs flayed madly from his high perch; his black hair spiked against the bright sky as he screeched his belligerence to the world.

Eagle yelled a string of words that the cabin dwellers did not understand. One string after another, he yelled, braving the few arrows that flew about him. Then, it all stopped; the arrows, the yelping, the sounds of massacre. It all stopped as the Indians stood staring at one of their own—*two* of their own,—and then, a miracle; they turned, whooping again as they disappeared into the forest.

For a good minute, silence covered the cabin. Lucy plunked into a chair and comforted Free. Cupid rested his head against a wall, the pistol dangling in his hand. Izzie had fallen to her knees. "Thank ye, Lord." She said, crossing herself.

Cassandra, still shaking in raw fear, stood outside next to Eagle, who handed her the baby. The entire grounds were covered in arrows—hundreds of them. Tears of relief filled her eyes.

"Thank you, Eagle." She whispered, for her breath still trembled in her throat. I don't know what you said to them, but you've saved us. I don't know how….but thank you."

"They no come back," he said, and trotted off toward the forest.

Chapter 21

upid was the first to reach Phineas, and the rest followed, knowing they could not leave the gruesome task to him alone. Lucy stood back, Kole in her arms, with Free hanging tightly to her skirt.

"He didn't deserve this end," Cassandra said, "Even if he *was* a scoundrel."

Izzie stood speechless— until Cupid knelt to the task of pulling the arrows from Phineas's back. "Oh, fie!" she said, turning away.

Cassandra and Lucy followed suit, as Cupid tugged on the stubborn weapons. "'Tis done," he said at last, and the women turned again in time to see Cupid flip Phineas onto his back.

"Oh, God," Cassandra shielded her eyes from those of Phineas, who laid eyes wide open, staring in horror.

"Look!" Izzie was down on the corpse like a buzzard. She pried open the fingers of his right hand, which had been tightly closed as if he held something too precious to drop during his frantic attempt of escape. Once open, Izzie gasped, for there, lying in the palm of his hand, were two Spanish silver coins. "'Tis here!" she exclaimed. "Did I not tell ye? 'Tis here!" She grabbed the two coins, turning them repeatedly in her hands.

"Pieces of eight," Cupid said, bending over to examine the coins, then reaching as if to pick one up.

Izzie quickly moved her hands away. "'Tis me land, 'tis me silver," she growled.

Cupid stood back and looked into the forest from which Phineas had met his demise. "More for da takin' in der."

"None of ye will 'ave me silver!" Izzie growled. "Hear me words, for they do not lie."

"The secret is out, Izzie. Finders, keepers. Cupid has just as much right as...."

"I'll 'ear none of it. 'Tis mine, and mine alone!"

"Don't you think you owe Cupid something for all the work he's done to keep us in comfort?"

Izzie's face scrunched into a ball of meanness. Her eyes narrowed, her eyebrows furrowed until they nearly touched. With her lips pursed, as if she were deep in concentration of an evil plan, she swooshed past her companions, past Kole, who reached a small hand out to his mother. She ignored him and headed straight toward the cabin.

"Where are you going?" Cassandra called out. "We still have to bury Phineas. Have some respect!"

But Izzie didn't stop. Instead, she continued toward the cabin. "Let 'im rot!" she yelled.

The next they saw of Izzie, Cupid was sweating over the digging of Phinehas's grave, which was to be near the same area in which he fell—far enough away from the cabin in case the forest animals should be attracted to the decaying body. As they didn't have enough supplies to spare a cloth with which to wrap his body, Phineas still lay where he fell and it would be a dirt grave for the poor soul. Izzie did not stop to pay her regards, but passed the freshly dug hole and continued into the woods, spade in hand.

"Who goin' feed da baby?" Lucy asked. Kole was already hollering for his mother's milk.

"You'd be turned into Social Services in my time. What a poor excuse of a mother you are. Kole has been screaming for hours, and what are you doing? Nothing that pertains to good sense or motherhood! I'd turn you in myself, if I could. And, oh boy, do I wish I could."

Dirty and disheveled, Izzie had come through the door at near dark. She took the screaming baby from Cassandra's arms and sat at the table to feed him.

"So? Where's the silver? Where are the riches that you're so willing to starve your own child for?"

"I shall not be tellin' none o'ye, for certain."

"Ha, I'll bet you didn't even find it, did you? Nope. You can't even answer."

Once Kole was asleep and in his cradle, Izzie ladled the remaining bit of stew onto her trencher and sat again at the table while Cupid snored lightly on his pallet against the wall. Lucy was either sleeping or laying quietly, listening. None could tell, but it was a wonder any of them could sleep through the commotion of Izzie's return.

Cassandra, too fired up from her tirade, sat at the table across from her. "I suppose tomorrow you'll be heading out on your goose chase again? What about Kole?"

"I shall feed the little savage first. Does that set right by your ladyship?"

"In my time, women have plastic bottles with rubber nipples. They pump the milk from their breasts into the bottles and put them in the refrigerator. That way, they don't have to always be on call."

"If you sayeth I need not be here to feed the child—I know of such things."

"Do you? Do you have baby bottles in this time?"

"We are not such buffle-headed fools, as ye think." Izzie went to the fireplace to take a pewter tankard off the mantel, returned to her chair, pulled a breast from her blouse and squeezed milk into the tankard. "Ye shall see who is the buffle-headed fool now, for ye have not thought to make a nursery cup."

"I suppose you think Kole is going to wrap his lips on that tankard and drink?"

"Make haste and bring me one and eight barleycorns[32] o'linen from Lucy's cradle."

"Barleycorns? What the devil are barleycorns?"

"Who is the buffle-headed one that knows not barleycorns? Eyes on me fingers, now," Izzie ordered. She set the tankard on the table and held her hands forward and apart. "This measure," she said, one naked breast hanging from out her blouse.

Cassandra did her bidding and cut a piece of fabric approximately six inches long with their pair of antiquated scissors. "Here," she said, setting it on the table. Izzie had by now switched to her other breast, attempting to fill the tankard. "The little savage has sucked me dry. Me teats are done till the morrow." She straightened her blouse and stood. "I shall feed him in the morn, then Lucy shall soak the linen in this milk and set it in the savage's mouth. His sucking should comfort him 'til my return. Lucy can make a watery gruel, or panada[33]. Tell 'er."

"Gruel...I don't know what the other is."

"When I find the silver—and mark me words, it shall be found—the cap'n'll sail me across the waters to the place he says I must give me request for more land. 'Twill be set then, done proper. Then we shall barter with the heathens to make more fields for the tobacco."

"*We*? Are you actually including us?"

"It cannot be done by one alone."

---

[32] *Barleycorns:* three barleycorns to an inch. 'Old Weights and Measures.'

[33] *Panada:* A 17th century breast milk substitute made with soaked bread in water

"Then you will have to pay us, Izzie. *Like I have a place to spend it?* We are not your slaves."

"I shall pay."

"In silver; *all* of us."

"Lucy is a slave. She receives no pay; she does me bidding."

"There are no slaves in the Americas in my time."

"Hmph. '*My time, my time,*' Izzie mimicked. "Blarney! 'Tis not *your* time, 'tis *my* time."

"You're exasperating."

"I'm off to bed. The morrow cometh early."

Cassandra snuffed the candles, thinking how odd it was to live by candlelight. Candles and oil lamps were a necessity if a person was to see anything in the darkness of night. Their candle supply was running low, which was of concern; but then, the others were ready for sleep when the sun set, and she should follow suit. *But I would be out to dinner with Bill at the club, or a restaurant where candles are lit for ambiance, not necessity!*

She removed her skirt, and lay on her mattress of branches and leaves stuffed beneath a rough linen cover. *How odd, she thought, that I have become accustomed to this life. That I can lie on this lumpy, poking mattress and be comfortable. That I can eat gruel, work in fields, plant tobacco—that I can love a man who has been dead many centuries!*

She wondered when he'd return. She rarely thought about Bill anymore. In fact, in comparison to Cupid and the Captain, Bill appeared as useless and shallow a person as she would ever hope to meet or associate with in her own time—*if* she should ever return. That thought brought a surprising pain to her heart, that she should leave this place. Perhaps life in the 21st century was not as good as she previously thought? Here was a life without tampons, toilet paper—or toilets! No choice of shampoos, perfumes, or clothing. No cars, television, newscasters, weathermen, computers, movie streaming, or cell phones. The list was exhausting to think about! A shocking revelation, but what began as a nightmare was now a life she found comfort in—despite Izzie's foul disposition. *And, of course, without any more Indian attacks!*

She didn't have to wait long for the return of the captain. The very next day, while she and Lucy were gathering oysters along the shore, a ship bearing full sail approached.

"looky dat!" Lucy exclaimed.

"I wonder if that's the captain's ship?"

"Meybe," Lucy said, her eyes shooting to Free who had fixated on plucking snails from the muddy edge of the incoming tide.

"Let's hope it is, or else I don't know why it's headed this way."

Eventually it dropped anchor, and the women watched as a small boat was lowered into the bay.

"Dey's comin'. Do ye tink 'tis pirates?"

"I don't know." Cassandra shaded her eyes from the sun. "They can't get too many people in that little dingy."

Lucy brushed the snails from Free's hand. "I go tell Cupid."

Shortly, Cupid arrived, pistol in hand, with Lucy and Free standing back at the edge of the forest.

Cassandra was quite nervous to see strangers approach, but with Cupid beside her as the boat came closer into view, she saw two men rowing, and one…no, two…*women!* She looked again to the rowers, and her heart thudded when she recognized Captain Strongbow. "He's come!" she said aloud. "It's the captain!"

Her patience wore thin, as it seemed an endless time before the small boat was close enough for her to yell out. "Captain!" she shouted, waving. He broke his rowing to wave back, and her heart leapt with joy.

When finally the boat could approach no further in the shallows of the bay, the captain and sailor jumped out and beached the craft.

Ignoring the others, Cassandra raced to the captain. "You're back!" she said, patting her hands against his chest as if to determine whether he really was standing solidly before her, or was a ghost—which he was—but still, she was beyond happy; he was solid, *and he's here!*

The captain reciprocated by wrapping an arm around her waist. "I cannot express my relief that you are still here, and safe, but we shall speak later." He turned to the sailor. "The trunk," he said. The sailor and Cupid lifted it from the boat, setting it on the ground. "You may go, Jack," and the sailor pushed off, rowing toward the ship.

"I believe you are acquainted with Goodwife Staples? The Susquehannock have slaughtered up and down the bay. Her husband was murdered—savagely," the captain whispered this to her ear. "She would not stay at the settlement, for it is in complete ruin, so many are dead."

Cassandra focused on the silent, young woman, and was shocked to recognize—just barely—Arabella Staples, and in such disarray! The neat and tidy woman who had befriended her on the island, now stood before her in a tattered and dirty bodice and skirt, with wisps of hair straying in wild abandon from what must have been, at one time, a very precisely orchestrated coiffure. Arabella seemed not to recognize her, for she made no reply to the introduction, stared blankly ahead, and approached the captain to link her arm through his.

"She is fearful to leave my side."

The other woman, the stranger, cleared her throat, gaining the captain's attention. "And may I introduce Goodwife Highgrove from England. She comes in search of her husband, Master Highgrove, but has been informed of his demise."

Cassandra's eyes shifted—no, *shot*—to Goodwife Highgrove, who now dabbed at her eyes with a lace-edged handkerchief at the mention of her husband, but managed to give a slight nod of the head. "Madam," she said.

In contrast to Arabella Staples, this woman wore clothing that was not torn and dirty. A fine, darkly dyed linen skirt had gathered water at its hem from the incoming tide, but aside from that temporary flaw, she was quite well dressed, a woman of some means. Beneath the water-stained hem peaked leather shoes of no distinction, being that only an inch or two showed. Her jacket was finely embroidered in various colors depicting vines, flowers and birds. It sported long sleeves, and over that draped an elbow-length linen cape tied at the throat with a large linen bow, the same color as the skirt. Atop her head sat a wide-brimmed hat of felt to shade her pale skin from the sun.

"Yes, Goodwife Highgrove," said the captain. "There was a skirmish with pirates that approached Goodwife Highgrove's ship as it sailed toward St. Mary's, but she was safely transported to the *Spirit of the Bay* upon the knowledge that her husband's grant sits upon the eastern shore, and I am familiar with the grant. Safety is an issue on both shores, however more so on the west, presently; so, I have brought Goodwife Highgrove here—at her request—to pay respects to her husband, and to secure her property."

Cassandra felt dizzy. Thoughts spun chaos in her head. She read perfectly well the underlying messages in the captain's commentary...*Izzie is caught in a serious lie.*

"Izzie is searching in the woods," She blurted, and then realized that it was a nonsensical comment. *Izzie! How will she wriggle herself out of this one?* Cassandra's heart thumped in trepidation. For a moment, she felt sorry for Izzie, wondering what would come from this shocking revelation—and what would become of them?

She attempted to still her shock. "Greetings, Goodwife Highgrove. Welcome to...to...Highgrove Chase." The woman nodded again in response, while continuing to dab invisible tears from her eyes—none that Cassandra could see.

"And, this is Lucy, and Free. Come here, Lucy." Lucy approached cautiously, Free in tow. She gave a brief curtsy in respect, and received nothing from the woman but a indiscernible tip of the head. "And, this is Cupid." Again, the woman barely acknowledged Cupid—barely looked at him— leaving Cassandra embarrassed at the snub of her friends, but trying to keep her temper in check; this was, after all, a different place in time with different social acceptability.

"'Tis to these fellow settlers that gratitude must be bestowed," the captain said, perhaps feeling Cassandra's tension. "...for they hath remained on Highgrove Chase to secure Master Highgrove's grant."

Good explanation, captain.

The woman did not comment.

"Please accept our heartfelt condolences on the death of your husband," Cassandra said, *and may you trip on a log.* "Now, come to our humble dwelling, as I'm sure you are aware that your husband's house was severely damaged. The captain and Cupid have repaired it the best they could, so that we would have a place to live." *And where there is no place for the likes of you.*

"Miz Izzie not goin' like dis," Lucy whispered as they walked behind Cupid, who struggled along with Goodwife Highgrove's trunk. The captain, with Arabella Staples still hooked to his arm, and Goodwife Highgrove presumably feigning grief, strode several yards ahead.

"Where we goin' put dem?" Lucy asked.

"Where we goin' put *dis*?" Cupid asked, his legs bowed with the weight of the trunk.

"Where dey goin' sleep?" Lucy was full of questions, as this was a very perplexing situation; conditions were tight in the cabin with five pallets and a cradle already taking up wall space.

Cassandra had no answers; she was thinking only of finding Izzie and warning her of the *real* Mrs. Goodwife's arrival. *What a mess!*

Chapter 22

Chaos! Goodwife Highgrove was, as expected, completely disgusted with the bedding accommodations—and everything in general. "You cannot expect me to sleep on…on *that*!" she said, scrunching her face in disgust at the captain's cot, which was always kept available for his use.

"Perhaps you would prefer the outdoors? Cupid and the captain will sleep under the stars, but if you wish…."

Goodwife Highgrove exhaled loudly, "Oh, I shall make do."

Cassandra left Lucy with the task of settling the Goodwife in, and approached the captain and Cupid who were now constructing pallets for their own use. Arabella stood nearby like a statue, silent, staring blankly.

"This is one heck of a mess," Cassandra said. "I'm going to find Izzie and warn her before she returns, or all hell will break loose. Even if I do warn her, there will *still* be hell to pay; she won't take this lightly."

The captain stood and wiped his brow, as he had been hunched over holding two long cuts of wood for Cupid to assemble into a bedframe

"How long will Arabella be here?" Cassandra asked, glancing at the nonresponsive woman.

"I know not. Where shall she go?"

This probably registered with Arabella, because she moved silently as a cat next to the captain, hooking her arm through his. He gave Cassandra a beseeching look, and shrugged. "I know not what to do, for she is fearful."

Cassandra approached the young woman. "Arabella, do you remember me, Cassandra? We're friends. We won't hurt you here. Would you like to come in the cabin and sit? You can play with the baby. There are two of them, now." Arabella's response was to tighten her grip on the captain's arm.

Cassandra sighed and stepped back. "Well, I guess it will take some time. Um, speaking of time, perhaps you and I can take one of our walks this evening?" She raised her eyebrows questioningly.

"I shall be more than delighted," he said, and her stomach did a somersault at the twinkle in his eyes.

A chill ran down her spine as she entered the forest. At first, she stared into the thick wall of brambles interspersed with the tall trees of red cedar and sweet gum, wondering where she should start; but then her memories of the Indian camp sprang to mind; *look for breaks in the brush, look for a deer path.* And there, off to the left, she spotted what was surely the path that Izzie had taken.

She followed said path, thin branches swooshing and cracking as she passed though. She looked closely for any diversion, any breaks that could represent a change in direction, and found none. The path led straight to a small clearing where she stood a moment remembering the magical moment—a moment so long ago in the beginning of this journey—when Izzie twirled in a circle of filtered, golden sunlight in a clearing such as this. It was such a contrast to the person she knew, but maybe—just *maybe*—that golden spirit of the forest lived within the rakish heart of Izzie Pratt.

"Now what?" she said aloud, snapping to the present. She sighed. She really needed to find Izzie. At least the knowledge of the arrival of Goodwife Highgrove *before* arrival to the cabin might help diffuse Izzie's fiery temper. "Izzie!" she called. Her voice reaching hollow and strange into the surrounding brush and trees. "Izzie! I have important information!"

She walked to the center of the clearing and turned a slow circle, all the while calling for Izzie, her eyes scanning for another path. "Answer me, Izzie! We must talk!" She thought she saw a break and squinted, her chin jutting forward as if it would bring a path so much closer into view.

"Pray tell, for what will you wake the dead with yer hollerin'?"

Cassandra spun around, searching for the face attached to the voice.

"'Tis Kole? Hath he fevers?"

"Where are you? Come out. Let me see you!"

She came from behind, stepping into the clearing holding a wooden chest to her breast. "'Tis Kole?"

"No, it isn't Kole." Cassandra was surprised that she even thought of the baby. "You aren't going to like this though. Consider this fair warning...." Curiosity got the best of her. "What do have there? It looks heavy. Is that....?"

"What think ye?" Izzie grinned, the gaps in her teeth seeming almost comical. "'Tis the treasure," she whispered. "Here in me arms is the future! 'Twill be no more grovelin' for the likes o' Izzie Pratt. Nay, for here in me arms is true Spanish silver." She grappled with the lid and struggled to turn the chest toward Cassandra. "Look!"

Cassandra moved forward. Her jaw dropped; it really *was* there in Izzie's arms! Phineas didn't lie after all! "You did it, Izzie! You found the treasure...." Then, a question of rightful ownership came to mind. Did the treasure belong to Izzie? Were they standing on Highgrove land? Certainly, it rightfully belonged to

Goodwife Highgrove in the first place. Perhaps they were outside the property boundaries? She put those thoughts aside for later.

"Listen, Izzie, close the chest, I have something to tell you. The captain is back, and he's brought two passengers. One is Arabella Staples from the island. Remember? She played with Free on the beach when we were there. The Indians attacked and killed lots of people, including her husband. The other passenger is…well, the other is…Highgrove's true widow."

Now it was Izzie's jaw that dropped. "Nah," she said. 'Taint so! 'Tis *me*, the widow of John Highgrove!"

"The captain told her we were watching over the property, keeping it safe. Don't lose your head; we'll think of something…something to get us out of this mess."

Izzie was quiet a moment. Her eyes narrowed and stared straight ahead; she hugged the chest tighter. "She an't gettin' the silver. She an't, ye 'ear me?"

"Put it back for now, wherever you found it. I don't need to know, if it makes you feel better. You must come with me."

"Perhaps the savages are in the woods watching? Perhaps they wait to steal the treasure!" Izzie frantically looked about, her eyes wide and wild. "What shall I do?"

"I don't think they know about the silver. Find a new place then. You can't walk to the cabin with a box of Spanish silver in your arms."

Cassandra waited while Izzie returned to the place from which she had slipped from the clearing, and returned empty handed. "We must rid ourselves of the imposter!" she said, as they trudged back along the deer path, single file.

Cassandra could do nothing but roll her eyes. "Izzie, *you* are the imposter!"

"O're me dead body. We shall rid ourselves of the woman."

"Get your head on straight," Cassandra scolded. "The only way we rid ourselves of the woman is to put her on the captain's ship. Only then, he'll take her across the bay to St. Mary's and the truth will be out. A thief—or thieves, meaning us all—will be arrested for sure. If I recall anything from history, justice is served swiftly and gruesomely in this century."

"Ah, 'tis a woman of righteous answers and history, 'twould toss aside our land—our toil—so easily. 'Tis no issue for me to cut the woman's throat in the night."

"Stop it!" Cassandra said, and then they were out of the forest. Ahead, across the tobacco field sat the cabin, smoke trailing upward from the chimney. Lucy was by the outdoor oven perhaps baking biscuits "You could at least pay your respects to Phineas while we're here. After all, you may not have found the coins without him."

Izzie stood at the foot of the mound of dirt that marked his grave. "Thanks be to ye, Phineas, for 'avin' the sense to bring me two silver coins as the savages shot arrows at your broad backside. Me heart is ever grateful. Thank ye, Phineas." She turned to Cassandra. "Does that satisfy thy righteous heart?"

Cassandra shook her head, disgusted. "You are the most vulgar, insincere and selfish woman I have ever met. Oh, and let me add *merciless,* willing to kill a woman you haven't even met yet, the *true* widow Highgrove, whom *you* happen to be impersonating." Enough said, and fuming, Cassandra walked off toward the cabin, Izzie's voice following from behind.

"Mark me words, I shall not leave this land; 'tis mine! The silver 'tis mine! With the coins I shall have more land and live in a house of comfort!"

Lucy, who was pacing back and forth in front of the cabin door, approached Cassandra with despair in her eyes, Free at her skirts and Kole in her arms. "Miz Cassie, dis in't goin' do," she said. "An't no mo' room for no mo' people."

"What's up?" Cassandra asked, as if everything weren't topsy-turvy already.

"Cupid, da cap'n, dat woman dat say notin', and dat bad woman, deys all in dere. An't no room for nobody. I goin' cook, but an't no room fo' cookin'...an't...." Lucy began to cry.

Cassandra took Kole from her arms. "I know, Lucy. This is a very bad situation. *And it's about to get worse when Izzie returns.* She sighed. She wanted to cry herself, but instead, hugged Kole. He tangled his chubby fingers into her hair, laid his head on her chest and sucked his thumb. *So sweet, this boy.*

Lucy didn't lie. The inside of the cabin was a jumble of pallets and people. The captain and Cupid were arranging a layer of boughs and leaves upon the crisscrosses of rope from foot to head and side to side of the new pallet frame. These created a support for a mattress—but there was no mattress, just the tree boughs. Cassandra groaned. "I hate to say it, but that doesn't look too comfortable."

"The woman hath not ears to hear, nor tongue to speak; surely she shall not notice discomfort." Goodwife Highgrove sat like a fat, ruffled hen at the table watching the melee, while Arabella sat across from her, quiet as a mouse, not responding a bit to the widow's comment.

Cassandra took a seat as well, in order to subtly prepare the widow for Izzie's entrance. "Goodwife Highgrove," she began. "Izzie Pratt will be returning shortly, and I...I feel I should prepare...." Too late, Izzie pushed open the door and stood a moment perusing the scene.

"Aha! 'Tis come to me attention that the cap'n has returned—with passengers—and here ye be, all a'clutter in our wee home." She closed the door and strode the short distance to the table.

Cassandra swallowed hard. "Yes, Izzie. You remember Arabella? And this is Goodwife Highgrove, widow of John Highgrove."

"Madam," Izzie said, bowing slightly. "'Tis me pleasure to know the woman from across the great sea, the woman who coddled Master John and sent him to the wild land of the Americas to meet his death amongst the savages."

All eyes turned to Izzie at this remark, as if there was not another thing in the room of any interest—and there certainly wasn't. Cassandra, quite horrified, shifted her view to the widow who appeared quite stunned for a moment, her eyes boring into Izzie, who remained standing before her at the table.

"I beg your pardon?"

"Did ye not send the miscreant[34] here? I am baffled!

---

[34] Miscreant: A lewd, wicked fellow. *The First Dictionary of Slang, 1699.*'

"I can assure you that Master Highgrove took it upon his own conscience to secure a place in this new land. 'Tis not thy business at any matter."

"Oh, but 'tis, for there in the arms of Mistress Pratt, is me child, and Highgrove's heir."

The widow looked to Kole, who now slept peacefully in Cassandra's arms. "Surely this is a farce! That...that child is a heathen... how dare you suggest that Master Highgrove produced a heathen bastard; preposterous!" She looked about at the stunned faces that watched this intercourse. "The woman is mad, can ye not see? Why, look, 'tis a heathen child and yet this woman (pointing to Izzie) proclaims it to be a child of my husband. Why, she has not the smallest measure of savage blood; 'Tis bad enough that she is of the Irish, but she hath produced a heathen."

Izzie ignored the protest. "Do ya 'ave issue across the sea? Do ya 'ave children to claim this land?"

"I hath not *heathen* issue." She now stood eye to eye with Izzie. "I hath not fornicated with savages. That is *not* the child of my husband. All eyes can see that naught but lies spill from the witch's tongue!"

"Izzie!" The captain now came to his senses. "I brought the Goodwife here as our guest. As widow of Master Highgrove and Mistress of this plantation. I beseech ye to mind thy tongue!" By the tone of his voice, it was not a request, but an order.

"Ha! See how ye look at me," Izzie said, her eyes moving from the captain, to Cupid, to Lucy, to Cassandra, and then to Goodwife Highgrove. "Look how ye've turned against me!"

"Izzie...we haven't turn...." Cassandra started, but Izzie was gone, out the door in a swish of red hot anger.

Goodwife Highgrove spoke first. "The woman is an imposter, Captain. I insist you take me to St. Mary's in the morrow, where I shall report her false claim. This is my husband's plantation, and that...that savage shall not make claim to what is rightfully mine."

Amen. Cassandra felt somewhat relieved that the cat was out of the bag; Izzie's identity theft and insatiable desire to become a person of importance and wealth, had backfired.

Jocelyn Miller

Chapter 23

Izzie did not return by sunset. Cassandra imagined she had returned to the chest of silver, and there pondered the situation for which she had placed herself in, and for which she felt no support.

Cassandra and the captain embarked on their planned liaisons at this time of evening, but even more important and necessary than their liaison in the woods (for which Cassandra felt the highest degree of impending passion) was the outcome of Goodwife Highgrove's intentions of relaying Izzie's false claim of the child to Governor Calvert's council.

"Do you think they know of Izzie as Highgrove's widow, across the bay? Will anything happen to her? I mean…she hasn't really caused any harm, just lied."

"I have discouraged Goodwife Highgrove from a journey to St. Mary's in the morrow. The uprising of the tribes has created more death and destruction—to what extent, I know not—but 'tis far too dangerous. Surely, the men across the waters must contend with the burials of their dead and the repair of damages."

"Why do they massacre when there is so much trading going on?"

The captain stopped in his tracks. "Do ye not know? We have come from the land across the sea to steal their lands, their food, their pride. We have come to rule over them, when they know not masters."

"Of course," she replied, feeling totally stupid. Of course she knew that, but somehow being here was different than reading it in a book. Here, the Indians traded; furs and corn for beads and trinkets, for fabrics, for advanced weaponry that they did not possess. It somehow seemed fair to Cassandra; it was commerce.

"We take their bounty, and give lies as promises."

"Eagle saved us, you know. We would all be dead now if it weren't for Eagle. I finally found out how he saved us; he told the marauding tribesmen that Kole was his child, and they left."

"Look!" the captain said, pointing to a trail of smoke emerging from the treetops deep within the forest.

"It's Izzie! I know it is, and I know where she is, and just as I thought. We should get her and bring her home."

"She hath made a fire. Perhaps she shall sleep in the forest tonight."

"We can't just leave her there."

"Perhaps 'tis best that she keep a distance from the Goodwife Highgrove this night."

"On second thought, perhaps we should keep a distance from Izzie's camp—for privacy, you know?" She smiled at the captain, desire running hot through her veins. "I wouldn't want her ruining our time together. After all, she can be a sneaky little mouse."

He took her hand, and they both looked toward the cabin to make sure none were watching. The sun had now set, and twilight prevailed. All appeared quiet at the home front as they slipped into the woods.

Once hidden away in the impending darkness, they settled onto their knees facing one another as he unlaced her waistcoat, and untied the linen strings that closed her shift, setting her breasts free. Her heart thumped wildly as her excitement grew with the new freedom. She relished his touch. She relished the fact that as proper and dignified as he was at all other times, his masculinity and desire were overpowering in these moments—*their* moments to take pleasure in each other, to relieve themselves of the toil and stress of surviving the harshness of their existence, of the conflicts that now lay before them; of the uncertainty of the future. If she were to disappear at this moment back to the 21st century, she would feel her true life was over.

If she had ever wondered what lovemaking was like in the seventeenth century, she was not disappointed; it was better with this man. This man was undoubtedly a *true* man, a man of the common kind who were unwritten and unnamed in history, one who was not possessed by the ever-changing, ever pressing technology of the 21st century, but a man who was in tune with his surroundings, a survivor of incredible hazards, a builder of civilizations, a pioneer in a new land—a pioneer with only basic tools, the knowledge of his predecessors, and two strong hands which now held her in heated passion. Most of all, he was a man sensitive to the plight of others, as displayed in his concern for the Indians, and in the wellbeing of their own little band of misfits.

They approached the cabin, satiated. Each time they lay together on the forest floor, the passion and pleasure increased. Each time, they bemoaned the fact of enduring the long daylight hours until they lay together again. *It isn't just sex, it's something more.* Cassandra sometimes worried that it was only lust the captain felt for her. He had mentioned the lust he felt in the beginning of their relationship; but then, when he said endearing remarks, or brushed against her during the day, or witnessed the way he watched her while she worked, she felt certain he loved her as much as she loved him.

Darkness overcame twilight, and Cassandra knew already that Kole was hungry, alerted by the shrieking coming from the other side of the front door as they neared the cabin. "How can Izzie do this to him? She's the last person on earth to be a mother." She was disgusted, not only with Izzie, but with herself for forgetting about the baby in her own lust for the captain.

"Miz Izzie not here, and po' Kole need his feedin'." Lucy was obviously at her wit's end. Kole squirmed in her arms, attempting to stick his little fists into his mouth, then aimed for Lucy's breasts. "Dat woman...." Lucy nodded toward Goodwife Highgrove, who sat at the table drumming her fingers. "Dat woman won' hold da babe so's I can make pap, or find Miz Izzie. Cupid gone lookin'."

"I shall not touch the little savage," Goodwife Highgrove adamantly replied while swatting Free's hand from her skirt. "Can you not control this negar child of yours? I do not want her filthy hands on me."

"Free!" Lucy called, and Kole shrieked even louder.

Cassandra's face grew red in anger. "Pardon me, Goodwife Highgrove, but in this house we do not abuse the children. If anything is filthy, it's your behavior."

Goodwife Highgrove shot to her feet. "Captain, please remove my pallet from this shamble and place it out of doors. How shall I sleep with the savage screaming? Nor could I rest within the same walls as his wanton mother...nor this impertinent woman who defends a negar child."

"Forgive me, Goodwife," the captain said. "I cannot remove the pallet as it hath been set and furnished with the bolster[35]. 'Tis best ye settle within the walls for safety." He spoke these words loudly, as it was quite a feat to be heard over Kole's screaming. "I shall search with Cupid," he said, leaving the women to a woman's dilemma.

Lucy handed the baby to Cassandra. "Sit, Miz Cassie. I make pap," she said, and busied herself preparing a mixture of bread and water. When it was mushed into a watery paste, she pulled a chair next to Cassandra's, and dipped a spoon into the mixture. "Hol' da babe."

---

[35] Bolster: Mattress

Kole wriggled and squirmed in Cassandra's arms, spitting out the first mouthful of mixture. It dribbled down his chin and onto his dress, but Lucy dipped the spoon again, and brought it to his mouth. "Eat, little babe. You wan grow big an' strong."

This time Kole smacked the mixture in his gums, his little legs kicking in excitement. "Lookie dat!" Lucy exclaimed. "He goin' eat!"

Spoonful after spoonful, he took the paste, smacking his gums and reaching for more. When at last he was full, Cassandra wiped his mouth with a rag and he fell asleep in her arms.

Arabella, having sat as a statue, surprised all by reaching across the table to touch him, but her reach fell short. "Sweet," she whispered to everyone's amazement.

"The mute woman speaks," Goodwife Highgrove said. She had watched the entire feeding process with contempt, and now her eyes turned to Arabella. "She hath not said a word from the time I first set eyes on her."

"She had quite a shock, Widow." Then, "Arabella, look at me." Cassandra was quite excited at the new gesture. "You spoke! Talk to us...please, we're your friends." But Arabella withdrew her hand and bent her head as if in prayer.

The door flew open smacking the wall with a loud *thud*. Kole woke with violent jerk, but settled quickly back into sleep. Izzie stood before them highlighted in the glow of the fireplace, a life-sized cutout against the black of night. Fire flickered in her eyes. "Ye filthy turncoats. I have come for me babe; I shall feed him now."

"Shush," Cassandra said. "He's finally asleep, no thanks to you. You left him to starve."

Of course Izzie could not reply. After all, she had left the cabin in anger, without a thought to the child and his hunger.

"Humph!" the widow said. "They hath fed your little savage, and at last I may uncover my ears from his screaming."

"I warn ye, do not call Master Highgrove's son a savage." The tone of Izzie's voice was frightening.

"He et pap, Miz Izzie."

"And *who* is the turncoat? Why thee, of course!" the Widow Highgrove said, now standing face to face with Izzie. "A woman who cares not for her own child—who leaves it to starve—is the turncoat; she turns against her own blood, savage that it is."

Izzie lunged for the woman's throat, wrapped her fingers around the widow's neck, pushing her backward onto the table. "Do not call the child a savage!" she growled, her face twisted into a sinister knot.

"Stop!" Cassandra yelled, standing quickly, her chair falling to the dirt. "Cupid! Captain!." She rapidly set Kole into his cradle.

Cassandra raced to the widow's aid, trying to pull Izzie (who was strong as a bull in this endeavor) from the woman; but Izzie's grip was too strong, her hands clenched around the widow's throat tightening like a vise. Cassandra pounded on her back. "Stop! You're in enough trouble already!" she screamed. "Where's the captain, for God's sake?" Lucy also tried to pull Izzie off the woman, and they finally succeeded. The widow stood, gasping, her hands clutched at her throat as she tried to catch her breath. Her eyes looked as if they would pop out of their sockets.

"Listen to me," Cassandra said, her hands gripped on either of Izzie's arms. "You will not take the baby from here, and you will not attack this woman again!"

Izzie shook loose from her grip, and Cassandra stood trembling in horror of what nearly happened. When the captain and Cupid arrived in haste, apparently having heard the commotion, she plopped her hands on her hips, and raised her eyebrows questioningly. "And just what in hell were you doing? Izzie damn near killed the widow!"

Izzie flew past the group and out the door. Cassandra followed, not about to let her return to the wilderness and leave poor Kole to scream in hunger again. "Wait a minute," she called, as Izzie walked a fast pace ahead. The night was black, but musically highlighted by an incredibly loud chorus of spring peepers; so loud, in fact, that Cassandra cried out again for fear Izzie couldn't hear her call over the cacophony of noise from the marshlands. "Izzie, stop!"

"Leave me be," Izzie said, facing Cassandra.

"Where do you think you're going? You can't just up and leave Kole without giving consideration to his hunger. We had a devil of.... Are you crying?" Even in the darkness, she witnessed a quick move of hand—a move to wipe away tears.

"What matter is it to ye?"

"For one, I didn't know you *could* cry."

"There is much ye don't know of Izzie Pratt."

"Izzie, you have to face the music. That woman is the rightful owner of Highgrove Chase. You can't kill her; it's out of the question. You have the silver, so why don't we move on? Perhaps we could head north to the island. The captain could take us...yes.... I have an idea. Perhaps you could buy land, your *own* legal land across the bay."

"Ha! Across the bay with them *tantivy-boise?*[36] Nay, not Izzie Pratt. I'll not 'ave those *fat culls*[37] and their busybody wives watchin' over me business."

"You're exasperating."

"'Tis me land, 'ere, where we worked our fingers to the bone plantin' tobacco. Me heart is 'ere. 'Taint no use poundin' me 'ead with fanciful ideas. Go ye to the other side, if 'tis thy desire, but 'ere I stay."

"And the widow? You tried to kill her, and you think she will let you stay? You can't be trusted!"

"Then I shall 'ave the land next over, the land across the clearin' where the treasure lay. I shall befriend the heathens, and they shall clear the forest, and I shall plant me tobacco. I 'ave me dreams."

"You have it all worked out, Plan B. And shouldn't you purchase the land from the Indians—or however it's done? It *is* theirs, you know. What makes you think they'll even want to help you?"

---

[36] *Tantivy-boise:* High flown church men in opposition to the modern church men. 'The first dictionary of Slang 1699'.

[37] *Fat culls:* rich fellows. 'The First Dictionary of Slang 1699'.

"Silver coin, and a heathen babe," she replied.

Chapter 24

"The big negar man, surely he shall stay?" The widow Highgrove was in a dither. Izzie had returned to her pallet in the crowded cabin the night before, turning her face to the wall, Kole beside her in his cradle. In the morning, Izzie announced that she was moving and taking everyone with her.

"Even the *mum-chance*[38]?" the widow asked, nodding to Arabella.

"Even she."

"'Tis glad I am that you hath come to your senses, considering 'tis not proper for a fine lady as myself to house with a common whore and her heathen child."

Cassandra tensed, waiting for another violent episode, but, fortunately, it did not come to pass. Izzie stood by the fireplace, chin up, her arms crossed over her chest. She appeared calm, but for certain her blood boiled at the remark. Lucy, who had stopped stirring the morning gruel at the widow's comment, returned her concentration to the morning meal. The pot now bubbled and

---

[38] *Mum-chance:* One that sits Mute. *The First Dictionary of Slang 1699.*

popped, which gave Cassandra a flash of dread as she was certain this was how Izzie felt at moment.

The widow approached the fireplace. "You shall need a survey of such property and present it to Governor Calvert for approval. For if it infringes upon my property, then it shall not be legal."

"And pray tell where is the survey for Highgrove Chase?"

"In my trunk."

"May we see it, Widow Highgrove?" Cassandra asked. *Now we're getting somewhere.* She went to the door to search for the captain, as it would be beneficial to have his input. What did she know about surveys? The captain and Cupid were nowhere to be seen, so she turned and studied the interior of the cabin and its inhabitants as she waited for the survey papers.

All women, *all women in the wilderness.* It struck her then how strong they were to survive the hazards that had befallen them: the shipwreck, the Indian villages, the trek through the wilderness, the planting of tobacco, and the Indian attack. *We are strong!* Even the widow Highgrove, who had crossed the ocean and survived a pirate attack—and now had to battle Izzie Pratt— was strong, too. Izzie, Lucy, little Free, and herself, were all women who had to survive together, to work together, to live together. She could not include the widow in that last thought, considering her attitude. It then occurred to her that perhaps Izzie had viewed *her* in the same way at their first meeting.

Lucy removed the bubbling pot from its hook, while the widow ruffled through her trunk. "Eat," she said, setting the pot on the table; but all continued what they were busy at, which was mainly standing still, waiting, except for Free, who left Kole's cradle and scurried to a chair. "Hungy," she said, wriggling in her seat, impatient for her mother to bring a trencher and spoon.

Lucy brought all the trenchers and spoons in their possession to the table, crossed her arms and looked from one frozen face to the next; Izzie stood near the fireplace, unsmiling; Widow Highgrove was bent over the trunk mumbling to herself.

Cassandra flashed a smile. "What would we do without you, Lucy?"

"Ah, here 'tis." The widow brought two rolled documents and set them on the table, seating herself across from Free. She unrolled a document. "This is the patent, as you can see. 'Twas sent by my husband."

She handed it to Izzie, sat beside her (and surely begrudgingly on both parts). Izzie barely spent a moment on the document since she couldn't read, and handed it to Cassandra, who was so confused by the handwriting and spelling of the words, she could barely make it out. "This is difficult for me to read," she said. "It's a shame it isn't at least typed. I'm not used to this kind of writing."

"Two idiots who cannot read...." The widow snatched the document from Cassandra's hands. "You do speak strangely. From where do you come?"

"Baltimore."

"I know only of Lord Baltimore. Where doth it sit?"

"Across the bay."

"Hmph," the widow replied. "I know it not."

"Perhaps it, uh, isn't there yet?"

"Pardon?"

"Oh, never mind." *Does Baltimore even exist in this time period?* No one seemed to recognize the name as a city. Baltimore was always there; it was her birthplace and her parents' before her. *If it doesn't exist, I don't exist...but of course I don't exist in 1644!* She quickly removed herself from *that* existential thought process; it was far too confusing!

The widow took up a scroll and read aloud. "From the tall notched cedar northwest, to the tall notched cedar northeast, 50 chains. From the tall notched cedar northeast, 50 chains to the notched cedar southeast. From the southeast notched cedar, 50 chains to the southwest notched cedar. Therefore, 50 chains to join the tall notched cedar northwest." She set the scroll on the table. "A square enclosure of *my* (she glanced at Izzie), Highgrove Chase."

"Chains? Oh, my God." Cassandra rested her head in her hands. "What the heck does 'chains' mean, and where are the men? Why are they never here when they're needed?"

"*Measuring* chains," Izzie chided, directing her comment to Cassandra.

Cassandra slapped the table. "Okay, let's go see if we can find the notched trees."

"We stay," Lucy said, indicating Free and Kole.

Cassandra, Izzie, and Izzie's nemesis, the Widow Highgrove, strode to the north end of the clearing. Cassandra blushed as they passed the spot of entry where she and the captain had conducted their passionate liaison the night before; the memory made her tingle.

Having arrived at the designated spot, Cassandra stared blankly into the forest. "This is a needle in a haystack! What does the notch look like? Anyone know?"

No one answered but continued scrutinizing every near tree, a tedious task considering there was a forest of them. Finally, Izzie shrieked with excitement. "Here ''tis! Come!"

Both Cassandra and the widow hurried their pace to view a manmade, deeply notched, six-inch long cut into a thick trunked tree that sat right at the edge of the forest. It was wide enough and deep enough to be recognizable. Cassandra copied the notch to memory. "This should make it much easier."

"This way!" Izzie was very excited now. She traversed the clearing from northwest to northeast in long strides, causing Cassandra and the widow to lag behind. Upon reaching the easterly outer edge of the clearing, Izzie was the first to spot the second notch. "'Tis here!" she yelled.

"This is like a scavenger hunt," Cassandra said, feeling Izzie's excitement at discovery.

Judging by her huffing and puffing as she trudged along, the widow was feeling the quick pace of the search. She stopped to rest a moment, and Cassandra stopped as well. Izzie raced onward past the outer side of the cabin, past the tobacco field, and straight toward Phineas' grave.

"It appears that this entire clearing may encompass Highgrove Chase," Cassandra said, for indeed, the first two notched trees ran parallel across the northern edge of the forest, and it appeared that the third tree would prove the supposition.

"'Twould make it simple, would it not?" the widow replied, pulling a hankie from her sleeve to dab her wet forehead, for the sun had risen and with it, the impending heat of day.

"'Twould," Cassandra said, rolling the unfamiliar word over her tongue.

Instead of following the clearing toward Izzie, they cut diagonally across the expanse, as Izzie was already pointing to the third tree. She yelled excitedly, but they could not hear her words. She waited patiently at the tree, then vividly came to life as they approached. "'Tis it! 'Twill be all of it, a square! The clearin' is Highgrove Chase. I shall take the land where the forest begins at Phineas' grave."

"Settled then," the widow said.

The evening meal encompassed a meeting of the minds regarding the abandonment of Highgrove Chase by Izzie and her crew. This was to take place as soon as land could be staked out and a deal struck with the Indians.

"If the Indians are at camp, I shall purchase the land."

"*If* they agree." Cassandra reminded.

"They shall." Izzie raised her eyebrows, defiantly.

I know you have the silver, but you don't know if they'll agree to a bargain. Of course she couldn't speak these words aloud, for the silver remained a secret; but still, would the Indians bargain? Would they agree to more hunting lands taken out from under them?

"Stake the land, Izzie, get approval from the weroance, and I shall sail ye and the widow across the bay to St. Mary's." the captain said.

"Of course," the widow replied. "I shall not stay in this place without comfort. I shall need a grand house built, and servants

servants to work the tobacco. I shall need more land, for more tobacco...." She eyed Izzie across the table. "Perhaps I should procure land beyond your Phineas' grave...."

Izzie slammed a fist on the table, to which all jumped an inch, including baby Kole in Lucy's arms. "Ye'll not procure a *barley corn* of me land, fat sow!" she yelled.

"'Tis not thy land as yet." The widow replied, loudly.

"Ladies, stop!" Cassandra pounded her own fist on the table and stood. "Must you continue this argument at the dinner table? Sit down and shut up!"

The widow glared at Cassandra. "Do not speak to me in such a tone!"

"All sit!" the captain ordered. "We shall eat our meal without agitation. Widow Highgrove and Izzie may discuss their differences afterward."

"And outside," Cassandra interjected. "Thank you, Captain," she said, touching his knee with her own beneath the table, for they sat side by side. She felt the warm touch of his hand as it caressed her thigh, thus sending a shock of tingles through her body. *Later.* She could not wait.

With the meal done, Izzie sat in a chair by the fire to nurse Kole, while Cassandra and Lucy cleared the table. Arabella—who had not said a peep since her remark about the baby—along with the widow, remained at the table, where the captain and widow perused the documents removed from the trunk. Baby Free ran circles around the table in a spurt of energy, giggling and screeching as Cupid lurched toward her each time she passed him at the table.

The widow shuddered at the high-pitched shrieks of joy coming from the little girl. "Please hush the negar child!" she yelled, apparently having reached her apex of tolerance. Kole, who managed to sleep through Free's expressions of joy, jerked awake in Izzie's arms at the sound of the widow's voice and let out a screech of his own.

"Now ye done it!" Izzie yelled, her face reflecting the dancing flames of the fire. "Now ye woke him!"

"'Twasn't I, but the screaming negar girl," The widow said, matter-of-factly.

Exasperated, Izzie stood and paced the fireplace, babe in arms. "If he in't goin' to sleep, then I shall pass 'im to you to slumber."

"I wouldn't touch the savage," came the reply.

"Did I not tell ye 'tis heir to Highgrove Chase? Did I not warn ye to not call this babe a savage?"

"Izzie…." Cassandra said. "Cool it. He'll go back to sleep."

The room stilled. Free sat on Cupid's lap sucking her thumb. The captain and the widow continued perusing the scrolls. Cassandra and Lucy washed the trenchers and utensils in a bucket of water.

It took Cassandra quite a while to adjust to her new non-sterile environment. The dirty bucket of dishwater always disgusted her and made her homesick for running tap water, dish soap and a dishwasher. When finished with the trenchers and utensils, the bucket would need to be carried outside and dumped. In the morning and afternoon, she and Lucy would take two buckets to the freshwater pond and fill up again for the day's use; one for washing, one for drinking. It was a tedious errand, day in and day out, lugging heavy buckets of water, but it was a necessity. It surprised and pleased her that none (especially she) had not come down with an intestinal disorder, a quite unpleasant experience for those who lived in a world without toilet paper or proper medication.

When the cabin door creaked open, breaking the pause of silence, Arabella and the widow shrieked in terror. Chairs flew backward as they stood. Arabella ran to a darkened corner, a high-pitched, ear-shattering scream spewing from her previously silent self. The widow clutched at the captain's arm and practically climbed onto his lap, but fell to the dirt floor as he shook her off and stood, firearm ready, and then relaxed.

"Greetings, Eagle," the captain spoke loudly, his voice rising over the shrieks of the women. He lowered his weapon. "You gave us a fright."

Izzie lowered the fireplace poker she had grabbed in haste. "Holy Mother of God," she whispered. "Can ye not knock?"

Cassandra's heart thumped wildly in her chest. "Thank God, it's just Eagle!" Everyone quieted except for Arabella, who appeared to melt into the darkness of the corner, wailing.

"Come in," the captain said. "Sit."

"That heathen shall not sit here!" the widow said, dusting off her large behind.

"Sit, Eagle," the captain repeated, then turned to the widow. "Eagle is of great importance to this plantation. He hath knowledge of tobacco, and therefore is an asset that you must treat with respect."

You tell her, captain, Cassandra wanted to say. All were getting quite tired of the widow's constant nagging and complaining.

"Just the man I want to see!" Izzie exclaimed.

The widow dragged her chair closer to the captain. Eagle was a frightening sight to those unaccustomed to parlaying with the tribes. As he strode across the room to the table, it was obvious that here was a very tall and physically powerful man. His legs looked as pillars of granite; muscles rippled from thigh to ankle as he strode, his breech clout shifting softly with each step. The widow gasped at the sight of his bare buttocks as he passed, but with a buttock so muscular, rounded and firm, none could help but stare.

Down the center of his skull, ran a full spike of hair. Bald on either side, the spike ran from forehead to back of crown, at which point it was gathered into a braid that ran to the middle of his bare back. The braid played host to a melee of decorative ornaments, such as bones, beads and shells. A spray of various feathers stood at the crown, secured with a tie of beaded hide, while the foot of a large bird, such as a hawk, or eagle, was threaded through his right ear, its claws fanning against his cheek; he was all decked out, as Cassandra noted, right down to the wide bracelet of copper banding each of his thick wrists, as well as a necklace of wampum and copper medallions. Slung over his shoulder was a woven quiver hosting feather-topped arrows for use with the long bow he carried in one hand.

"Trouble come," he said in his matter-of-fact voice as he sat.

Cassandra's eyes grew round at this news; they didn't need more trouble. Nobody did. Up and down the bay, the settlers were burying their dead and rebuilding.

"More ship come," he continued. "More people come, make trouble."

"What kind of trouble?" the widow asked, but not to Eagle directly. "Ask him, Captain. What kind of trouble?"

"Who wiraohawh[39] crenepo?" Eagle asked.

"Noungasse Highgrove," the captain replied.

"Hmph." Eagle's eyes bore into the widow, causing her to shuffle in her seat. "Why doth he stare?"

"Sizing you up, most likely. He does that to people." Cassandra said, well remembering his staring eyes during the dugout trip to the island. It now seemed years ago, just as her previous life had faded into memory. "Like," he had said then, in reference to herself. She wondered if he still felt the same?

"Hair face come, take land. No hunt. No food. People have hunger."

Cassandra looked at Izzie, who had excitedly sat beside Eagle. But after his explanation of the 'trouble', her brow furrowed, her eyes squinted, and her lower lip popped forward. It was the 'deep in thought' look that Cassandra knew so well. "Perhaps this is not a good time to ask Eagle if...."

---

[39] *Wiraohawh:*Algonquin for 'fat'. *wiraohawh crenepo:* fat woman.

Algonquin language collected by William Strachey

"How would ye be knowin' what I would ask Eagle?" Izzie cut her off, her face morphing back to normal.

Cassandra raised her brows. "Because I know you by now, that's why; and I know what you want—land."

Eagle waited patiently for this short outburst to conclude before continuing. "Tribes angry. See more ship come."

"Oh, well. That is all? 'Tis to my advantage that more ships come. I shall hire indentured servants for the plantation," the widow piped in.

"Are you deaf, Widow?" Cassandra watched the woman's face for any sign of empathy. "Eagle just said that the Indians are unhappy with more people arriving. The Indians are starving. It's obvious that you have no clue what this land is really like. Unhappy Indians mean death and destruction, in case you haven't figured that out yet. Eagle saved us from one attack, but who knows if he can save us again, should there be another attack."

"Nonsense! Do we not trade with the heathens? Do we not bring the word of God?"

"The word of God does not feed the Indians, Widow." The captain now spoke. "Hunting and fishing feeds the Indians. Their villages and gardens feed the Indians. We hath brought naught but disease and hunger."

All eyes fell to the widow, Izzie's included; but for her it was mostly likely not concern for the disappearing lands of the natives, but for concocting a plan to acquire the land adjoining Highgrove Chance—without starting an Indian war.

"I go," Eagle said, rising, and just as he arrived, he left, silently—with Izzie trailing at his feet. Cassandra followed, curious to hear how she would handle asking Eagle's help in procuring land from the Indians, when he had just explained how angry the natives were regarding their loss of property.

"Eagle, me good friend!" Izzie called, rushing to keep up with his wide strides. He stopped and waited, looming over her as she approached, and looking quite the wild man in his attire; *wild but beautiful,* Cassandra thought.

She watched from a distance, not catching every word Izzie said, but here and there she caught a word or two and was able to put it all together. Knowing Izzie's determination, she knew what the conversation was about anyway. It was a one-sided conversation, as Eagle, in the polite way of the native, stood patiently waiting while she gesticulated and spoke. When finished, he remained silent. Then, with a jerk of the bow in his hand, Cassandra heard loud and clear his answer. 'No!' he said, and walked off toward the forest.

Izzie looked after him a moment, stamped her foot, and turned to see Cassandra watching. "Are ye me shadow, now?"

"You and the widow, you don't listen and you don't understand. Worst of all, you don't care!'

"Care for what? The savages? Ha, and why should I be carin'? Are they carin' for Izzie Pratt? Are they carin' for the departed souls what blood they spilt hither and yon? I 'ave me good silver to give the savages, and I 'ave me heathen babe. Kole is sure to be me foot into the longhouse, aye?"

"For your information, you still need a grant from the Governor, whether the Indians are with you or against you."

"I shall 'ave me grant." She swooshed past Cassandra and headed for the cabin.

"You don't speak the language, so who's going with you to barter with the Indians since Eagle won't go?"

"Who else but the cap'n?" she replied over her shoulder.

Chapter 25

Izzie straightened her shoulders, stuck out her chin and followed Captain Strongbow through the palisade gate into the Indian village. She had promised him to never, *ever* request more land from the Nanticoke Nation if he would just, this once, be her translator. He reluctantly complied.

Cassandra followed behind Izzie as they entered the compound. As with Long Feather's village, the roundhouses and gardens were neatly spaced. The village center firepit, a gathering place for celebrations and storytelling, was not so different than the 21st century. Hadn't she sipped wine and sat with friends at the fire pits in backyards in her other life? Hadn't she sipped the Indian grog, sat at the fire pits at the Indian camps watching ceremonial dances?

Memories of Long Feather flooded her mind as they were greeted by the villagers, and she wondered what had occurred after she left him—after he realized she was gone? *Did he search?* Had he missed her? She imagined Otter had been furious at the disappearance of her treasured pouch.

As in previous times, women and children followed the trio, chattering excitedly in their own language. As always, Izzie's red hair was a topic of conversation; but more so was the papoose she insisted on Cupid creating for her to carry upon her back, Indian style, with Kole as the charm. He bobbed along, his shock of straight black hair and darker skin was an obvious draw of attention; for what was this native child doing on the back of the red-headed woman?

That question was answered through Captain Strongbow when the *weroance, Ahshowcutteis*,[40] of this particular section of the Nanticoke Nation, rose from his seat in the longhouse to examine the child, who now fidgeted on Izzie's lap. He directed a question to the captain, who answered in the native tongue. Izzie had already given the captain instructions on the explanation that was to be given; "Tell 'im I had the pleasure of a sava...uh, *native* man, as 'usband for a wee bit o' time." Cassandra could only roll her eyes at the tangled web of lies Izzie spun as she forged her way through life.

"Tell 'im I 'ave me a bag o' silver to give 'im for the land." She jangled the pouch she had created from a piece of traded fabric. "'Tis all his."

"He asks of the blue-eyed one." The captain looked slightly alarmed as he relayed this to Cassandra. "He tells me the *weroance Meqwanoc's* blue-eyed wife had vanished from his village, and he wondered if you were she." He then turned to the *weroance* and spoke more words in the native tongue.

"What did you tell him?" Cassandra tried to keep the fear from her voice; she could never return to Long Feather!

"I told him you are my wife."

"I hope he believed you."

"What sayeth he of the land?" Izzie asked, impatiently.

"He doth think on it. 'Tis more hunting grounds gone, should he comply."

"Tell 'im 'e is free to hunt on the land, but not the clearin', for that is where we shall plant the tobacco. Tell 'im I shall trade more silver for savage workers."

---

[40] *Ashshowcutteis:* Cardinal. Algonquin language collected by William Strachey

The *weroance* looked suspiciously at Izzie and said a few words.

"He sayeth the white faces tell lies and break promises," the captain relayed.

Izzie stood, a move that briefly startled the *weroance*. He subtly moved his hand onto the tomahawk handle that lay beside him. Izzie did not flinch, but held Kole outward. "Tell 'im I 'ave a child of his people, and I do not break me word." Kole squiggled at this disrespect of dangling in the air, and let out a holler. Cassandra swore she witnessed the *weroance* stifle a smile.

Izzie's strong display worked. It was agreed. The *weroance* would come in a fortnight for the staking of the land. Should he agree, Izzie would hand him the bag of silver.

"'Tis mine! 'Tis mine!" Izzie jumped about the inside of the cabin, kicking up so much dirt that everyone had to move to the outside until the dirt settled. The *weroance* had come that day, to see the land she had staked out as her desired property. Perhaps her requested land had not been as large as he originally thought it would be, or perhaps it was the existence of Kole that unknowingly persuaded him; but he agreed to the exchange, and the bag of silver changed hands. Another bag of silver changed hands for the promise of workers to come.

"It's not quite yours, yet." Cassandra said. "Let me remind you that you still need a patent from Lord Calvert before it's official; that will be your only legal proof."

"I know 'tis mine, patent or none. 'Tis me destiny."

"Ha!" the widow laughed. "Thy destiny is naught but whoredom and poverty."

"And thy destiny is to be the fat sow what stands a'fore us!" Izzie quipped. "I shall be with ye when we cross the bay, and ye'll see that I 'ave me patent on the return."

"I care not what you do, but do not tread on what is mine."

The group reentered the cabin once the dirt settled, except for Cupid and the captain, who crossed to the woodpile to gather more wood for the fire. Free jumped ahead, always the sprite. Lucy carried Kole, while the widow huffed proudly forward through the threshold, elbowing Izzie out of her way to enter first. Cassandra watched this abrupt and rude move as she edged Arabella through the doorway. Surely Izzie would blow, for her fuse was short— and especially when it came to the widow.

"Give me the babe, Lucy," Izzie ordered, momentarily ignoring the widow's insult. She sat at the table, exposed a breast, smirking and staring at the widow, who sat across from her against the fire. Kole latched to the nipple quickly.

The widow exhaled in disgust. "I shall be glad to leave this heathen hole of common women, and ye shall be gone at my return." she said.

"And a good riddance to ye, fat sow," Izzie was quick to reply.

"What joy it shall be to not lay eyes on the common whore and her savage babe...*and* the negars." she added. "They belong in the barn with their own kind."

"Lucy!" Izzie yelled, and Lucy quickly scrambled to her side to take Kole from her arms. He hollered in protest to be pulled so abruptly from his meal.

Oh, oh...."Please, Widow Highgrove...." Cassandra began, but her voice was diminished by another outbreak from the widow.

"The child should be drowned in the river! 'Tis a sin against God to fornicate with a heathen, and yet ye have no shame, but coddle the child!" Both women stood, their insults flying across the table at one another.

Izzie's face grew as red as her hair. Kole, robbed of his meal and sensing the tension in the air, wailed in anger.

"I cannot bear another moment of this woman and her bastard. If ye have no courage to do the deed, I shall!" The widow moved toward Lucy, who looked pleadingly at Izzie, hugging the baby even tighter.

"Give me the heathen!" the widow demanded.

Cassandra stepped to intervene. Izzie rounded the table in a second flat, but before she could reach the woman, Arabella, who had previously sat as stone, slipped as quick as lightning to move between them.

It was chaos. The air was so full of choking dust from the scuffling of feet, that visibility had diminished dramatically. In the midst of this melee of tempers gone awry, the widow gave one piercing cry before falling to her knees, then onto her face. A final cloud of dust rose from her prone body.

Time stopped still as all looked to the floor, stunned. It happened so quickly that none could have guessed that the silent Arabella, apparently feeling the danger to Kole, took the scissors from Lucy's basket and stabbed the woman in the back, the deadly shears protruding grotesquely between the widow's shoulders, from which blood now seeped darkly onto her beautifully embroidered waistcoat.

"Mother of God!" Izzie made the sign of the cross. "She's kilt the woman!"

For a moment, Cassandra's eyes met Arabella's. "What have you done?"

"She thought to hurt the babe," Arabella answered, as if it were a simple event that needed no further explanation.

Izzie gave the widow a swift kick to make sure the woman was dead. "Ha! The mum-chance hath saved me the effort!"

"Have some respect!" Cassandra ordered.

"The woman was naught but a thorn in me side."

Cassandra looked to Lucy, but she, Kole and Free were gone—as was Arabella.

Within seconds, the captain entered the cabin, obviously having run, for his breath was shallow. Lucy and her charges followed behind.

"Mistress Staples hath run into the forest," the captain said. "Cupid shall find her and…." His eyes fell to the widow lying on the floor, her face to one side, staring blankly. The captain straightened his back, his face stern "What hath occurred here?" he asked gruffly, looking to Izzie for an answer.

"'Twasn't I," she said. "Though I cannot say twas a sad event."

"It wasn't Izzie, Captain, it was Arabella."

"What reason would the young woman have to kill the widow?" he demanded.

Lucy stepped forward, Kole still in her arms. "She goin' drown da babe, cap'n. She comin' at me like da debil!"

"'Tis the truth?" he asked of Cassandra.

"She said she was going to drown Kole in the river; and as she came at Lucy to take the baby, Arabella must have grabbed Lucy's scissors from her sewing basket and stabbed the woman. The widow fell where she lay." She shuddered. Lucy's scissors were long and sharp.

"And a good marksman she is!" Izzie's elation was growing. "The widow is gone, and 'tis me land once more."

"We must bury the woman, and I shall have to take Arabella across the bay, where she shall have judgement put upon her."

"No! You can't do that, Captain. Arabella is not in her right mind, she was protecting Kohl!"

"'Tis the proper thing to do, and 'tis up to the court to decide her punishment."

"What will they do to her, then?"

"She may be hung, if found guilty of murder. 'Tis what is done for the crime. Perhaps she shall have a lesser judgement."

"No! She's not guilty of anything, and I will not let you take her; she is not in her right mind."

"Do not disobey the laws of this land!"

Cassandra stood back, surprised that the captain could say such a thing to her, and in such a tone of voice! This was the captain, *her* captain, her love;, and yet he admonished her for wanting to save her friend from the gallows. "You can't talk to me in that tone!"

A surprised look spread across the captain's face. "Woman," he said. "I am bound by the laws of this land. Murder is a punishable crime and 'tis my duty to deliver such persons for judgment and punishment."

"And my duty is to protect the innocent from injustice!" *Since when? When did I become so righteous?* She nearly didn't recognize herself, and could not believe she was yelling at the man she professed to love—but perhaps this was not a period in time in which she could accept such harsh judgment and laws for one like Arabella Staples, who was mentally incapable of making good decisions? "You're a pirate, for God's sake," she yelled. "You sure don't act like one!"

"I am in the service to this colony! I protect the bay from all intruders, I do not protect criminals."

"Oh, you certainly pulled the wool over my eyes, *Captain* Jonathan Strongbow. I thought you had a conscience—a heart."

"Quiet ye down!" Izzie yelled. "Can we not get the widow to her grave? 'Tis a ghastly sight, the fat sow lying dead at our feet."

A far sight far worse than the body of Widow Highgrove laying in the dirt was the removal of the scissors from her back. During this operation, the women removed themselves and the children from the cabin, to stand outside like a bunch of nervous hens. Cassandra observed that Free did not seem at all fazed by the excitement of Arabella's act and the mayhem that ensued; but then, she was still young. Indians, starvation, slaughter, it was all part of her new world. Free and Kole would grow up understanding the dangers. *A rough land for children, and now we have murder to contend with, and murder by one of our own!*

"She gone." Cupid's appearance startled the women, for they did not hear or see him approach. Izzie, normally fearless, jumped at the sound of his voice; everyone's nerves were on edge

. "Cupid, ye cannot surprise a person in such a manner, or we shall 'ave more than the widow's grave to tend to this night!"

"She gone. 'Tis dark , and she make no sound."

"Just what we need, a murder and a missing mute," *and a disagreement between me and my lover.* Cassandra was totally exasperated, not to mention exhausted. "What a mess," she mumbled.

The morning dawned with frigid chill between Cassandra and the captain. She had not spoken to him after their final parlay of words the night before. All attention was put to the burying of the widow. The captain and Cupid dug her grave beside her departed husband.

"Twas da las' cloth." Lucy moaned, having to relinquish her last piece of fabric..

"The cap'n is wantin' to wrap the fat sow before the buryin'—as if she would know otherwise. Poor Phineas 'ad no cloth."

"He feels it's the proper thing to do, Izzie."

"Ha, because of her fancy station? Were I to die, wouldst ye wrap me body in the last piece of cloth? Am I not o' equal standin' on this earth? Nay, 'twould be the dirt for me, and no cloth to keep it from me mouth."

"We could pull your skirt up to cover your face," Cassandra said, slyly.

Izzie shot her a nasty look. "Hold they tongue, and let us be off to bury the witch and be done with it."

Chapter 26

Izzie stood proud as punch at the edge of the clearing. "Did I not tell ye I would 'ave me land one day? I shall 'ave more, and more, and more, for here 'tis not where Izzie Pratt ends her journey."

"You're very sure of yourself. I've got to hand it to you, pursuing your dreams the way you do, by hook—or by crook."

"Éist do bhéal[41]*!* The sow is dead and the land 'tis mine; and the rightful heir, Kole Highgrove."

Cassandra shook her head. "How the devil will you pass Kole off as the son of Highgrove, when he looks the way he does? Do you think the settlers are blind fools?"

"They need not see the babe."

"*'Oh, what tangled webs we weave '*[42].... Izzie, it won't work." Your lie will catch up to you. True, they don't know you across the bay, but they've seen you at the island professing to be the Widow Highgrove, and Kole wasn't born at that time. If they see him now,

---

[41] *Éist do bhéal:"* Gaelic for 'shut your mouth'.

[42] *"Oh, what tangled webs we weave:"* From Alfred Lord Tennyson's poem, "Marmion".

they'll have caught you in a terrible lie, and who knows what the punishment is for that? Hopefully, not the same as for Arabella— should the captain ever find her." *Arabella.* The night she disappeared into the woods, was the last they saw of her, despite Cupid and the Captain's desperate search, a search that went on for a week until they had to give up.

Izzie fell silent, perhaps thinking over the thought of punishment for the crime of confiscating another's land by a trail of lies; at least that's what Cassandra hoped she was thinking.

"Ye are but a damper to me spirit," Izzie replied, and turned to look again at her new property. "But, look! Look how they work, the savages."

To Cassandra's surprise, it was the Indian women who appeared to clear the land, that day. As she perused the clearing, she noticed that much had already been removed, and wondered how they could have worked so fast. She also felt somewhat guilty, watching them lug heavy branches from the clearing to deposit them into the woods at the spot Izzie had designated. Some women carried babies on their backs, now and again stopping to breast feed. Kole would have blended in perfectly.

"The savage men sit on their arses while the women work," Izzie said as they traveled back through the woods until they came to Phineas' grave. "See how the tobacco grows!"

Several yards ahead lay the tobacco field, and indeed it *had* grown—chillingly so. Cassandra did a double take; *it wasn't like that earlier when we passed by. It wasn't this hot, either.* She felt dizzy with confusion.

"Where is thy tongue, woman? Is it not beautiful?"

"Yes...yes, it's beautiful. It's growing fast." Her head was spinning; time had moved forward again, and in such a short span! Sweat dripped from her forehead in the oppressive humidity. *Think...think...think.* The tobacco plants were just about an inch high when they left the cabin that morning, and the air was dry and cooler. Now, a short time later, the plants had grown two feet and she was dripping from the humidity! She sat on the stump of a tree—the remainder of one that had been used for the repair of the cabin wall. "Go on ahead. I'll sit by Phineas for a while; I'm not feeling so good in this heat."

"Thy choice of company is befuddlin'." Izzie shrugged and sashayed back to the cabin, overlooking the field of tobacco as she went. Cassandra, too, overlooked the field, but in shock. *Something's happening to me....* The dizziness did not subside, so she laid her head on crossed arms in her lap. *Something's happening. Heat stroke, maybe....*

Perhaps she had fallen asleep sitting on the stump. The air felt oppressively humid, and she was clammy with sweat. Something had disturbed her; but afraid to open her eyes for fear the tobacco had grown another two feet during her nap, she remained with her head in her lap, eyes closed.

"*Noungasse.* Sky Bu." The voice sent shivers down her spine. "*Noungasse,*" he repeated. "*Caumorowath!*[43]"

She remained seated, not moving, panic running rampant through her veins.

"Cuttachcum![44]"he ordered.

She had no choice but to raise her head to see first his calves, his thighs, muscular and strong; then, his loin clout which covered the parts of him that she remembered so well in her nights at the Indian camp, coupling in the dark of the longhouse, Otter and Crane surely listening in silence as passions ebbed and flowed.

His form was magnificent; the bronzed chest, shiny in the heat of summer; his strong, hairless face, marked in tattoos of red and black; his long feathers worn as a crown, and ornaments of bone woven into the thick, black braid that lay over one shoulder. His age, she couldn't tell—ageless, handsome, strong—and he filled her with terror.

---

[43] *"Caumorowath"* Come! Algonquin language collected by William Strachey.

[44] *"Cuttachcum!"* Look! Algonquin language collected by William Strachey.

She shook her head. "No, Long Feather. I can't go with you." Tears sprang to her eyes, not in sadness, but in fear of being ripped away; ripped away from this life that she had so settled into. Ripped back into a life of servitude in the Indian camp as his wife, and far from her beloved captain.

He reached into the pouch that tied to his loin clout, and to her shock and surprise, pulled out her Cartier watch and dangled it before her eyes!

She stood, abruptly. "Where did you get this? Did Otter have it?" Momentarily overjoyed, she reached to take it back but he quickly returned it to his pouch.

"Cuttachcum!" He signaled her to follow.

"No. I won't go." She shook her head to make her point clear.

In one swift move, he lifted her from the stump, flinging her over his shoulder. She protested; she screamed; she kicked, all the time knowing it was a futile effort. The captain and Cupid were fishing at the river. Izzie and the others were in the cabin; no one would hear her scream.

He ran deftly through the thick woods, dodging the trees and brush. The forest passed in a highspeed blur of bumps and jarring impact, as her abdomen slammed against his powerful shoulder sending shards of pain into her gut. She pounded his back until he stopped, breathless, and set her on her feet. She had no clue as to where they were, dizzy as she was from the painful run, but it seemed he had run far.

"Noungasse," he said, jabbing a finger into her chest. In his mind, they were husband and wife. "Sky Bu." He then jabbed a finger into his own chest.

She felt woozy, unbalanced from the run, but shook her head in protest. "No. I am not yours." She said this angrily so that he would understand.

He took her chin into his powerful hands and stared into the blue of her eyes. "Sky Bu." His voice had softened, and a sadness filmed his eyes. *"Noungasse."*

Tears filled her own eyes, and she feared they would be misread. She had enjoyed this man, but she had not enjoyed the lack of communication, nor Otter and Crane, who held nothing but distain for her. The work at the Indian camp was overwhelming and never-ending. It was not her world, and she could not—*would not*—return. If so, she would run away again. She did not love him; she had suffered a moment of lust for him, perhaps out of fear and uncertainty brought about by the strangeness of the situation.

Because her 21st century life had been torn from her, she would settle for the tobacco plantation, Izzie, Lucy, and the children; but she could never return to the Indian camp and the droll life that lay ahead there. Her world was now with Captain Strongbow, be he at sea, or be he at home. If he was so entrenched in the morals, laws and plights of the 17th century, then so be it. She would not protest. She would accept the fate that brought her to this harsh land; it was all she had left.

Long Feather's palm struck her cheek with such force, that she flew backward, landing hard on the ground. The sting of it brought her back to the situation at hand. Anger encouraged her. "What did you do that for, you brute?" She stood to her feet, wiggling her jaw to make sure it wasn't broken.

"Noungassee!" This time he yelled the word, obviously his patience having been spent in the one softened moment. Before she could protest, he flung her over his shoulder once again, and ran like the wind through the forest, she, bouncing painfully and helplessly along.

"Muttahohoons![45]*"* The voice that echoed through the forest was *not* that of Long Feather, for his breath came short and

---

[45] *"Muttahohoons!"* "Stop!" Algonquin language collected by William Strachey

strained with the stress of her weight. Long Feather stopped in his tracks.

Cassandra was abruptly set on the ground and pushed out of the way. "Eagle!" she said, her eyes focusing on the Indian she knew as friend. He stood several yards ahead, blocking Long Feather's path. She was beyond surprised and very relieved that she may be rescued; but Long Feather did not appear pleased at all

"Keij[46]!" Long Feather practically growled the word to which Eagle replied with a raised tomahawk.

"Oh, my God, Eagle!" She screamed. "Watch out!" No doubt a fight was about to ensue. Long feather shouted a few words to her, which she assumed were 'get out of the way', and she complied, stepping away, ever fearful of what was to come. She could smell the testosterone and rage.

Long Feather raised his own tomahawk, and the men circled one another, but now knives had been pulled from sheaths. They crouched like stalking cats as they tread the circle, muscles rippling and eyes piercing; for both men were in top form, toned and strong. Then, as bucks in rut, they collided into a combustive clash of grunts and yells. Words she did not know burst from the two titans of the forest as they clashed and battled. When they separated to circle again, Cassandra saw that both were bleeding from wounds.

"Stop!" she yelled. She could not bear to see either one so brutally killed before her eyes! "Stop! Don't do this!"

Panic was full blown as she tried to intervene; a dangerous move at best. Twice she was knocked to the ground, and twice she rose to try again. She grabbed blindly for a hold on Long Feather's body, reaching only the hide pouch attached to his clout. She clenched it tightly in her fists, pulling with all her might; but this meager move did naught but rip the pouch from its hold.

---

[46] "Keij!" Get out, get away, get you gone. Algonquin language collected by Strachey

Long Feather now had Eagle pinned against a tree. She pounded his back with the pouch, time and time again, smacking it between his shoulder blades; but he ignored her attempts and raised his knife, ready to plunge the blade into Eagle's chest. When she wrapped her arms around the knife wielding arm, Long Feather yelled, knocking her aside.

It could have been a futile move, considering the man's strength, but this brief second gave Eagle a chance to wriggle free of the knife. Again, the men crouched in their circle. A fight to the death was how Casandra perceived the scene, for there appeared to be no end to the confrontation, and if there were, it was sure to be deadly.

She could not let this happen and groped for a weapon— anything that would make an impact. Her fingers found only a short, thick stick. She rose, stick and pouch in hand. "Stop!" she screamed, running forward— just as the men collided, ramming her between their chests.

Chapter 27

Cassandra staggered to her feet. "Stop! Don't fight!" Confusion set in, for when looking about for the fighting foes, she saw nothing but a darkened expanse, except for a stream of daylight filtering in through a windowpane. "Long Feather? Eagle? Where are you?" She looked to her hands, but there was no stick, and no pouch. *Where am I?* Silence settled around her as she stood in the musty attic. Her eyes fell to the opened trunk, and then to the small chest, and next to it, a large key. It looked so very familiar, but as she bent to retrieve the key, a phone rang. *Phone...phone...answer the phone.* She found it beneath a pile of yellow lice-eaten papers scattered next to the key.

A man's face jumped at her from digital screen, along with the name 'Bill'. For a moment, she didn't know how to make the ringing stop, but then recall swiped her finger across the man's face. "Bill?"

"Hello, baby. You sound surprised. Of course, it's me. Who else? Are you alright? Your gaggle of girls are wondering what happened to you since you didn't show up for lunch. They've called several times, but you never answered."

"Club? Bill?"

Silence. "Are you alright? You sound strange. I'm coming over."

"I have to think," she said, and hung up.

Bill...billbillbillbillbill. Who is Bill? Where is everyone?

Cassandra dropped the phone and head down the stairs. Once at the foyer, she proceeded to the kitchen and sat in silence at the cook's table. The kitchen clock read 3:00, ticking away the minutes as she sat staring out a window that framed a distant pool and guest house.

"My God, I'm home—but, where was I? What's happened? What happened to those people?" *Were they real? Am I crazy?* She spoke to no one, just the emptiness of the kitchen. Its cupboard doors lay open, exposing bared shelves—shelves that silently told the story of the sterile loneliness of an empty house.

What was that all about? She was terribly shaken.

The doorbell rang, and she glanced at the clock. 3:35.   She felt very tired, but dragged her body the long walk to the front door to look through its peephole; an empty house was a beacon to thieves.

"Bill, what are you doing here?" she asked, opening the large beveled oak door

"You said you had to think. Think about what? You sounded strange, so I hightailed it over here. You're not smoking the funny stuff, are you?"

"Don't be ridiculous. Look, I'm tired. I need to think."

"See, there you go again. Think about what, exactly?"

"I mean...I need to rest. I didn't sleep well last night."

"Hey, not so fast. We have a date tonight, remember? The dinner dance at the club."

She rested her face in her hands. "This is too much," she whispered, but not quietly enough.

"What's too much? What's wrong with you? This morning you were happy about the dance. What's changed that?"

"I...I...okay. I'll meet you there. What time?"

"7:00. I knew you'd come around. See you later, doll face." He pecked her on the cheek, and she watched as he climbed into his Mercedes and drove off around the circle and down the tree-lined drive. She looked at her wristwatch to see how much time she had before getting ready for the club, but there was no Cartier watch sparkling on her wrist. It was gone, and she remembered that it was in a leather pouch...*in the forest?* "I'm so confused! *It's not in a forest. How ridiculous!* I must have dropped it in the attic. I'll get it tomorrow."

The house was empty of furnishings, drapes, food—everything was gone—except for one can of coffee, and her bedroom and bath. She still needed to pack it all up, but, because there was no food in the house, dinner at the club actually sounded good. In fact, food sounded exceptionally good, and she realized that she was unusually famished.

She laid on her bed and drifted off to a dreamless sleep. When she woke, the golden, fading light of a setting sun shone through her bedroom windows.

"Ahhh." The tub was piping hot. *Just what I need after such a crazy dream!* Relaxing in the steamy bath gave her time to reflect on the mysterious memories that flooded her mind. Had she fallen, hit her head and passed out in the attic? What could account for the strange experience of time travel, sex with the native man, sex with a sea captain—and on the forest floor at that! *What an imagination! And that crazy red-headed woman, who was she? What a strange dream—or, was it a dream?* She couldn't shake the feeling that there was something more to the dream...something...*something.* It was so real.

She slipped into a basic black, body-fitting sheath, spiked heels to match, some glitzy jewelry for accent, and headed off to the club. The monthly dinner dance was always fun, and the food divine. *Forget the dream, have fun tonight.*

The valet greeted her as she pulled up under the overhang to the front doors of the club, and drove off to park her BMW. It felt strange being at the club, though she was a very familiar face and well greeted. *Why do I feel uncomfortable?* It felt all wrong—the dress, the jewels, the fake smiles—as she passed the regular staff on her way to meet Bill and the group at their usual reserved table; and there they were: Pepper and Ron, Sandy and Bob, Rebecca and Josh, and Georgine and Sal. The gang were all there.

"You missed our lunch today, Cass. We had a great time tearing Wanda apart. That bitch did it again, you know. She slept with Samantha's husband, and now Samantha's ready to kill." Pepper tossed her black, shiny head of superbly cut and trained, dyed black hair, which fell perfectly back into place, as highly trained and superbly cut hair will do.

Pepper was one of Cassandra's nearest and dearest friends. Of course, she had plenty of near and dear friends, all in the same upper class as she; all coming from large estates, fancy cars and big money.

"Oh, you should have been here!" Pepper said. Cassandra felt uncomfortable at the nauseating, smug look on the face of her friend, the gossiper, but didn't know why Pepper's remark had rubbed in such a bad way. Normally, she would have bitten the bait on that one.

Pepper's husband, Ron, shook his head. "Don't you girls have anything better to do than sit around and gossip all day?"

"Oh, shush," Pepper replied. "Honestly, you are getting to be such a bore!"

Everyone laughed, except Cassandra, who sat trying to chase thoughts of the strange dream from her head while the waiters bustled around from table to table carrying trays of hors d'oeuvres.

A tray of bacon-wrapped water chestnuts appeared before her face. "Would you care for one?" a female voice asked; a *familiar* voice.

"Why y...." Cassandra turned to thank the woman— and froze. "Lucy! Is that you?" Surely it was, for the woman was the spitting imagine of the woman in the dream!

"No ma'am, my name is...."

"No!" Cassandra jumped to her feet, accidentally knocking the tray from the woman's hands. It crashed to the floor sending water chestnuts helter-skelter. "You're Lucy. I know you are! Where are the others?"

"I—I'm sorry, ma'am." The woman stooped to retrieve the tray, then gingerly stepped around the fallen hors d'oevres as she departed. "We'll have this cleaned up in a jiffy," she said over her shoulder.

"Jeez, you scared that poor girl to death," Pepper said. "What was that all about? Who's Lucy? What others? What are you talking about?"

. "I'm sorry, guys, but I have to go. Urgent business." It was official; she was surely losing her mind!

"But you just got here," Bill complained.

"Sorry Bill. You stay. I've got to go."

"What's got into you?"

"Ghosts," she said. "I'm haunted by them."

She couldn't get to the attic fast enough. On went the attic lights and up she went, directly to the trunk from which she had taken the chest, which still lay unopened on the floor. Its copper hinges and straps were nearly black with tarnish and age. Decayed wood showed its years in several places, leaving little of its original color.

It's so familiar, she thought, as she carefully descended the stairs, chest and key in hand. Flipping on the overhead kitchen lights with her elbow, she placed the chest on the table, and sat.

I know this chest. She closed her eyes and thought back to the dream, trying to shake up memories. *I've seen this chest before....* She turned the key in her hands and a picture came to mind: a forest and a red headed woman. The woman held something in her arms, clutching it tightly to her chest as if she feared it would be taken from her. The woman was familiar, the red hair, the dark eyes, the strange grin.

Cassandra clenched her eyes tightly, trying to keep the picture in mind. It had something to do with the chest; she was sure of it. After a few moments, the answer came in a brilliant flash of white light. "Izzie!" she said aloud. "My God, it's Izzie and she has the chest of Spanish silver!" *But who is Izzie? How do I know her name?*

Cassandra rested her head on the chest's tarnished straps. It was courage she needed at this moment, courage to unlock the chest, for it would be easy to lift the latch, but she stalled, remembering—trying to remember—everything about the strange dream. It had been so real, and now, after seeing Lucy—or someone who looked like Lucy— at the club, she was terribly confused. *But who is Lucy, anyway?* Now, with the familiar chest in her hands, she was quite shaken.

She turned the key, and the lid creaked as she lifted it from its base to rest it open and lopsided on a broken hinge. Papers, yellow and tinged with age, sat inside. She was afraid to lift them for fear they would disintegrate in her hand. *I should take these somewhere for help...a historical society?* But, she couldn't wait. Instead, she took a breath and gingerly lifted the top paper, which nearly tore in half at the intrusion. Squinting, she realized it was impossible to decipher the flourish of the letters and language, though she was sure it was English, but faint and unreadable to one who never studied the writing of the day. The date, she could read with much effort: 30th day of October 1648. Her eyes scanned the paper to the bottom signatures. "Ifa...b...e...l. Ifabel? P...r...a. Oh, my God, Isabel Pratt!" Beneath the name was an 'X' mark. Chills ran up her spine.

She lay the paper gently on the table. "How could this woman's name be in my attic? She's a dream...a spirit... unless...no...no...I couldn't *possibly* be related to that character." *Could I?"* She shuttered in disgust that her proud family could be related to the toothless, relentless whore of her dream. *Who is she, and why do I think she's a whore?* Then, she gingerly lifted the second paper from the chest. This one was not so wordy. It was much shorter, and bore a wax seal—or part of a wax seal—which quickly slipped off the paper and onto her lap. *Damn.* She retrieved it from off her dress and placed it on the table.

Again, her eyes traveled to the signatures on this second piece of paper. Again, Isabel Pratt appeared, but below her 'X' was another name. She squinted, reading out loud the faint and fancy letters. "C...a...p...t...a...Cap-tain...Captain!" Her heartbeat accelerated as she jumped ahead to the next word. "J... *it can't be*...o...n." She jumped to the next word without finishing the first. "F...t...r...o...Strongbow! Is this for real?" She felt faint. What were these names doing in her attic? *Did I really know these people?* What was the chest doing in her attic?

There was yet another paper. With her heart thumping wildly, and her hands sweating, she lifted it from the chest. This paper appeared to be a bit different; still old, but not as tinged with age as the others. The flourish of the letters were the same, but there were two seals at the bottom, though both had fallen off leaving blotches of red where they had been. As with the others, she scanned to the bottom signatures and nearly fell off her chair; without a doubt, was written the name 'Kole Pratt." There was not an 'X' mark by his name, but a crude signature, as if the signee could write. She stared at the signature. *Kole! He grew up, and he could write...but how do I know this?*

Cassandra raised a few inches off her seat and onto the balls of her feet, hovering over the chest to peek inside for more papers, but saw none. She now stood to fully scrutinize the inside of the chest, and there, tucked into corners at the bottom, were two objects. One was a dirty, uneven disc. She picked it up, turning it in her fingers. Shivers ran up her spine. *Is it...a piece of eight?* "Spanish silver...it can't be!"

She set the coin aside and reached again inside the chest for the last object. No sooner was it out of its containment, that she dropped it to the table as if it were on fire. Cassandra stood out of her chair, staring, stepping backward. There, filthy and crusted, barely recognizable, was her Cartier wristwatch, and she remembered *everything.*

Chapter 28

assandra, how nice to see you again, and under much better circumstance."

"Agreed, Charles." He was the family lawyer. He and her father had been friends ever since she could remember. He was a part of the family in many ways, knowing all there was to know about the Pratt affairs—or so she hoped. She hadn't seen him in person since the reading of her mother's will.

"So, young lady, what can I do for you today? The estate is under contract and moving along smoothly. What are your plans for the future?"

"At the moment, I'm just trying to…well…I'm trying to figure out what to do with all the stuff that was left in the attic. I need to be out of there in one week, as you know. This is kind of what I need to talk to you about."

Attorney, Charles Oliver, sat back in his leather desk chair. Through the immense window behind him stood the city, its skyscrapers sentries to the Inner Harbor, and Fort McHenry which lay just across the waters, a testament to the wonderful country in which Cassandra now sat. *So much history, and I think I was there, watching the beginnings.*

"So?" Charles said.

"Oh, sorry. I guess I was daydreaming for a moment. Here's what's going on. I came across some old papers in the attic and I'm just wondering the connection to my family—that is, if you have the information."

"What papers are these?"

"I think they're old land grants from the 1600's."

"Did you bring them?"

She lifted a briefcase from the floor. "They're in here, but you must be very careful. If you have protective sheets, that would be great. We're totally cleaned out of everything at the house."

Charles called for his secretary, who brought the sheets and helped Cassandra get the documents into their protective covers.

"They're not at all easy to read, but they date back to 1648, and the names included are "Isabel Pratt, Captain Jonathan Strongbow, and the last one is Kole Pratt. I need to know if you have any other papers or information with these names."

Charles sat quietly for a moment after viewing the documents, the fingers of both hands interwoven into each other. "I do."

"You do?" Cassandra was incredulous. "What do you know about these people? If they're related in some way to my family, why didn't my father ever tell me?"

"Your father was a very busy man running the Pratt empire."

"So, what do you know about Izzie Pratt?"

"Izzie?"

"I mean, Isabel."

Charles called his secretary on the intercom. "Sheila, please bring me the Pratt deed files."

Sheila brought a large binder, setting it in front of her boss. Charles leafed through the pages, until he found the ones he was particularly interested in, and turned the binder to face Cassandra.

"We don't have identical copies of the documents you brought, but we do have these copies, which I believe reflect the same transactions. Of course, they've been transcribed to be readable; the English at that time was a bit difficult to read, despite the impressive handwriting. You'll see that Isabel Pratt made a deal with a native chief—I can't exactly say his name correctly...."

"Ahshowcutteis," she said, without realizing she had spoken out loud.

Charles looked aghast. "How did you know that?"

Cassandra shrugged. "Uh...I guess I picked the word out of the old documents." *Still thy tongue, woman, you can't tell him you met an Indian chief who lived four centuries ago!*

"Hmph. Well, this woman, Isabel Pratt, purchased the right to land from this particular chief, Asho...whatever his name. She then managed to officially, from Lord Calvert himself, acquire grants and patents for not only that land, but the neighboring land. It's mentioned somewhere in the documents that she had a half-breed son named Kole. Perhaps that's why your father never mentioned it."

Sweet baby Kole. She could envision his mocha skin and jet-black hair, and the big toothless smile that melted her heart.

"This half-breed, Kole, must have been a smart guy, because despite the prejudice at the time, he managed to acquire even more land in his adult years, not only on the Eastern Shore, but on the western as well. From there, well, Cassandra, it just accelerated, and here we are."

"So...you're saying that these old documents are legit?"

"I'm saying that this Isabel Pratt person is your ancestor, and apparently an important one. She came early to this country and, unknowingly, began the empire that you benefit from today."

Cassandra felt numb as she left the office. She felt numb as she drove her BMW back to the estate. She felt numb when she entered the mansion she had called 'home' all her life. In the kitchen, she replaced the deeds into the chest; it was, without a doubt, a very special chest. *I really was there. Those were my people!*

She made a cup of coffee—the only drinkable thing in the house aside from tap water—sat at the table and cried. She wasn't quite sure if she cried for the loss of her parents, for the loss of the life she knew in the 21st century, or for the life she lost in the 17th.

"What's wrong with me?" she asked herself. "I have everything here: friends, clothes, cars, money; and I have Bill. I can live first class anywhere in the world. Why am I so sad?" *The world wide web is at my fingertips. Cell phones, airplanes, toilet paper, tampons...shopping malls...lots and lots of restaurants...new clothes...real doctors. No more hunting, fishing, scavenging, starving. No more crazy red-headed woman named Izzie Pratt. No Cupid, no Lucy, no darling little Free. No Kole...no captain.*

"My captain." She would never see his dark-lashed blue eyes again, nor hold him close beneath the starry sky. She would never hear his voice, nor stare in awe at his handsome stature as he stood at the ship's wheel, the wind gently fluttering the billowy sleeves of his shirt. She would never again see Chesapeake Bay in its natural state, the way it lay virgin before the Europeans came to clutter the lands, to build empires, to rob the natives of their homes. She would never know how Izzie... Izzie!" She shot to attention, nearly knocking herself over as she stood.

"It was Izzie! The old woman in the dream; it was Izzie!" It seemed a hundred years had passed since the initial dream, but it was crystal clear now. Izzie wanted her to know that it all started with she, Isabel Pratt. That without her endurance of the harsh land, without her fortitude and belief in her dream, without her foresight and gumption to push onward, there would not be a Pratt empire. There may not even be a Cassandra Pratt.

"And you kept your name, Izzie...you didn't lie. You stayed true to yourself."

Now, there was one thing she knew for certain; she wanted to go back. She wanted to go back knowing what she knew now. She wanted to know what happened to Eagle and Long Feather. She wanted to be with the crazy red-headed woman, with Lucy and Cupid; with the children...and her captain.. Yes, she wanted to be there at the time before the skyscrapers, before cell phones, computers and automobiles. She wanted away from the country club life, from her catty friends, and even from Bill. She wanted a life with the captain, to sail on the beautiful bay void of mansions dotting the shore. She wanted to roll up her sleeves and be a part of her future; she wanted it *desperately*. She wanted a life with meaning.

"Take me back!" she said her hands gripping either side of the chest. "How can I get back? Tell me!" She pulled the chest to her, as if it would sprout wings and fly her away from this world. "I don't want to be here! If only time would...*time*.... I wonder...."

She opened the chest, gently lifted the papers and retrieved the watch. It was very corroded, making it difficult to see through the crystal to the hour at which it had stopped. Holding it every which way, she turned the watch face in her hands until she could read the numbers through the corrosion: 11:18. She looked at the kitchen clock. 11:15. *Three minutes. Maybe it's worth a try; maybe that's the magic hour.*

Her stress level rose as she fumbled with the clasp, as the severe corrosion was not obliging. "Damn!" She looked at the kitchen clock. 11:17. "Hurry, damnit!" She frantically fumbled until the minute hand hit the number 18, and the clasp locked; *Snap*. It was on!

Tick...tick...tick. The kitchen clocked moved its precise pace forward into the future, occasionally interrupted by the faint call of a bird from beyond the window. Otherwise, the kitchen sat as still as death, and all that remained to indicate prior existence of human life in the empty house, was a cold cup of coffee.

THE END

Other books by Jocelyn Miller

Tanglewood Plantation

Tanglewood Plantation II, Adventure in the Everglades

Tanglewood Plantation III, Adventure in New Orleans

Broken Chords

Terror River

All available at

www.amazon.com

ABOUT THE AUTHOR

Jocelyn Miller writes from Chesapeake Bay and the Florida Gulf coast. Her interests in history, genealogy and time travel, are woven into her tales through the fictional lives of characters who find themselves suddenly transported centuries into the past and delivered face to face with their ancestors. Adventure, ghosts, paranormal romance and salty characters abound in a Jocelyn Miller novel--along with a lesson learned by its heroine.

Jocelyn lives happily by the waterside with her husband of many years, two Yorkshire terriers, and one aggressive parrot.

www.ingramcontent.com/pod-product-compliance
Lightning Source LLC
Chambersburg PA
CBHW070846250626
47159CB00003B/956